Outstanding praise for the novels of Holly Chamberlin!

SUMMER FRIENDS

"A thoughtful novel."
—*ShelfAwareness*

"A great summer read."
—*Fresh Fiction*

"A novel rich in drama and insights into what factors bring people together and, just as fatefully, tear them apart."
—*The Portland Press Herald*

THE FAMILY BEACH HOUSE

"Explores questions about the meaning of home, family dynamics and tolerance."
—*The Bangor Daily News*

"A dramatic and moving portrait of several generations of a family and each person's place within it."
—*Booklist*

"An enjoyable summer read, but it's more. It is a novel for all seasons that adds to the enduring excitement of Ogunquit."
—*The Maine Sunday Telegram*

"It does the trick as a beach book and provides a touristy taste of Maine's seasonal attractions."
—*Publishers Weekly*

THE FRIENDS WE KEEP

"Witty, yet quietly introspective."
—*RT Book Reviews*

Books by Holly Chamberlin

LIVING SINGLE

THE SUMMER OF US

BABYLAND

BACK IN THE GAME

THE FRIENDS WE KEEP

TUSCAN HOLIDAY

ONE WEEK IN DECEMBER

THE FAMILY BEACH HOUSE

SUMMER FRIENDS

LAST SUMMER

THE SUMMER EVERYTHING CHANGED

BEACH SEASON
(with Lisa Jackson, Cathy Lamb, and Rosalind Noonan)

Published by Kensington Publishing Corporation

The Summer Everything Changed

Holly Chamberlin

KENSINGTON BOOKS
www.kensingtonbooks.com

KENSINGTON BOOKS are published by

Kensington Publishing Corp.
119 West 40th Street
New York, NY 10018

ISBN-13: 978-0-7582-7534-9
ISBN-10: 0-7582-7534-X
First Kensington Trade Paperback Printing: July 2013

eISBN-13: 978-0-7582-7535-6
eISBN-10: 0-7582-7535-8
First Kensington Electronic Edition: July 2013

10 9 8 7 6 5 4 3 2 1

Printed in the United States of America

As always, for Stephen
And this time, also for Peggy

Acknowledgments

My deepest appreciation goes to John Scognamiglio for his guidance and friendship.

Many thanks to Chris of Longfellow Books here in Portland. His dedication to writing, writers, and readers is unsurpassed.

Thanks also to Julia Einstein, friend, painter, arts educator, and longtime Mainer. To Sage, Olive, and Cait at Se Vende, thank you for serving my passion for jewelry—and for good conversation. To Judy Sowa for the gift of her fine work—and her potatoes. Last but never least, to my mother, Joanie—for everything.

This is in memory of Mackintosh Donner.

A mother is the truest friend we have,
when trials, heavy and sudden, fall upon us . . .

—Washington Irving

Chapter 1

It was a typically beautiful afternoon in early June when the call came in.

Afterward, Louise liked to refer to it as "the fateful call." Her daughter, Isobel, chose to refer to it as "the call that changed everything." Either phrase was appropriate, because with absolutely no warning or preparation, Louise Bessire, owner of the Blueberry Bay Inn in Ogunquit, Maine, found herself deep in a mostly one-sided discussion with a wedding planner to the stars.

"Yes, yes," she said. "I see." She did not see, not at all. She could hardly believe what she was hearing from this person calling herself Flora Michaels. "How many guests did you say? That many?"

Louise leaned against the kitchen sink and put her hand to her head, where she suspected there would be a big pain very soon. At forty-two Louise still had the slim, lithe figure she had had at twenty-two. Mostly, that was due to genetics and next, to nervous energy. She was five feet eight inches tall, with thick blond hair, darker now than it had been when she was younger. Usually, she wore it hanging straight to her shoulders or up in a messy bun; today, she had gone for the bun. At the moment she was dressed in one version of what had become her summer uniform—a pair of white jeans, a fitted T-shirt, and comfortable wedge sandals. Another version might have substituted capri pants for the jeans and flat sandals for the wedges. These days, Louise didn't have much time to spend on worrying about her wardrobe.

The inn's kitchen was located at the back of the house, and during the busy season it served as home base for the Bessire women. The walls were painted a cheery yellow. The floors, originally pine, had been replaced with good ceramic tile some years back. Windows all along the back wall, against which stood the sink and a long working counter, let in plenty of natural light. The backsplash tile was a springy green that worked nicely with the yellow of the walls. A big round clock—black-rimmed, white-faced, black-numbered—hung over the kitchen door, which opened out onto a small, semi-enclosed space for storage of gardening equipment, and then onto the backyard.

Though the room was off-limits to guests, it was still a bit of a showcase and, of course, spotlessly clean. The appliances were restaurant grade, as the inn served breakfast from seven until nine o'clock and in mid-afternoon provided tea, coffee, and homemade pastries in the parlor.

The meals were thanks to Bella Frank, a sixty-five-year-old local woman who had trained in her youth as a chef. After a lifetime of supporting her children by doing the books for her husband's hardware store and taking odd jobs when they presented themselves, she welcomed the opportunity to prac-tice her passion. Louise felt beyond lucky to have Bella as an employee. Before buying the inn, she had had absolutely no experience in any area of the hospitality industry; she had never even waited tables, let alone cooked for potentially fussy strangers.

The table in the center of the pleasant room was an old, scrubbed-pine piece; it was the first bit of furniture Louise had bought for the inn. It was here that Louise and her fifteen-year-old daughter, Isobel, ate their meals together. It was where Isobel was sitting at that very moment, watching her mother intently. Louise felt a bit like a slow-moving bird being eyed by a hungry cat. Occasionally, Isobel mouthed a questioning word that Louise thought might be "what" or maybe "who," and her right hand was making a spasmodic gesture Louise interpreted as "hurry!" Isobel wasn't known for her patience. She was the kid who had to give you the birthday present she had bought you as soon as she got it home, even if your birthday was weeks away, just because she couldn't wait to see your pleased reaction. She was also the kid who routinely burned her mouth on cookies fresh out of the oven because she simply couldn't wait until they had cooled off.

Isobel, on the cusp of sixteen, was tiny, about five feet two inches tall, and her complexion was much darker than her mother's, closer to that of her father's side of the family. Her hair, too, was darker than Louise's, more of a golden brown than blond. Her eyes were a very deep blue—in contrast to her mother's light blue eyes—but like the Jones side of the family, she was very slim. At the moment she was dressed in—well, not a version of a uniform, because every day Isobel emerged from her bedroom in an entirely new and unpredictable outfit. Today that outfit consisted of a pair of bright green Converse sneakers; a tan crocheted skirt (with a silk lining) that came to mid-calf; and a man's blue oxford button-down shirt tied up at the waist. In her ears she wore hoops studded with turquoise stones; both wrists sported an assortment of bangles and rope bracelets; on her right hand she wore a massive faux gold ring set with a triangular bit of pyrite; and on her left hand she wore a Lucite ring in pink and orange. The Lucite ring had belonged to Louise when she was a child.

"But I don't—" Louise was interrupted, again, by Flora Michaels. "Well, yes, that's possible, I guess, but—" And again.

Isobel rolled her eyes, and her leg bounced with curiosity.

Louise turned away. Isobel's excitement was making her nervous. Well, more nervous than she already was and had been since buying Blueberry Bay Inn a little over two years earlier, just after her divorce from Isobel's father had been finalized. The purchase had been partly whim, and partly dream; she had presented a tiny bit of a plan, and had taken a hell of a lot of a risk. Louise still wondered if she had been entirely in her right mind when she signed all those papers at the closing.

Still, there were aspects of her life as an innkeeper she enjoyed, and she downright loved the inn itself. The house had been built around 1880 and had remained in the possession of the Burke family for generations. Around 1993 the last of the Burkes sold it for far less than it might have been worth if failing fortunes hadn't rendered it almost uninhabitable. The new owners restored it from the near wreck it had become over time and converted it to an inn they called Blueberry Hill. Somewhere in the early 2000s the name was changed to Blueberry Bay. Louise wondered if the association with the famous 1950s Chuck Berry song had occasioned too many annoying questions like, "So, did Chuck Berry ever stay here, or what?"

The last owner had painted the big old building white, and the doors and window shutters a dark green. On the first floor, to the left of the entrance, was a parlor for the convenience of guests on a rainy afternoon or evening. It had a working fireplace, several large and comfortable high-backed armchairs, a couch that was just the right degree of saggy (that, according to Isobel), and a scattering of small antique occasional tables.

A smaller room across from the parlor, now called the library, housed the reception desk, a rack of tourist guides, stacks of local magazines and newspapers, and a collection of books amassed haphazardly over the years by the various owners of the inn. There was also a big supply of paperbacks abandoned by summer visitors. Those with steamy covers Louise had stuck up on the higher shelves. The inn did not allow children, but still, Blueberry Bay did have a certain reputation to maintain. That, or Louise was becoming prudish in her early middle age.

The breakfast room was beyond the parlor. There was a private table for every guest room, each one set with an eclectic assortment of old crockery, china, and silverware Louise and Isobel had scavenged from antique shops and flea markets. Each morning, Louise refreshed the tiny vase at the center of each table with offerings from the garden, a bit of Queen Anne's lace or a single peony or, later in the season, a bloom of hydrangea.

A small powder room was tucked in under the stairs. It had been installed fairly recently, within the last ten or twelve years, and like all of the other bathrooms at the inn, it boasted modern facilities along with touches of New England charm, like the basket of whitened seashells that sat on a shelf over the toilet, and a print showing the crew of a lobster boat hauling in their catch. (Louise had to replenish the contents of the basket on a regular basis; guests seemed to feel a compulsive need to steal the shells.)

On the second floor, at the back of the house, were Louise's bedroom, Isobel's bedroom, and the bathroom they shared. At the front of the house, there was a large guest room with an alcove big enough to serve as a sitting area; this room offered a private bathroom. From the window you could see a bit of Perkins Cove—at least, you could make out a few roofs and beyond them, on a clear day, a bit of horizon.

There were three medium-sized guest rooms on the third floor. From the front room you could see a wide strip of the energetic Atlantic, silvery blue in a certain light, bright teal in another, and deep navy in yet another. There was one shared bathroom in the hall.

The attic, off-limits to guests as was the kitchen, might have been a treasure hunter's paradise except that by the time Louise bought the Blueberry Bay Inn, all of the attic's antique and vintage contents had long ago been dispersed. Now, the room contained remnants of her own past, including boxes of her childhood toys and report cards and even the dried and crumpled corsage she had worn to her high school junior prom; mementos of Isobel's not-so-distant childhood; and things from the Massachusetts house Louise couldn't bear to part with but couldn't quite live with, either. Like the hideous oil painting her mother had given her one Christmas. It was one of those awful landscapes bought at a "starving artist sale" in some run-down office park. The trees didn't look like any trees Louise had ever seen, and the lake resembled a pit of boiling oil. Still, her mother had meant well . . .

The basement, ugly, large, and utilitarian, was also off-limits to guests. It was home to the industrial-grade washing machine and dryer (Louise did the inn's laundry herself, though Isobel thought she was nuts for bothering when there was an affordable local service that could handle the washing, drying, folding, and delivery), the boiler, and all those other loud and nasty-looking machines necessary for operating a building.

The inn's front porch was, in Louise's opinion, the building's best feature—long, deep, and charming. There, one could practice the fine and almost lost art of "porch sitting." A guest could daydream, doze, wave to people driving by in cars or cycling by on bikes or strolling by on foot, read, or sip a cool drink.

The front yard sloped gently from the base of the porch, and the landscaping was simple but pretty—no opulent water features or ugly garden gnomes or reproduction "wishing wells" for Louise Bessire.

The backyard was about half an acre of perfectly manicured grass, with a gazebo sprouting smack-dab in the center. No doubt the gazebo was a bit of an eyesore to those who didn't care for excessive Victorian detailing such as its ornate tracery and vaguely grotesque sprouts of curlicues. Isobel thought it gorgeous; Louise tolerated its presence because guests seemed to find it something to *ooh* and *aah* over.

Overall, the Blueberry Bay Inn was the epitome of New England picturesque. If it lacked that "wishing well," complete with pail and crank, you could find one down the road on the property of one of the kitsch-loving summer residents.

"Yes, that sounds—" Again, Flora Michaels interrupted. "Okay, I'll expect—"

Louise finally managed to end the call with a series of thanks and assurances, neither of which she felt were particularly genuine. She put the phone beside the sink and turned back to her daughter.

"Violet," Isobel said.

"What?"

"Your face is violet. No, wait"—Isobel squinted critically at her mother—"maybe lavender. Yeah, that's more accurate. So, I'm dying already. What was that all about? Who's getting married? Someone we know? Do I have an excuse to buy a new dress? Something awesome and vintage and maybe covered in lace? I don't have anything covered in lace. Pink might be good, if it's not too bubblegum. A pretty dusty rose might be a nice change for me. Or maybe buttercup yellow."

"Uh, in a sense it's someone we know," Louise replied, as she sank into a chair at the table. "I don't know if the occasion justifies a new dress, though . . ."

"Mom, come on! Tell me!"

"You know that television show, *Tell Me You Didn't Just Say That?*"

Isobel shook her head. "No. I mean, I've heard of it—it's a sitcom, right? But I've never watched it."

"Well," Louise went on, "that was a wedding planner. It seems that two of the stars, someone named Ashley Brooklyn or something like that, and a Jake or a Blake, I can't remember exactly, want to get married at a traditional, charming New England inn. In short, they want to get married at the Blueberry Bay Inn."

Isobel jumped from her seat. Louise was surprised she had kept still this long.

"Mom, this is amazing," she cried, pacing excitedly. "This

could really be fantastic for us. For the inn, I mean. Imagine the publicity!"

"Yeah. Fantastic, if I don't totally mess up and wind up losing the business." *How Andrew would gloat,* she thought, *if I had to declare bankruptcy.* But maybe that was being unfair to her ex-husband. He wasn't a gloater. He would simply shake his head, lips compressed, and say something on the order of: "I told you a country inn was a bad idea." In Andrew's opinion, Andrew was always right. Annoyingly, as the opinion of much of the world proved, he was, indeed, most often right.

"Mom, come on," Isobel was saying, her hands on her hips, "how hard can it be to throw a wedding? You've been to dozens of weddings, I'm sure. So buy a few magazines, get some cute ideas, and voilà."

Louise stared. Isobel's general optimism and enthusiasm really could be viewed as an astounding naïveté. She decided not to comment on her daughter's personality quirks. "We're not throwing anything," she corrected. "We're—hosting, I guess would be the right word. We're hosting a wedding for a minor celebrity couple. Oh, it sounds awful! What am I thinking? I can't pull this off!"

"Mom, don't be a Gloomy Gus. How did they find out about us, anyway?"

"Online. Where everyone finds out about everything. Oh Lord, I must be out of my mind. I'll call the wedding planner right back and say that something came up and—"

Louise made to rise, but Isobel gently pushed her mother back into the seat. "Mom," she said, leaning down and looking her squarely in the eye, "you'll do no such thing. Come on, where's that fighting spirit, that gung ho attitude? Where's that devil-may-care woman I know so well?"

"Gung ho?" Louise couldn't help but smile. "Devil-may-care? Are you feeling all right?"

"Of course. I'm just trying to encourage you. And I'll be here to help every step of the way, don't forget that."

And she would, Louise thought. Isobel was a person of her word. "Are you sure I turned lavender? Not sickly mint or icky puce? Not disgusting pea soup?"

"You like pea soup," Isobel pointed out. "Especially when it has ham in it."

"Answer the question."

"Periwinkle!" Isobel cried. "That's the word I was looking for. You turned periwinkle."

"Periwinkle?" Louise felt her stomach drop heavily into her lower intestines. "Crap," she said. "What disaster did I get us into?"

Isobel squeezed her mother's shoulders. "It'll all be okay, Mom. I have a feeling our lives are about to change in ways we never even dreamed possible. Isn't it exciting!"

Louise managed a pathetic smile. "That's one word for it," she said.

Chapter 2

CITYMOUSE

Greetings, Dear Readers!

Gwen, my sidekick extraordinaire, my partner in daily adventure of the most varied kind, was extra Gwentastic yesterday when she unearthed a treasure beyond compare at the very bottom of a lopsided cardboard box stuffed under a shelf at Say It Again, one of our favorite hunting grounds, on Route 1 in Wells. With her usual (careful) vigor she rooted through layers of old and delicate lace, some of which threatened to fall apart in her hands, to finally uncover a sterling silver, monogrammed calling card case!! It's even got a silver mesh chain on one end so you could carry it around your wrist when you went a-calling.

Here's a picture of her find. And, well, the owner of the shop admitted he hadn't even known it was there, at the bottom of that old box. Desperately afraid we wouldn't be able to afford to buy the case, Gwen and I held our breaths, but in the end Mr. Green was *molto generoso* and sold it to us for a very reasonable price indeed. It now resides with its rescuer, Gwen, who likes to imagine the full name of whoever sported the initials *A. C. P.* Allison Catherine Peterson. Or maybe Ann Carol Paulson. We'll never know the truth—A. C. P. will remain for us a missing person—and there's something really poignant about that.

But, in other news, LouLou and I are celebrating our two-year anniversary in Ogunquit and at the Blueberry Bay Inn, and the almost-two-year anniversary of CityMouse. Time flies when you're having fun, doesn't it? (Does anybody know who first said that? Truer words were never spoken!)

How deluded I was when first I came to what I truly thought to be the wilds of Maine! I've seen the wilds now—our first summer here, LouLou and I ventured north one weekend (before our lovely inn got underway) and spent a few days in Greenville at a teeny, family-run motel on Moosehead Lake, and that, my friends, is splendidly rural and wild and supposedly chock-full of moose though we didn't see a-one—and let me be clear that Southern Maine is not wild nor is it unkempt or in any way messy. It only goes to show that so much of what we think we know we don't know at all—it's all so much misinformation and bad marketing and prejudice. So the lesson here is not to make snap judgments and to keep your mind open until you can make an informed decision all on your own.

But one thing I learned in these past two years is that it's not what is around you but what you carry inside of you that makes you happy in one place or another, that makes life here or there merely bearable or actually, in fact, happy.

And one of the things I found that I do carry inside of me is style and the love of fashion for the FUN of it, so that even if most of my local pals don't share this quirk of mine, YOU do, everyone who reads this blog and everyone who is HERE with me so that I never feel alone!

To all you style gals back home, it's City-Mouse signing off for now with moose hugs (eergh!) and lobster kisses (ow!) from Maine.

Isobel posted the blog and closed her laptop. It was true, she thought. So much had happened since her father had left the family and her mother had decided to move north to Maine.

She had been sad to leave her friends, some of whom she had known since kindergarten, and her school, where she was a top student and popular without trying to be. And for about a moment she had grumbled mightily about moving to what she had thought of as a hick town where she was convinced no one had ever heard of fashion, let alone the concept of style. But grumbling did not sit well with Isobel. She was not negative by nature or given to self-pity. It wasn't too long before her spirits rallied and she began to look forward to the move with excitement.

Besides, she had been eager to get far away from her father and all he represented—their former so-called perfect family life.

The first few weeks in their new home had been really tough. School was out for the summer, so there was no convenient way for Isobel to meet people her own age. So when she wasn't helping her mom with Blueberry Bay Inn stuff, she found herself spending an awful lot of time online, reading through style and fashion blogs (Tavi Gevinson was her heroine, though she admitted to being a lot less ambitious than Tavi seemed to be), idly wish-shopping for vintage on eBay, and scrolling through QVC's website for stuff she couldn't afford and didn't need. In short, she was busy being generally unproductive.

And then, because Isobel Amelia Bessire was not happy being unhappy and unproductive, one day it had occurred to her that she could stop wasting precious time and pour her energy into writing a blog of her own. After all, she thought that someday she might want to become a writer, or maybe a stylist or a buyer. This venture could be practice for her career!

It hadn't been difficult to come up with a tagline—"You can't take the city out of this girl!"—or a mission statement—"To find and cultivate style even in the wilds of Maine." She had altered that statement a bit now to something less bellicose and challenging—"Style is where you make it."

The blog allowed her to keep in touch with at least some of her friends from at home in Massachusetts, though she had to keep reminding herself that this was now home, Ogunquit, Maine, and that the sooner she accepted that fact, the better her life would be. She would re-achieve the peace of mind and contentment and all that other good stuff she had once possessed.

And she was well on the way! For example, she had totally

lucked out in meeting Gwen Ryan-Roberts. They had run into each other on the grounds of the Ogunquit Museum of American Art. Gwen was there taking pictures of the giant wooden sculptures by Bernard Langlais. Isobel and her mother were strolling the lovely gardens out back. The three had struck up a conversation, and the rest, as it was said, was history.

Gwen had a real gift for photography (she was currently obsessed with the urban street photos of Scott Schuman, known as The Sartorialist), and she drove her own car, which was lucky for Isobel because without a car, you were virtually a prisoner in your home.

Together the girls spent hours hunting out local thrift, re-sale, and antique shops, buying what they could afford, and taking pictures of anything that struck their creative fancy.

Over time the blog had become a lifeline for Isobel, especially as her mother had become increasingly busy with the running of Blueberry Bay. And as her father, almost imperceptibly at first but more obviously over time, had become less and less of a presence in their lives. It was to be expected. He was remarried. He had two little stepdaughters. He had his big career, as he always had. He had his life.

And Isobel had hers, complete with CityMouse. Sometimes she wondered if she came across as kind of hyper on the blog, but the thing was that the writing just seemed to come out the way it came out and she didn't want to censor that or edit herself the way she did for a paper at school or even an e-mail to a friend. Except, of course, that she would never allow herself to say mean or nasty stuff about anyone on the blog, not that that was a struggle, as Isobel liked to think (and she was right) that she didn't have a mean or nasty bone in her body. Maybe an impatient bone or a moody bone (or two), and maybe even on occasion a pissy bone, but not a mean or a nasty one.

Yeah, it was all good. Isobel looked around her room and smiled. The walls were painted a bright, deep pink (her mother

had once called them magenta but Isobel thought that raspberry was more accurate) and hung with framed posters of
European capitols and famous works of art. To the right of
the room's narrow closet hung a small oil painting Isobel had
removed from the breakfast room because she loved it so
much and wanted to be able to look at it whenever she
wanted. It was by a local painter named Julia Einstein, and it
showed a view of a garden from an upstairs window. The
colors were bright and happy, the image bold and confident.
The painting energized Isobel. Not that she needed much
outside help in the energizing department.

The furniture consisted of a jumble of pieces she had wanted
to salvage from their house in Massachusetts, in spite of her
mother's assurance that the Blueberry Bay Inn came already
largely furnished. That didn't matter to Isobel. Some of the
pieces she had shipped north hadn't been meant for use in a
bedroom but that didn't matter, either, like the old book-
stand, the kind that you found in private libraries and museums. Lacking a gorgeously illuminated medieval text to
display on it, Isobel piled on the latest editions of *InStyle* and
Vogue.

The rest of her book collection was stacked every which
way on shelves Isobel herself had nailed into the walls (with
some later corrective help from Quentin Hollander, the
seventeen-year-old local guy who worked at the inn full-time
during the summers and part-time off-season). Isobel liked to
read almost as much as she liked to write. In addition to a
good old-fashioned (but recent edition) dictionary, there was
her mother's battered college copy of *The Riverside Shakespeare,* a complete hardcover collection of the Harry Potter
series, paperback copies of the Hunger Games series, a book
about the life and career of Coco Chanel, and a very expensive book about El Greco, who was one of her favorite
painters. That had been a Christmas present from her father
a few years back; the quality of the colored plates was outstanding. The rest was an eclectic mix, from a secondhand

copy of a book about birds of the Northeast, a coverless copy of Hemingway's *The Sun Also Rises,* a first edition of Daphne du Maurier's *Rebecca,* and a book about jewelry written in England in the 1940s. That she had found in Yes!, a cool secondhand bookstore on Congress Street up in Portland.

The bed was the same one she had been sleeping in since she was first out of a crib. The current bedspread was a paisley print that Louise found riotous; Isobel thought it was restful.

On the floor (under piles of magazines and clothing, the latter clean but often rumpled) was an old wool carpet her parents had bought on a trip to Paris when Isobel was small. She had always loved it, and rather than leave it behind in Massachusetts, as her mother was inclined to do, the carpet, with its intricate design worked in maroon, goldenrod, and deep green, had journeyed north.

All in all, the room was what some people, the kinder ones, would call an organized mess, and what other people, the less kind, would call a train wreck. Yes, the room was cluttered; Isobel was a collector by nature, not a minimalist. A "pack rat," Mrs. Brown, the housekeeper back in Massachusetts, had called her before she had refused to attempt to clean under the piles of clothes and magazines and books heaped on the bed and littered across the floor.

The inn had a small staff of housekeepers, three teenaged girls from Macedonia, none of whom were allowed into Isobel's room. It was her haven; it was sacrosanct. And what looked like junk to some people, was considered treasure by others.

Isobel leapt from the desk chair. Speaking of treasures, she had promised Gwen she would call her when the latest post was complete. There were endless whimsical baubles and fantastic oddities still to find!

Chapter 3

"Yes, yes, I heard you the first time, Ms. Michaels. Yes, I'll be sure to get those measurements to you as soon as possible."

Flora Michaels sniffed loudly. "See that you do." She ended the call without a good-bye.

Louise fell back onto the bed, letting the phone drop at her side. God, she longed for a nap but she couldn't justify one just yet, not when there was so much to do. There was a new guest checking in later that afternoon, and a professional painter was coming by to give an estimate for repainting the gazebo. And, of course, there were the measurements of every room on the ground floor of the inn (why?) to get to the wedding planner.

Maybe if she just closed her eyes for five minutes . . . Nope. Wouldn't work. Closed eyes led to serious snoozing. Louise sighed and sat back up against the pile of decorative pillows.

As messy and disorganized as Isobel's room was, Louise's was neat and ordered. She had painted the walls a very soothing azure blue; the floorboards were wide pine painted white. Here and there, like at the foot of the bed, were scattered throw rugs in a dusty rose color. A comfortable armchair from their former house in Massachusetts, one of the few pieces she had brought along to this new life, was positioned to allow a view of the backyard and the grove of pine trees that marked its boundary. The chair was one of her fa-

vorite pieces, already on a third upholstering, this time in a
pretty sea-foam green that contributed to the room's cool
and peaceful feel.

There was a small, rather dainty desk in which she kept a
box of old-fashioned writing paper, and a good Cross pen
she had gotten as a thank-you gift for her work organizing a
fund-raising event for a local charity back in Massachusetts.
Two checkbooks, one for her personal account and one for
the inn's; a roll of stamps; and a stack of bookmarks Isobel
had made one summer in day camp completed the stash. The
bookmarks were cardboard strips (unevenly cut) on which
Isobel had pressed Queen Anne's lace under a layer of clear
shelf paper.

A hefty-sized bookcase was stocked with favorite titles
Louise wanted at hand at bedtime, including a copy of every
Elizabeth Peters and Barbara Michaels novel published to
date. She had read each novel at least three times and would
no doubt read each novel three additional times. In Louise's
opinion, you stuck with a good thing, especially when the
good thing was a favorite author. Recently, she had succeeded
in getting her friend Catherine hooked on Peters/Michaels,
but Isobel was proving a tougher case. She was still favoring
some of the older teen series, though recently Louise had seen
her engrossed in a copy of *The Great Gatsby*. There was
hope yet.

The bed was new, one Andrew had never seen let alone
slept in. (He had never visited his former wife and his always
daughter in Ogunquit, and Louise suspected that he never
would.) She had treated herself to high thread count sheets
and an expensive down comforter covered in a luxurious
silky fabric somewhere in shade between the azure walls and
the sea-foam chair. If the room looked a bit like an under-
water grotto, so be it.

In addition to the window facing the backyard, there was
one facing the narrow side yard. Louise had hung white sheer
curtains for the warm months; in the fall and winter, she re-

placed these with curtains of heavier fabric. Though there was an air conditioner in the window facing the side yard, Louise rarely used it. The room was nicely cross-ventilated; only on those nasty humid days when temperatures crawled into the nineties (this was a common enough occurrence in Southern Maine) did she crank up the AC a few hours before bedtime.

Louise sighed. She knew she would spend less and less time in this lovely haven as the busy season took hold, and she strongly suspected that this summer, what with the celebrity wedding looming, her sleep schedule would be pretty severely reduced. It worried her. She was already drinking way too much coffee just to keep awake past three in the afternoon, and if she weren't careful to exercise some self-control, the one homemade pastry she snuck around ten each morning would turn into two pastries. What would happen from there was anyone's nightmarish guess. Being active—supervising the housekeepers (who, being intelligent, energetic, and hardworking, didn't need much supervision), or discussing a change to the breakfast menu with the cook, Bella Frank (who had her own firm ideas about what to serve the guests), or asking Quentin to take a look at the dishwasher or some other appliance (which, often enough, he had already earmarked for repair)—didn't necessarily mean you were conscious while doing so.

Louise fought with her eyes, which insisted on closing, but she knew it was a fight she was not going to win. She got off the bed and went down to the kitchen.

"Knock, knock."

Louise turned to find Catherine, and her dog, Charlie, at the kitchen door.

Catherine King was fifty, an early retiree from a very successful career as what Louise thought of, without any disrespect, as a "corporate something or other." She was a bit shorter than Louise but taller than Isobel (not hard to do, according to Isobel herself). Her hair, once bright red, had deep-

ened in color to a sort of burgundy, and she wore it tied back
or up in an old-fashioned but becoming French twist. Her
eyes were very green and her skin was very white. Though
she spent a fair amount of time outdoors these days, a lot of
it painting *en plein air,* she managed to avoid burning or tan-
ning through a combination of sunblock and protective
clothing. "If I'm an object of ridicule in my long sleeves and
floppy hats, so be it," she pronounced. "So far I'm the only
one in my immediate family who hasn't gotten skin cancer."

"Any room at the inn?" Catherine asked.

"Yes, and I was just about to make some coffee."

"Ah, music to my ears. Any water for Charlie?"

Catherine rarely went anywhere without her dog, Princess
Charlene, a five-year-old chocolate lab she had found at a
shelter shortly before moving to Ogunquit from a wealthy
suburb of Hartford, Connecticut. Her career had kept her
too often on the road and too busy to be a proper parent to
an animal, especially to a dog. Now that she was retired she
was reveling in her first adult relationship with a four-footed
creature.

"Why Princess Charlene?" Isobel had asked when Catherine had first come to Ogunquit, only months after Louise and
Isobel had established residence.

"Because that poor young woman seemed so in need of
rescuing for a time, remember?" Catherine had said. "Just
like my baby. Mind you, I don't so much think that Princess
Charlene of Monaco needs saving anymore. She seems to
have found her footing."

Isobel loped into the kitchen just then.

"Hi, Catherine, bye, Catherine. Hi, Princess Charlene,
bye."

She was out the back door in a flash.

"Does Isobel ever sit still?" Catherine said. "That's a
rhetorical question."

Louise placed a French press pot of coffee on the table,
along with two mugs. Both women took their coffee black.

"Only when she's writing her blog. And then her leg is bouncing."

"Huh. Lucky gal, she'll probably never have to diet." Catherine took a sip of her coffee. "Ah, that's magic," she said. "You know, even though you and Isobel look nothing alike, there's no mistaking you for anything other than mother and daughter. It's a look in the eye or something. It's really quite extraordinary. Two peas in a pod. The apple not falling far from the tree."

"Uh-huh."

"Just uh-huh? What's on your mind?"

Louise drained half of her cup of coffee and then told her friend about the phone call from the celebrity couple's wedding planner. Catherine listened without comment.

"And the next thing I knew," Louise finished, "I was saying yes. I think she mesmerized me. There was something odd about her voice, something compelling, almost threatening. It was like I didn't dare say no!"

"Have you signed a contract yet?" Catherine asked.

"No, I haven't seen it yet, so technically I'm still in the clear if I decide to change my mind. Though, for all I know Flora Michaels could have the power and prestige to blacken my name if I did bail now . . ."

Catherine shook her head. "You won't change your mind."

"Who says I won't? This is a huge commitment. Maybe too huge for me."

"I say you won't. You'd be nuts not to grab this challenge. This could set you up for years to come. You could really make it big. And other clichés denoting success."

"What if I don't want to make it big?" Louise argued, pouring herself another half cup of coffee. "What if I'm fine just making it medium?"

"Medium is boring."

"Maybe for you. I've always kind of liked medium. It's comfortable and—"

"Boring. Anyway, when the contract comes in, you had better let me review it. Lord knows I've reviewed a contract or two in my time."

"Would you? I'd be grateful. I don't think I've ever read a contract in my life. Dealing with the mortgage papers on this place almost sent me to a rest home."

"What are friends for if not sharing expertise?"

"What expertise do I share with you?" Louise asked, genuinely curious.

Catherine made a show of considering the question, twisting her mouth and wrinkling her nose. "I don't know. I'll have to give it some thought. In the meantime I will admit that you make good coffee."

"Well, that's something."

Catherine stood. "Come on, Charlie. We've wasted enough of Louise's time. She's got a celebrity wedding to plan."

Charlie finished slopping water onto the kitchen floor and led Catherine out the door.

Louise smiled to herself. Being with Catherine, even if only for a few minutes, always cheered her. And having someone she considered a best friend was almost a brand-new experience for her. It wasn't until she was muddling through the divorce that Louise realized she hadn't had a best friend in years, maybe not since grammar school.

Sure, there had been the women she volunteered with, and the mothers of Isobel's classmates, but there had never been anyone really intimate. And she had never spent much time wondering why she had no close female friends. Her life was very full without them; besides, she had always considered Andrew the best friend she could ever have.

And look how that had turned out! A woman should never sacrifice female friends for the sake of a male friendship, even that of a husband. There was plenty of good emotional energy to go around. You just had to use it. Too bad Louise had learned that lesson so late in her life.

Catherine was, Louise thought, a good role model for Isobel. Not that she herself was so bad a role model, but Isobel's having several older women she could admire and try to emulate couldn't hurt. Louise's own mother hadn't been much of an inspiration, though she had been a kind and loving woman. She had been fearful by nature and had grown increasingly timid as she aged. When Louise wasn't finding her mother and her trepidations supremely annoying, she was finding them pitiful. Neither feeling had made her think of herself as a good or dutiful daughter.

But enough of the past. Louise sat at the kitchen table and opened her laptop. There was an inn to run, guests to satisfy, and a celebrity wedding to host. Assuming, of course, that she was capable of doing such things . . .

Louise stared blankly at the screen saver; it was a photo of Isobel at the age of two. Once again, she was overcome by an awful feeling that she was reaching too far. The hospitality industry was a notoriously fickle business, not for the faint of heart or those without serious financial backing. And in Louise's case, she felt the added pressure of proving to her ex-husband that she, too, could be successful in business.

Besides, if she failed and lost the business, what then? She would have to get a regular job (if she could find one; she had been out of the workforce for over sixteen years), and that meant uprooting Isobel once again. Even if she decided that it was financially smarter to stay on in Maine, they couldn't stay in Ogunquit. They would have to move north, maybe to South Portland, somewhere more affordable than a vacation destination.

No, Louise thought, determinedly opening one of her accounting files. Isobel had been through too much upheaval already. Louise would have to make the Blueberry Bay Inn and their life in Ogunquit work. She remembered all too clearly what Isobel had gone through in the months after her father's defection—the sleepless nights, the crying jags. Isobel blamed her father for having hurt her mother and for having wantonly destroyed what was, in her opinion, a perfect family.

"I hate him," she had declared to her mother, days after her father had moved out of their home and into one of those sterile furnished apartments in downtown Boston, meant for people in town on extended business trips and/or those in Andrew Bessire's unhappy situation.

"Don't hate him," Louise had said, fighting her own feelings of despair. "Be angry if you need to be. I am. I probably will be for a long time. But don't hate your father."

"Don't you hate Dad right now?" Isobel had demanded.

"No," Louise had said, honestly. "Hate is exhausting and it's unproductive. I hated someone once—you know who I'm talking about—and it didn't help me heal. It was only when I forced myself to let go of the hate that I got better inside."

Isobel had known that her mother was referring to the man who had stolen her innocence, the college boyfriend who had repeatedly hit her until one day, in an attempt to escape his anger, Louise had accidentally stumbled down a flight of stairs and wound up in the hospital with a concussion, a broken wrist, a cracked rib, and a fractured ankle. What Isobel didn't know and might never know was that that episode had cost the life of Louise's unborn child. Her first daughter, the one she had not been able to protect.

"Well, I hate Dad right now," Isobel had declared, "and I think I have a right to!"

Louise had let that outburst go without comment. Maybe Isobel did have a right to hate her father. Anyway, you really couldn't legislate emotions. What a person felt, she felt.

"And don't tell me that you forgive Dad for cheating on you," Isobel had added.

"I'm working on it," she had told her daughter.

"Why bother?" Isobel asked.

"Because forgiveness is good for your peace of mind," Louise had recited. She believed that. She did.

Well, Isobel had come a long way since those first painful months. She was nothing if not resilient; it seemed to Louise that Isobel had been born that way. She only hoped that as

Isobel aged and life took its occasionally brutal toll, she would never entirely lose that sense of wonderment and enthusiasm for life that marked her as special.

Louise closed the laptop, got up from the table, and grabbed her car keys from the hook on the wall. She had dallied with her thoughts long enough; there was so much work to be done. Right after she inspected the room that had been prepared for the new guest checking in later, she would drive to the Hannaford in York and raid the magazine section for wedding-related publications. She had learned long ago, in the early days of giving dinner parties for Andrew's colleagues and their spouses, that when all domestic inspiration failed, you turned to Martha Stewart.

Chapter 4

CITYMOUSE

Dear Lovely Readers:

Help! Sartorial crisis!

Just the other day while rummaging through Miss Kit-a-Cat's closet (with permission, of course), I came across a pair of dark red cowboy-like ankle boots. I say *cowboy-like* and not full-blown *cowboy* because the designer (a name I didn't recognize) sort of nodded at the Cowboy Boot and then did his (or her or their) own thing with it. Which is totally fine by me because not only am I not a cowboy/girl, I also don't play one on TV. (Hmmm . . . though that might be fun.)

So here comes the crisis. Miss Kit-a-Cat gifted me the boots, which she says she forgot she even had and had never worn because they were too small. (The boots were a gift. I have no other details so they must be top secret!) But neither the gifting nor the forgetting is the crisis. The crisis is that I don't know how to wear them!!!! Meaning, red cowboy-ish boots could, in some situations, be really, really tacky in the not-cool-at-all sort of way. You would think that with my vast experience dressing myself, I of all people, City Mouse herself, would be able to meet this dilemma with vigor and a sense of, "no biggie, I'll figure it out," but that's not what's happening at all! *Quelle horreur!*

Here's Gwen's portrait of said boots. Nice, huh? And the heel is a perfect height for daily walking wear. (I've been clomping around the inn wearing the boots in place of slippers, just to get their feel—but only when the guests are out, of course!)

Any and all assistance in this matter of vital importance would be greatly appreciated, so start sending me your brilliant ideas. I just know there's an ensemble out there, taking form in someone's creative mind, that includes the red cowboy-ish boots.

Au revoir for now!

Isobel posted the blog after one last check for unintended grammatical errors (intentional grammatical errors were sometimes allowed) and closed the laptop. She experienced a feeling of intense satisfaction when she had completed a piece of writing. Well, only if she thought the piece had merit.

Isobel thought often about how writing was a lot like acting (not that she had ever done any acting, but she was making an educated guess), meaning that even "your voice" on paper was only one of your voices or only one way your voice could sound at any given time. So even when you were writing in your journal, supposedly with only your own self as an audience, you were speaking to yourself with another self or another version of your listening self. It was inevitable, she thought, and kind of freaky. How did you ever get down to an authentic, totally normal, and real voice? Maybe you couldn't. Maybe it didn't matter. This sort of puzzling dilemma was one of the things Isobel really enjoyed about writing. There was such weirdness and ambiguity to it all, even when you were being hyper aware of style and grammar and rules. Odd turns of phrase and disturbing, alien thoughts could intrude and change the entire tenor of what it was you were trying to say—or what it was you thought you had wanted to say. It was true, from what Isobel had found, that you only really discovered your topic or your message through the act of writing. Strange.

Isobel came back to earth at the sound of a car in the driveway. She guessed it was Gwen; she had said she would try to stop by around now. She dashed downstairs and out onto the porch to see her friend getting out of her car.

Gwen Ryan-Roberts was a year older and a grade ahead of Isobel. She was also about a head taller and a good deal wider. Her face was downright cherubic—full cheeks, sparkling brown eyes, and dimples when she smiled—but Gwen liked to set off the angelic aspect of her appearance with short hair dyed a different improbable color every week. At the moment she was sporting a lilac mass; the week before her hair had been kelly green. She was also somewhat of a master makeup artist and could drastically change her look with a few artful strokes of a brush or pencil. Today, black eyeliner and heavy false lashes had given her a sultry air. If the sultry eyes didn't exactly work with the pastel hair, that was a decision Gwen had made consciously. She described her style as "inconsistent" and "provocative."

Gwen and her brother had been adopted by Will Ryan and

Curtis Roberts, Gwen when she was six and Ricky years later, when he was only eighteen months. He was now ten. Gwen hadn't known her brother until he came to live with the Ryan-Robertses. He was, in biological fact, her half brother. Ricky's father was Puerto Rican; Gwen's dad was, as Gwen put it, a mutt, someone of indeterminate cultural roots, a bit Irish, a bit German, a bit English, a bit whatever. The mother, about whom Gwen spoke with a frown, was an on-again, off-again drug addict. That was all that needed to be said about her.

"I kind of like not knowing much about where I come from," she had explained to Isobel early on in their friendship. "I mean, my fathers have the names of my biological parents, and some basic medical information. But honestly, I don't care about knowing more. I have a feeling I'd be disappointed if I did. Besides, I have two loving parents right there with me at home. No, I'm happy right where I am."

Isobel waved as Gwen climbed the stairs to the porch.

"Nice day, huh?" Isobel said.

Gwen shrugged. "If you like sunny and warm, with a good breeze, sure."

Their childhoods had been so very different. While Isobel had been living the pampered life of a suburban only child, complete with two-week summer swimming camps and brand-new clothes each season and her own spacious room with private bathroom, Gwen had been transferred among several lower middle class, hardworking foster parents, forced to be content with crowded public swimming pools and hand-me-down clothes, and the cramped family bathroom down the hall. But the girls had emerged from their respective childhoods with intelligence and curiosity and kindness and passionate interests in common—style, shopping, and the arts.

Today Gwen was wearing a kimono-inspired top in cobalt and emerald and black over black leggings. In an odd way, it complemented Isobel's simply styled but vibrantly colored maxi-dress—more cobalt, a dash of jade, and a hint of what might be called peridot or spring green. That happened pretty often, as if, Isobel thought, the girls were on the same sartorial wavelength.

They sat side by side on the top step of the porch.

"I just posted the red boot dilemma," Isobel informed her friend.

"Life is tough for CityMouse, isn't it?"

"Ha-ha. How's Ricky?"

"He's fine. Loving day camp, especially the archery lessons."

Isobel's eyes widened. "They let a child handle a real weapon?"

Gwen shrugged. "Blunt-tip arrows? Believe me, for what my parents are paying, I'm sure the camp takes all sorts of precautions. And, has all sorts of insurance."

"Huh. Hey, so I have big news." Isobel told Gwen about the celebrity wedding Blueberry Bay Inn would be hosting later in the summer.

"Yikes," was her first response. "Your mom is a tough cookie to take on Hollywood types. They're different from you and me, you know."

"Oh, it won't be that bad. Weddings are happy occasions." Even, Isobel thought, her father's wedding back in December, exactly a week before Christmas, had been a happy occasion. Well, for him if not entirely for her.

Gwen gave her the look Isobel had come to recognize as the "are you kidding me?" look, with the emphasis on the first syllable of "kidding."

"Don't you think you and your mom should at least watch that show, whatever it's called?"

"Why?" Isobel asked.

"To get some sense of the happy couple?"

"But the characters probably have nothing to do with the actors."

"I wouldn't be so sure. From what I've heard—and seen— a lot of times an actor takes on the personality of his character and has trouble shaking it off. You should hear the stories my parents tell."

"But they're talking about stage actors, right?" Isobel said. "Aren't theater people notoriously different from film and television people? Quirkier or more superstitious or something?"

Gwen shrugged. "Whatever. I just think it would be smart—at least that it couldn't hurt—if you watched the bride and groom at their day job. Actors come to believe their own publicity machines, you know."

"I guess."

"I suppose it's inevitable when you've got a camera trained on you every single moment of the day," Gwen went on. "I mean, these people can't even run out for a quart of milk without someone snapping a shot and publishing it with some awful heading about how limp their hair looks or how their pants don't fit right. What a weird way to live. After a while you must want to be the characters you play. At least a character is something to hide behind."

"Yeah. Like how a voice on the page, a narrative voice, is also something you can hide behind. Or something you can use to fool people, if that's your thing."

Gwen nodded. "The unreliable narrator. So I guess there are going to be a lot of paparazzi types at this shindig. And maybe a horde of fans, too, waving autograph books."

"Or body parts. I read somewhere that some people like their favorite celebrities to sign a body part."

"That's beyond pathetic," Gwen announced. "No wonder the really big celebrity types have so much disdain for the public."

"Disdain is never really justified," Isobel argued. "At least, I don't think it should be. People should really try to be understanding of each other."

Gwen laughed. "Isobel, you really are kind of naïve, you know that? I'm not saying there's anything wrong with it. Frankly, I find it refreshing. It's so easy to be cynical and suspicious. I think it takes more courage to be—well, nice and kind."

Isobel shrugged. "Well, I'm not trying to be anything in particular."

"I know. You were just born that way. And I was born—not that way."

"You're nice and kind!"

"Maybe. I certainly want to be nice and kind. But I'm not very positive by nature. I can put up a good show, but my default mode is caution and cynicism and suspicion."

"Well, I like you just the way you are. If it matters."

Gwen smiled. "It matters," she said.

Chapter 5

"So, that's that," Louise said. "The wedding of the century—in the minds of the bride and groom, anyway—is going to take place on my front lawn."

James whistled. "Wow. That is big news."

James Chappell and his longtime partner, Jim Goldman, were sitting at the kitchen table with Louise. A half-empty coffee cup stood before each of the men. Louise had come to realize that she seemed to attract people who liked coffee as much as she did. Take Catherine, for example. And James and Jim, already each on his third cup of the day; Jim took his coffee with two sugars and cream; James took only a splash of low-fat milk.

The couple had been visiting Ogunquit and the Blueberry Bay Inn every summer for the past fifteen years. Although the first summer Louise had run the inn things were not perfect—Louise had never been a landlord, and in spite of months of research she found herself taken by surprise almost daily by unexpected domestic crises of the plumbing and mechanical variety, and by the sometimes frighteningly odd demands of guests—the men didn't complain, and they had come back this summer for another three-month stay in the large guest room on the second floor. Sure, they could rent a house for the months or even buy one, but the inn lifestyle suited them just fine. Who wanted, they said, to be responsible for the bills when the plumbing went haywire?

They had enough responsibility with the, as James called it, "gargantuan pile" they owned back in New York's Hudson Valley.

"I'm not sure I've got what it takes to pull this off," Louise admitted now, draining the last of her coffee and getting up to bring the French press pot to the table.

"Don't be so sure," Jim said. "You know, the last owner of this place didn't know anything about marketing. You've done so much better at getting the name out there in the two years you've owned the inn than he did in the twenty-some odd years he owned it."

"Yes, well, I can't say that I've done anything so unique or innovative. I mean, it's not like I've claimed to have discovered a dashing, sea captain ghost in the attic."

"Hmmm. As far as I know," James said, "Ogunquit lacks a genuinely haunted inn. If only we could hold a séance, see what we can find . . . We could advertise on all the travel websites . . ."

"Oh Lord," Louise said, "that's all that needs to get out! I could lose business if people think the inn is really haunted."

"Or you could reinvent your business," James said. "You could cater to the ghoulish thrill seekers. But the truth is, Blueberry Bay Inn is not haunted. We would know. Jim is a sensitive. No need to hold a séance with him around. The specters would be flocking."

"Are you really a sensitive?" Louise asked Jim. "Wow. Were you ever menaced by an evil spirit? Did you ever feel a spirit touching you? Is what they say about cold spots being evidence of ghosts true? What about disembodied voices?"

Jim put his hands to his temples in mock despair.

"So you're not totally opposed to ghosts, then?" James asked with a laugh.

"Oh, I'm opposed," Louise said emphatically. "Especially when they're on my property. But I am interested."

"Well, this wedding should put you on the map, ghosts or no ghosts."

"Yeah, as a disaster zone."

"Louise," Jim said firmly, "it's time for an attitude adjustment."

"Yeah," James added. "Don't become a self-fulfilling prophecy. I think I will fail, therefore I will fail."

"It's just that I've never done anything without a safety net," Louise explained. "Either Andrew had my back or I was working as part of a team—you know, all those volunteer committees—where we all shared blame and responsibility and success. Frankly, I'm scared witless."

"Let me suggest that you use the energy the fear generates for a better purpose."

Louise looked at Jim as if his head had suddenly sprouted bean shoots. "Please," she said, "give me something I can use."

"In other words, take hold of your fear and transform it into forward action."

"You got a how-to manual for that?" Louise laughed. "Sorry, Jim. I know you mean well and your advice is probably very good—for someone who knows how to accept it."

"So what outrageous demands has this Flora Michaels person made so far?" James asked.

"Well, nothing terrible," Louise admitted. "It all seems normal enough. Actually, the most unusual thing she's asked for so far are detachable seat cushions for the folding chairs, and I'm pretty sure they won't be too hard to find. You know something? You're right. Maybe I am being a drama queen. Maybe everything will be okay, after all."

James stood from the table. "Now there's the spirit. Let's go, Jim. We're going to miss prime people-watching time."

The men left for the beach, canvas bags over shoulders and ergonomic folding chairs under arms.

Quentin came through the kitchen door then, a bandana around his head, his light blue T-shirt stained with sweat, soil on the knees of his old jeans. "I've gotta run to the hardware store, Mrs. Bessire," he said. "Can you think of anything you need while I'm out?"

Louise thought about it for a moment. "Honestly, Quentin, I probably do need something, but for the life of me I can't think what. Of course, the moment you drive away it will come to me."

Quentin grinned and went off. Louise knew she was lucky to have him working for her. From what she knew of Quentin's home life—which admittedly wasn't a lot, other than the fact that his father had passed away suddenly a few years back, leaving a wife and four children—he could use what money he could make. But Louise suspected that need alone wasn't what made Quentin the dedicated, hardworking young man that he was. Quentin had character, which was saying an awful lot these days.

No sooner had Quentin gone than Catherine made an appearance at the kitchen door, loaded with her painting gear—a portable easel slung over her shoulder, a camp chair, and an enormous satchel that held her paints, brushes, two small canvasses, and other miscellaneous but vital items an on-the-go artist needed.

"I'm just stopping by to say hello." She held up a plastic to-go mug. "You wouldn't happen to have any coffee going to waste, would you?"

"You just missed James and Jim," Louise said, taking the cup and filling it half with coffee and half with ice, the way Catherine liked it when she worked outside in the summer heat. "They were off to the beach."

"What is it they do for a living, exactly? Do you know?"

"Not really. James told me once that they work for themselves. Whatever they do, it enables them to escape from the rat race for three months a year. I hardly ever see either one on a cell phone or using a computer."

"Maybe once they're in their room at night they continue to build their empire."

Louise shrugged. "As long as they pay—and it's always in

advance, by the way—they could be Lex Luthor's right-hand men for all I care."

Isobel came into the kitchen then. "What about Lex Luthor?" she asked, opening the fridge and peering inside.

"No hello?"

"Hey, guys."

"Hey," Catherine said. "Well, I'm off to channel Woodbury or some other notable Maine artist. Wish me luck."

"You don't need luck," Louise told her. "You have talent and desire."

"Darling friend," Catherine replied, her hand on the doorknob, "everyone needs luck."

"Everyone needs good luck," Isobel amended, shutting the fridge.

"I thought that went without saying. See you later, alligator."

Louise smiled. "See you in a while, crocodile."

"You guys should get married already," Isobel said, when Catherine had gone. "You get along so well. It's pretty cute."

"That's exactly why we won't marry," Louise replied, laughing. "Not enough arguing to keep things interesting. Well, that and the fact that neither of us is gay."

"Yeah, but lots of women your age change teams," Isobel pointed out. "Look at that woman who was on that old show you used to like. *Family Ties*. I heard that she's with a woman now. And there's the woman who played Miranda on *Sex and the City*. Cynthia Nixon. She's legally married to a woman and they have a baby together."

"Well, that's nice for them."

"Yeah. I think it's hormonal. Or maybe it's that a lot of women finally feel safe being who they really are. No more having to hide behind a person that someone else thought they should be. Whatever the reasons, it's perfectly normal."

"Be that as it may," Louise said, "what do you mean by 'women my age'?"

Isobel smirked and shrugged. "You know. Old."

Louise made a playful swipe with the dishrag she had been using to dry a mug. Isobel squealed and dashed out of the kitchen.

Louise was aware that her mood had lightened considerably since only an hour ago. She wasn't alone in this new life after all. Yeah, the business of the inn was her responsibility, but there were people who had her back. There were people who had faith in her abilities and who were sure she would succeed.

In fact, she felt pretty good about her life right then. She mentally reviewed the afternoon thus far: the lively conversation with James and Jim, Quentin's generous offer to stop at the store, Catherine's unexpected friendship, her daughter's unconditional love.

Jake and Amber? Jordan and Montana? Now all she had to do was get the bride and groom's names straight.

Chapter 6

CITYMOUSE

Greetings and Salutations!

Today, I would like to pay tribute to The Jimmies. (See Gwen's portrait below. The Jimmies are sitting in the charming gazebo behind the inn, enjoying an early evening cocktail, or what they call a "liquid sociable." Whatever it is, isn't it a gorgeous shade of pink? And don't you just love their full and beautifully kept beards??) Together and separately they have reinforced for me the commandment or rule or truism that style is all about being who you are, and if who you are is genuine, then you have great and ever-lasting style.

But do you know how rare it is for people— okay, I'll say it, especially girls! Especially teenaged girls! Don't hate me!—to be comfortable in their own skin and to really know who they are and say "nope" to stuff that everyone else is wearing but that really isn't true to themselves? (Wow. Did I get all twisted in *theirs* and *themselves* or what? Grammar can be brutal.) It's rare. Really rare and sometimes it feels like it's getting rarer, that everyone (exaggeration there) is copying everyone else (is that even possible?????) and that real, true, individual style is just not something you come across a lot.

Like when LouLou and I take a road trip to Portland and walk down Congress Street and stroll down to Exchange Street and watch the boarders and art students and dropouts and guys and gals in their endless twenties, it's like wading through a sea of sameness. How did it come to pass that hipness and hipsterism is now uniform? How did it come to pass that looking "cool" could be so deadly boring and repetitive? Sometimes I think that if I see one more porkpie hat I'll start to scream and never ever stop! Just because something is declared "all the rage"—by some fashion industry marketing types!—doesn't mean you have to buy it and wear it! Let's face it, kiddos—not every head looks good under a porkpie hat! Not every pair of legs looks fantastic in jeggings or coated jeans or hot pink tights!

And then just when I think I'm going to die (not literally) of boredom or frustration (I wonder if you can be both bored and frustrated by something at the same time; I think so!), one amazing boy or one wonderfull girl pops right out at you and everything about him or her says, "Hey. I'm just me. And me is fantastic," and hope springs again in my breast, and, but I'm guessing here, in LouLou's breast, too.

So, here's a photo of this guy we saw outside of Space Gallery on Congress Street. We snapped it with his permission of course— to do otherwise would be rude. And it all works, from the very seventies mustache (which somehow avoids looking cheesy) to the dress shirt buttoned right to the starched collar, from the flared, cuffed dress flannels to the pink leather brogues on his feet.

Pink leather brogues!

Remember: *Chacun a son gout!*

CityMouse is signing off.

Isobel closed her laptop. *Well,* she thought, *I really spoke my mind this time!* She smiled as she remembered one of her first conversations with The Jimmies. The three of them were in the kitchen; the men were the only guests allowed into that inner Bessire sanctum.

"So, you're both named Jim," she had said.

"Yup," blond Jim in the plaid shirt said. "Officially, James."

"So, when someone calls out, 'Hey, Jim,' do you both, like, turn?"

"Sometimes," brunette Jim in the striped shirt said.

"Well, doesn't it kind of drive you nuts?"

"It used to," both said at once. "But not anymore."

"What can be annoying," blond Jim in the plaid shirt added, "is when people decide to differentiate us by calling us Jim One and Jim Two."

"Or Blond Jim and Brunette Jim," brunette Jim in the striped shirt said.

"Or Big Jim and Little Jim. Please!"

"Wait a minute," Isobel had said, literally snapping her fingers. "Why doesn't one of you go by your middle name?"

Both men had laughed. "Because," blond Jim in the plaid shirt explained, "we have the same middle name, too. Martin."

"What are the odds!"

"In fact, I now go by James," said brunette Jim in the striped shirt. "It helps."

"Isobel!"

That was a voice from the present; it was her mother, calling from the first floor.

"I'm coming!" Isobel shouted, and proceeded to tear down the stairs.

Chapter 7

The parking lot was full, jam-packed with cars from as far north as Canada and as far south as Connecticut. Finally, after three turns around the perimeter of the lot, Louise found a space, narrowly beating out another driver who was too busy poking at her phone with her thumb to realize not only that she was passing an open spot but that Louise was easing her own car into it.

Louise chuckled to herself. *You snooze,* she thought, *and you lose. Or, you text and you—You what?* Someone with more imagination than she had would have to come up with a new word that rhymed with text (the verb) so she could complete that sentence. You texted—and you wound up vexed? Nope. That wouldn't do.

Louise got out of the car and immediately began to sweat. It was one of those sultry days southern Maine could be plagued with, the air heavy with humidity and absolutely motionless. Louise fanned her face with her hand—a ridiculously futile gesture—and headed toward the pedestrian walkway.

First stop, the party store for anything swan-related she could find. Flora Michaels had asked (demanded) she supply representations of the bride's mother's favorite animal. Catherine had argued that Louise should have refused this request (demand) as outside the parameters of her contract, but Louise had been feeling generous for some unidentifiable reason.

And after that chore was accomplished, she would pay a visit to the Banana Republic outlet. Not that she needed any new clothes, but you never knew what incredible find you might stumble across on an outlet's sale rack. Isobel had not gotten her talent for bargain hunting from nowhere.

Louise's attention was suddenly caught by the sight of a couple standing dead center on the pedestrian walkway, forcing shoppers to make their way around them. They were a rough, unkempt-looking pair. The woman was badly overweight. The man wore glasses that had been repaired with silver duct tape, and a baseball cap turned backward. Both had on baggy jeans and T-shirts emblazoned with the brand names and logos of popular alcoholic beverages. The woman clutched a cloth tote bag that had seen better days.

Louise's instinct, finely tuned, told her that the man was an abuser.

It had been a long time since she had experienced a similar feeling, a gut-based knowledge of trouble. It had been back in Massachusetts, when she had been working as a volunteer at a safe house for battered women and leading workshops for young girls and—

The angry honking of a car horn brought home to Louise the fact that she had stopped in the middle of a lane of traffic. She hurried to the pedestrian walkway. The couple was still there; they seemed to be deep in conversation. Correction, Louise noted. The man was talking and gesturing wildly. The woman's mouth never opened; occasionally, she nodded. Louise continued to watch them without seeming to.

Her experience as an abused woman had made her even more concerned for the happiness of other women than she might have been if she had not gone through such an ordeal. At least, that was how she saw it. Making lemonade out of the lemons tossed into her lap? Maybe. Her experience had made her more attuned to the needs and well-being of others.

That was probably not uncommon. Not everyone who suffered transformed into a selfish, bitter being.

The man was talking now on a cell phone. The woman was staring at the sidewalk. Louise continued to watch them.

Only months after her miscarriage—as soon as she could get around without the aid of crutches—Louise had begun to volunteer at a safe house for battered women. She had felt it was a moral duty. Which was not to say that it was an easy thing to do. There were days, especially in the beginning, when the weight of sadness emanating from the residents felt impossible to bear and she longed to run (or in her case, hobble) out through the back door and never return. But she stayed and learned and did what she could to help and was glad for it. She was grateful for her own survival and realized time and again just how lucky she had been in the end.

Her fearful mother had questioned her choice of work; she had wondered if it would be healthier for Louise to "put it all behind her," to try to forget what had happened to her. Nancy Jones had thought it best that her daughter avoid associating with people who could only serve to remind her of what horrors she had been through with Ted.

But avoidance wasn't an option for Louise, not back then and not now, here in this parking lot. She felt the frustration mounting. She knew in her gut that the woman in the Jack Daniels T-shirt needed help—she knew it!—but there was little if anything Louise could do for her. If she dared approach the woman—if somehow the man turned away long enough to allow an approach—it was entirely possible, even probable, that the woman would lash out at Louise, even roundly defend her companion.

Some people sought abusive relationships for serious and complicated reasons. Riding to the rescue, even armed with proof of wrongdoing, was not to be taken lightly. You couldn't assume that every victim was willing to be saved. So many of them were simply too afraid to let go of the hell they knew for a hell that might prove to be worse. And some victims simply couldn't be saved. That was a grim fact.

Louise watched now as the woman searched in her dirty tote bag; the man, now off his cell phone, made gestures of impatience with his hand. The woman handed the man a lighter and he lit a cigarette. Did she imagine it or did he blow smoke directly into her face?

The couple turned away from Louise, and a moment or two later, his cigarette abandoned, they disappeared into the Old Navy outlet. Louise fought the urge to follow them. Better sense prevailed. Because, of course, there was the possibility—however slim—that Louise was wrong about the couple. Even the most perceptive of people occasionally misread a situation. And abusers were notoriously skilled at misleading those around them. A lot of times, their victims learned that skill, too. It was all about survival and protection. Protection of yourself and of those you loved.

Louise took a deep breath, not easy to do on a hot and humid day. She had struggled not to become an alarmist; she had resisted the impulse to see crises everywhere. That would be to morph into another version of her mother, and how miserable and small life would be then. Besides, she was wary of crusaders; some of the crusader types she had met over the years seemed to want people to be victims of injustice in order to validate their own personal mission. Not all, of course, but some.

Louise reminded herself of why she had come to Kittery in the first place, not to seek out (to imagine?) victims of domestic violence, but to purchase items for the wedding. As quickly as she could, Louise completed her task; swan-themed items proved easy to find. When she came out of the store she scanned the parking lot for any sign of the couple she had been surreptitiously watching. They were gone and it was likely she would never see them again. She could only hope that the woman—if indeed she was being abused—found the strength to turn to a friend, a family member, or a crisis center before it was too late.

Before what she lost to her abuser—her self-esteem, a child's life, even her own life—was beyond retrieval.

Chapter 8

CITYMOUSE

Good day, Everyone!

No self-respecting Mainer, even one as newborn as I am, can avoid paying tribute to L.L. Bean. And as a Maine blogger, I can't go a moment longer without extolling the Beauty of the Bean—the legendary company whose designers are masters of color as well as of utility. The summer sweaters, the winter boots, the canvas totes! And though in general my personal sartorial style tends to be more oddball than what La Bean offers, even I have found classic pieces of such durability and, well, class, they have found their way into my wardrobe. Take, for example, the lemon-yellow rolled-neck cotton sweater LouLou bought for me the first time we made an excursion to Freeport, home of outlets galore. The color makes me happy, happy, and so I feel pretty jaunty when I'm wearing it.

"Isobel!" It was her mother, calling from the front hall. "Are you ready?"

"Coming!"

LouLou calls! I'm off for now, so best wishes to all and the next time an L.L. Bean catalog shows up in your mail, buy something from it. You won't regret it, I promise, and CityMouse does not break her promises.

Isobel closed the laptop. She wouldn't actually post the blog until later, when she had had time to add Gwen's photos—one of Isobel in the yellow sweater and another of Gwen wearing her own favorite Bean piece, a men's hunting jacket. In spite of the fact that Gwen was grossed out by the notion of hunting (though she did eat venison and even moose), the jacket really worked for her. Maybe it was the juxtaposition created by the pink cashmere scarf she usually wore with it . . .

Isobel dashed downstairs and out onto the front drive.

"What were you up to?" her mother asked as Isobel slid into the passenger seat.

"Writing."

"Of course. Should have known."

The day was perfectly clear. If there was a cloud in the sky, Isobel couldn't see it. As the Bessire women drove into downtown Ogunquit, Isobel felt her spirits soar for no specific reason—well, other than the fact that it was a gorgeous day and she was psyched about the summer ahead. There would be the week with her father in Newport and adventures with Gwen and now, the celebrity wedding in late August. At the very least the wedding would be a hoot.

"I'll be about a half an hour at the accountant's office," her mother said as she drew the car to a stop. "I'm sure you can occupy yourself while I'm gone."

"No problem. And then we'll head down to Wells to check out that new secondhand clothing store, right?"

"How could I have forgotten? You've been reminding me every hour for the past day."

Louise waved and pulled off into the slow-moving yet somehow frantic summer traffic of downtown Ogunquit. Isobel hurried to one of her favorite little shops; it sold lots of prettily packaged lotions and handmade soaps. She peeked inside and saw that it was mobbed with tourists, so she decided to window-shop until the crowd departed.

A display of bejeweled hair clips held her attention for a good three minutes; they were both hideous and gorgeous at the same time.

Isobel finally turned away—and bumped smack into a chest. It was attached to a guy. He was tall, a bit over six feet, Isobel guessed. His eyes were blue (she knew that because his sunglasses were sitting atop his head), surrounded by lashes and set off by eyebrows that were very dark in contrast to his hair. That was blond and wavy and sun-streaked; she didn't think it was the result of a box of dye. She didn't like dyed hair on a guy. (Was that sexist? she wondered.)

He was wearing a pair of low-riding (but not too low, ugh) dark jeans and a paler blue linen shirt, partially tucked in and open at the neck. On his feet were European-influenced loafers. On the middle finger of his right hand he wore a thick silver band; there were tiny silver hoops in his ears.

"Oh, I'm so sorry!" she cried.

"My fault," he said, though Isobel knew that it hadn't been. "I'm Jeff."

"I'm Isobel."

"So . . ."

"So . . ."

They laughed.

"Are you from around here?" Isobel asked, kind of amazed at her boldness. She didn't think she had ever talked to such an incredibly good-looking—and older—guy before. It was a bit unnerving!

"Yeah," he said, "born and bred. But I go to school in Vermont, Worthington College. You might not have heard of it. It's a small and private school, kind of an experimental learning environment. Anyway, I'm home for the summer, working for my father."

"That's nice," Isobel said. "I mean, that you work for your family. Your father, I mean. What do you do?"

"I'm helping him with some personal business. You must have heard of my father, Jack Otten."

Isobel shook her head. "No, sorry," she said. "I don't think so."

"Really?" Jeff's eyebrows went up with surprise. "Well, the Ottens have kind of been established here for generations. And, no doubt, we'll be here for generations to come. You might have heard about the new youth center in Yorktide? My father financed the construction. Protecting the future of our young people is something he believes in strongly."

"Wow," Isobel said. She was genuinely impressed. And that explained Jeff's clothes, she thought. She could tell they weren't from a bargain basement. And if they were from a bargain basement, she wanted to know which one!

"I've never seen you around," Jeff was saying. "Are you here on vacation?" He smiled disarmingly. "That might explain why you don't know about my family."

"Oh no," Isobel said. "I live here. My mom owns the Blueberry Bay Inn."

"Yeah, okay. I heard the place had new owners."

"Well," she corrected, "we're not exactly new. We've been here for almost two years now."

Jeff laughed. "According to us native Mainers, you're still 'from away' and will be when you've been here for twenty years."

Isobel laughed, too. "Yeah. I've heard that. Well, we like it here so that's all that matters."

Jeff gestured off right, toward the beach. "What's not to like?"

"Well, winters can be a bit harsh . . ."

"That's when a lot of us head down to Florida. When we're not in school, that is. Or, like my dad, troubleshooting a corporate crisis in Dubai."

"Dubai?" Isobel repeated, pretty much stunned. She had never met anybody who knew somebody who had been to Dubai. "Really?"

Jeff shrugged. "It's just a city like any other city."

Isobel didn't know about that, but before she could comment Jeff was offering to drive her wherever it was she was going. "That's my car right there," he said. "The Jaguar."

"Oh, that's okay," she said, glancing toward the car and back again. Wow. The Ottens must have a serious amount of money if they could afford a Jaguar—and a convertible one!—for their son. Sheesh. "I'm waiting for my mom. But thanks."

In truth, though the idea of getting into that cool car with a gorgeous guy sounded pretty awesome, it also sounded a bit scary. He was, after all, a stranger. A friendly, incredibly good-looking stranger, but still. Isobel was not dumb.

"No worries," he said. Jeff raised his hand in a gesture of farewell. "Maybe I'll see you around town."

Isobel watched him get into his car, put his sunglasses back in place, and pull out. He didn't wave or look back at her. Well, she thought, why should he?

Her mom pulled up to the curb a moment later.

Isobel got into the car, aware of the smile on her face.

"You look like the cat who ate the canary," Louise commented.

"I have yellow feathers sticking out of my mouth?"

"Ha. And gross. What happened?"

Isobel shrugged. "Nothing."

"You're grinning for no reason?"

"Do I need a reason for grinning? Other than it's a beautiful day, the birds are singing, and I'm happy?"

Louise laughed. "Guess not."

Wow, Isobel thought, as her mother pointed the car in the direction of Wells. That was completely atypical behavior on her part. She always told her mother everything. What had made her—well, lie? Because choosing not to tell her mother something—especially something that couldn't possibly worry her—was the same thing as lying, wasn't it?

Well, maybe not really the same.

As they drove south toward Wells, Isobel decided that even though she doubted she would ever see Jeff Otten again, or at least not for a very long time, she wasn't going to tell anyone about their meeting, not even Gwen. It felt like her little secret—and she realized with a little rush in her tummy that she felt both guilty and excited about keeping it to herself.

Weird.

"Penny for your thoughts?" her mother asked as they passed one of the elaborate miniature golf courses along Route 1.

"Huh?"

"You're unusually quiet."

Isobel smiled her best angelic-daughter smile. "I thought you'd be grateful for the respite."

Chapter 9

"They want what!?"

Isobel was with Gwen, no doubt engaged in blog-related behavior, photographing a funky bit of clothing or trolling a Salvation Army or Goodwill store for hidden treasures. That left Louise alone in the kitchen with poor Quentin, the unfortunate witness of Louise's end of the latest call from Flora Michaels.

"Pink doves? They want to release pink doves after the ceremony? I don't think the town is going to allow the release of a flock of dyed birds . . ."

"Well, that's your concern, not mine," Flora Michaels snapped. "You need to make it happen."

"Me?" Louise heard her voice squeak. "Why me? Wait a minute, are the birds trained? Won't they poop on everyone's head? Will they come back?"

"How do I know? Just clear it with whoever you need to clear it with in that sleepy little town of yours."

Flora Michaels ended the call in her usual abrupt manner.

"Pink doves," Quentin said. It wasn't a question.

"What am I going to do, Quentin? I need more staff to deal with this crazy wedding, but I can't afford to hire more staff! Or maybe I just need to take a step back and think calmly about this whole thing . . ."

"It's a dilemma, for sure," Quentin said in his usual, unperturbed way. If the guy ever got flustered, Louise had yet to see it. Then again, why should he be flustered about a flock of pink doves? That was her problem.

"If you don't need me inside," Quentin said now, "I'm going to mow the backyard."

Louise nodded and Quentin left. No sooner had he gone than Flynn Moore made an appearance at the kitchen door.

"Afternoon, Louise. I came by to take a look at that cranky food disposal."

Louise smiled gratefully. "Thanks, Flynn. Can I get you a glass of lemonade first? Bella made a pitcher before she left this morning. It's pretty amazing."

Flynn accepted the offer. Nobody in his right mind turned down Bella's food or her lemonade. Louise knew better than to ask Bella for her recipe; whatever secret ingredient went into her lemonade to make it so tasty would forever remain Bella's secret.

Flynn was a handsome man of sixty, tall and lean, though what there was of him was solid muscle. For years he had been the owner and beloved manager of an extremely popular and successful restaurant/music venue known as The Jive Joint. A few years back he had sold the enterprise for a very nice profit, and instead of journeying south as so many northerners did as soon as they could manage it, Flynn had opted to stay put. He still lived, alone, in the house he and a few friends had built thirty years ago, a post-and-beam construction that was as practical as it was beautiful. These days, from what Louise could tell, Flynn spent a good deal of his time being a helping hand around town. Just the other day she had seen him on a top rung of a sickeningly tall ladder outside Mrs. Berkeley's house down the road. And today, he was here to crawl under the kitchen sink, at no charge other than some chitchat and maybe one of Bella's muffins.

Chitchat they did, and then Flynn got to work. Louise busied herself with cleaning the fridge and thinking about the celebrity wedding that was looming. She wondered if Flora Michaels had ever been married, and if she had, Louise wondered if she had inflicted on herself a wedding planner. The thought was actually amusing, the imperious wedding planner getting a dose of her own medicine. Wedding planners. How long had they been around, anyway? Back when Louise had gotten married, a woman planned her own wedding, with the help of her best friend (if she had one; Louise had not) and her mother. Then again, she hadn't been born and raised in a world where people hired caterers to feed their picnic guests. You did that yourself, with a bowl of home-made potato salad, a package of hot dogs, and a tray of cupcakes made from a mix. Maybe wedding planners, like party planners, had always been around, for the relative few who could afford them.

"All done," Flynn announced, bringing Louise back to the moment.

"Thanks so much, Flynn," she said, closing the door of the fridge. "I owe you one."

Flynn grinned. "As long as there's some of Bella's baked goods on hand, or a glass of lemonade, we're even."

Catherine came by just then, half-running through the kitchen door after Charlie, who was straining on her leash.

"Afternoon, Catherine," Flynn said with a grin.

Catherine caught her breath before responding. "Flynn."

"And how's the Princess today?"

In response, Charlie threw her considerable bulk against Flynn's legs and turned up to him a look of abject adoration. Flynn obligingly scratched her head until she had had enough of his attention. For the moment.

"Ladies, I'm off. Louise, call me if that food disposal acts up again."

"I will, Flynn. And thanks again."

When he had gone, Louise turned to her friend. "Flynn likes you."

"He likes everybody."

"You know what I mean. He *like*-likes you."

Catherine hooted. "Are you twelve? He's a nice person.

Like I said, he likes everybody and everybody likes him back."

"Look, the first thing he said to me, after 'hello' and 'I'm here to fix the food disposal,' was 'where's Catherine'. All I could tell him was that you were out and about somewhere with your easel and paints and canvasses. No doubt if I had been able to tell him exactly where you were creating a masterpiece, he would have hightailed it off in hot pursuit."

"I think it's cute the way you hallucinate."

"Hilarious. Where are you two off to now?"

"Obviously," Catherine said with a frown, "I'm not off to the beach, what with that ridiculous law about not allowing dogs in summer."

"Well, it does make some sense," Louise argued.

"It's not the dogs' fault if there are piles of poop along the sand, it's the fault of the idiot parents who don't clean up after them."

"Be that as it may . . ."

"Oh, don't worry," Catherine said, with a dismissive wave of her hand. "I'm not going to violate any laws. I want to keep a good reputation here, especially if I'm going to live out my days in this little town. I know I'm still eyed with suspicion by a good portion of the old locals. You are, too, my friend."

Catherine took her leave then, the Princess leading the way, as princesses are wont to do.

When she had gone, Louise thought about what Catherine had said just before Charlie had pulled her off. The town was eying her with suspicion. Yikes.

And how would the townspeople feel about a celebrity wedding in their midst, especially one hosted by a newcomer? She hadn't once considered it, but now that she did consider it, she felt a little sick. She couldn't imagine the town elders appreciating a media circus, no matter the immediate business it might bring to store and restaurant owners. "I just might have committed social suicide," she said aloud.

Maybe she should have talked to Flynn before signing that contract. Maybe he could help her research local laws about the release of dyed birds . . . Dye couldn't be good for a bird, could it?

And neither could lack of water be good for a plant. Louise filled two plastic watering cans at the kitchen sink and went out to the porch to tend to the hanging plants.

A few moments later, a very sleek and very shiny car Louise hadn't seen before made its way up the drive and came to a stop. A young man got out of the driver's side.

"Mrs. Bessire?"

"Yes," Louise said, setting down the watering can. "I'm Louise Bessire. May I help you?"

The young man extended his hand. As she took it, Louise noted that it was nicely manicured. Not a farmer then, or a fisherman. Well, certainly not either if he drove a Jaguar!

"I'm Jeff Otten," he said, "of the Ottens on Ocean Circle. On behalf of my family, I want to extend a welcome to Ogunquit. I apologize for it being so terribly belated. I thought one of my parents had certainly stopped by before now. I myself would have come by, but I'm away at school most months. And most summers I'm off traveling. But this year I'm sticking around town, helping my father with the business."

Louise smiled. "That's very nice of you," she said. "To come by and welcome us."

"My pleasure. If there's anything we can do for you, here's my card. Just give me a call."

"Well, thank you. I think we're all settled in," Louise said, "but you never know!"

Huh, Louise thought as the young man got back in his car and disappeared around the curve in the road that would take him toward the heart of town. *That was nice of him.* She looked at the card. JEFFREY RICHARD OTTEN, V.P., OTTEN CORPORATION. Contact information followed.

She made a mental note to ask Flynn about the Otten family the next time he came around. She had heard of them, of course, everyone had, but beyond the common knowledge that they were wealthy, had lived in the area for generations, and were active in state politics and their local church—facts that were true for just about any of the old families thereabouts—she knew nothing else.

Well, Louise thought, when Isobel started to date, and it would probably be before too long, she hoped she would choose someone with the good manners of a Jeff Otten. Too many young people these days were rude and disrespectful and—

Whoa. Louise grimaced. Where did that burst of grumpy old lady come from?

Hmm. She wondered how the Ottens would view the wedding of celebrity couple Emory and Drake. Or Kassandra and Mack. Or whatever their names were. As one of the leading families of the area, their opinion probably carried a whole hell of a lot of weight. They might even have the influence to drive the Blueberry Bay Inn out of business . . .

Louise sighed and went back to watering the hanging flowering plants. Well, it really was too late to pull out of the project now. As her mother had been fond of saying, she had made her bed and now she must lie in it. Fatalistic and depressing to the end, Louise thought. Good old Mom.

Chapter 10

CITYMOUSE

Salutations!

I just discovered that Miss Kit-a-Cat has the most fun book in her library. It's a big picture book called *My Love Affair with Jewelry* and it's all about Elizabeth Taylor's passion for collecting (buying, as well as getting as gifts) exquisite rings and earrings and bracelets and necklaces and even tiaras! I don't know much about her movie career—or about that infamous love affair with Richard Burton, who looks kind of hot in an older-guy-from-the-old-days sort of way—but I'm going to find out!

At some point Ms. Taylor supposedly said, "Big girls need big diamonds." I guess she was talking about herself, what with all of her mondo diamonds, like, for example, the Krupp, though she looks kind of tiny in pictures. (People who mocked her when she gained weight as she aged and because of battles with her personal demons should be ashamed of themselves. Who among us is perfect, huh? And enough with women and weight, already! Sheesh!) Anyway, no matter her physical stature, her personality certainly was enormous!!!

Anyway, the book made me think. I'm only fifteen (almost "sweet sixteen"—uh, right!), and already I've collected so much neat stuff, from beaded purses from the 1950s to funky pins from the 1970s to newer stuff that just looks great. Will I continue to collect until I'm old and gray? Will I someday start weeding out my collections of baubles and bangles, and replacing pieces with, I don't know, more expensive stuff, or more boring stuff, or maybe even more weird-er stuff? And in the far, far future, will there be someone I can leave my stuff to, like a daughter or a granddaughter? Who knows! Maybe I'll turn out to be a minimalist, though honestly, it's kind of hard for me to imagine myself liking less instead of more!

But I guess that's part of the fun of life, right? You just never really know what to expect. Except for death and taxes, which is something my father always used to say, and maybe he still says it but I wouldn't know. (Hey, Dad? You out there?)

Isobel stopped typing. She debated deleting those last lines. True, she hadn't heard from her father in almost two weeks; his periods of prolonged silence were becoming more usual, but it was still troubling. She really didn't want to end the post on a grim or a whining note. *The heck with it*, she thought, letting that shout-out to her father stand. Isobel's fingers flew across her keyboard once again.

The awesome LouLou surprised us last night with a homemade apple pie that was worthy of Julia Child (genius!) and left us groaning in warm, crusty, oozy delight! Gwen had her slice with ice cream and proclaimed the gustatory experience one of the best in her sixteen years. (Isn't that a great word—*gustatory???* I came across it recently in an article and loved the sound of it in my mouth but had to look it up in my big old trusty dictionary, as it was new to me. Context told me a bit, of course, but it's always good to confirm that you really know what you think you know.)

Here's a picture of the ceramic pie plate in which LouLou baked her latest masterpiece. It weighs about fifteen pounds. Okay, maybe about two. And, as you can see, it's a really interesting shade of turquoise. (I'd love a scarf that color. Must keep out an eye!) Lou-Lou found it at a yard sale a million years ago and remembers paying less than a dollar for it. Less than one hundred pennies! (Note to self: Start rolling your pennies, dimes, quarters, and nickels.)

I don't know how she does it, our LouLou, working from dawn to dusk and sometimes beyond, catering to all sorts of personalities and planning to host the wedding of the century (that's all I'm allowed to say about

THAT), while keeping a genuinely sweet smile on her face and managing to look *très chic* all the while!

Well, every good thing (and bad, I suppose) must come to an end. So long for now, Dear Readers!

Isobel posted the blog and put her laptop to sleep.

And she thought about Jeff Otten.

Her mother had told her about how he had stopped by to introduce himself and to offer any help they might need "settling in." Well, that had been very nice of him, but why would a guy like Jeff Otten be likely to pay attention to an obscure mother and daughter (obscure compared to people like the Ottens!) taking up residence?

Anyway, she guessed he hadn't said anything about his having met her in town, which was a little odd. Then again, she hadn't said anything to her mother about their running into each other—and that was the really odd thing. She knew she should say something soon, even if they never saw Jeff Otten again, because what if, just what if, he actually liked her? It was not good to start a relationship with a lie of omission, even if the lie was to her mother.

Whoa! Isobel thought. Talk about jumping to impossible conclusions, thinking that Jeff Otten might actually *like*-like her! Sure, she had always been popular in school with both boys and girls, but she had never had a genuine boyfriend. A few guys had asked her out (the first when she was nine and he was eight! She remembered thinking it was totally funny and laughing and then, when the boy started to cry, wow, she had felt so bad!), but not anyone she liked enough to say yes to. There was plenty of other stuff to do besides hold hands with some guy you could barely tolerate, like so many of the girls she knew from school did. Or, worse, have sex—oral or other kinds—with some guy just because you were "supposed" to be having sex.

Anyway, Isobel didn't really know who all these teens were who were supposedly having sex. She wasn't one of them, and neither was Gwen. Isobel had concluded that a lot of guys at their school were probably put off by Gwen's fiercely independent appearance and her perfect grades; she had heard the term "man repeller" (from that cool fashion blog) used about Gwen and about herself, too, once. Maybe in a big city it would be different, but in a small town there just wasn't a whole lot to choose from, and on the whole, people chose what was familiar, not what was wearing pink hair one week and green hair the next. It was understandable, if often frustrating.

As for Isobel, her mother's own cautionary tale hadn't put her off guys or scared her or resulted in anything negative or restricting like that. On the contrary, her mom's forthrightness about her own bad experience and her being so involved in the education of girls (all those workshops about girls' empowerment she had led!) had made Isobel feel pretty strong and smart about things.

And even though her father had become inattentive (to put it mildly) in the past two years, for a long time he had been a positive role model of true manly behavior. Well, maybe that very fact—his good behavior—had made his veering so wildly off course that much more difficult for Isobel to accept. If he had always been a bit of a slacker, then the contrast to what he was now—an absentee father—might not be so brutally clear.

Bottom line was that Isobel liked guys and was excited about the whole dating thing. Her basic nature was positive; she insisted on seeing the good before the bad, on seeing the potential for love before the possibility of hate. She just didn't assume the worst about people, and she was kind of proud of that. Not that she was a saint or anything, but she didn't look at the world and its inhabitants as inherently or necessarily flawed. Why should she? That option seemed too depressing. Maybe, like Gwen had said to her recently, being positive was a lot more exhausting than being negative, but that was just the way it was with her.

Isobel realized that she was smiling. So, Jeff Otten had come by the Blueberry Bay Inn . . .

Chapter 11

Louise had been out of bed uncharacteristically early, unable to sleep. All night she had been anticipating what she knew was going to be an unpleasant day. Today she was to meet the formidable Flora Michaels in person. Try as she might—and her imagination was a fertile one—she had little clear idea of what to expect, other than a nightmare of bossy behavior and miscommunication.

At exactly 10 a.m. a Hummer painted a strangely nauseating combination of red and purple (Louise cringed; some people's tastes!) roared up the drive of the Blueberry Bay Inn and came to an ungraceful halt by the foot of the porch, spewing gravel over the bottom steps. Three people climbed out of the vehicle, two men and a woman.

Louise and Isobel stood on the front porch, ready to receive wedding planner to the stars, Flora Michaels. At the first sight of her, Louise decided that the woman's name was about the only normal or inoffensive thing about her. She was painfully thin (Isobel had whispered that she made Rachel Zoe look robust and Victoria Beckham downright fat); the veins in her arms and hands protruded to a startling degree, and the tendons in her neck, not to mention her cheekbones, threatened to burst through the taut skin. Louise had a huge urge to run for a can of Boost and call for an intravenous drip.

Making the wedding planner's awkward appearance even

more disturbing was the fact that she was wearing the most absurd outfit Louise thought she had ever seen other than on a couture runway. It appeared to be one piece, but whether it was in fact a sort of dress or a sort of jumpsuit, neither Louise nor Isobel could determine. It also appeared to be constructed of a variety of fabrics in strips of varying width, sewn together with crudely obvious stitching. The garment, Louise thought, would depress even the jolliest clown.

The shoes were beyond absurd, more (bad) architecture or (bad) sculpture than functional footwear. How she could walk without severe injury to her spinal cord was anyone's guess, and more than once during the course of the day (more like tens of times) Flora Michaels tottered dangerously as she made her precarious way across the back lawn or down the sloping front lawn, forcing Calvin Streep, her trusty and ever-scowling assistant, to grab at and steady her before she pitched to the damp grass face-first. Louise had been tempted to offer a pair of her Keds to the woman but realized almost as immediately as the idea had come to her that Flora Michaels would probably rather commit a particularly nasty suicide before sliding her narrow feet into a pair of something as common as a pair of sneakers, let alone sneakers belonging to another woman.

It was impossible to guess Flora Michaels's age. Louise decided on "indeterminate" as the nicest way to put it. The woman's makeup was flawless but in a heavy, masklike way, which was as fascinating as it was frightening. Her hair hung to her shoulders and was artfully and professionally colored in the ombre fad, but it was so thin that her scalp was clearly visible at the crown of her head. Too many extensions, Louise thought, that or poor nutrition.

Not once during the interminable day did she let go of her handbag, which was approximately the size of a chunky one-year-old and the shape of a—well, of a chunky one-year-old. Except that chunky one-year-olds weren't known to come in a puce and kelly green print. Isobel dubbed the bag The Incubus, for reasons she chose not to share. Louise was reminded of the enormous handbags carried by one of her favorite Elizabeth Peters's heroines, and then felt bad for having made such a poor comparison. She doubted Flora Michaels had ever brilliantly fought off the criminal element with her own appendage as had Jacqueline Kirby. When Louise helpfully suggested Flora Michaels set the bag down in the parlor, she was met with a look of such horrified disbelief she really wondered for a moment if she had committed a serious social blunder.

There was something both pitiful and disgusting about the woman; after only moments in her presence, Louise felt simultaneously sad for and repulsed by her. Isobel declared her the most unstylish fashion-addicted person she had ever seen, and that, she said, was saying something.

Worse, Flora Michaels's personality was as entirely devoid of charm as was her appearance. She treated Louise with a condescension that bordered on pathology and ignored Isobel as if she were a sticky, obnoxious toddler and not a well-mannered, well-groomed, and perfectly articulate fifteen-year-old. (Isobel didn't seem fazed by this treatment, but it made her mother's blood boil.) As for Flynn and Quentin, unobtrusively on hand for minor and unexpected emergencies, they, wearing jeans and plaid shirts, were well beneath her notice. Louise again thought it odd for someone whose profession required her to handle and satisfy Bridezillas and their mates to display such toxic behavior, but maybe that was the key to her success, she thought, being more awful than any awful client could be.

"You must be Louise Bessire," the wedding planner said, thrusting her bony hand at Louise, who gave it a very careful shake. She noticed as she did (how could she not?) that the nails were bitten down to the quick. "I, of course, am Flora

Michaels. And this," she added, jerking her head in his direction, "is Calvin Streep, my assistant."

"Executive assistant," the man amended blandly. He did not put forth his hand.

Calvin Streep was a sour-faced specimen, also of indeterminate age, and as comfortably padded as his boss was skeletal. Louise was immediately reminded of that awful old nursery rhyme about Fat and Skinny and the pillowcase race. Calvin Streep clearly despised his job or, perhaps more accurately, he despised Flora Michaels. He practically snarled his obsequious responses to her questions and demands, and when her back was turned he produced the most amazing expressions of loathing Louise had ever seen out of a horror film. At least his clothing was inoffensive. He wore a lightweight cream-colored linen suit with a pale blue oxford shirt and pink silk tie. On his feet he wore sensible and very expensive loafers, complete with shiny pennies. The only incongruous note was struck by a rather large gold and ruby ring he wore on the pinkie of his right hand.

Before a half an hour had passed, Louise had decided that Flora Michaels and Calvin Streep could easily have been invented by Charles Dickens, should he have decided to continue his career from the grave, or by some other, still living writer who specialized in macabre and obnoxious characters.

In addition to her assistant, Flora Michaels had brought a photographer with her, whom she failed to introduce. He was a bald, gruff-looking older man in head-to-toe camouflage (why camouflage? Louise wondered). The moment the three had climbed out of their Hummer (why a Hummer? Isobel wondered), Flora Michaels loudly directed him to "photograph everything," which he proceeded to do—from the wide expanse of the front lawn to the details on the antique lamp shades in the parlor, from the lacy wood tracery of the gazebo to the hand towels in the first-floor powder room.

By eleven o'clock, Louise was approaching the limit of her patience. She stomped into the kitchen, where she found Isobel flipping through a magazine at the table.

"Mom, what's wrong?" Isobel asked loudly. "You're periwinkle again!"

"I'll tell you what's wrong! That—that creature! Well, if she thinks I'm going to replace that lovely old carpet in the front hall because the blue doesn't match the blue of her client's eyes, she's crazier than I assumed."

"Good for you, Mom," Isobel said. "Stand your ground. Wait. Really? The carpet has to match her eye color?"

"Not her eye color," Louise said with a grimace. "His. The groom's."

"Ah. Jake."

"I think it's Blake, actually," Louise said. "Or maybe it's Zack. Zack Dakota."

"That doesn't sound right, either. Whatever."

At exactly noon, Flora Michaels announced a break in the activities. Louise had provided a simple but substantial lunch, which she and Bella laid out in the breakfast room. Flora shrank from the buffet as if it offered toasted bugs and baked entrails and instead installed herself on a straight-backed chair in a corner of the room, where she sipped a fluorescent yellow concoction from a plastic bottle she had fished out of her monstrous bag. (Isobel murmured that the painfully bright liquid had "cancer causing" all over it. "I mean," she said with a shudder, "that color is not found in nature!")

After glancing briefly, and with disdain, at the buffet, Calvin Streep took himself off into town for what he called "a proper meal." The photographer, whose name no one seemed to have caught, grabbed a sandwich in passing and continued to document every square inch of the inn, with the sole exceptions of Louise and Isobel's rooms. Louise held firm in spite of Flora Michaels's whining demands for access to their personal space.

"More for us," Louise said with a sigh, surveying the untouched potato and green salads Bella had graciously prepared. Louise, Isobel, Flynn, and Quentin ate in virtual silence. When they had finished their meal, Louise packed the remainders for Quentin to take home. If Flora Michaels wanted coffee later in the day, she could damn well send her assistant into town for a cup.

When Calvin Streep returned to the inn an hour after he had gone, Louise detected the slight but unmistakable scent of alcohol. His eyes were brighter, as was his attitude. Louise found that she couldn't blame Calvin Streep for his indulgence. She might take to boozing at lunch or worse if she had to work for Flora Michaels.

Louise was in the backyard with that estimable creature when she said, "Have I mentioned that the couple have demanded a miniature carousel? Well, they have."

"What do you mean by miniature?" Louise asked, hoping to clarify the conflicting images that had leapt to mind.

"Small, my dear," Flora Michaels replied, in a tone that betrayed just what she thought of such an idiotic question. "Tiny. In that vein."

"Yes, I understand what 'miniature' means. What I mean is, is the carousel small enough to sit on a table?"

"What? No, it's an actual working carousel."

"For children?"

Flora Michaels's tone was now glacial. "There are no children invited to this wedding."

"Okay, so . . . Who's going to ride this thing?"

"No one is actually going to ride it. Lord!" Flora Michaels attempted to stamp a foot and tottered dangerously. Louise did not reach out to steady her, and the wedding planner eventually righted herself.

"So, people will just stand by looking at it go 'round and 'round?"

Flora Michaels shrugged.

"How tall is it?" That was from Flynn, who had appeared

at Louise's side like, she thought, a saving angel. "What are the dimensions?"

With a sigh of great exasperation, Flora Michaels fished in her monstrous bag and retrieved a folded catalogue. "There," she said, handing the catalogue to Flynn. "Page thirty. Pictures and the specs."

Flynn frowned down at the page and made several odd noises that sounded a bit like a lawn mower's engine spluttering. "Won't work," he declared, thrusting the catalogue back at Flora Michaels. "Fire hazard."

Louise frowned and nodded in what she meant to be a wise way.

"How could a carousel be a fire hazard?" Flora Michaels demanded, waving the catalogue.

"You think it runs on wishful thinking?" Flynn snapped. "Nope. No way. That's a death trap of a machine you're talking about. You'd never get the insurance."

Flora Michaels thrust the catalogue into the depths of The Incubus and squinted around the yard.

"Can the gazebo be relocated?" she asked suddenly.

"It most certainly cannot!" Louise cried. What in God's name might that cost! And where were they supposed to relocate it to? Louise wondered.

"Why not?" Flora Michaels demanded. "It's just a stupid little building."

Flynn's face took on an expression of extreme gravity. "Too much torque involved in the deconstruction and your leverage would completely collapse the infrastructure, causing the internal fuse lines to crack and run the risk of combustion. Also internal."

Louise fought mightily not to collapse in laughter. Where had Flynn learned to lie so creatively?

Flora Michaels sighed. "I told them that holding an event in the backwoods was a mistake . . . Calvin!"

Her scream—not a cry, a genuine scream—caused both

Louise and Flynn to wince. Across the yard, Quentin and Isobel clapped their hands over their ears.

"We're done here for today," Flora Michaels announced,
turning back to Louise.

Calvin, who appeared to be sagging by this point if the
beads of perspiration on his forehead were any indication of
fatigue (or an oncoming hangover), grabbed his employer's
arm and half-dragged her across the yard and around to the
front of the inn. Louise and Flynn, Quentin and Isobel, followed in silence.

Calvin Streep got behind the wheel of the Hummer. His
boss crawled in next to him, and the enigmatic photographer
and his piles of equipment installed themselves somewhere in
the vehicle's massive darkened interior.

There had been no farewells, no thanks, no more bony
hand to shake.

"I hope he knows how to drive that thing," Quentin said
as they watched the Hummer speed off down the narrow
road, a clear menace to vacationers not on the watch for
military-style vehicles and to local farmers rambling along in
their pickup trucks.

Flynn shook his head. "The photographer didn't say a
word all day. Not one. Amazing."

"Smart man," Quentin said with a nod.

Isobel sighed dramatically. "Geez, it was like a reality
show around here today. Seriously crazy in that, 'oh come
on, this has to be scripted' sort of way. You know, fiction
being stranger than truth."

Louise grabbed her daughter's arm. "You don't think . . .
Oh my God! Do you think there really are hidden cameras?
You don't think that creature planted microphones in the
ferns or behind the couch cushions? I saw her creepy assistant lingering over by the chaise in the parlor . . ."

Isobel rolled her eyes. "Mom, you need to relax. No, I
don't think they hid any cameras or microphones. Besides, I

think in reality shows the cameras are right out there. Everyone knows they're being filmed."

Louise let go of her daughter. "Well, it's too late to back out now. We are well and truly committed to this disaster."

Flynn cleared his throat. "You do realize that stick figure, Florabelle whatever her name is, needs this wedding to go off without a hitch as much as you do. She's a pain all right, but in the end, she's your ally. Keep that in mind and don't let her get to you."

"He's right, Mrs. Bessire," Quentin added. "Someone like that, her bark is way worse than her bite."

The men's words made sense, but at that moment, Louise could take very little comfort in sense. "I think," she said to the group, "that I need a drink."

Chapter 12

CITYMOUSE

Greetings, my Fellow Travelers on the road to—well, on the road to somewhere fun and happy and stylish!

Gwen and I were digging through LouLou's storage closet up in the attic yesterday—it was one of those drizzly, gray, and icky humid days when the only place you want to be is in an attic (even though it was hotter and wetter up there than downstairs, so why were we there????) unearthing fabulous treasures—when suddenly, Gwen shrieked and I shrieked and then we were each holding up a shoulder of a paisley maxi-dress in the most vibrant shades of blue and green and purple. With much clatter of our sandaled feet and an unfortunate bang of my knee against the doorsill (you should see my psychedelic bruise), we ran downstairs and hunted down LouLou, who (though very busy with Blueberry Bay business) told us— get this!—that the lovely dress we were clutching (carefully) once belonged to my grandmother!!!

"In fact," LouLou said, finger to her chin, "I think I have a picture of her wearing it." And she proceeded to hunt out an old photo album, one of those faux leather–bound thingies, where she found a white-bordered "snapshot" of her mother wearing the dress! My (young) grandmother is standing kind of self-consciously, or so it seems to me, in front of a house LouLou recognized as a neighbor's. The grass is green (though the colors in the photo are faded), so it was either spring or summer. And you can see the tail end of a car, some old monster from the late sixties, back when cars were as big as boats and, in my opinion, often gorgeous.

Then LouLou went on to say: "I remember being really surprised when my mother bought that dress. It was so unlike her to wear something that would call attention to herself. I remember suspecting a friend had talked her into buying it. Anyway, I don't remember her wearing it more than this once, but then again I was pretty young at the time. I remember finding it in the back of her closet after she died and I was going through the house. I couldn't believe she'd kept it all those years. It must have meant something to her after all. I guess that's why I kept it, too."

The dress now hangs in my closet, and I'm saving its first reappearance for a special occasion. It's a little long, so LouLou will have to hem it when she has the time. (I'm hopeless with a needle and thread, and don't let me near a sewing machine—*quel désastre!)*

I wonder how I'll feel, wearing a garment that once belonged to my ancestress, a woman who, from what I know from LouLou, was very unlike me. She was, according to legend and lore, shy and unassuming and not very self-confident at all. I most certainly am not shy (!) and I do tend to assume and I think I've got a pretty good sense of confidence in my self and abilities and all that.

Anyway, some people believe that a feeling or a spirit can cling to possessions over time, sort of a psychic residue deposited by the owner of those possessions. But maybe that's only when the person who owned the thing (a hat, a bit of jewelry, a dress) was a force of nature, someone unlike what my poor grandma was said to be.

I have no idea. Hopefully, someday I'll find out!

'Til next time, My Friends!

Isobel closed the laptop and sighed deeply. She felt tired and more than a wee bit grumpy. Faking exuberance wasn't as easy as some people made it out to be, even when you were faking it on paper—or a screen. Talk about being an unreliable narrator!

And her bad mood was all her father's fault. She had found the e-mail from him that morning; he had sent it in the middle of the night. With no warning, he had cancelled their vacation in Newport, Rhode Island. Isobel had been looking forward to touring those massive old mansions, and strolling the Cliff Walk, and shopping the boutique stores in town, hunting out little gifts for her mom and Gwen and Catherine, and finding something weird and wonderful that she could talk about on CityMouse.

True, Vicky and her daughters were to have been there, as well, but Isobel had even been looking forward to spending some time with her stepmother and stepsisters. Why not? They hadn't done anything mean to her, unless you could say that by having an affair with a married man Vicky had knowingly committed an act of meanness . . . Whatever. Isobel did not like to hold a grudge. She was the sort of person—and, according to her mother, always had been—who gave a person the benefit of the doubt not once but twice, and sometimes even three times.

Except, it seemed, when it came to her father.

Andrew Bessire had given no explanation for the cancellation other than "a pressing work matter." Isobel had no real reason to doubt him, but at the same time she did doubt him, of course she did. And she wondered if he would send Vicky and the girls to Newport without him. Probably. But of course he couldn't send Isobel, as well. Her presence, without her father being there as a buffer, might not appeal to Vicky. Isobel had only met her stepmother once, and that was at the wedding just that past December. She had been perfectly pleasant to Isobel, but, as any bride, she hadn't had time to stop and exchange more than greetings with any of her guests.

To argue that she should have made time for her new step-daughter, as Isobel's mother had argued—maybe a private breakfast that morning, before the ceremony—was futile now, after the fact. It was what it was. To argue that Vicky should have made an effort to meet Isobel long before the wedding was also moot. Besides, for all Isobel knew, her father was to blame for that, too. Maybe he hadn't wanted them to meet. Isobel could understand that. He probably had been afraid that she would lash out at Vicky. Not that she had ever been the type to lash out at anyone, for any reason. But given the fact that Isobel had outright refused to see or talk to her father for several months after his awkward, faltering explanation of why he was leaving his wife and child, Andrew Bessire might be excused for considering his own daughter an unknown quantity.

Isobel got up from the desk chair and wandered around her room, idly kicking aside whatever stuff her feet encountered. It didn't matter what disappointment she was feeling in her real, off-screen life; whatever it was she hid it from her readers. The blog was a determinedly happy place. She would never allow her own personal misery (or even just a bad mood) to leak into its domain. Okay, she had shouted-out to her father the other day . . . But that was the first and the last time she would let a bit of angst infect CityMouse.

Isobel stopped her wandering and flopped onto the un-made bed. She had told her mother about her father's e-mail over breakfast that morning. Her mother had dropped the piece of toast she was buttering and had then begun to apologize, almost as if it was her fault that Isobel's father was a jerk.

"I am so, so sorry, Isobel," she had said, her eyes wide with concern and an emotion a little too close to pity. Somehow her mother's reaction, though there was nothing wrong about it, made Isobel even angrier with her father and a little bit angry with her mother, too, something she couldn't immediately understand.

Isobel shook her head as if to clear away the uncomfortable memories. She got up from the bed, closed her door firmly behind her, and went downstairs. Gwen was just pulling up to the inn. Her visit was unannounced and very welcome.

Isobel waited for her on the porch, under the huge hanging

baskets of orange and yellow petunias. A variety of ornamental grasses were flourishing in the beds at the foot of the porch, along with a row of giant hosta plants that had fought the good fight against marauding deer. Quentin was to be thanked for that. He had spread some homemade concoction his family had used for generations around the plants, and whatever the magic ingredient, it had caused the deer to go off elsewhere to feast. The white wicker rocking chairs on the porch gleamed in the sun. Next to each one was a low table on which drinks and magazines and books or even feet might rest. At one end of the porch, a wooden love seat, painted white and amply cushioned, awaited tired guests.

"My father cancelled our vacation," Isobel said without preamble, perching on the railing. "Something came up at the office."

Gwen sank into one of the rocking chairs. "That's too bad. You must be disappointed. And angry."

"Oh, I'm not angry," Isobel lied, wondering why she was lying. Who was she trying to impress with a show of noble maturity? "Really. What's the point of being angry?"

"I'd be angry in your situation," Gwen said. "I think it would be normal to be angry. Not to say you're being abnormal . . ."

"Thanks. Personally, I think I am an eminently sane teenager. Which is saying a lot."

The girls were silent for a time. Two massive blue jays were screeching at each other in an azalea bush, and an enormous local cat by the name of Ivan the Terrible was stretched out low to the ground, slowly and patiently but determinedly slinking his way toward the unsuspecting birds.

"My dad is such a cliché!"

Isobel's sudden exclamation caused Gwen, absorbed in the antics of the fauna, to jump in her seat and the blue jays to fly off and Ivan the Terrible to turn his massive gray head toward the girls and glare.

"I mean, midlife crisis much?" Isobel went on. "What did

he do, read a how-to manual? Step One: Trade in the older wife for a younger model. And Mom heard that he upgraded his sports car again. I should have known something was up when he first bought the vintage Corvette. How boring! Next thing you know, he's going to get hair plugs. Maybe he's even wearing a man girdle!"

"His behavior is a tad clichéd," Gwen agreed calmly. "Look, I'm not trying to defend your father—he did cheat on your mother—but are you sure that's all it was, a midlife crisis? Maybe he really wasn't happy with your mom. Maybe they were incompatible deep down."

"Are you saying there's something wrong with my mom?" Isobel's voice squeaked in disbelief.

"Of course not. Your mom is fantastic. It's just that not everyone is meant to live happily ever after with a particular person. My dad Will was with someone for almost ten years before he met my dad Curtis. He totally thought he'd spend the rest of his life with that guy and then he was dumped. And then he met Curtis."

"And happily ever after?"

Gwen shrugged. "So far."

"Well, I still think that my dad was a weenie for what he did to my mom, and to me. He duped us. He made fools of us."

"You are angry at him for canceling the trip. Admit it."

"I admit nothing," Isobel proclaimed. "It's no big deal. I mean, sure, I was looking forward to Newport, and he could have called me. Come on, an e-mail headed 'sorry, kiddo'? 'Maybe next year'?"

"An e-mail? That was pretty lame."

"Well, maybe next year I won't be available. We'll see how he likes that!" Isobel shrugged and left the railing for the comfort of the rocker next to Gwen's. "Okay, that sounded pretty childish," she admitted. "But I do have a life and I can't be expected to be at his beck and call, right?"

"Right."

"I mean, Vicky isn't so bad. At least she's smart. She was a trader on Wall Street at one point so she has brains. Not that I understand anything about high finance, but it might have been nice to spend some time with her. And her kids are cute enough. They were adorable at the wedding. Matching green velvet dresses with a crown of ivy in their hair. Well-behaved, too."

"Yeah."

"At this point I wonder if they even remember me. I only met them at the wedding. Kallie and Karrie. I made a point of remembering who was who. *L* comes before *R*, Kallie comes before Karrie, meaning Kallie is older."

"That was smart of you," Gwen commented.

"Kids hate being called the wrong name. They understand the disrespect it implies."

"You'd make a good big sister."

Isobel huffed. "If I had the chance. But, whatever."

"Yeah. Their loss."

The girls were quiet for a time, during which Isobel was very stern with the resentful feelings that insisted on lingering in her heart. Or in her mind, wherever feelings really lingered. She did not like to feel bad or angry. She. Did. Not.

Gwen broke the silence between them. "Did you ever really mourn the loss—relatively speaking—of your father?" she asked.

Isobel laughed loudly and heartily. "Are you kidding me? I was an emotional wreck for weeks. Crying all the time, the whole thing. I wouldn't even talk to him for, like, three months or so."

"Okay. But why did you stop crying and all that? I mean, were you really done with the grieving process or were you just bored with it?"

"What kind of question is that?" Isobel asked. "Really!"

Gwen raised an eyebrow at her friend. "Well, you know, patience isn't your strong suit. It's no surprise to anyone who knows you even a little that you like to keep moving, and fast."

Isobel silently admitted the truth of that assessment. Look at what she had been doing mentally just a few moments ago—chasing away unpleasant thoughts. But before she could frame an answer to Gwen's uncomfortable questions, the sound of a motor and the appearance at the curve in the road of the car it belonged to intruded.

"Who's that?" Gwen said. "I don't recognize the car . . ."

"Oh my God," Isobel whispered. "It's Jeff Otten."

"How do you know Jeff Otten?" Gwen whispered back.

"Never mind now," she said, wondering if she should stand or stay seated or just go ahead and pass out.

Jeff brought the car to a smooth stop in the drive and got out. "Hi," he said, climbing the stairs to the porch and shifting his sunglasses to the top of his head.

"Hi," Isobel said. Still sitting, she gestured to Gwen. "This is my friend Gwen."

Jeff nodded briefly at her and looked back to Isobel. "I was in the neighborhood and I thought I'd stop by."

"Oh."

Jeff held out the bunch of loosely tied orange daylilies he had been holding down by his side. "And give you these. Welcome to the neighborhood."

Isobel did stand now, and accepted the flowers. "Wow," she said. "Thanks. They're beautiful. Thank you."

Jeff smiled. "I'm glad you like them." He pulled back the sleeve of his taupe-colored linen blazer and checked his watch. "Well, I've got to run. See you around."

Isobel just nodded. And she probably smiled back. She watched as Jeff got back into his car and drove off. If he had acknowledged Gwen in his parting, Isobel didn't know. She was in a sort of daze. She sat back down in the rocking chair, bumping heavily into one of the arms as she did.

"Ow," she said.

"So, spill," Gwen directed when Jeff had reached the end of the drive, safely out of earshot. "Where did you two meet?"

"In town," Isobel said. "We literally bumped into each other. Wow. I can't believe he brought me flowers. That was so nice of him."

"Hmm."

Isobel frowned at her friend. "What's wrong?"

"Nothing. It's just that they look an awful lot like the flowers from Mrs. Baker's front yard. The woman down the road, the one with the antique carriage on the lawn?"

Isobel laughed. "I know who she is. And daylilies are daylilies. How can you tell which garden they come from?"

Gwen declined to answer the question. "You're not seeing him or anything, are you?" she asked.

Isobel shrugged. "No. Why?"

"I don't know. It's just . . ."

"Just what?"

"Just nothing. Probably exaggerations. I heard something once about his being a troublemaker."

Isobel laughed again. "That's ridiculous. Jeff? He's so nice. People are probably just jealous of him because he's so cute and his parents have money or something. There are always people who can't stand when other people are happy or lucky or good-looking."

"Yeah. Maybe."

"Besides," Isobel pointed out, "you were the one who warned me about how catty people in small towns can be. The rumor mill running twenty-four/seven and all."

"True. But . . ."

"Anyway, this is only the second time I've laid eyes on him."

"Okay," Gwen said.

"We most certainly aren't dating."

Gwen skillfully raised one groomed eyebrow. "Methinks the lady doth protest too much."

Isobel felt herself blush. "Well, would it be so terrible if he did ask me out and I said yes? Assuming, of course, my mother agreed." *And I bet she would,* Isobel thought, remembering her mother's almost glowing report of Jeff's visit.

"He's nineteen, I think. Maybe twenty."

"So?" Isobel sat up as the thought finally occurred to her. "Wait a minute. Do you like him?"

"God, no! I mean, he's not my type at all!"

"Whew. I mean, if you liked him I couldn't go out with him. It wouldn't seem right at all."

Gwen smiled. "You're a pretty cool gal."

"You're pretty cool yourself," Isobel said honestly. "It's a pact. No guy ever comes between us, okay?"

"Okay. But can you imagine how many women throughout history have made that pact and broken it without blinking an eye? I bet the number is in the millions. Trillions, from the Neanderthals on out."

"Yeah. But it doesn't have to be us. We don't have to be a cliché of the backstabbing woman if we choose not to be."

"True. How many people really understand that they have the right, the ability, the privilege of making choices about their lives?" Gwen asked rhetorically. "Every single day, big choices and little choices. It's like, so many people just walk around on automatic pilot . . . What a waste."

"Well, we know about choices," Isobel stated firmly. "And we're not going to grow up into zombie adults who do everything just like their neighbors do it and who dress exactly like the guy in the next cubicle and who—Gwen? Are you listening?"

Gwen, whose head had swiveled in the direction of the side yard, abruptly turned back. "What? Oh yeah. Cubicles."

Isobel leaned forward to look off to Gwen's left. Quentin was at the far end of the side yard, busy trimming a hedge. He was muscled but wiry, not far from skinny, and for the first time Isobel noted that he moved with a kind of masculine grace.

Isobel sat back and laughed. "So *that's* your type!"

"It's not because he's good-looking," Gwen said, defensively. "Well, it's only partly because of that. He's really smart and really nice. And his eyes are so brown. And when he smiles . . . Wow. It's . . . just, wow."

"His hair is pretty great, too," Isobel said. It was. It was a soft brown and loosely curled and made a kind of halo around his face. She doubted he ever had to comb it. Of course, Jeff's hair was pretty great, too, even greater then Quentin's.

"So, what are you going to tell your mother about the flowers?"

Isobel thought about that for a minute. Well, she hadn't told her mom about meeting Jeff in town. So, how would she explain a "complete stranger" stopping by the inn with a gift of flowers? But maybe her mother wouldn't consider Jeff a complete stranger. After all, she had met him. But would her mother believe that he had never met Isobel before today? Isobel's right leg began to bounce as it often did when her mind was wrestling with something.

"The truth, of course," she said. But maybe she would just leave the flowers tucked away in the gardens out back, among their own stand of daylilies. If anyone noticed four flowers not rooted to the ground, they would more than likely attribute the destruction to the pesky groundhogs or the ravenous deer.

"You know, daylilies are kind of an odd choice . . ."

"Gwen!"

Gwen grinned. "I'm just saying."

Chapter 13

The Blueberry Bay Inn was fully booked for the Fourth of July holiday, which was a good thing, of course, but it also meant there was no holiday for its keeper. But that was all right. Louise had known the kind of life she was getting into when she bought the inn. Sort of. Knowledge gleaned from the reports of others was never the same thing as knowledge gleaned from your own gritty experience.

So, while Isobel and half of the town was at Gwen's family's house for their annual blowout party, Louise was busy sticking a broom as far under the fridge as it would go without snapping. An olive had escaped from its container and she was damned if she was going to let it mutate into an alien life form in her kitchen.

The job at hand wasn't exactly mentally taxing, so as Louise poked, she thought about times past when the Bessire family would roll the Fourth of July celebrations right into Isobel's birthday celebrations. On the Fourth itself there would be a visit to the town-sponsored fireworks after an afternoon barbeque at the Bessire house, to which the entire block was invited. On the fifth the Bessires would travel to Cape Cod for a lobster and clam chowder dinner. And on the sixth, Isobel's birthday, the family spent the day in downtown Boston.

While Louise and Isobel shopped, Andrew hung out at a sports bar; he was a rabid baseball fan. He joined his wife and daughter for cocktails at five (not at a sports bar) and then they went off for dinner at the Union Oyster House. That was Isobel's unlikely choice. She loved the old wooden booths and the rickety stairs to the second floor. Plus, even as a small girl she had loved oysters Rockefeller. Go figure.

"Aha!!" Louise cried. The olive, slightly smushed, had emerged. She picked it up with a paper towel and threw it into the trash.

Next on her agenda, cancel the order for the tables and chairs Flora Michaels had requested and then rejected, and place a new order for a different set of tables and chairs. "Shouldn't Flora Michaels be doing that sort of grunt work?" Catherine had questioned. Louise had shrugged. "Sometimes it's just easier to go along than to try to fight her."

But there were some occasions when a good fight was in order.

The happy couple, it seemed, would be staying in a luxury suite at a luxury resort in Kennebunk. Louise guessed there was a limit to their interest in old-fashioned charm, especially once the cameras ceased to roll. Blueberry Bay Inn was not the sort of place that offered Jacuzzis and in-room massages. So be it. But Flora Michaels had wanted to book James and Jim's room for an "A-list surprise guest" who did enjoy roughing it at an old-fashioned inn. Louise had outright refused.

"They are loyal guests and they're paid up through the end of their stay," Louise had said firmly. "There's no way I'm kicking them out for anyone."

Flora Michaels had backed down, but only after Louise had agreed to find the "A-list surprise guest" a room at another inn or bed-and-breakfast, a near-impossible task as every room in town was usually booked months in advance of summer. (Where the hell were all the other guests staying at such relatively last-minute notice? A campground in Wells? It seemed the bride and groom didn't know or care. Neither did Flora Michaels.) After some finagling and promises she hoped she could fulfill, she managed to get the bigwig a room and called Flora Michaels with the good news.

"Louise, dear," Flora Michaels cooed, "how sweet of you to go to all that trouble! Unfortunately, our guest won't be able to attend after all, something came up in Paris, so if you could just cancel that reservation, that would be awesome."

What could she say to that? When Paris called, you answered. And she never passed up an opportunity to do something awesome. Blushing with embarrassment, Louise had called the manager at Loon Isle and ate a heaping portion of humble pie. "You still owe me," Gus pointed out. "Now I've got an empty room to fill. Again."

The new table and chair order placed online, Louise treated herself to another cup of coffee. She wondered what Catherine and Isobel and Flynn were doing at that very moment. Not only had she been forced to miss the party at the Ryan-Roberts house but also to miss (well, to postpone) Isobel's birthday celebration. They had planned a day in Portland that was to include a massage at Nine Stones, a lovely spa on Commercial Street, lunch at the Portland Lobster Company, a visit to the museum, and, of course, shopping at all of their favorite stores.

The night before, while she had been sitting with Catherine on her little deck, drinking wine, Louise had told her how bad she felt having to cancel on her daughter. Catherine had said what any good friend was supposed to say.

"You're not required to be a saint," she had stated flatly. "End of story."

But there was more to confess. "I was a teeny bit relieved when Andrew called off their vacation," Louise had told her. "Of course, it would be a positive thing if Isobel developed a decent relationship with Vicky, but I would probably like it better if they never met again. Am I crazy? I feel jealous of a relationship that doesn't even exist but that probably should exist, at least for Isobel's sake."

"*Au contraire,*" Catherine had replied, "I think you're

pretty gosh darn normal. What would be odd is if you were working to make Isobel and Vicky BFFs."

"Really? You don't think Isobel and I are too close? Sometimes I wonder if I've smothered her or if I interfere too heavily in her life."

"About that you're asking the wrong person," Catherine admitted. "I look at your relationship with Isobel with something between admiration and raging envy."

"Oh. Thanks, I guess. You know, Isobel and her father used to be so close. I can't help but wonder if she's really as all right with things as she seems to be."

"Do you think she's pretending she's over the pain?" Catherine asked.

"No," Louise said, "not pretending. Not really. But I worry that maybe she decided she just doesn't want to deal with any more bad feelings. She can be terribly impatient . . ."

"Don't assume trouble. If there's no smoke, there's probably no fire."

"True. But if you don't properly grieve it all comes sneaking back at some point, the pain, the anger, and it can be that much more intense."

"Yes," Catherine said. "But maybe Isobel is simply one of those ridiculously resilient people. They do exist, though I suspect they're a rare breed."

Louise remembered finishing her second glass of wine and wondering if she should have a third. "There's one more thing I feel I should confess," she had said, still considering the important question of more wine, "if you don't mind being my confessor."

"Confess away. Though I have no official power to absolve."

"You know, Andrew made no attempt to introduce Isobel to Vicky before the wedding last December. He had a million reasons why he wanted to keep them apart—some downright cowardly, other reasons having to do with Vicky's messy divorce—and so I dropped the issue."

"You feel guilty for not forcing your daughter to meet the woman who had an affair with her father?"

"Well, yeah," Louise said. "I mean, my motives were entirely selfish. In the interest of peace I probably should have pushed Andrew to—"

"No," Catherine interrupted, "you probably should have done just what you did. Let Andrew handle the introduction. Really, Louise, his behavior, good or bad, is not your responsibility. You might have thought that it was when you were married—it seems to me, and maybe I'm wrong, that a lot of wives feel responsible for their husband's actions—but no more."

"Innkeep! Innkeep!"

Louise came back to the moment with a start. Thank God Mr. Peters, a pompous little pastry shop owner from Connecticut, who declared Bella's baking skills sub-par, was only staying for one more night. He treated her as little more than a slave. Louise went out to the front hall to deal with his latest urgent and no doubt utterly ridiculous demand.

Chapter 14

CITYMOUSE

Happy birthday to the United States of America! Mountains of thanks to the Founding Fathers who did the arguing and the thinking and the writing, and mountains of thanks, too, to the Founding Mothers who kept them fed and clothed while acting as sounding boards through the grueling process of framing the constitution. I am forever grateful.

Today I'm posting a photo taken by my father of LouLou and me on the Fourth of July, back when I was two days away from my fifth birthday. How cute is the little outfit LouLou has me wearing, a matching shorts and T-shirt, pale blue and sprinkled with a pattern of little flowers. And how sophisticated is LouLou's nautical-themed ensemble—the navy and white striped boatneck shirt, navy shorts, and white boat sneakers. We both look very happy and relaxed. Well, I suppose it's pretty normal for an almost-five-year-old to look happy and relaxed. What troubles did I have back then? Nothing that I can recall, except maybe not being allowed to have three scoops of ice cream for dessert. Sigh. I've always had a weakness for dairy (calcium is good for you!) . . . Maybe I'll stop at the ice cream shop in the Cove and get a scoop of maple walnut and maybe one of butternut crunch, too, just for the heck of it . . .

Here's a fun quote to keep in your head as you munch on hot dogs and slurp down pink lemonade and make party chitchat with your friends and neighbors. The always-stimulating Coco Chanel is quoted as saying:

"You live but once. You might as well be amusing."

Though CityMouse would add: but not at the expense of others.

So, happy Independence Day to all and everyone—and please be safe when on the road and handling fireworks!

"Heads up!"

Isobel ducked, narrowly avoiding being hit by a wildly thrown Frisbee. The Ryan-Roberts party was in full swing. She had felt bad about leaving her mother to the wolves, as it were, and had offered to stay at the inn to help troubleshoot any crisis that might arise, but her mother had pointed out that Quentin was there and he was a big help, more like three people than one. Then Isobel had felt bad about Quentin not getting a day off, but there was nothing she could do about that except bring home some cupcakes or brownies from the party and hope he was still around to enjoy them.

Jim and James were also missing from the celebrations; they had gone to a party at a friend's in Booth Bay. Otherwise, it seemed as if a good number of the town's year-round residents, as well as those who summered there regularly, made an appearance at some point.

Catherine had driven Isobel to the party. Flynn More was there, as were the town librarian, Nancy, and her partner Glenda. Most of the McQueen clan of the Larchmere Inn had made an appearance—Craig and his wife, Anna; Hannah McQueen and her wife, Susan, along with their two children; Tilda and her second husband; and the estimable Aunt Ruth, with her longtime and, at first glance, unlikely companion, Bobby, a retired lobsterman. (Ruth McQueen had been a corporate bigwig for a large part of her life.)

There was also a bunch of people Isobel didn't know by name, only by sight, like the two guys who came to town each summer from Los Angeles to perform at the Ogunquit Playhouse, and the older woman who volunteered at the Ogunquit Museum of American Art. She was probably, Isobel guessed, in her late eighties and was wearing what Isobel called Ladies' Attire. The woman's dress was modest in the extreme, complete with white lace collar and cuffs. It was made of two different materials—a sheer top layer over a denser bottom layer in a very pretty peach color. In the crook of her elbow hung a cream-colored framed purse with delicate silver hardware. Her jewelry consisted of a string of pearls around her neck, a pair of clip-on pearl earrings, and a narrow wedding band on her left hand. To Isobel, the woman seemed a figure from another, more gracious time. She doubted the woman even felt the heat in that restricting dress—and if she did, she certainly wouldn't admit it!

Jeff's family, however, was not in attendance (Gwen confirmed that), and Isobel had no idea if they had been asked or not. She thought it might be inappropriate to question the guest list. Besides, for all she knew the Ottens moved in a much more rarified circle than Gwen's family. There was still an awful lot about her new home she didn't know or understand. The intricacies of small-town living were not to be learned and absorbed in a hurry. And information was doled out in dribs and drabs, only when a newbie was deemed worthy of receiving the information. It would probably take years before Isobel and her mom were in possession of half of what the longtime residents knew.

The party was a great success. There were horseshoes and badminton for the adults, though after a few games early in the afternoon, these activities were mostly abandoned in favor of eating and drinking and chatting. An inflatable kiddie pool, meant, of course, for the few babies and toddlers at the party, was rapidly taken over by two ten-year-old girls who spent the rest of the day in the pool (legs hanging over the side), applying handfuls of sunblock, posing for their camera phones, and giggling maniacally.

"Teenage disasters waiting to happen," Gwen noted darkly.

Isobel was compelled to agree. "Girls gone wild, in training."

Gwen's father Curtis had cued up hours of music featuring the work of some local musicians like Eric Bettencourt, singer and songwriter out of Portland; Joyce Andersen, an amazing local fiddle player; the Lex and Joe blues and jazz duo out of Ogunquit and Kennebunk; and Lady Zen, also out of Portland. Curtis had also cued up some classic favorites guaranteed to get people into a festive mood—songs by The Beatles (everyone, even the ten-year-old girls, seemed to know the lyrics to at least a few of the songs) and Bon Jovi and even The Clash (that surprised Isobel).

The food had been provided by a small but popular local catering company owned and operated by a husband-and-wife team who worked out of their home in Yorktide. There was everything from corn on the cob to lobster rolls, from clam chowder to green salads, from strawberry shortcakes to brownies (several of which Isobel snatched for Quentin, whose sweet tooth was well known). For the adults there was beer and wine, and for the kids and whoever wasn't drinking alcohol, there was bottled water, diet soda (under protest as neither Will nor Curtis were fans of soda or junk food), and juices.

Ricky spent most of the afternoon playing war with some friends. The boys were each equipped with huge water shooting assault rifles, and in spite of stern warnings from parents, a fair number of guests found themselves "accidentally" sprayed. *Boys*, Isobel thought. What was it about violence that seemed to attract them? Something on a hormonal level, no doubt. It was not her immediate concern.

Charlie ran around off leash with the other dogs whose parents had been invited, including two chunky but hugely energetic pugs named Beatrice and Eugenie who were, beyond a doubt, the cutest little dogs Isobel thought she had ever seen.

"If I ever get a dog," she told Gwen, "I'm getting a pug. They're so velvety."

"And they snore a lot. I'll stick to my cats. By the way, have you seen Hamlet? He's been harassing this one poor little cardinal that comes around even though I've asked him politely not to."

"And cats always do what they're told."

Gwen shrugged. "I can try. And he listens when he's in the mood. Hey, what's with all these people naming dogs after European princesses?"

"What's with you naming cats after Shakespeare's characters? Hamlet. Laertes. Henry the Fifth?"

"Quoting or making reference to Shakespeare needs no excuse," Gwen replied loftily. Isobel was forced to agree.

The afternoon passed quickly, as fun times mostly do. It was only after many hours, when a good deal of the food had been consumed and the younger set of guests had fallen asleep in the laps of parents, did Isobel experience a sudden pang of loss. She saw Gwen standing in between her parents, an arm around each dad's middle. Curtis leaned down and kissed Gwen atop her hot pink head. Will smiled fondly at his daughter.

Isobel had to look away. She wasn't jealous of Gwen. She couldn't be jealous of someone she loved, even when that someone's happiness highlighted her own unhappiness. Envy was the green-eyed monster (kind of unfair to green-eyed people, and wasn't Shakespeare at least partially responsible for that slander?), and you didn't want him hanging around. It was just that her birthday was in two days, and try as she might, she couldn't seem to banish the memories of the fun birthday times she had shared with her mom and dad.

Though Isobel still wouldn't admit it to anyone, her dad's canceling the vacation had really hurt. And in spite of her denials she was angry, too. She had sent him an e-mail in reply to his. "I'm really disappointed, Dad," she had written, plainly. "I was really looking forward to spending some time with you."

His response was brief and almost lighthearted. "Really sorry, kiddo," it had read. "Nothing I can do about it." Disappointment had been heaped upon disappointment.

Still, Isobel really, really hated to feel angry with someone, even if it could be argued that that someone deserved her anger. She didn't like displeasing anyone, and to be angry with someone made her feel somehow guilty or wrong. *Isobel*, she told herself—and quite sternly whenever she felt she was getting grumpy about someone—*move on!*

Isobel grabbed a lobster roll (her second) from one of the tables laden with food and gobbled it down. Food helped one's mood, too, especially when it involved mayonnaise.

Her father, it had to be said, had sent a perfectly nice card from Hallmark. But it was too little too late. Isobel had barely glanced at it before stuffing it in a dresser drawer. There had been no personal note, and no present, and no phone call. Her father had expended the least amount of effort for her birthday. Maybe he had even asked Vicky to pick out the card; it seemed possible. Isobel couldn't help but wonder what he had done for his stepdaughters' birthdays earlier this year. Helped bake a seven-tiered cake? Dressed up as a clown and made balloon animals? Bought each of the girls a pretty little pony?

At least the signature on the card had been his. He had signed Vicky's name, too. Isobel wondered if Vicky knew that he had. She suspected that Vicky didn't care either way. Really, why would she? Isobel was out of sight, all the way up north in Maine. It must be easy to put her out of mind, as well.

Move on, Isobel had told herself. *Don't dwell on the negative!* Besides, it wasn't as if everyone in her life was ignoring her. Just the day before, she had received a birthday card from—of all people!—Jeff Otten.

Her immediate reaction had been one of intense excitement. It had taken a few minutes before she wondered how Jeff had known it was her birthday. There were lots of easy ways you could find information about people. Okay, sometimes maybe not ethical ways, but Jeff Otten hadn't struck her as some sort of creepy stalker type. Not driving a car like he drove and being the son of a man who was pretty much a local celebrity.

Anyway, she had kept the card from her mother (and from Gwen!), like she had kept the gift of the daylilies from her, and the fact that she had met Jeff in town, three acts of almost unprecedented secrecy. What was it about Jeff that made her want to hide him away and treasure his attentions in private? Or maybe it had nothing to do with Jeff at all. Maybe she was just growing up, needing her proverbial space.

Isobel stared off at the row of pine trees at the back of the yard. Whatever. She wasn't really worried about what she had done, or had failed to do.

"There you are." Isobel blinked; Gwen was standing directly in front of her. She hadn't been aware of her at all.

"It's almost time for fireworks," Gwen went on. She held out her hand; Isobel grasped it, and they made their way to where Curtis and Will had arranged a small (and carefully controlled) fireworks display. When every party guest was gathered within a safe distance, Will lit the first fuse. There were cries of joy and excitement. The dogs barked. The ten-year-olds exclaimed, "Awesome!" The boys punched their fists into the air.

For her part, Isobel fought back tears. Ceremonies of any sort always made her cry. Parades were the worst. She hadn't been able to attend Ogunquit's Memorial Day Parade back in May; she had learned her lesson the year before when the trolley ferrying three ancient veterans from WWII came by. She had burst into tears and hadn't been able to stop crying pitifully for almost a quarter of an hour. Sometimes, being a sensitive person could be a liability.

Now, Isobel looked around at the smiling group gathered in the Ryan-Roberts's yard. It was a beautiful evening and it had been a really fun day. She had stuffed herself with yummy food and had tried her hand at badminton (she had been awful!) and had sung along with Gwen and her fathers to that song Lex and Joe played about Memphis women and fried chicken (it was hilarious). She had even got to cuddle with one of the pudgy pugs!

Yeah, the verdict was in. She was happy with her life here in Maine. So what if her family wasn't perfect. Whose was? Anyway, it wasn't as if her parents were criminals. Her mom was great (her biggest failing seemed to be a tendency to worry too easily, which wasn't exactly a sin) and her dad had his moments. (He probably was really busy with work.) Isobel knew she had things a whole lot better than a whole lot of other kids.

She had, for another thing, a truly amazing best friend. She turned to Gwen and smiled. Gwen smiled back.

Yeah, it was all good.

Really.

Chapter 15

Louise rubbed her forehead and hoped that the ibuprofen she had taken a few minutes earlier would kick in soon. Stress-induced headaches were becoming annoyingly frequent. She was not amused.

Louise sat up straight in her chair; slumping never helped anything, certainly not clear thinking. And she needed to think clearly if she was going to solve the latest supremely annoying request made by Flora Michaels. Hand-embroidered hankies for each of the wedding guests? Really? And even if such things could be found in this machine-dominated age, why should it be Louise's responsibility to provide them? It should not be her responsibility. Her contract said nothing about such duties. So then why hadn't she come right out and told Flora Michaels to go to Hades, instead of hemming and hawing her way out of the phone conversation?

And then, just to make matters a little more interesting and a lot more frightening, there was the question of the electrician's bill. It was way higher than Louise had estimated—how had she made such a mistake?—and she was worried she might not be able to pay it all on time. She had plenty of experience balancing a budget through her volunteer work, but for some reason she really couldn't explain, working carefully with someone else's money was a whole lot easier than working with her own. No doubt a therapist could help her root out the answer to that provocative dilemma.

In short, Louise Bessire, sitting (slumped again) at her kitchen table, was suffering a very grave case of self-doubt.

Vicky Bessire could pull off this whole inn thing, she thought morosely, as well as the celebrity wedding, with her eyes closed, her hands tied behind her back, and her ears stuffed with cotton. Unlike Louise, Vicky was very close to perfect.

Consider her career. Vicky had been some sort of bigwig on Wall Street. Even after she had married Dan and moved to Boston she had kept her hand in it, commuting to New York several times a month. She had retired after the birth of her first child; after the birth of her second, she had established a home-based company called Bumblestiltskin. It sold expensive, handmade baby and toddler clothing to women who could pay a hundred bucks for a onesie. It was, as far as Louise knew, a great success. No doubt Vicky's children were geniuses, too.

Grr. Louise got herself a cup of coffee; what was that, her fourth one today? Maybe her fifth. So her stomach would rot out. Louise almost laughed as the thought of a sick stomach led her to a mental picture of Vicky's first husband. Dan Holmes was one of those all-too-common insufferably smug corporate lawyers who condescended to everyone he met as a matter of course. When he learned that Louise wasn't gainfully employed, his attitude toward her became that of a patronizing older uncle toward a sweet but not very bright niece. It had infuriated Louise, but at the same time she knew there was little she could do about the situation. Nothing she said or did would budge this man's opinion of himself as an exalted being.

Back then, before all the craziness had happened, Louise had thought that Vicky was nice enough, if a bit of an odd choice for Dan's wife. She had imagined him with that sweet-but-not-very-bright-child sort, and Vicky was anything but. She was fast-talking and intelligent, well-educated and witty.

She was also exceptionally pretty, in that heart-shaped face, perky little nose, and big blue eyes way so many men—and the camera—seemed to love. She was like Kelly Ripa with an MBA—a deadly combination.

Not that Louise and Vicky were ever likely to be friends. In college, Louise had majored in European literature and art history. Vicky had majored in economics and political science. Louise wasn't religious. Vicky was very involved in her church. Louise was a bit of a loner. Vicky admitted to a very active social life that included vacations with her women friends (what happened in Vegas stayed in Vegas?).

The couple had been in Louise's home only once, but the memory of that evening still rankled. The four of them had been at one of those boring command-performance corporate parties when Dan and Andrew got the brilliant idea of skipping out. They had gone back to the Bessires' house, where Louise had served Vicky a drink, had listened to Vicky compliment the living room's décor (her comments had seemed genuine), had admired her children (Vicky had a phone loaded with photos), and had even (God, how embarrassing in retrospect) given Vicky her recipe for banana spice bread. Did a woman like Vicky have time to bake? Yeah, she probably did. A woman like Vicky made time for everything she wanted to do, and more.

Andrew's betrayal, when it came, had seemed that much more painful because Louise had shared a pleasant evening with her rival. If Andrew had revealed an affair with some—to Louise—anonymous, unknown woman, the pain might have been a bit more manageable. And the men . . . Though they had never been close, there was the unsavory element of poaching in Andrew's choosing to run off with Dan's wife.

Louise shuddered at the thought. She got up from the table and put the empty coffee cup in the dishwasher. She spotted a glass on the sideboard. It was one of the more expensive ones she and Isobel had bought when they had first come to the inn, a red cut-glass goblet dating from around 1930. She wondered what it was doing out of the cupboard. She reached for it and it slipped from her grasp, shattering into thousands of tiny pieces.

"Damn!" she cried. Vicky, she thought, wouldn't have been so careless with such a valuable piece. Louise carefully swept the shards of the glass into a dustpan and then more carefully spilled them into a paper bag, which she placed in the trash.

There was no way Andrew could help but compare his first wife to his second, Louise thought now. And he would find Louise lacking—in business experience and savvy, in looks (if only because Vicky was almost ten years younger than Louise), and most definitely in ambition.

Louise slumped down at the table with yet another cup of coffee. How had she gotten on to this upsetting (and pointless) train of thought? No use fighting it now; she knew it was here to stay. In fact, might as well indulge the trip down memory lane . . .

Louise had begun to suspect something was wrong in her marriage almost in spite of herself. The clues were subtle; it was months before she identified them as worrisome. Andrew was coming home from the office later and later, though he never mentioned the trouble that demanded his attention. He was increasingly distant, yet increasingly pleasant in a bland, polite way. He bought several new suits, though the ones he owned were barely a year old and in fine condition. When she asked him if he was okay—"You seem a little bit, I don't know, distracted lately"—he smiled and replied, "I'm fine." He didn't tease her about her concern, which he would have done if everything had indeed been okay with him.

By then, Louise had felt that she had no choice but to launch an investigation. She felt dirty spying on Andrew; after all, he was her best friend, and all she had to go on were vague suspicions. But she went ahead and read his e-mails; she checked through his Internet history; she went through his wallet looking for receipts that didn't make sense and even inspected the contents of his briefcase and the pockets of his clothing. She did everything but break into his office and hack his computer there (not that she knew how to do such a thing), but found nothing at all suspicious.

But rather than admit she must have been wrong to think Andrew's eye had been wandering, she took one last desperate step. She hired a private investigator. Within three days he had brought her photographs of Andrew leaving a hot-sheets motel in a neighboring town. There were also several shots, taken only moments after the ones of her husband, in which a woman (wearing a printed silk scarf around her head and large dark sunglasses) was seen emerging from the same motel room. Coincidence? A legitimate, though unorthodox business transaction? Unlikely.

Louise, deeply shocked, had considered keeping silent about what she knew. If Andrew were just having a fling, then it would most likely end when the novelty wore off, and things between husband and wife could resume their normal pattern. But the not knowing became a nightmare and by week's end Louise had confronted Andrew.

Again, she was deeply shocked when he immediately admitted that the relationship with Vicky Holmes (Vicky Holmes!) had been going on for close to a year. He told her that he and Vicky wanted to marry. He had, he swore, planned on telling Louise soon. He and Vicky were tired of the sneaking around. How noble of them, Louise had thought. How absolutely freakin' noble.

Louise finished the reheated coffee and considered the wisdom of making another pot. An angry noise from her stomach convinced her to pass on that idea. Maybe a glass of milk instead, followed by a shot of Pepto-Bismol—because the trip down memory lane wasn't over.

Those first weeks after Andrew's defection had been horribly painful; her conflicted emotions were enough to drive her mad. Did she want Andrew to come back? Was she afraid of life without him? Did she still love him? Did she believe she could forgive him? None of the questions had easy answers. Yes, she wanted him back—until further thought revealed that no, she did not. No, she could never forgive him—until in a sentimental moment she knew that of course she could, and would, forgive him.

And then . . . A few weeks after the news broke, Dan had called Louise and asked if they could meet to commiserate. Slightly suspicious—did a man like Dan Holmes know how to commiserate, especially with a woman?—but not being in the strongest or most clear-thinking state of mind, Louise had agreed.

Before the appetizer had arrived, he had made a blatant pass at her, suggesting they finish the evening back at his place. Dan made other, more specific suggestions as to what might happen once at his place, one involving a restraining apparatus, but Louise had promptly blocked the suggestions from memory.

She had been disgusted. She doubted Dan was at all attracted to her; clearly his suggestion of a sexual romp was a crude attempt to get back at Andrew in the only way such men knew how—by stealing (or, in this case, borrowing; Louise was in no doubt this would be a one-night event) their property.

She had turned Dan away quite firmly, and though he was visibly annoyed by her rejection, he said no more on the subject, paid the check (bizarrely, they had finished their meal), and made sure she got safely into a cab at the end of the evening. There was something to be said for the courtesies.

The next morning, after a restless, almost sleepless night, Louise had been tempted to tell Andrew about Dan's proposal. It was doubtful he would be jealous. He might even laugh. And, he might tell Vicky, which would complete

Louise's humiliation. Better, she had decided, to keep that little bit of scandal to herself. And it wasn't even scandal, was it? For all practical purposes, both she and Dan were single.

Fortunately, after that one night, Dan had let her be. Not long ago she had heard from an acquaintance back in Massachusetts that he was remarried, and that this wife, Dan's third as it happened, was not only younger than Vicky, she was far better-looking (if somewhat artificially enhanced) and dumber than a bucket of hair. No defying the powerful Dan Holmes for Wife Number Three. (What, Louise wondered, had happened to Wife Number One? Had she been a typical Starter Wife, unthreatening and well-behaved? Whatever she had been, Louise hoped that now she was kicking butt and causing trouble in a new and fantastic life.)

Absentmindedly, Louise wandered over to the sink, picked up a sponge, and began to wipe its already clean surface. She supposed Andrew had to deal with Dan on some level, what with his being the father of Vicky's daughters. Knowing for sure that Dan made life difficult for Andrew might bring a smile to her face . . . She wondered if she should send a casual inquiry to one of her old acquaintances back in Massachusetts, someone who might have some dirt on the Bessire-Holmes family dynamic. Dirt she could gloat over. Dirt to warm the cockles of her heart, whatever they were.

Nah. Louise was above that sort of thing. More was the pity. She sometimes found herself thinking that it would be fun not to care about things like decency and respect. But she was stuck being a decent and respectful person, thanks to nurture, nature, or a little bit of both.

Louise looked up from the sink and saw Isobel in the backyard, filling one of the bird feeders. Her mouth was moving; no doubt Isobel was talking to the birds. They didn't seem at all afraid of her, fluttering close to her head and darting into the feeder even as Isobel poured the seed. Isobel as a modern-day Saint Francis.

Louise smiled and felt happy tears prick her eyes. Happy

tears, and tears of gratitude. Her daughter was a true joy in her life.

She tossed the sponge away. And if she, Louise Jones Bessire, had produced such a rare treasure of a human being, how could she fail to figure out how to pay a bill or host a stupid wedding?

Chapter 16

CITYMOUSE

Howdy, Style Wranglers!

Wranglers? Now where did that come from?

Come to think of it, I dreamed last night of being on a ranch that was scary-beautiful in its isolation and harsh, stark landscape— the jagged outlines of a mountain range in the distance, miles of nearly naked land, mini dust storms and tumbleweeds skipping devilishly along the dirt. Still, at one point I remember feeling so dream-frustrated that there were no places to shop or even to browse within walking distance and no cars on the ranch and so the only way to get to the stores was to ride there on a horse but I was dream-terrified of getting up on one of those huge, albeit gorgeous and noble beasts . . .

I guess that all means that in waking life I can't wait to get my driver's license so I can zoom up (okay, LouLou, within the speed limit) to Portland whenever I can to shop the fantastic stores. Not that I don't love shopping with LouLou—I do, I do!!!—but sometimes, well, lately it's more often than not, LouLou is super busy tending to the Blueberry Bay Inn guests (whom we love, one and all) and simply can't be forced behind the wheel of our Beloved Family Vehicle and pointed north. And though Gwentastic Gwen is always willing to chauffeur yours truly, why shouldn't she get to be the passenger once in a while and relax and enjoy the scenery?

Anyway, Portland is simply packed with fun shops like Encore and Material Objects and Find and Second Time Around and the Flea-for-All (not a shop really, and open only on the weekends but worth a visit; it's a combination flea market, antique show, and crafts fair) and Little Ghost (my favorite store name ever). Oh, and not to mention Stones 'n Stuff and Se Vende and . . . Well, I could go on and on.

And since these style seekers are on a budget (wah, but who isn't?) and can't afford to purchase every single gorgeous item we covet/desire/crave, we are super grateful to the shop owners who allow us to photograph these items (without, of course, leaving anything sticky or icky on said items) and share them with our readers.

So, here for your enjoyment are a few photos of items Gwen and I did not purchase (for a variety of reasons) but were allowed to share with you via CityMouse. They are, from top to bottom:

*A plastic change purse in the shape and image of a doll in the traditional dress of Holland; the zipper runs along the bottom of the full skirt; circa 1970;

*A tiny Wedgwood plate in the classic (soothing) blue with white figures; said figures are dressed in Classical garb and seem to be performing a dance while waving garlands overhead;

*A very heavy statue of the Egyptian goddess Bastet, or, as I'm told, also known as Bast; as you can see, Bastet is an extremely elegant feline. (Hint to self: I think Gwen would like this statue or one like it for her birthday next April . . .)

Now, on another note altogether . . .

Some people say that becoming sixteen is a landmark of sorts, a big deal, a turning point, the stuff of angst-ridden novels. But others, well, others say—or I think they say because I don't know; all I have to go on is their actions and you know what is said about actions in relation to words! Anyway, some people say that a sixteenth birthday is just like any other birthday, no great shakes, no big whoop, nothing to write home about, not even worthy of a phone call or a card with a personal note.

But whatever the truth about the Big One Six, I want to offer many and heartfelt thanks to those who tried and succeeded to make my sixteenth birthday a really special day. Love and hugs and kisses to them, especially LouLou, Gwen, Miss Kit-a-Kat, Blue-Bella, and The Jimmies.

Remember, Dear Readers, life is good!

Isobel finished posting the entry and closed her laptop. Life really was pretty good. Big deal, so her father had let her down. The other important people in her life certainly had not. The night of her birthday there had been a small and very lovely party in the kitchen with Isobel and her mother; Catherine and Princess Charlene; Gwen; and James and Jim.

Bella had made a scrumptious cake, with hazelnut cream between the vanilla cake layers and mocha-flavored icing on the top and sides. Everyone clamored for seconds, and thanks to Bella's generous notion of large, there was plenty to go around. They had shared a bottle of prosecco, with a small glass each for Isobel and Gwen, never to be mentioned outside of that room.

Gwen had given her a brooch made of brass and studded with colored glass stones. It had been part of a costume worn in a production of *As You Like It* that her father Curtis had directed years earlier in Boston.

James and Jim gave her another painting by Julia Einstein, this one depicting a glass jar, the kind used to put up preserves, standing on a rough wooden table, a spray of forsythia sprouting from the jar's open mouth. No one had ever given her a work of art before, and it was a very special first occasion.

Catherine gave her a gift certificate to Longfellow Books in Portland, and a pretty generous one, too. Her mom, the promise of a day together in Portland still there, had handed her a package wrapped in shiny purple cellophane. "Just a token," she said. "A little something to mark a big occasion." Inside the package was a cotton scarf the exact same turquoise as the ceramic pie plate on which Louise made her famous apple pie. Isobel was ecstatic.

By the end of the night the absence and the neglect of her father had been long forgotten.

And by the next morning, when her mother had asked if she wanted to come along with her while she ran some errands, Isobel, wearing her new scarf and her new pin and feeling pretty spiffy (she loved that word!), had jumped at the chance to tool around town and people watch.

They were stopped at a light along Route 1 in Wells when she saw Jeff. He was standing by his car, which was parked in the lot of a garage and repair shop. His sleeves were rolled to the elbow, leaving his muscular forearms bare. He was wearing another pair of fantastic jeans that emphasized his slim hips and flat stomach . . .

Isobel was seized with the desire to touch him. She realized that her stomach was whirring and that she felt very close to passing out or to . . . She wondered if sexual attraction was always associated with nausea. She hoped not. That would be a sick joke on the part of the Universe or God or Odin or Xena, Warrior Princess or whoever had organized this whole thing called Life on Earth and tossed it into existence. Sheesh.

"Are you okay?" her mom had asked.

"Mmm, hmm." Isobel hadn't trusted herself to say more. Jeff was now leaning into the car's open hood . . .

"What is taking so long for this light to turn?" Louise grumbled.

As far as Isobel was concerned, they could sit there all day, as long as she could continue to watch Jeff.

"Oh," her mother said suddenly, "there's that nice young man who came by the inn. Jeff Otten."

"Oh?" Isobel asked, doing her best to feign nonchalance. "Where?"

"Over there in the gas station. Or garage or whatever it is. The guy leaning over that gorgeous car."

"Oh. That's him?"

The light turned green—"Finally!" Louise exclaimed—and they drove on. "Yeah, that's him. He's good-looking, don't you think, in that Armie Hammer or Chris Hemsworth sort of way. Big and blond."

Isobel shrugged. "Sure, I guess."

"Thor, with his hammer and whatever other weapon or tool he wielded. I can't remember now. Wow, it's awful how the memory deteriorates."

"Mmm."

"I mean, maybe Thor didn't carry anything but a hammer."

"Yeah."

An image of Jeff wielding a hammer—or maybe an ax—his sleeves rolled up past his elbows, his shirt buttons mostly undone, threatened to send Isobel into a fit. She resisted the urge to peer into the rearview mirror. She wondered if Jeff would think she looked pretty in her new scarf.

But she would probably never know.

Chapter 17

Catherine let out a monstrous sigh. "What a freakin' awful day."

"You, too?" Louise asked.

The women were in the kitchen. On the table Louise had put out a selection of cheeses (all made in Maine), some good bread (ditto; it was easy to be a well-fed locavore in Maine), a dish of cured green olives, her own homemade tapenade, and a plate of shortbread cookies baked that morning by Bella. There was also a bottle of sauvignon blanc from Chile and a bottle of Malbec. Each bottle was almost half-empty and the women had only been at it for a half hour.

"I wonder if this is really what it all comes to in the end," Catherine mused, sipping her wine.

"What?"

"This. Sitting at a friend's kitchen table, drinking."

Louise grinned. "And eating. Could be worse."

"Yeah. Maybe this is all that really matters. Hanging out with someone who gives a shit about you in spite of your annoying qualities."

"Something's got you in a funk. Spill."

"Well, if you must know, I got a call from this woman I knew back in Connecticut."

"Bad news?"

"Not for her. She's getting married. First time. She's forty-three and he's fifty. She made a point of telling me that I shouldn't lose hope. Her hubby-to-be assured her that lots of men were willing—willing!—to date women my age."

Louise grimaced. "You must be kidding me."

"I wish that I were. And I hadn't heard from this woman since I moved here two years ago! What possessed her to call me now? I'll tell you what possessed her. The need to boast about her man-hunting prowess. The need to make me feel bad."

"Sounds like quite the bitch. Poor guy."

"Oh, I don't give a crap about him. He's an adult. He should have figured out before now what he's getting himself into."

"True."

"You know, I've been accused of being too fussy when it comes to men. Me, fussy! That's ridiculous. I've been in several serious, healthy relationships. But none stood the test of time, or the guy just wasn't the right one to marry. And in one memorable case, I wasn't the right gal to marry."

"Ouch."

Catherine shrugged. "Why must there always be a reason for something to have happened or to not have happened? Why must we attribute events or non-events to human agency when maybe there's something else at work?"

"Like what?" Louise asked.

"Like a random occurrence in a random universe. Or God. Or Fate. Or sheer dumb luck, good or bad. It should be enough to say, I have never met someone I wanted to marry. It needn't be made into a psychological drama."

"In other words, shit happens."

Catherine smiled. "Crudely put, but exactly."

"Well, I'd have to agree. Though some people do seem to bring misery on themselves," Louise noted. "I think my mother was one of those people. Not that anything horribly traumatic ever did happen to her. But she always expected it to, and I think she was half-disappointed when it didn't. She was all about doom and gloom. I'm afraid I inherited—or learned—some of that attitude."

"What a waste of time and energy, anticipating misery, when the fact is it's going to come at some point, anticipated or not."

"Right," Louise agreed. "Worry is interest paid on a debt that might never come due. Andrew taught me that, actually. The man has nerves of steel. Well, that or he's so supremely arrogant he fully believes he can conquer any crisis that might come his way."

"A helpful attitude in a career like his. Or in any career, I guess."

"But pride cometh before a fall," Louise said. "My mother taught me that, and it's a hard lesson to shake entirely. First, you have to really understand the difference between healthy pride and unhealthy arrogance and assumption."

"Yeah." Catherine seemed to be considering something . . . "Did you know that my situation is called 'circumstantial infertility'? Well, my former situation, as I'm no longer really in the running for a pregnancy. I mean, I'm not officially menopausal until my period has stopped for over a year—I think—but I'm close enough."

"Huh. That's kind of an odd term," Louise said, "but it could be way more offensive."

"Yeah. It's all right. You know, why shouldn't I have held out for love and marriage, in addition to motherhood? Yeah, I wanted a child. But I also wanted a loving husband and a committed relationship."

"You're preaching to the choir. In other words, you don't have to convince me."

"I know what preaching to the choir means. Sorry. That sounded snippy. And thanks."

"No worries. It's a sensitive subject. You know about my seminal experience, losing that first baby. It's colored the rest of my life. Not a day goes by when I'm not aware on some level or another of that lost child."

"It must be horrible . . ."

"You get used to it, like you get used to most things in life . . ."

Catherine snorted. "I'm not sure I'll ever get used to how carelessly, casually cruel people can be. One so-called friend actually had the nerve to say to me that if I had really wanted kids I would have just gone ahead and had them. As if a kid was the equivalent of a pint of ice cream. You want the ice cream, just go ahead and buy it already. The message there is, stop complaining. You should have adopted or settled for Mr. Less Than Right."

"It's amazing how some people have the nerve, the audaciousness, to pronounce on another person's desires! The only person who really knows how badly you wanted a family of your own is you. And it behooves those of us you tell to believe you."

"Behooves, huh?" Catherine smiled. "But seriously, thanks. You're right, of course. You know, even worse than idiotic presumption is the pity. Poor barren woman . . . What a horrible word to use, isn't it? Barren. As if the very essence of my womanhood is a dry and dusty wasteland."

Louise nodded. "Pity is rarely easy to accept, even when you want it, and we all do, sometimes. How do you handle it?"

"With humor, of course. Inside, however, I harbor visions of wreaking bloody havoc. Or, at the very least, of smacking her smug face until I'm the one feeling pity for her. And it's always a female who says such stupid things. Why is that?"

"Women feel they have immunity, given the subject matter?" Louise suggested. "I don't know. I'm sure there are plenty of men out there voicing their moronic and hurtful opinions to women who can't properly fight back."

"Probably. Except in my world—I mean, the corporate world—if any man dared mention the subject of motherhood or marriage or sex, he'd be out on his can with a sexual harassment suit."

"Thank God for small favors! But then why can male—
and female—politicians get away with making crude and ig-
norant and downright insulting pronouncements about
women whenever and wherever they please?"

"Don't get me started on politicians! But as for God . . .
Do you know the very worst thing someone ever said to me?
That God didn't want me to be a mother. That He knew I'd
be a terrible mother so He saved me—and the unborn
child—from the experience."

Louise gasped. "That's appalling. And incredibly stupid.
Who are these people with a hotline to God, anyway? And
why doesn't God tell them to stop calling?"

Catherine laughed. "Can you imagine the scene? I wish I
were a comedian, maybe Louis C.K., so I could write a
sketch showing God trying to let down a loonie gently. Or
maybe not so gently. Maybe God gets a restraining order on
the fanatical caller . . ."

"Restraining orders often don't work as well as they
should," Louise pointed out. "If I were God I'd just send a
lightning bolt and be done with the loonies."

"I think Zeus is the one with the lightning bolts. The He-
brew and Christian God sends plagues."

Louise shrugged. "Same thing. Far more efficient than taking legal action."

"And then there are the women who say, 'You have no
children? Oh, my, God, you are so lucky! I have four and I
haven't slept in ages!' They smile when they say that, of
course. Some of them laugh. A few of them tell me how
young I look, and that it must all be due to a stress-free,
'childless' life."

"Ow. I'd be tempted to punch someone who said that
to me."

"I've come close," Catherine admitted. "Only my incredible self-control stopped me. Oh, and once I was even told
that it was a good thing that I didn't have kids because it al-

lowed me to concentrate on myself. What the hell does that mean?"

"I'm assuming that helpful soul meant that as a child-less—or as some like to say, a child-free—person, you were able to take up a variety of costly and time-consuming hobbies."

"Yes, that sounds like quite the life, doesn't it? What do you think of my raising carrier pigeons? Or maybe collecting model trains is the way to go. Knitting? Bonsai? Extreme mountain climbing?"

"I always thought macramé would be a fun hobby . . ." Louise mused.

"Macramé? Hmm. I used to enjoy macramé when I was a kid . . . And was it just last year that macramé was said to have made a fashion comeback?"

"Really? You'd have to ask Isobel about that. I'm afraid I don't keep up with the trends these days."

"Trends are boring," Catherine pronounced. "Isobel would agree."

"Forget about trends. I'm going to eat this last bit of goat cheese unless you want it."

"Go ahead. I've got my eye on the cheddar. You know, these perimenopausal years are pretty hellish. I have this awful sense of my body mocking me. The whole system that makes us so biologically special was useless in my case. Before, when I was younger, at least it was of some potential value. But now, my period feels like a sick joke my body's playing on itself."

"That's awful. Really, I don't know what to say to console you."

Catherine shook her head. "Oh, there's nothing to say and I shouldn't be whining."

"I don't think it's whining to bemoan—okay, let's say to mourn—the loss of something as important and as potentially powerful as the ability to bring new life into the world.

I think you've got a very justifiable reason to mourn. Or to whine and rant and rave."

"Thanks. Hmm. I shouldn't have let you eat that last bit of goat cheese . . ."

"Sorry. But hey, your life isn't so bad the way it is, is it?" Louise asked.

"God, no. I had a fantastic career that allowed me to retire early with plenty of money. Face it. If I had married and had children, my career would have taken a backseat. It's just that the life I have now is entirely different from the life I imagined I'd have."

Louise nodded. "I think a lot of people can say the same. Maybe most people. I grew up with this boy who was an amazing runner. He won every medal you could win and was in training for the Olympics when he broke his leg. And that was it. The leg healed badly and a career as a track star was out of the question. He was only seventeen and everything he had planned for his life was suddenly scrapped."

"Yikes. Whatever happened to him?"

Louise smiled. "Last I heard he was a college track coach. So, I guess he found a way to make the dream come true after all."

"I wonder if he's an example of the rule or an exception to it."

"And I wonder if he's happy or bitter."

"I once dated a guy who was bitter," Catherine said. "From morning 'til night, it was all about what rotten luck he had always had and how he could have been a great success if only the world hadn't been against him from the start. Honestly, I don't know how I stood it for so long."

"Why did you go out with him in the first place?" Louise asked.

"I was young. I mistook bitterness for brooding masculinity. Too many romance novels as a teen, I guess. I didn't make that mistake again, I assure you."

Louise nodded. "Ah, yes. Young women really do have a knack for turning a guy's annoying character traits into evidence of heroic suffering and his faults into charming quirks. A tendency to throw punches becomes evidence of unfathomable bravery."

"And moodiness means he's a poetic soul when really, he's just a nasty son of a bitch."

Louise laughed.

"I wonder," Catherine said, "if that sort of thing is as common with today's young women as it was when we were young, or when our mothers were growing up. Take Isobel or Gwen, for that matter. Neither strikes me as likely to make a complete ass of herself over a totally unsuitable guy."

"They might be an exception to the rule," Louise said. "Let's hope they are. And let's hope we're not so biologically determined that a future generation can't break a mold that's clearly destructive to our well-being."

"Well, I hate to be the pessimistic one—or, as I would prefer to call myself, the realistic one—but I think we humans—we women, to be more exact, for the purposes of this conversation—are indeed pathetically predisposed. If we don't convince ourselves that guys are romantic heroes, we'll never sleep with them and thus the end of the human race. Which, of course, might solve a lot of problems for the planet, but it ain't gonna happen without some weirdo dropping a bomb."

"Always lovely chatting with you!"

Catherine executed a mock bow from her seat.

Louise poured a bit more wine into her glass. "Getting back to one's expectations of one's life," she said, "I certainly never expected to be divorced. I knew it was a possibility, of course, but I never counted on it! I was so in love when I married Andrew, and he was so in love with me."

"Really?" Catherine asked. "Were you really both in love?"

"Absolutely. Even Andrew will still admit that. Which

only makes the whole divorce thing that much more depressing, I think."

"Yes, I suppose it does."

There was silence for a long moment, and then Catherine said, with some urgency, "When do you give up? When do you say, okay, it's not in the cards for me to get married? Okay, it's not in the cards for me to have a baby of my own?"

"You could still meet Mr. Right," Louise pointed out.

"Sure, anything's possible! The world could come to a raging nuclear end tonight. Lady Gaga could decide to enter a convent. Well, actually, I could see that happening . . . Anyway, even if I do meet the right guy we won't be having a baby together, that's for sure. Not the old-fashioned way, at least."

"You haven't made peace with this yet, have you?"

"Nope," Catherine said forcefully. "I haven't. And maybe it's about time I did. Bitterness, as we have noted, is not an attractive quality."

Louise nodded. "It's very bad for the skin."

"Please pour me more wine. And forgive me for chewing off your ear."

"You're my friend."

Catherine took a sip of the Malbec and smiled. "That's your expertise, you know. One of them, anyway. You're a good listener."

"Thanks."

"No, really. It's a gift."

Louise laughed. "Not when Isobel is rambling on about her latest costume jewelry purchase it isn't! Then, it's a liability."

Chapter 18

CITYMOUSE

Greetings, My Friends!

Today I want to talk about jewelry. Well, pretty much every day I want to talk about jewelry (hehe!), but today especially, as yesterday afternoon I found the most amazing little piece at, of all places, Reny's. Gwen and I drove down to the store in Wells because Gwen needed some new basic T-shirts (she likes to layer them, which is something she does quite skillfully), and I thought, why not tag along?

So while Gwen examined the stacks of T-shirts for just the right assortment of colors in the scoop-neck style she adores, I carefully poked my way through the small and somewhat haphazard rack of jewelry until, just when I was beginning to despair of finding a treasure, what should I stumble upon but a braided, brown leather bracelet studded with a row of crystals set in bronze right down the center of the braiding. Sounds pretty common, no? Well, yeah, in one way it is pretty common, but in another way it's very much its own statement. See Gwen's photo, below. The piece has character somehow, I don't know how or where, exactly, but the character is there. Character and a good weight on the wrist. It feels solid but not too heavy. I love it!

Don't ever forget that it's the little things that can make an ordinary day one of distinction!

More on jewelry: I've been collecting vintage jewelry for the past few years, stuff by Miriam Haskell (I've only been able to afford one pin so far); those gorgeous, colorful pins in the Juliana style (ditto); some good rhinestone pieces (with only a few stones missing here and there). I would dearly love to stumble upon a Marena pin. They were made in Germany and some are available on eBay but the hunt is part of the thrill for me so I hunt on . . .

Note to self: Attend a live auction soon!

Over the years (don't I sound ancient!), I've amassed a good stash of old crystal stuff (clear and colored), and two Bakelite bangles (one studded with colored crystals), a super-long set of blue pearls for a whopping five dollars (okay, they probably aren't real pearls but I don't care, they're lovely).

And someday I'm going to inherit from LouLou and from my grandmother via Lou-Lou, a platinum and diamond wedding set (the main diamond is a marquis cut, which has always struck me as the height of elegance!), as well as a few other heirlooms, like a gold and pearl brooch and a gold and diamond stick pin. But as long as LouLou can wear the family pieces in good health, I wouldn't dream of pressing her for them. (Really, LouLou, I swear.)

I can't possibly wear all the jewelry that I have collected at any one time (does anyone know where I could get an extra set of hands, ankles, a neck, etc.?), but I can gaze and admire and wonder, and sometimes a piece calls out to me in a definitive and very loud voice and demands to be taken out for a day or even for an hour. So I'll sit down at the kitchen table to watch a TV show, maybe *American Pickers* (LouLou has a crush on Mike; I love the friendship between the guys, and Danielle is beyond cool!), or maybe *Auction Hunters* (Ton is such a gentle giant!), or *Auction Kings* (I think Paul is adorable! Those dimples! And Cindy kicks butt!), all decked out in bits of my finery, clip-on earrings (ow!), noisy charm bracelets, huge cocktail rings (one is never enough), and multi-strand bead necklaces, and everyone is happy—bracelets, rings, and all!

So I anthropomorphize inanimate stuff. Doesn't everyone?

But I just have to tell you about a non-bauble purchase, a 1970s brown leather trench coat that LouLou and I found at Encore in Portland back in March. The coat, which comes to just below my knees, is beyond cool. You can almost hear the sound of one of those classic bands like Earth, Wind & Fire playing the minute you slide an arm into one of the very narrow sleeves. Now all I need to hunt down is a pair of knee-high vintage '70s boots and maybe a suede patchwork bag and I'm off to the disco! (Does anyone know where I can learn to do The Hustle? Wait, maybe funk would be more my thing . . . Yeah, I think that it would!)

It's CityMouse signing off until next time!

Isobel closed her laptop. It had been really hard to keep focused on jewelry and funky old clothing when all she really wanted to write about was her upcoming date with Jeff. But CityMouse was not the place for gushing about guys, nor was it the place for anything really personal. CityMouse, the voice, was, after all, a persona, and while she didn't lie about her real self (she did anthropomorphize inanimate objects!), she also didn't reveal too much about that real self—like how she felt about her father.

Or like how she felt about Jeff Otten.

He had stopped by the inn again the day before; she happened to be on the porch at the time. When he got out of the car, all she could see in her mind's eye was how incredibly sexy he had looked the other day at that garage in Wells. She could hardly look at him now without blushing. Maybe she did blush.

He came up the porch steps and sat in the rocker next to the one in which she was sitting. They exchanged what Catherine called "pleasantries." And then Jeff asked her if she would like to have dinner with him.

Isobel had really, seriously thought she was going to faint dead away. With every bit of her strength she summoned what she hoped were the right, normal words: "Sure. I'd like that." And then she had had to add, "But I'll have to ask my mother for permission." She had felt embarrassed and very, very young admitting that, but Jeff had smiled kindly.

"That's cool," he had said and had given her his cell phone number. "Just call me when you've talked to her."

So she had talked to her mother. She told her that Jeff had asked her out. And without planning to, she also told her about having met Jeff in town that first time. She kept the fact of the gift of flowers to herself. And the fact of the birthday card, too.

"Why didn't you tell me you'd met him?" her mother had asked, sounding not exactly mad but definitely puzzled. "Especially when I told you he stopped by the inn?"

"I don't know, really," Isobel said after a moment. "I guess I thought it wasn't important." That was a bit of a lie, too. Isobel had begun to feel increasingly uncomfortable with the conversation, but there was no escaping it if she was to get her mother's permission to go out with Jeff.

"It's odd that he didn't mention it that day he stopped by the inn," her mother went on. "Well, he probably assumed you had told me."

"I'm sorry, Mom. Really."

"Well, no harm done."

And then her mother had admitted she had asked around a bit about Jeff. Catherine, she said, knew nothing about him but had heard the usual and not very interesting facts about Mr. Otten. Flynn had been a bit more helpful; he had served with Jack Otten on various local committees and for a year on the town zoning board. The senior Otten was generally polite if a bit pompous. He gave generously to his church and to local and state representatives of his political party. He had recently funded the construction of a youth center in Yorktide.

About the Ottens' younger son, Jeff, he had nothing to say. "He flies under the radar from what I can tell," Flynn said.

About the Ottens' older son, Michael, he had much to relate. "The guy was golden from the get-go. Straight-A student, all-around athlete, volunteered at the hospital, kids' cancer ward, when he was old enough to get around on his own. Went to Northeastern and then on to graduate school somewhere in California. Last I heard he was heading up a research division at a big pharma company, headquartered in Basel. Nice kid, too. Always had a pleasant word for people he met, whether on the street or at some hoity-toity party his parents hosted. It's no wonder Jeff is a quiet one. Michael would be a very hard act to follow, even if Jeff should want to."

"Does he want to?" Louise had asked.

"No idea," Flynn had admitted with a shrug. "Like I said, under the radar."

Jim and James knew nothing about the male Ottens and only a little about Mrs. Otten, and their source, they freely admitted, a well-known local boozehound, was unreliable at best. Still, what they knew was harmless. Sally Otten made monthly overnight trips to Boston to shop and have dinner with old friends (she had gone to Boston College), and she patronized the bar at MC Perkins Cove with some frequency, often alone. "One martini and she's gone," James said. "Never drunk, always polite, and she's a generous tipper."

"Did you talk to Quentin and Gwen, too?" Isobel had asked her mother. She wasn't sure how she felt about—well, about her mother's interrogation of the community!

"No," her mom said. "Honestly, I thought it might embarrass you if I did."

But I'm already embarrassed, Isobel realized. But all she said was, "Oh."

"Anyway," her mother went on, "the point is that everyone I talked to had something good to say about Jeff or his parents. So I guess it's okay for you to go out with him."

Isobel managed a sincere smile. "Thanks, Mom," she said.

Her mother gave her a quick kiss on the cheek and left the kitchen in search of Quentin.

When her mother had gone, Isobel wondered, Why had she been withholding information from her mom? And she had downright lied to her that day they spotted Jeff in town and Louise had pointed him out and Isobel had pretended she had never seen him before . . . But that little fact seemed to have slipped past her mother, or else for some weird reason she had decided not to bring it up. Either way Isobel was relieved.

And why had her mother been seeking information about Jeff and his family like a private investigator?

Isobel sighed. Like it or not, their relationship was changing. That was inevitable, of course; all relationships changed over time. People got closer and then more distant and then maybe closer again. Stasis wasn't something that applied for any length of time to human beings and their behavior.

Besides, she thought, all that mattered right at that moment was that her mother had given her permission to go on a real date with Jeff Otten! And she had survived the call to Jeff.

It had been her first call to a guy other than her father, and she was inordinately pleased to find that her voice was steady. She even, she remembered later, cracked a little joke. At least, she thought that she had. Some of the conversation was a bit of a blur. She hoped he didn't think she was one of those ditzy types . . .

Well, it was too late to do anything about the call now. They had a date. Jeff would realize soon enough that she was an awesome gal and that you could be interested in appearances—style and fashion—and at the same time just as interested in what informed those appearances—personal choices, cultural preferences, varying ideologies! If she did say so herself, she was one smart cookie!

Chapter 19

Louise was in the kitchen, attempting to concentrate on the inventory she was reviewing—Bella had compiled (by hand) an impressive and detailed list of every baking and cooking supply on hand. Her thoughts kept dashing away to the fact of Isobel's first date.

She had hoped it would come later—say, when Isobel was eighteen, or maybe even twenty-two (well, she was kidding about that). At the same time, she didn't think there had been much to gain by refusing to allow Isobel to go to dinner with Jeff Otten.

She had always envisioned both she and Andrew greeting the lucky young man at the door, Andrew grilling him (politely) about his intentions, while she stood off a bit to the side, smiling enigmatically—just enough to unnerve the kid. But Isobel's father was not part of this momentous event. So be it.

Louise could barely recall her own first date. She had been fifteen, or maybe fourteen. She did not remember the boy's name. They had gone to a local place for pizza and a soda. He had tried to take her hand on the walk home, but she had snatched it away. He had not asked for a second date.

Four cans of condensed milk. What did Bella need with condensed milk? Louise wondered. Three boxes of raisins. That made sense. Three boxes of baking soda.

Thank God, Louise thought now, that Isobel was far

savvier than she herself had been at sixteen. Louise, unlike her daughter, had lived a very sheltered existence. The family had not traveled farther than Cape Cod from their home in Wakefield, and that only once a summer. They did not make it a habit to go into Boston. Mr. and Mrs. Jones were friends with only two other couples, one of whom had no children, the other of whom had a much older son and daughter. What Louise knew of boys was gleaned from the few television shows she was allowed to watch and from observing the boys at school.

The latter experience told her that a lot of boys liked to play sports. A fair amount of boys were good in math and science. A few were natural-born cutups. One or two were troublemakers. In short, she had learned nothing useful. By the time she got to high school, Louise still knew next to nothing about the opposite sex.

It would be a long time before she realized that boys and the men they grew into were just like girls and the women they became—flawed and vulnerable, awful and lovable. In short, that boys and men were human beings. If you cut them, they bled, and most times they complained loudly about it. If you were nice to them, they smiled and were mostly nice back. If you challenged them, they rose to the challenge or they scuttled away like frightened mice. If you betrayed them, they cried and got angry and acted out like any woman scorned. Men weren't all that different from women. That's what a lot of women and some men most needed to understand.

"One small bottle of cream of tartar." Louise frowned down at Bella's inventory. Whatever that was, it didn't sound appetizing. "One can crushed pineapple." *Who*, Louise wondered, *had bought that and why?*

By the time Louise had gone away to college (a huge concession from her parents, who had not been able to turn down the scholarship money the college had offered their daughter), she was no longer a virgin but she was still woefully naïve about men, and she stayed that way—at least until the start of her junior year of college, when she had fallen so hard and so completely for Ted Dunbar.

He was a good-looking guy. His hair was dark and wavy; his eyes were almost black. If he had a tendency toward a little fat around the middle, well, it was only a tendency. His smile was broad and came easily. In fact, in the first weeks of their relationship, Louise couldn't remember him ever frowning, not even when his favorite football team lost an important game, not even when she had forgotten to pick up a six-pack on the way home from classes.

Ted had dropped out of college in his freshman year (school just wasn't his "thing," he explained), and for the past two years had been working at a garage—when he was working, which, as Louise came to learn, wasn't all that much. Still, things were fine at first. Ted was often charming, and he was a decent enough lover—when he wasn't drunk. Still, he made up for routinely passing out on her couch by making dinner (his repertoire was limited, but he didn't burn the hamburgers or serve the spaghetti mushy) or by doing the laundry (his, not hers). He didn't talk much about his family. One night, after four or five beers, he mentioned a brother who had left home at sixteen and hadn't been heard from since. And there was a sister. She had gotten pregnant at fifteen; the baby had been adopted at birth; the sister was now eighteen and living at home with the parents.

Ted, in short, seemed like a sweet but harmless ne'er-do-well. But Louise had gotten in way over her head. Over time, Ted went from borrowing money from her, swearing he would pay it back, to stealing from her wallet while she was asleep, to announcing that he was going to take whatever money she had on her for his own needs—like spending hours at a dive bar with his buddies. Over time, Ted went from yelling at her when he was mad to pushing her, to hitting her.

But the abuse escalated so artfully, and was so skillfully

executed that for a long time Louise hadn't been at all sure what was happening. It was tempting to blame her parents, at least partly, for having ill-prepared her for evil in human form. Tempting, but unfair.

How could a woman like her mother, afraid of her own shadow, so wrapped up in her own convictions of personal disaster, have had the acuteness, the sensitivity, to detect real danger to others?

Her father, too, had been useless. He was a typical man of his generation and the ones before it, emotionally obtuse, seeing only what was before his face. She had no doubt he loved her, but he was entirely incapable of showing or proving that love in any way other than paying for food, shelter, and what he could afford of an education.

If you said you felt fine, he believed you.

If you said you felt sick or sad, he sent you to your mother.

He wasn't a bad man, just a limited one. Other people's motives were as hidden and unknown to him as his own motives were hidden and unknown to himself. When Louise was in the hospital after the fall, he was entirely inarticulate, with grief or shame or anger, Louise never knew. He probably didn't know, either.

At her college graduation her father had shaken her hand, his expression one Louise thought of as slight puzzlement. At her wedding he had danced with her once, as was expected, but he hadn't said a word as he held her, stiffly and at a distance.

"Two dozen eggs. Four pounds of coffee beans. Three boxes of tea bags; one, decaf."

Louise's mother had drunk only decaffeinated tea and coffee. Her father had consumed nothing stronger than ginger ale.

When Mr. and Mrs. Jones, that repressed and fearful couple, had died close to a decade back, within a year of each other, each taken by an aggressive cancer, Louise had felt sorrow but not violent loss. She had been sad but not undone. In retrospect, it had been shockingly easy to get past their deaths.

A noise at the back door startled Louise from her thoughts.

"Good afternoon, Mrs. Bessire."

No matter how often or how strenuously Louise had begged Bella Frank to call her by her first name, she would not comply, so Louise had given up the fight.

"Good afternoon, Bella. What brings you by?" she asked.

"I'm afraid I haven't finished reviewing the inventory yet . . ."

"I picked up these blueberries at that little farm stand we like. Don't know how Fred can afford to sell them so cheap, but he can and I'm grateful for it."

"So are the guests. And so am I! What are you planning for the morning? Muffins? Scones? Pancakes?"

"All that and a nice pound cake, too."

Louise paid Bella for the berries, which really were ridiculously inexpensive, and stored them in the fridge.

"Do you have a moment?" she asked Bella, as the other woman headed for the door. "Or do you need to run off?"

Bella looked down at her considerable girth. "I'm long past my running days, my dear. What's on your mind?"

"Oh, I was just wondering if you knew the Otten family. I'm not looking for dirt, really," she hurried to assure Bella. "It's just that Jeff Otten has asked Isobel for a date. He seems like a very nice young man, but . . ."

"Sure, I know them somewhat. It's been years now, but I used to work for them serving at their fancy parties." Bella smiled. "I have such fond memories of Michael! I guess just about everyone who ever knew him does. He was about ten or eleven, I guess, back when I worked for the family. Charming boy, always polite, very smart."

"What about Jeff?" Louise asked.

Bella shook her head. "I don't recall much about Jeff. He was very young then, an adorable little boy if ever there was one. He looked like one of those little blond cherubs you see in those old-time paintings. But neither boy was allowed to spend much time hanging around while an adult party was going on so . . ."

Yes, Louise thought. Young children underfoot at a party was a disaster waiting to happen. "What about Sally Otten?" Louise asked then.

"A lovely woman from what I could tell. Soft-spoken. Kind. She always paid us in cash and sent us home with the leftover food. I guess these society types don't actually eat all that much, always on their diets and whatever."

Louise smiled and recalled the dainty eating habits of some of the society women she had known from her volunteer days back in Massachusetts. Lunchtime with those women had been a real trial. All Louise had wanted to do was chow down and refuel for the long afternoon ahead. All the society women had wanted to do was talk about how fat they were and nibble a small side salad. Dainty habits—or middle-aged-onset anorexia.

"There was one funny thing I noticed one time . . ."

Bella's words caught Louise's attention. "Oh?" she said.

"Well, I was passing through the hall between the kitchen and the dining room when I came across Mr. and Mrs. Otten. He seemed really angry. I mean, he was talking in a hushed voice but I could tell he was upset. She was, too." Bella shrugged. "But it could have been he was angry at one of us or maybe the brand of gin he liked had run out. Or did he drink vodka? Anyway, my point is, he could have been angry about anything. Or nothing. Not necessarily his wife."

"True," Louise said. "And we both know that husbands and wives fight over the most inane things."

Bella laughed. "Yes, we do. In my house, most times it means that one of us is hungry. Well, maybe I said too much. People shouldn't look for trouble and hidden meanings. There's enough trouble right out in the open to occupy everyone's time."

Bella left then, off, she said, to do her own grocery shopping. When she had gone, Louise thought about what Bella had told her. Overall she felt reassured by her assessment of the Otten household. And really, how many times during a dinner or cocktail party at the Bessire house had she and Andrew shared a tense or slightly angry moment? Many times, when, as Bella had surmised, the alcohol had unexpectedly run low or the hors d'oeuvres had gotten burnt or one of the guests was being drunkenly belligerent.

Louise sighed and sat down at the table with Bella's inventory. It was high time she focused on the moment at hand.

Jeff was not Ted. Isobel was not Louise.

She had to believe that everything would be all right.

Chapter 20

CITYMOUSE

Greetings, My Friends!

I am currently having a problem with black.

Now, let me clarify that rather startling statement. It's not that I don't like black. In lots of sartorial circumstances and fashion panic situations, black is the best if not the only way to go. Black leather trench coat? No-brainer. Black satin clutch? *De rigueur!* Black patent leather Mary Janes? Every girl should have a pair by the age of five. Little black dress? Enough said.

No, the nature of my problem with black is—and this is going to sound weird—it makes me want to vomit.

This happened once with forest green. I'd always liked forest green, and then one day about four years ago, out of the blue (ha! It's funny how we use colors in our expressions, like, "I'm in the pink," and "the company is in the red," and calling someone who is cowardly "yellow," and saying you "feel blue" when you feel sad), I looked at something forest green (it was a wool coat of LouLou's) and I felt downright sick to my stomach. It was the oddest sensation. A color made me want to throw up. A nice color, too, not something harsh or overly bright or false; a negative reaction to a color like that would be understandable. That aversion, that gut reaction against forest green, lasted for about a year, and then, boom, just like that, it was over and I could look at the color again and say, "Wow, that's really restful and soothing."

I hope this troublesome problem with black goes away quickly. I mean, black is kind of hard to avoid—it's everywhere! I even had to ask Gwen if she could not wear this great black cotton sweater thingie she wears a lot, at least for a while, until my tummy feels better in the vicinity of its inkiness.

Sigh. I guess I am an odd duck!

And now a word about something really important. Yes, more important than black and my problem with it. (I mock myself.)

I want to go on record as saying that I am one hundred percent with the Photoshopping protesters. No, make that one thousand percent.

A person might assume—and be forgiven for it—that someone interested in style might also be a fan or advocate of falsity and pretense, but that person would be dead wrong about me.

I believe in and try to promote (on this blog and in my daily life) authenticity and genuine self-expression. I believe in the importance of individuality. Difference and variety are the spices of life.

Look, I'm no psychological expert, so I can't say if looking at images of perfect girls makes imperfect girls anorexic or otherwise damaged, but come on, it certainly doesn't help! Sheesh!

I'm aware (and you probably are, too) of websites that promote extreme thinness—thinspiration sites, I hear they're called—and other websites that go so far as to promote anorexia, which is a disease and a nasty one at that, as a goal, a choice one might really want to make. Where do I begin to express my dismay! To choose to be ill is an illness. How can people not understand that? It's all just too sad.

And on a related note—when will the media (i.e., all of us by our consuming it and so, allowing it—and I am as guilty as anyone) stop harassing women about their looks NO MATTER WHAT THEY LOOK LIKE? For example, and this drives me nuts, a woman is supposed to be thin we are told, no matter her age. But when a fifty-some-odd-year-old thin woman like Meg Ryan or a forty-some-odd-year-old woman like Sarah Jessica Parker is torn apart because the veins in her arms and hands are prominent, she's blasted for that, too! Damned if we do and damned if we don't! We can't win!

I am tearing my hair out. To eat a cheeseburger or not—that shouldn't be the most burning question a woman faces!

But maybe we can win. Think about how it would feel to win—to be proudly who and what you are, societal pressures be damned! (More use of the word *damned* . . .)

Deep breath. I'm coming down off the soapbox now and saying farewell for the moment. Dear Readers—be true to yourselves!!!

Isobel posted the blog and closed her laptop. In spite of her determination to keep autobiographical elements on the blog to a minimum, for about a second she had been tempted to drop a little hint about her upcoming date with Jeff. But only for a second.

Privacy was a notion Isobel took seriously, though sometimes she thought she was the only one of her generation who did. That was an exaggeration, of course, but all you needed to do was spend even fifteen minutes on Facebook or Twitter to realize that an awful lot of people had never learned or maybe had forgotten that "too much information" was not only unnecessary but downright ugly. Why did some people think anyone would possibly care where they got their afternoon coffee, and how their routine dental appointment had gone, and if they had woken up that morning with wicked crease marks on their face? Boring! Somewhere (probably online!) she had read that there were people so addicted to social media outlets that they spent eight hours a day on the sites. What?!

Isobel jumped up from her desk chair. Enough interior ranting! There was a very big and very important decision to make: What should she wear on her date?

Jeff was exactly on time.

Isobel opened the door. She was wearing a pale yellow sundress with a scooped neck, fitted bodice, and full skirt, circa 1962. A lightweight white cotton cardigan was draped over her shoulders, held in place by a gold-tone sweater clip she had found at one of her favorite vintage stores.

Jeff was wearing another pair of awesome jeans and a black, fitted T-shirt that made it pretty clear his abs were amazing. Over that he wore a semi-structured linen blazer in taupe. His shoes were the ones he had been wearing when they had first met in town.

"Hi," she said.

"Hi," he said.

"So . . ."

Jeff smiled. "Can I come in?"

Isobel's hand flew to her mouth. "Oh gosh, yeah, sorry!"

"Is your mom here?" Jeff asked when he had stepped inside.

"She's in the kitchen. It's this way."

Isobel led him to the back of the house where her mother was sitting at the kitchen table, her laptop open, a well-used notebook and pen next to it.

"Mom, Jeff is here." Isobel stood, her hands folded in front of her, like one of the girls from *The Sound of Music*. She felt extremely awkward. It was weird.

Louise got up from her seat. Jeff put out his hand to shake hers.

"It's nice to see you, again, Jeff."

"The pleasure is mine. I wanted to let you know that we'll be at Barnacle Billy's if you need to reach us. And you have my cell phone number; it's on my card."

"Yes, I have it right here." Louise pointed to the fridge.

She had used a magnet in the shape of a mushroom to hold Jeff's card in place. "But I doubt I'll have a reason to interrupt your evening."

"Well, thanks for allowing Isobel to have dinner with me."

Isobel's mother downright beamed. "You're welcome," she said. "Have fun."

The drive from the inn to Barnacle Billy's in Perkins Cove took about four minutes, but finding a parking space looked like it was going to be a big challenge.

"Yikes," Isobel said. "We could be here awhile!"

"No worries." Jeff summoned the young parking attendant and gave him a folded bill (Isobel thought it was a twenty but that seemed outrageous; she figured she must have been mistaken), and when Isobel and Jeff had gotten out, he drove Jeff's car around two cars ahead of them to the only empty spot in the lot. She had seen her father do that once, give a parking attendant money to get them a space ahead of other people. She remembered how her mother had scolded him; she had said it was an unfair practice and that he should be ashamed to use his money to cheat others less fortunate. At the time Isobel hadn't given it much thought; she hadn't had lunch and just wanted to get into the restaurant and eat. Now, she felt a bit weird about what Jeff had done. Her mother was right, it was kind of unfair . . . But she knew she could be naïve; it was probably just the way things were done in the world of adults out on the town—and obviously, now she was one of those adults!

They sat at a table for two on the gorgeous terrace; Jeff held the chair out for her. (*Wow,* Isobel thought. *Seriously old-fashioned and pretty nice!*) The garden at Barnacle Billy's was lush and beautifully tended. It overlooked the water where the private pleasure boats were tied up; farther down the Cove were the working fishing and lobster boats, along with a few tour boats that were super-popular with the tourists.

"It's so pretty, isn't it?" Isobel said. She wondered if that remark was lame.

Jeff smiled. "I knew you'd like it out here. I reserved the table yesterday. Usually they don't take reservations for the terrace, but my dad is pretty tight with the owner so . . ."

A young waiter took their order. Jeff asked for a seltzer; Isobel was glad he wasn't drinking even though the ride back to the inn was so short.

Jeff asked her about school and wanted to know her favorite subject. He told her a funny story about Mr. Becker, the tenth-grade math teacher, who had been at the school since the seventies and who was well known to be a "leftover hippie." He reminisced about homecoming weekends and explained that although the football coaches repeatedly begged him to join first the junior varsity and then the varsity team, he had refused. "I'm not a big fan of competition," he told her. "Except when it's against myself. I'm always trying to better my own standards and my own performance in life."

Isobel thought that was a very mature character trait.

He asked politely if Mr. Bessire lived at Blueberry Bay Inn with Isobel and her mother. Isobel had guessed that question would be coming. When she had first moved to Ogunquit, she had prepared a stock answer for the people at school and she pulled it back out now, only adjusting for the passing of time.

"My parents got divorced about two years ago," she said. "My father is remarried and lives in Massachusetts." That's all she would say about that. It felt like betrayal to share a woman's misery with a guy you hardly even knew, even someone as nice as Jeff Otten.

She asked about his family and he told her a bit more about his father, how he had inherited a pretty successful business from his father before him and how he had grown it to more than twice the size it had been. "He's a very impressive guy," Jeff said. "I hope to become half the man he is."

Isobel had nodded and said, quite seriously, "Oh, I'm sure you will be!" Jeff shrugged and looked down at his meal. She thought he might have been blushing, but it could have been a trick of light from the low candle on their table.

When he spoke of his mother, it was with real affection. "She's great," he said. "She was the perfect mom when I was growing up, always there, always supportive, milk and cookies waiting when I got home from school, the whole nine yards. Now that I'm an adult, she spends a lot of her time working for one of her favorite charities. It helps support children with cancer. And she supervises the staff at the house, of course, and makes my father's life at home as smooth as possible. And believe me, with the stress he's under every day, that's a big job. She does it beautifully."

Isobel almost cried. She was so pleased to learn that Jeff respected his mother's contribution to the Otten family. It took intelligence to recognize and appreciate the value of a stay-at-home parent's efforts.

It wasn't until much later that night did she remember that Jeff had an older brother. Michael, she thought his name was. She wondered why he hadn't mentioned him when he had told her about his family. But it was no big deal. She would ask Jeff about Michael at some point down the line.

Jeff didn't say anything about her clothes, but he did tell her at one point that she was beautiful and would look pretty in something hot pink, something, he pointed out, like the dress another diner was wearing. Isobel had never liked herself in hot pink, but she had smiled and said, "Thanks," though Jeff's words hadn't exactly been a compliment. Still, the fact was that he was thinking about her as they sat together eating lobster rolls and steamers, not focusing on something else. Right?

They were back at the inn by ten o'clock, as Jeff had

promised. They stood on the porch, away from the cool glow of the overhead light and the dimmer light coming from the windows of the parlor. Isobel felt intensely nervous and excited and afraid and eager all at once. How could she have made it to the ripe old age of sixteen without having been kissed by a boy? It seemed impossible . . .

He kissed her gently, with just enough pressure of his lips on hers for her to know they were there, but not enough to be aggressive. She was a wee bit disappointed by his restraint, though of course she knew that he was being a gentleman for her sake. She was, after all, only just sixteen. Really, it was something else to like and admire about him!

"Good night, Isobel," he said. "Will you let me see you again?"

Isobel nodded. She wanted to shout, "Yes! Of course!" but figured that probably wasn't exactly a sophisticated response.

Jeff grinned. "Great. I'll wait until you get safely inside."

Isobel closed the door behind her and watched him drive off from one of the narrow windows on either side of the front door. Before she had turned away from the window, he had sent her a text. **GRT TIME.** She smiled broadly but also hoped that he was paying attention to the road. After all, they were going to go out together again—but only if Jeff made it home safely!

There were no guests in either the parlor or the library. The kitchen, too, was empty. Her mother was asleep; at least, she was in her room. Isobel wondered if she was waiting until she heard Isobel's bedroom door close behind her before she got into bed for the night. Isobel kind of wanted to talk to her mother, but she was also kind of glad she was let alone to savor the memories of the night.

Isobel went up to her room and got ready for bed. She lay awake for some time, replaying the date, wondering if she had sounded smart, if she had come across as funny or as too young or as just perfect or . . .

She was finally falling asleep when she heard the sound of her phone. It was Jeff, sending her another text.

MISS U, it read.

MISS U 2, she replied.

Isobel shimmied down under the lightweight summer covers and smiled into the darkness. This business of dating was fun, she thought. And then she fell asleep.

Chapter 21

Louise was barely out of bed two mornings later when her phone chirped like a bird, indicating a text from her former husband. It could wait. Louise didn't do social media or most other tech-related things before she had consumed a good deal of coffee. So it was not until she was showered and dressed and in the kitchen gratefully drinking her second cup of French roast that she read Andrew's text. She didn't know what she had expected to hear from him, but it wasn't this.

She was glad Bella had gone to the powder room and that the servers were busy in the breakfast room because the word she expelled was not one she would have wanted anyone to hear. Anyone but Andrew, that is.

"Bastard," she said now. It was accurate and far cleaner than the first word that had come shooting out of her mouth.

He had a right to have sex with his wife, a right to make babies with her, but for God's sake, couldn't he break this news in a more mature way?

V PRGGRS!! the text read. **DO OCT.**

Sophisticated! What the hell had happened to the man she had fallen in love with and married, the man who would write love letters in his terrible handwriting, the man who would take the time to bake a cake from scratch for her birthday, even though the results were consistently lopsided?

Louise sighed. She would have to tell Isobel, but she really didn't want to just yet. Isobel was so happy about the attention she was getting from Jeff. Her first date had gone so well . . . It would be cruel to spoil her pleasure with yet another—disappointing? difficult? disturbing?—announcement from her father.

But maybe telling Isobel soon was the smarter thing to do. Andrew might approach his daughter on his own, and Louise didn't want Isobel finding a similarly crude message on her phone, at least not without first having been prepared.

Another cup of coffee later, she called Catherine from the porch, away from prying ears. (She had caught one of the current guests, a hulking woman of about sixty-five or so, lurking outside of the kitchen the other afternoon, her ear cocked toward the kitchen door. When asked if she needed assistance, the woman had had the nerve to take offense and mutter something about the prying proprietress. . . .)

"Hello," her friend said.

"Guess what?" Louise responded, without a proper greeting.

Catherine sighed. "I hate when people say that."

"My shit of an ex-husband knocked up his wife."

"I see. Well, that is news. When is the blessed event to occur?"

"October."

"I wonder if this has anything to do with his canceling Isobel's visit?" Catherine mused. "Either way, I'm so sorry. It's bad timing for you, isn't it, this news?"

"Bad timing for Isobel, too," Louise said. "First he cancels her visit and now this."

"You can't be sure Isobel will mind so terribly, can you? I mean, she wrapped her head around the fact of two stepsisters prettily easily. Then again . . ."

"Exactly. Then again, this kid is Andrew's."

"And in some ways then, a part of Isobel. Something she shares with her father and not at all with you."

Louise frowned. "Thank you for pointing out that all-too-obvious fact."

"Sorry. I call them as I see them."

"Yeah, no worries. I have to go. Thanks for listening."

Catherine said, "Anytime," and ended the call.

Louise went back into the kitchen. It was the time of the morning that she usually enjoyed. The inn was blessedly empty; guests had gone off on their adventures, Bella and the housecleaning staff had finished their work for the day, even Isobel was usually out with Gwen or off on an excursion of her own, novel or notebook in hand.

Today, however, Louise found the silence to be evidence of isolation, not of peace and quiet and strengthening solitude. Andrew's news had shaken her. She didn't know why, but the idea of his having a child with Vicky had never even occurred to her. "Stupid," she pronounced to the empty kitchen.

Louise had been so intensely grateful for Isobel and Andrew had seemed so contented, too, neither had even mentioned the notion of having another child. She wondered now if that had been a big mistake.

Andrew had known about the miscarriage, of course, and had been appropriately horrified and sorry for her. He also knew that the baby had been a girl. Louise had not known this until the awful end, at three months into the pregnancy. A nurse had asked if the child had a name . . .

Had the nurse asked for the name of the father? Louise could not for the life of her remember. Father. That was a cruel joke. More like drunk, angry, barely conscious source of sperm . . .

Louise picked up the teakettle and put it down again. There was much to do—guest rooms to be inspected, bills to be paid, dirty laundry to wash—but she felt disinclined to do any of it. What she suddenly wanted to do more than anything—and even though she hadn't had the impulse for well over a year—was to call Andrew and demand closure, real closure this time. . . .

With Herculean effort Louise talked herself off the ledge. She had learned the hard way that most times when you said you wanted closure, what you really wanted was an entirely different ending to the story that had already ended. Demanding closure—more than once or twice, anyway—was not a way to heal. It was evidence of an emphasis on your own pride and damaged ego. To demand on having the final word was, she had come to realize, to demand the right to a spoken version of the nastiness running through your head like a dirty, swollen stream, roiling with broken branches and dead fish. So—and it had been difficult—she had stopped pestering Andrew with calls and letters, had stopped insisting they have a final conversation when what she really meant by "conversation" was that Andrew shut up and listen to her abuse.

Closure with Ted had looked like something very, very different, Louise thought now. She had gotten a restraining order after the accident, but he had come to see her in spite of it, full of the usual meaningless apologies and excuses meant to elicit pity for a misunderstood and downtrodden man. Closure had then involved the police. And therapy, to help heal her bruised ego and come to terms with the loss of the baby. And then, of course, closure had involved the slow, painful healing of cracked and broken bones.

Not many months after Louise's fall, Ted had been arrested for punching some guy in a bar fight. He was back out on the street after that again where, exactly seven months after the date of Louise's miscarriage, he had died a particularly fitting death—if one could say that without being totally callous. Ted Dunbar was shot and killed by the brother of a woman he had attempted to rape. The avenging brother was no prize, either. It turned out the gun he had used to kill Ted was stolen and he had had a string of drug-related arrests trailing behind him for years. Louise had no idea what had become of the man who had unknowingly removed the scourge from her life.

And that was just fine, because she had horrible people in the present to deal with, like Calvin Streep. He could be even nastier than his boss, and that took some doing. He called around noon with a series of demands that went from the merely annoying to the undeniably absurd. There had to be bottles of hand sanitizer not only in the bathrooms but also in every room of the inn. There also had to be a variety of deodorants and perfumes on hand for freshening emergencies. The groom, it seemed, was a fastidious sort. "If one was inclined to be nasty about it," Calvin Streep cooed, "one might be tempted to say that he has a mania about personal cleanliness." And it would be utterly divine if she could also manage to have a few professional seamstresses standing by the day of the wedding. The bride, Calvin Streep explained with faux honey in his voice, "liked her chow."

When Louise had finished spluttering and protesting— "Why isn't Flora Michaels handling that sort of thing?" and "But I'm only the innkeeper, not a . . . a hygienist!"—there was a long moment of deadly silence. Louise braced herself.

"I don't know how you're used to doing things up there in the boondocks," Calvin Streep pronounced in icy tones, "but down here in civilization we are accustomed to getting the job done in a timely manner and exactly as the client has requested it."

"Look, all I'm saying is that I really don't think providing dressmakers and deodorant is my responsibility. If you read my contract, you'll see that—"

"Are you saying you want to break your contract, Ms. Bessire? Because I'm afraid Ms. Michaels's lawyers will have something very interesting to say in response."

"No, no," Louise replied wearily, "I'm not breaking any contract, I'm just—"

"Then we understand each other," Calvin Streep said with false cheer. "Good day, Ms. Bessire."

Louise stuffed her cell phone into the front pocket of her jeans. She wished she had an old-fashioned phone, the kind with a hard plastic receiver you could smash down onto the cradle, a statement-making kind of phone.

In lieu of that, she could only hope that Calvin Streep choked on the lemon slice in his luncheon cocktail or the olive in his four o'clock martini. For someone like him, the social embarrassment alone would be punishment enough. The thought made her smile. It was the first smile she had been able to muster all day.

Chapter 22

CITYMOUSE

Hello, Dear Readers!

The great and magnificent Diana Vreeland was quoted as saying, "The only real elegance is in the mind; if you've got that, the rest really comes from it."

I think that what Ms. Vreeland meant by elegance of the mind (that's my slight rewording) was a habit of contemplation or consideration before action. In other words, the habit of inquiring before making a judgment.

And I think I see what she meant that everything else flows from your state of mind, from the purity of your thoughts, from the clarity of your feelings about things.

I hope I'm not totally wrong!!!!

Ms. Vreeland, the French actress Jeanne Moreau, and even the American actress Anjelica Huston, have been termed *"jolie laide"* by those who think about such things. I like this term and the idea it denotes. It's a very interesting and I think a very liberating idea. I wish more women (and girls) would embrace and claim their own individual and possibly unconventional or irregular or off-kilter beauty against the cultural or societal standards (I think they might be separate things, though they are certainly related) of beautiful.

It has been said that Beauty is in the eye of the beholder. The problem is that from the time we can understand the adults around us, we're told that beauty should look like A and not like B. So how can you learn to develop a truly personal sense of beauty when your thoughts and perceptions have been shaped and guided (some would say wrangled or coerced) by your culture's standards from the beginning? It's really hard for most people (I think) and not as hard for some (like me, and that's not bragging, it's just a fact) to take an honest look at those cultural standards (of the moment—they're always changing over generations!) and say, "Okay, that's one way of looking at things. But hey, here's another way! And wait, here's yet another way! I think I like this third way best . . . At least, for now!"

"Knock, knock."

Isobel looked over her shoulder. "Hey, Mom. What's up?"

"You busy?"

"Just finishing this post." Isobel rapidly typed out a closing line. "And—done."

Isobel's mother came into the room and perched on the edge of the unmade bed. "We got some news from your father this morning," she said without preamble.

Instantly, Isobel felt wary, and afraid. *Please,* she thought, *don't let Dad be sick.*

"What is it?" she asked, feeling far more trepidation than she let on in voicing those three simple words.

"Vicky is pregnant."

Later, Isobel remembered feeling absolutely nothing in that moment. Numb. Not happy, not sad. And then she had said: "He called?"

Odd, she thought, even then, that this was her first question. And if he had called, why hadn't he asked to talk to his daughter?

"Well, no."

"Then how did he . . . Oh, please don't tell me it was another lame e-mail."

"Actually," Louise said, her tone neutral, "it was a text."

"What did it say, exactly?"

Louise shook her head. "That's not important. The message was clear."

Isobel jumped up from the desk chair and paced through the clutter on the floor. "He's such a coward!" *And,* she added to herself, *he certainly has no elegance of mind.*

Louise declined to respond.

"I mean, he didn't even have the nerve to tell you he was cheating!"

"To be fair," Louise replied calmly, "he said he had planned on telling me soon."

"Yeah, right. I believe that."

"Can't you give your father the benefit of the doubt?"

"No," Isobel said emphatically, throwing her hands into the air for emphasis. "I can't."

"Anyway," her mother went on, "we should be happy for Vicky. We should wish her a healthy pregnancy and birth."

"Of course," Isobel agreed, however grudgingly. "Do we have to send a card?"

"No. But it would be nice. If you like, I'll buy one and sign it from us both."

"Okay. You can buy it but I'll sign my own name." *It's not Vicky's fault that my father is a jerk,* Isobel thought. *It's not her fault she got fooled. Smart women get fooled all the time. Look at what had happened to my mother all those years ago. And look at what had happened to her in the more recent past . . . Really,* Isobel thought glumly, *it's a miracle anyone ever trusts anyone. But that is negative thinking and unproductive and . . .*

"The child will be your half sibling," her mother was saying. "I know that's big."

Isobel hadn't yet taken in that interesting fact. Now, she did. Wow. This child would be a flesh-and-blood relative. They would share DNA. They might even look alike. "Yeah," she said, her tone deliberately light and careless, "but it's okay. I probably won't even see him or her more than a few times in the next twenty years. I'm sure I won't be invited to birthday parties and graduations, let alone the wedding."

"Isobel . . ."

Isobel sighed. "Sorry, Mom. I can't help but feel a bit— grumpy. The situation is just a bit—weird."

"Yeah. It is. And don't be sorry."

"It's just not something I was expecting. Though I guess it's perfectly normal. People get married and have babies."

"Yeah," her mother said. "A lot of them do. Look, are you going to be okay? I should get back to work. Calvin Streep has issued a demand from the bride for hand soaps in the shape of lobsters and clamshells, and I have absolutely no idea if such things even exist. Though they're probably for sale in some awful tourist shop."

"Yeah," Isobel said. "I'll be fine."

"You sure?"

Isobel managed what she thought was a reassuring smile. "Sure."

Her mother kissed her cheek and left the room.

Isobel sank onto her bed. Her mind was racing; her emotions were a muddle. Where to begin sorting out this news and all it might mean for her?

She had never given much thought as to why her parents hadn't had more children. Now, she wondered. It might have been for any number of reasons, all very normal, like economics (though her father did make a lot of money) or health issues (had her mother had a really bad pregnancy?).

But for some reason—Vicky's demand? Or his own desire?—her father was having another child now. A child of his middle age. Isobel guessed that she was no longer child enough for him. "The thrill of me has worn off," she said quietly to the otherwise empty bedroom. "Imagine that."

And then she thought of Jeff, of his killer smile, of how he had sent her a birthday card back when he had hardly even known her, of how he had taken her to such a pretty place for dinner. Suddenly, she felt very anxious to see him, and soon.

And then, as if summoned by her need, her phone rang. It was Jeff.

Boy, Isobel thought, smiling to herself. *Summoned?* She was even more of a romantic than she had realized!

"Hey," she said.

"You sound upset," Jeff replied. "What's wrong?"

She was shocked—pleasantly—that he could tell from a one-word greeting that something was bothering her. But still, she hesitated to tell him what.

"Oh, nothing," she demurred. "Just something with my dad. It's all right."

"Are you sure you don't want to talk about it? You know I'm here for you, right?"

Isobel didn't answer immediately. They had only known

each other a very short time. How could Jeff be sure he wanted to be there for her when he hardly knew her? Then again, it was an awfully nice thing to say.

"Yes," she said. "I do know. It means a lot to me. Okay, I just found out that my dad and his wife are having a baby."

"Good for telling me," Jeff said heartily. "No secrets, okay? You need to understand what you mean to me. You need to know that you can rely on me for anything."

"Okay."

"Good. Well, I've gotta go. I promised my dad I'd look over some reports for him. Good night, Izzy."

Isobel tried to hold her tongue, but the tongue was a slippery thing. "Um," she said, "I kind of don't like nicknames." Actually, she hated them except in the blogosphere and even then, not for herself.

Jeff laughed lightly. "Really? But you're such an Izzy. It's so—bubbly. So full of life."

Isobel thought about that for a few seconds. At the moment she certainly didn't feel bubbly or full of life. But mostly she was a happy person; pretty much anyone who knew her even a little could attest to that.

"Well," she said, conquering her final bit of reluctance, "I guess it's okay."

"Good. It'll be my special name for you. No one else will be allowed to call you Izzy."

No one else would want to, Isobel thought, but then, when she had hung up, she felt ungrateful. Jeff cared about her. He had the right to give her a nickname that pleased him. It was the least she could do for her boyfriend. *Boyfriend!* That word still sounded so odd. Isobel Amelia Bessire had a boyfriend. Whoa.

It was almost an hour later when Isobel, sitting at her computer, realized that Jeff hadn't actually said anything about the news that her father was having another child. But that was okay. Lots of guys were really bad talking about emotions. Guys liked to fix problems; they saw emotions as puzzles to be solved. They were totally misguided about that, but there wasn't much women could do but accept their wrong-headedness as inherent and unchangeable. It wasn't cause for anger!

Isobel got up from her desk and looked into the mirror that hung over the dresser.

"Hello, Izzy," she said to her familiar reflection.

And she felt only slightly embarrassed and only a little bit like a stranger to herself.

It was the teeniest bit exciting.

Chapter 23

"Cockles. I am having cockles this evening."

Louise smiled. "Cockle to your heart's content. I think I'm going to have a steak. A gal could use some red meat on occasion."

Catherine nodded. "Maybe cockles and a steak . . ."

The women had gone for dinner at MC Perkins Cove, owned by the justifiably famous Mark and Clark of the justifiably famous Arrows Restaurant. At their request, Norman, the manager, had seated them upstairs at a table by the window. It was midweek; only two other of the tables were occupied, though the bar was full.

The view from both the first and second floors of the restaurant was the best in Ogunquit. Here, you could see the rocky strip of beach, the beginnings of the romantic Marginal Way, and the vast, magnificent expanse of the Atlantic. Now, at seven thirty in the evening, the sky was a series of blues, from indigo to peacock to powder and back again. A few early stars were pinpoints of light in an otherwise moody display.

Back at Blueberry Bay Inn, no doubt oblivious to the sky, Flynn was on call in case of emergencies. The women had left him settled at the kitchen table, a pot of coffee, a plate of Bella Frank's scones, and a stack of *National Geographic* magazines at hand. He admitted he hadn't done much traveling in his lifetime, and was unlikely to do any in his future, but he had always been an armchair adventure traveler. "In my fantasies," he told Louise once, "I'm as familiar with the Amazon jungle as I am with the back of my hand."

The women ordered—cockles and a steak for Catherine; steak and a salad for Louise—and settled in for what each hoped to be a restorative evening. But before long, and as was natural, Louise steered the conversation to Isobel.

"I want her to be more established as her own person," Louise said, "before I venture back into the world of dating. It's one of the reasons I'm really glad she has the blog. She's shown initiative with it, and if she wants to she could take it really far. I know she and Gwen have talked about expanding. I just don't know how competitive Isobel wants to be. Competition has never been her strong suit."

"I wouldn't know about that," Catherine said, "but the blog is definitely good work. But you're right. She could further challenge herself. The blogosphere is 'where it's at.' And there's money to be made. I would be more than happy to lend a hand if she wants to explore getting some advertisers or partnering with a store or a brand for a promotion."

"Thanks, Catherine. You know, I'm even glad that Isobel has Jeff in her life. Which is not to say that I'm not keeping an eye out for trouble. The last thing I want to happen is for Isobel to lose her life in a boy's. What a disaster that would be, my daughter a Stepford girlfriend."

Catherine laughed. "I find that very hard to imagine. Stranger things have happened, of course, but Isobel is so— Isobel. She's so self-sufficient, so a person unto herself. I can't see her giving up all that she's become—and all that she's becoming—to follow the lead of just anyone, especially a boy."

"Well, as we've noted in an earlier conversation, girls do stupid things for a boy's attention. And I've got my own history to prove that."

"Are you thinking of taking the risk again?" Catherine asked. "You know, the risk of doing something stupid?"

Louise shrugged. "Maybe. But finding a man is not a priority."

"Good thing, because we certainly didn't move to a town teeming with eligible middle-aged heterosexual men," Catherine pointed out. "Which was actually part of the appeal for me. There's so little statistical chance of my meeting anyone it's easy to let the whole notion slide into oblivion."

"Except there is Flynn Moore. And from what I understand, he's been single for a good many years. Did you know he was married once, when he was very young? I heard she left him for one of the musicians who played at his club."

"You don't say? That's fairly tacky. And there was no Mrs. Moore after that?"

Louise shrugged. "I'm guessing there was a woman or two along the way, unless his heart was entirely broken. But as far as I know he never married again."

"Huh. Well . . . we did go to a movie the other day. And we got coffee after."

"Aha!"

"Aha nothing. You and I go to the movies."

"Oh, come on, Catherine. That's not the same, and you know it."

Catherine grinned. "Well, I'll admit he is quite attractive. And he's so—unflappable. I find it—well, attractive. I've met—hell, I've dated—drama queens in my day. It's refreshing to spend time with a man who doesn't chew your ear off with tales of woe."

"The strong, silent type?"

"Well, sort of. I mean, Flynn can hold a conversation, as you know. It's not like he communicates in grunts and moans. It's just that he doesn't go on about himself. You know how so many men are: 'Enough about me. What's your opinion of me?' "

Louise thought of Andrew in some of his less-than-fine moments of self-absorption. There was, for example, his habit of turning off a light when leaving a room—even if someone else was still there, using that light. If Andrew wasn't using it, it wasn't being used. She had come to realize that even his obsessive concern with his health had more to do with vanity than with an attempt to prevent an early death. Andrew liked to look good in his expertly cut suits. Not just good. Perfect.

"Earth to Louise?"

"Oh. Sorry. Just thinking about the ex."

"Better to think about the future ex. You know what I mean."

"I do," Louise said. "But I haven't met anyone I could be interested in. Anyway, I'm not opposed to using a dating service when—"

"When what?"

"I'm not sure what I was going to say," Louise admitted. "When the time comes when I realize that I'm lonely. When the time comes when I really want to have sex again. Like I said, it's not a priority. I guess I'm still gun-shy."

"Well, that stands to reason."

Yes, it did. How terribly painful it all had been, Louise thought, especially the time between her having the evidence of Andrew's affair confirmed and finally confronting him; the time spent working up the nerve to ask the questions she really didn't want to ask, to hear the answers she really didn't want to hear. Could she risk her newfound peace of mind ever again? She wasn't sure she would want to bother.

"So, Isobel took her father's news all right, then?" Catherine was asking. "No worrisome delayed reaction?"

"Not that I can tell," Louise said. "She hasn't mentioned Vicky or the baby since our one conversation. I guess there's no reason she should . . . And I'm kind of hesitant to bring up the subject again. Why prod at a wound that might already be healed? Or, at least, a wound that might be well on its way to being healed."

"Isobel does seem resilient, if a tad hyper at times. I don't mean that as an insult, please know that."

"I do know that," Louise said. "It's true that Isobel isn't someone to dwell. That's good, mostly, but sometimes I wonder if she goes deep enough when it comes to her own feelings. I don't mean her opinions; God knows, she's serious enough about those! But I do suspect that she might be developing into one of those people who avoid unpleasant feelings, rather than confront them."

Catherine laughed. "Well, to some extent that describes all of us, doesn't it? Only a masochist enjoys probing the nasty depths of hurt and anger and shame."

"True. But as I learned the hard way, not facing the facts of what's really going on in your life—and not facing how you really feel about those happenings—leaves you in a very vulnerable place, unable to know how to handle a big crisis when it hits."

"No doubt that's true. But we should probably try to talk about something pleasant. After all, this evening is costing us enough. Not that it isn't worth the money, but if we wanted to depress ourselves by solving other people's problems, then we could have stayed home and done it on the cheap. No insult to Isobel."

"You're right. You usually are."

"About some things. Everyone is usually—or often—right about some things."

"Do you think? I'm not so sure. Take my parents, for example. They—"

"No thanks! I'd rather not take them. Now, how about dessert?"

Louise considered this suggestion for about a second. "Yes," she said. "Let's have dessert. But I don't want to share."

Chapter 24

CITYMOUSE

Good day, Dear Readers!

Thanks to everyone who shared her ideas about how to wear the red cowboy-ish boots! Your ideas, one and all, were wonderfully creative and whimsical and some were even outrageous!

I wore the boots yesterday (okay, it was way too hot to wear boots, but I was so eager to begin the experiment, and as we all know, patience is NOT my strong suit!) with SassySarah's suggested outfit of high-waist navy shorts and a silky pale blue T-shirt tucked in neatly and the whole thing totally rocked. Red paired with blue—yes, even pale blue—just works. Next time I wear the boots (when the weather cools down—boy, were my feet hot and no doubt stinky!) I'm going to try them with My-Stuff's suggestion of a swingy black skirt, patterned tights, and a big, chunky turtleneck sweater. And if my brain freezes and seizes up again, I'll be begging for more ideas from my loyal and very, very creative readers! You are all an inspiration to me!

So, here are Gwen's Gwentastic photos of the boots and me in them. That's Blueberry Bay Inn in the background. Quite charming, no? The hollyhocks are in bloom though the lilacs are long gone, which is too bad. I just love their scent, and now I have to wait another year for them to bloom again! (Patience!) And to the left of the inn you can sort of see a bit of the virtual forest of pine trees that encloses our backyard like a circling arm of green spookiness. The good kind of spookiness, the kind populated with fairies and sprites and whatnot. No mean old goblins or spine-chilling wraiths here!

Today I would like to close with what I find to be an inspirational quote from Helen Gurley Brown (and if you don't know about her, please look her up online! She is, for our generation, a controversial figure, but controversy can start dialogue and that can lead to revelation!):

"What you have to do is work with the raw material you have, namely you, and never let up."

I love this idea! It totally coincides with what I so firmly believe in—the importance of being an individual, of being who you really are and not who or what someone wants you to be. And once you recognize you for you, you take an inventory of the strengths and yes, even of the weaknesses, and you get out there and LIVE YOUR LIFE to the best of YOUR UNIQUE ABILITY. (Caps very intentional.)

So, Dear Readers—onward and upward!

Isobel posted the blog, closed the laptop, and sighed. Her mind was still itching from the awkward conversation she had had with Gwen the other day. She hadn't told Gwen about her date with Jeff until the morning after the fact. If Gwen had been hurt, she hadn't admitted it; she had, however, admitted to being puzzled by the timing of Isobel's news.

"Did you think I was going to try to talk you out of going?" she asked.

"Well, no," Isobel had said. But maybe she had been afraid that she would have to defend her decision to see Jeff. After all, Gwen was the one who had told her she had heard that Jeff was a troublemaker . . . "Anyway," she went on, "we had a really nice time."

"He didn't force you to kiss him or anything, did he?" Gwen had asked.

"No way!" Isobel cried. "What kind of person do you think he is? And do you really think I would go out with a creep!"

"No, of course not. But what if you didn't know he was a creep at first? Creeps are notoriously good at pretending not to be creeps."

"Gwen!"

Gwen had smiled. "All right, all right. I'm just playing the cautious friend."

"And I thank you for your concern, really."

Isobel got up from her desk. Everything between her and Gwen was okay. She shouldn't be worrying. Besides, Jeff was due any moment!

* * *

"I really love this little town," Isobel said. "It always feels so—happy."

Jeff smiled down at her. "That might be because you always feel happy."

They were walking along Maine Street in Ogunquit. The sun was high and bright, and the air was mercifully humidity free. Well, almost.

"Hey, look!" Isobel said. "There's my friend. Come on, I want to introduce you."

Jeff let himself be hurried across the street, where Catherine and Charlie were waiting for the light to change.

"Catherine!" Isobel called. The older woman smiled and waved.

"Hey, fancy meeting you here," Catherine said when Isobel and Jeff had joined her.

Isobel smiled. "Jeff, this is my friend Catherine."

"Hi," he said, extending a hand. "Nice to meet you."

But before Jeff and Catherine could touch, Charlie began to growl at Jeff. And then she crouched, and for all Isobel could tell, it looked as if she was going to leap at him. Catherine instantly got Charlie under control, but it wasn't easy—Charlie was strong and tenacious. The dog continued to growl and stare intently up at Jeff.

And in those horrible few seconds, Isobel saw a look flash across Jeff's face and she was sure he was going to kick Princess Charlene. But the look passed as quickly as it had come, and Isobel was now beyond certain that in her own moment of fear and panic she had imagined it.

Jeff's next words proved her right. "Hey," he said with a laugh. "I guess not everybody likes me after all! Well, no worries."

"I'm sorry, really," Catherine said, pulling back on Charlie's leash to further settle the agitated dog at her feet. She frowned, her eyes narrowed, and looked from Jeff to Isobel. "I've never seen her act like this."

Isobel knew her mother's friend pretty well. And she didn't think Catherine sounded—or looked—very contrite. But what did Catherine have to frown about? Jeff was the one who had almost been attacked!

"Generally," Catherine went on, patting the dog's head, "she likes everyone."

"She was just being protective of you," Jeff said amiably. "She must be a good watchdog."

Isobel took Jeff's arm. "We should go," she said. " 'Bye, Catherine."

Catherine mumbled something that might have been "Yeah." When they were several yards on, Isobel looked back over her shoulder to see Catherine still frowning down at her dog. She still thought Catherine looked more puzzled than angry.

"I'm so sorry that happened," Isobel said to Jeff. "Charlie's a shelter dog. She might have a bad history. Maybe some man who looks like you hurt her once, before Catherine adopted her."

"You can never trust a mutt," Jeff replied forcefully. "My dad only buys dogs from a well-respected breeder. It's the same thing with adopted kids. Unless you can pay for the best, you really never know what you're getting. And even then, it's a crapshoot."

Isobel stiffened. Surely, Jeff knew about Gwen and Ricky being adopted. It was such a small town; everyone had to know. Besides, Gwen's parents were both men and Gwen had to have been born of some woman somewhere. And to talk about adopting a child in terms of making a purchase was . . . It was kind of sick. She didn't know what to say.

But maybe Jeff's remarks were simply the result of the scare he had just experienced. Yes, she thought, that was probably the case. Anger and fear and adrenaline . . .

"Hey," Jeff said, taking her arm now as she had taken his earlier. "What's wrong? You're frowning. Are you still upset? Hey, I'm not hurt."

Before she could reply, Jeff put his arm around her waist

and pulled her to him. He leaned down (automatically, she stood on her toes) and kissed her tenderly but fully on the lips. When he released her, Isobel felt her face flame. It had been her first daytime, in-public kiss, and she felt terribly adult, and terribly—well, terribly important.

What if someone she knew had seen her being kissed! How awful! How wonderful, too!

They continued to walk, her hand held firmly in his. And even if Jeff wasn't still shaken by the incident with Charlie, Isobel thought, she was sure Jeff hadn't meant anything really critical. She had read somewhere that adoption was a scary idea for some people. That was all it was. She was probably being oversensitive again. That, and naïve. Other people had opinions different from hers, and they had a right to those opinions. Just because Gwen (and Isobel's mother and Catherine) pretty much thought the way Isobel did about the big and important stuff didn't mean that Jeff had to think that way, as well.

Isobel became aware of a man walking toward them on the crowded sidewalk. He was dressed in typical tourist garb, complete with baseball cap and white crew socks. But his clothes weren't what caught Isobel's attention. It was his dog.

Really, Isobel thought, it was one of the goofiest-looking little mutts she had ever seen. She couldn't help but smile.

Neither could Jeff. "Now there's a face only a mother could love. Is he friendly?" he asked the man, who had stopped to allow them to admire his four-legged friend.

"Friendliest little guy ever!" the man replied. "Go ahead, pet him. His name is Freddie."

Jeff crouched and the little dog went wild with wriggling excitement as Jeff tickled him behind the ears. "Hey, Freddie, hey, little guy," Jeff cooed.

"Got him from a shelter back home in New Jersey," the man said, beaming proudly. "Took one look at him and fell head over heels."

"I can see why," Jeff said, standing up.

The man took his leave of them with a friendly "Have a nice day."

See, Isobel thought. *I was too quick to judge Jeff.* It was a bad habit to get into, making snap judgments, especially negative ones.

Jeff ducked into a store to buy a cup of coffee. He was gone only a moment. "What are you looking at?" he asked when he rejoined her. He was frowning. "Are you looking at that guy by the pickup? Did he look at you?"

Isobel shook her head. "What guy? What pickup—oh, I see it. No, I'm looking at that woman, the one in the big straw sun hat. I'm not sure, but I think that's a Marena she's wearing."

"A what?"

"Her brooch. I'll be right back. I just have to ask her about it."

Isobel had been right, and the woman was pleased as punch that someone so young could recognize such an old piece. She had bought the brooch in an antique store in New York City some years ago. Isobel thanked the woman for sharing her story. Jeff was still frowning when she returned.

"You should be careful approaching strangers," he said.

"In Ogunquit?" Isobel laughed. "It's a fantasy town! Nothing really bad ever happens here."

"Even in Ogunquit." His tone was stern. Isobel fought the urge to laugh again, this time more loudly.

"Well," she said, "it's not like I'd go up to some drunk guy or some lunatic raving on about the end of the world at the top of his lungs."

"Make sure you don't. You really thought that brooch was beautiful?"

"Oh yes. And it's one of a kind. That's part of the appeal. Why? Didn't you like it?"

"I thought it was hideous. Frankly, I think you would look horrible wearing something like that. You're much too delicate. It was—grotesque."

"Oh." Isobel wasn't quite sure how to process this—comment? This criticism? Maybe Jeff was just one of those guys with traditional notions about jewelry. Her own father could never understand why her mother would choose to wear a crystal quartz point on a rough leather cord when she had a platinum and diamond necklace in her jewelry box.

"No," Jeff was saying, "I see you in something sparkly and feminine, like diamonds."

Isobel laughed. "Well, sure, diamonds are great, too! They're a girl's best friend, after all. Oh, I've been meaning to ask if you want to go to the Barn Gallery to see a show that's opening Wednesday night. I think the party is from five to seven."

Jeff shrugged. "Art's not really my thing."

Isobel didn't know quite what to say to that, either. (Jeff really spoke his mind, just like she did!) How could art not be someone's "thing"? She could see how a specific genre or style might not be to someone's taste. For example, she wasn't crazy about Surrealism. But art, in general? Art was—well, it was huge! Jeff must have meant that the sort of art the Barn Gallery usually displayed didn't impress him. Maybe he didn't care for seascapes or still lifes.

"Well," she said, "I could go with Gwen and her family. They all love art. Even Ricky."

"I've got a better idea. Why don't we go to see *Die Again Now?*"

"I'm not really into action movies," Isobel said. "They're so violent. They upset me for days afterward."

"Oh, come on, it'll be fun. Look, I'll order the tickets online right now."

Jeff took his iPhone out of his pocket before Isobel could protest.

Oh well, she thought. *I can see the show at another time. Though it's too bad I'll miss the opening. Openings are fun. You get to meet the artists and there are usually some yummy miniature quiches or bacon-wrapped shrimp being passed around* . . .

"Done," Jeff announced. "Two tickets for the five-thirty show."

Isobel smiled. "Okay," she said.

Who knows? she thought. Maybe the movie would change her mind about action flicks. Anything could happen if you just gave it a chance and kept an open mind!

Chapter 25

Catherine's house, on Ledge View Road, had been built in the early 1980s by a middle-aged couple that had peacefully grown old inside its walls. When Catherine bought the house a little less than two years earlier, it was in as pristine condition as when it had been built, thanks to its conscientious owners, now passed.

The walls and pine floors of each room on the first floor were painted white; the effect was of whitewashing, cool, crisp, and clean. All of the windows, on both floors, were large, some even appearing to be oversized, making the house bright with natural light. Even on a rainy day the house avoided being gloomy. Catherine boasted that her electric bill had never been lower.

The living room was inarguably oversized. A few throw rugs provided splashes of color underfoot while paintings in a variety of styles and media covered a good deal of the walls. There was a series of tiny oil paintings, still lifes, set in large ornate frames and hung in a horizontal row. A triptych—an abstract image of sand dunes—dominated an entire wall. And since moving to Ogunquit, Catherine had fallen in love with the work of local (though Midwestern-born) painter Judy Sowa. She owned several works, including a very large piece—an image of the Muse of History from a work by Vermeer—that hung over the fireplace in the living room. Louise's favorite of Catherine's collection of Judy Sowa's work was a smaller work, a copy of a Bronzino portrait of Laura Battiferri, a sixteenth-century gentlewoman and poet, originally painted around 1555–1560.

The furniture was minimal but comfortable—a love seat, two armchairs, and an ottoman for each chair, upholstered in a pale tan—with a liberal sprinkling of chocolate lab hair. A low coffee table set before the love seat completed the room's uncluttered décor.

Catherine's study, in contrast to the living room, was a smallish room stuffed with furniture, including a monstrously large maroon velvet armchair, two ladder-back chairs, and a low table with an elaborately carved wood base and a green marble top. The floor was mostly covered by an old but still vibrantly colored Oriental rug. Built-in shelves on two walls were crammed with books, an eclectic group that included novels by long-dead as well as contemporary authors, a collection of Restoration plays, the ubiquitous *Riverside Shakespeare,* biographies of men and women of European and American fame, and a hefty collection of good-quality art books. Another Judy Sowa painting hung next to a painting by another local artist, Michael Palmer. A sleek laptop sat on an old oak desk that was way too large for the space it occupied. Next to the computer were stacks of magazines (everything from *Time* to *Rolling Stone*) and newspapers (Catherine had the *New York Times* Sunday edition delivered, and she kept up with all of the local papers, including those out of Portland and Portsmouth).

The kitchen was state-of-the-art, and, in Catherine's opinion, totally wasted on her. She had never had time to cook much—too often on the road, too many late nights at the office—and now that she did have time, she had discovered she didn't care for it. Hence the stack of take-out menus on the bar top and the fridge bare of all but a few essentials—a carton of low-fat milk, a half a pound of butter, several jars of jellies and preserves from Stonewall Kitchen, a jar of pickles, and in the freezer, a few packs of frozen shrimp, easy enough to toss on the indoor grill.

The powder room was decorated in peach and pale green, and there was the ubiquitous shallow bowl of white seashells, along with a similar bowl of green and blue and amber pieces of sea glass. Sea glass was something guests liked to steal even more than seashells, which was why Louise kept her own collection tucked away in her room.

The second floor consisted of Catherine's bedroom, a small guest room, and a large bathroom. Louise had seen the bedroom only once, and that on her initial tour of the house; Catherine took her private space quite seriously, as did both Louise and Isobel.

There was always music playing from the stereo system in the living room, not too loudly but not too softly, either. At the moment Madeleine Peyroux was crooning her version of an old Patsy Cline hit.

Charlie was asleep on a braided rug in front of the fireplace. Every once in a while a paw would twitch. Louise wondered if human beings would ever know for sure what went on in the minds and hearts of four-legged animals. More was the pity if they didn't.

The women settled on the love seat, each with a cup of coffee.

"Did Isobel tell you I ran into her and Jeff in town the other day?" Catherine asked.

Louise shook her head. "No. At least, I don't think that she did. I've been so preoccupied lately what with this wedding and the usual assortment of fussy guests . . ."

"Well, I did run into them. And I have to tell you that Charlie had a very unusual reaction to Jeff. In short, she tried to bite his head off."

Louise looked quickly to the sleeping dog; at that moment she was the epitome of peaceful laziness. "What?" she said. "I don't believe it."

"Believe it. She barked at him, growled, snarled, the whole bit. I had trouble holding on to her. Seriously, I thought she was going to break free and knock him down. I've never seen her take against someone so completely, especially not within a few seconds of meeting him. I have to say, it made me wonder about Jeff's character. You know what they say about animals having a better sense for character than we dumb humans."

Louise glanced again at the slumbering lump of fur. "I'm shocked," she said. "Jeff is such a nice young man. I don't think you should read too much into Charlie's behavior. Jeff's done nothing but treat Isobel with respect and kindness."

"I'm not saying he's a criminal," Catherine pointed out. "I'm just saying that Charlie's reaction was odd."

"Charlie probably smelled something on him she didn't like. Maybe he was wearing cologne. Some dogs don't like those artificially sweet smells. Come to think of it, I might bark if a guy wearing too much cologne got too close to me."

"Maybe," Catherine conceded. "Anyway, I thought you should know, but maybe I shouldn't have mentioned it."

Louise shrugged. "Oh, it's all right. Well, I've got to get going. Duty calls."

Once back at the inn, Louise opened her laptop and went to Isobel's blog. She read the latest post and smiled. Isobel seemed to have so much fun writing CityMouse. And there were so many comments from Isobel's fans. Louise noted several recent messages from a girl who had been a friend of Isobel's back in Massachusetts. Huh, Louise thought. She hadn't heard Isobel mention Maureen in over a year . . .

That was one of the things Louise thought she might not have fully considered before uprooting her daughter and transplanting her to Maine—the friendships she would have to leave behind. But Isobel had offered very little resistance to leaving Massachusetts, aside from some initial grumbling about moving to a backwater. It was almost as if she couldn't wait to get far away from her father and the life she had known with him.

Louise had felt much the same way. Moving north to Maine had been like running away, and running away was rarely a good thing in the end—unless, of course, you were running away to save your life and there were simply no other viable options. But in Louise's case there had been other options, of course there had been. She could have stayed put, either in the house she and Andrew had owned together or in another house, one without the memories. She could have gotten a job with regular hours and far less risk to her (and Isobel's) financial future and to her sanity.

Louise exited CityMouse and closed her laptop. She wondered if Isobel had told any of her old friends back in Massachusetts that she had a boyfriend. She realized she had no idea of the nature of Isobel's relationships with anyone other than Gwen. Maybe there were no more real friends from "back home."

And maybe Gwen was enough. Gwen and me, Louise thought. *Because, of course, Isobel has me—if no longer her father.*

Andrew and Isobel. There had been times throughout the years when Louise had felt downright jealous of the relationship they shared. She remembered now how once a month they had gone on a breakfast date to the local diner for French toast and sausage. Isobel probably never knew that her father paid for that indulgence with an extra-rigorous session at the gym later that afternoon. His usual breakfast was a bowl of high protein cereal with nonfat yogurt and sliced fruit. Andrew had always taken his health seriously; both of his parents had died of heart-related disease before reaching sixty. There was that—and there was Andrew's aforementioned vanity.

Even in the final months before the big reveal, when Andrew must have been almost wholly occupied with how to extricate himself from his marriage, he had never missed a breakfast date. "But while we were eating our French toast," Isobel had remarked later, after the divorce, "and talking about the new bird feeder we were going to put up in the backyard, all he was thinking about was when he was next going to see Vicky. I feel like such an idiot. I feel like I was being used."

Well, what could Louise say to that? She, too, felt that she and her daughter had been duped, fooled, and mistreated by Andrew Bessire.

Once Andrew had moved out of the house, Isobel had refused to see him. That last breakfast date had taken place well over two years ago. Louise wondered if Isobel ever thought about those mornings, or if she had cut all emotional ties to the old rituals and habits. She hadn't asked her daughter those questions, not directly. She didn't know if they were the sort of questions she should be asking.

Louise got up from the kitchen table. She thought about what Catherine had told her earlier. She had defended Jeff to Catherine so strongly, as if her faith in him was absolute. Why? Because she had to believe in him as a good and decent person. The idea that she had unwittingly allowed her daughter to date a jerk was deeply unacceptable; it was not a possibility she was willing or able to entertain.

"I'm a good mother," Louise told the kitchen. "I would never let anything bad happen to my daughter. Never."

Chapter 26

CITYMOUSE

Bonjour!

Today I want to share with my Dear Readers some snaps Gwen and I took while at the beach yesterday. Ogunquit Beach (also called Main Beach; it stretches from Ogunquit on into Wells) is considered one of the most beautiful beaches in the world, and hey, I'm down with that! The Marginal Way, which starts in Perkins Cove and winds its way along the rocky coast and into town, isn't technically part of the beach, but it's definitely an essential part of the Ogunquit experience. The view from the cliff path is spectacular and dramatic—you're looking out over the wild Atlantic Ocean!

So, about Photo Number One. This family of five from Toronto is almost too cute to be real, but trust me, they are real and they were super-nice about letting us take their picture. Look at how the seven-year-old boy is hamming it up for the camera! Mom looked smashing in her neon pink two-piece and Dad's sun hat is the hippest goofy sun hat I've ever seen. The twins—two years old in September, we learned—are named Sam (Samuel) and Pam (Pamela), and they love swimming in a pool but are still kind of afraid of the ocean. (I don't blame them! Icky seaweed, jagged rocks, crashing waves, oh my!)

Now, Photo Number Two. Here's a couple Gwen and I have seen several times this summer and last. They were on their way back home after a morning of rest and relaxation before the hordes arrived and the sun hit its full height. I boldly asked them how long they had been married (I guessed, as both were wearing bands on the fourth fingers of their left hands), and they graciously told us that they had tied the proverbial knot six years ago, after the death of their respective spouses, to whom they had been married for a bazillion years or so. How lovely that these people— Martha and John—found each other in the golden years and were courageous enough to take another emotional leap of faith.

Last but not least, Photo Number Three. Here are two BFFs—really! These two women told us they are fifty-eight years old and have been best friends since grammar school. Gwen and I were impressed and hope to be our own version of these ladies someday. The hat on Maryanne was a gift from Julianne; we love its impossibly wide brim. Julianne's necklace was a gift from

Maryanne; the beads are real lapis lazuli, a truly luxurious stone beloved by the ancient Egyptians, and we all know they could do no wrong in the style and taste department. Each woman is married (with kids, and Julianne has a grandson), but they don't let that stop them from spending three or four days alone together in Ogunquit every summer. Here's to friendship!

Finally, when our work was done for the day, Gwen and I sank to the sand and grabbed a well-deserved rest, complete with ice cream cones, strawberry for Gwen, vanilla for me. For once I got behind the camera and took a photo of Gwen—here she is in a lovely cover-up in a flowy, chiffony fabric. The green and tan print works perfectly with this week's emerald hair. And here I am in a black retro one-piece; the woman who wore this back when it was new must now be une femme d'une certain age, as the French say. (The French really do have a way with words.) The suit is in near-perfect condition, so I'm guessing the original owner did not wear it to do daily laps in a chlorinated pool!

All in all it was a wonderful day. There's nothing like the beach for attracting all sorts of people in one happy, feel-good place.

Have a sunny summer's day, Everyone!

"Um," Gwen asked in a whisper, "why did he come with us on this excursion anyway?"

Isobel, Gwen, and Jeff were in a vintage clothing shop called Good Old Days. It occupied most of the first floor of a big old Victorian farmhouse out on Springfield Road and had an eclectic selection of clothes and accessories from the 1920s through the 1990s.

"Uh," Isobel replied, also in a whisper, "he's my boyfriend." It was the first time she had ever said those words to anyone but herself. She hoped it was true, that Jeff really was her official boyfriend. How did you know about something like that? Did someone make an announcement? *How,* Isobel thought, *can I be sixteen years old and not know this?*

"Well, I know he's your boyfriend," Gwen was saying, "but doesn't he have better things to do, like, I don't know, hang out with his guy friends? You can see he's bored out of his mind. He should be in a sports bar, cheering on the Red Sox. Isn't that what most straight guys do if they're not actually playing sports? Eat nachos and watch sports?"

Isobel started to respond with something like, "Yeah, but—" when she realized that she had no idea who Jeff's friends were. She assumed he had friends—after all, he was so nice and good-looking!—though he hardly ever mentioned anyone, and the one or two times he had mentioned a name, it was that of a guy he knew from school in Vermont. Jeff had pointed out that this guy—Terry—was the son of someone rich and powerful, or maybe the son of someone nearly famous. She couldn't remember, exactly. Did Jeff really have no other friends? She remembered how he had asked why she hadn't invited him along to the beach the other day. He had seemed a bit put out, even a bit hurt. "It's just that I'm crazy about you," he had said. "If I could, I would spend every minute of my days and nights with you."

She had felt enormously flattered and then, a tiny bit worried. It was a big responsibility, meaning so much to someone that they wanted to spend all their time with you. But with her characteristic optimism, she had dismissed those tiny worries. Maybe Jeff was the proverbial Lone Wolf. Maybe he liked it that way. That was all right. Actually, it was kind of cool, being the One and Only for the Lone Wolf.

"He's just being supportive," Isobel said to Gwen, finally.

Gwen glanced at Jeff, who was standing a few yards away, arms folded across his chest, yawning. "I guess," she mumbled. "But I wish he didn't have to lurk like that."

Isobel laughed. "He's not lurking. Come on, Gwen!"

"Well, if he has to be here maybe he could actually help us. Not that we need help, but he could offer to be useful. Carry my tripod or something."

"You don't have your tripod today," Isobel pointed out.

"Whatever."

"He offered to drive us wherever we wanted to go. You were the one who insisted on driving your car."

"I didn't insist. I prefer to drive myself. Us. Besides, he drives too fast."

"He does not! Only sometimes."

"Once is all it takes," Gwen said in an ominous tone.

Isobel turned toward a circular rack of dresses. Gwen could be so dramatic! Why did she have to make her question Jeff's being with them as anything other than, well, normal? She took a deep breath. They were having a nice time. There was no need for drama, even if Gwen thought there was.

Her eye stopped on a dress and she carefully removed it from the rack.

"What did you find?" Gwen asked, joining her.

Isobel studied the dress for a moment before answering, "The seams are in good shape, it's got all its buttons, which are very cute—see? They've got a tiny running horse stamped in—and the length is just right. I adore the V-neck. It's not too low, but it would really frame the right necklace. What do you think, Gwen?"

"I think it's cool," Gwen said. "The color is so unusual. Like a cross between watermelon and, I don't know, Orangina. It's definitely a summer statement. Is there a brand name?"

"The label is cut out. I'm guessing maybe a Forma, about ten, twelve years ago."

"Good call."

"Jeff?"

Isobel turned to Jeff, and held the dress up against her.

"What do you think?" she asked.

Jeff raised his eyebrows in an expression of disbelief. Or was it puzzlement?

"What?" she said. "You don't like it?"

For answer Jeff turned away and idly began to flip through a rack of plaid work shirts.

"Good thing he doesn't have to wear it," Gwen muttered. "So, are you getting it?"

Isobel hesitated. "Well," she said, "maybe not . . ." She returned the dress to the rack. She wasn't sure it was a great idea to purposely choose to wear something your boyfriend didn't like. If it were an accident, then no worries. But it could be kind of insulting to be all, *hey, I know you loathe and despise this dress but I'm wearing it anyway.* Wouldn't it? She wasn't so sure she would do that to her mother, either, or to Gwen . . . But would her mother or Gwen even care what she wore as long as Isobel herself liked it?

"It would look great on you," Gwen said, emphatically.

Isobel shrugged. "I'll think about it. It's not like I need another dress right now . . ."

"Since when is need the issue?" Gwen sighed. "Whatever. If we're not going to buy anything, let's get going. Are you coming with me?"

Isobel didn't answer immediately. She really didn't want to abandon Jeff; he had driven his own car and could take off whenever he wanted to, but . . . Poor guy, she thought. He was probably bored beyond belief. As a rule men didn't like to shop. Everyone knew that. It really had been nice of him to offer to come along. "You go on," she said finally to Gwen. "I think I'll hang out with Jeff."

Gwen shrugged. "If he exceeds the speed limit, tell him to slow down. 'Bye, Jeff," she called out.

Jeff didn't react. "He must not have heard you," Isobel said. "I'll tell him you said good-bye."

"No worries. Have fun," she said, and headed out of the store.

Jeff was at Isobel's side the moment Gwen was gone. "I thought she would never leave. Now we can be alone."

"Didn't you hear her call out good-bye?" Isobel asked.

"No," Jeff said. "Did she?"

"Yes."

"Oh."

"So, you really don't like that dress? Gwen thought it would look good on me."

Jeff laughed and drew her into his arms. "Izzy," he whispered, kissing the top of her head, "what am I going to do with you?"

Chapter 27

Louise sat at the kitchen table, her laptop open in front of her. She had started out almost an hour and a half earlier browsing online for wedding inspiration. She yawned hugely and wondered where the time had gone.

It was amazing what a time sink the Internet could be. You hunted down your information with very little fuss and then four hours later you raised your swollen eyes from the screen and didn't know where the hell you were. Daily Mail UK Online? Why were you reading that trash? And how in God's name had you gotten to a site about some new, supposedly fantastic handheld vacuum and from there, on to a site that promised to double your financial investments within a week? "And don't get me started on all the websites about cats and their wacky antics," Louise mumbled to the empty kitchen. They were more addictive than anything else, like the one about Maru, the Japanese Internet sensation who in one clip managed to stuff himself into a box about one-eighth of his bulk . . .

Enough! Louise got up from the table and began the preparations for a press pot of coffee. She smiled a bit wickedly as she did. Flora Michaels had sent a panicky e-mail (odd, as her usual tone both on-screen and off was icy indifference) saying that the bride was rumored to be four months' pregnant. Flora Michaels and Calvin Streep were on their way to her home in a desperate effort to convince her not to postpone the nuptials. A "bride with a bump" was chic nowadays, Flora Michaels stated, as if trying to convince Louise of this interesting fact. The bride must be made to understand this!

Louise had no sympathy to offer the bride or the wedding planner; she thought the rituals surrounding celebrity pregnancy and motherhood were ridiculous. Consider the frantic rush to erase any trace of the pregnancy! It was pretty insulting to the baby, when you thought about it. Mummy loves you but Mummy doesn't want anyone to know she gave birth to you. For her part, Louise had been thrilled by her child's birth, and proud to bear the stretch marks.

Louise poured a cup of fresh coffee and savored the first sip. *Ah,* she thought, *here I am enjoying life's simple pleasures when no doubt the celebrity couple's agents are frantically selling print and online rights to magazines and newspapers and Internet venues.* What a lot of fuss for what came down to just a party. You could get married in a courthouse or on a rowboat and save yourself the time and expense. What mattered were the vows, not the venue.

Her own wedding had taken place in a Universalist Unitarian church, with only about twenty people in attendance. They had honeymooned in Italy, a week in Rome and another in Ravenna. And the early years of the marriage had been really wonderful, filled with laughter and joy and the sheer fun of a child in their midst.

Where, when, why had it gone wrong?

Andrew's excuse for leaving her had been inarguable. He said that he had fallen out of love with her. What did that mean? Louise had wondered. Andrew couldn't quite say. Clearly, he didn't find her physically attractive any longer. They hadn't had sex in almost eight or nine months, but that wasn't terribly unusual for long-married couples, was it? Maybe he had become bored by her, by the meals she routinely cooked, by the TV shows she routinely watched, by the turns of phrase she routinely used, but she had become kind of bored by him, too. That was usual, also. Your spouse wasn't supposed to entertain you every day of the year. That was what television and movies and books and music were for. And friends. And children. And big fat cats like Maru . . .

Thankfully, James and Jim came into the kitchen just then, interrupting thoughts that threatened to become morbid and quickly.

"We just thought we'd see if you wanted anything special from Portland," James said. "We're on our way up there now for lunch at our favorite Mexican restaurant."

"And you know we're going to stop at Brown Trading while we're there," Jim added.

Louise smiled. "How about you see what goody you can find me for twenty dollars," she said. "I doubt it's going to be caviar, but . . ."

"Deal."

No sooner had the men gone out through the front door of the inn than Catherine, sans Charlie, came knocking at the back door.

"Am I interrupting?" she asked.

Louise smiled. "Yes, but nothing that can't be interrupted. Slightly sad thoughts that were threatening to get very depressing very soon."

"Oh good. I mean, good that I'm not interrupting happy thoughts. I guess. Anyway, I wanted to bring by that book I was telling you about." She held out a fat trade-sized paperback for Louise to take. "*The Historian*. You'll love it, trust me."

Louise glanced at the back cover and put the book next to the computer. "Thanks. Honestly, I'm not sure I'll have time to read it until after the wedding from Hades has come and gone . . ."

"No worries. Save it as a well-deserved treat."

"My list of literary treats is getting longer every day. I just bought a copy of *Bring up the Bodies* by Hilary Mantel. Of course, I'll have to reread *Wolf Hall* first. My mind has become a sieve . . ."

"Just wait until you hit the menopausal years. Or, as they are also known, the 'mental pause' years. You'll think back upon your old self as a rocket scientist."

"Yikes. That bad, huh?"

Catherine's response—her open mouth indicated that she was about to say something—was interrupted by yet another visitor at the back door. This time, it was Jeff Otten.

"I hope this isn't a bad time?" he asked, smiling from Louise to Catherine.

"No, no, come in," Louise said.

She would have to have been blind not to notice the massive bouquet of flowers cradled in the crook of his left arm. At first glance Louise could see that there were lush pink peonies and pale green bells of Ireland and quite a few white roses. It was a pastel symphony. The entire bundle was protected by shiny cellophane and tied with a pink satin ribbon.

"These are for you," Jeff said, offering the bouquet with a touching solemnity.

Louise took it gently. "It's gorgeous!" she exclaimed. "Catherine, look at this!"

"It's a stunning piece," Catherine agreed.

"I know the owner of the shop pretty well," Jeff said, with modesty. "He owed me a favor actually, so . . . "

"I have to put these in water immediately." Louise went to a cupboard for a vase and busied herself filling it with water. The flowers, she thought, would look lovely in the parlor, but she was sorely tempted to take them up to her own bedroom. Guests didn't have to share every aspect of her life!

She turned the water off and became aware that Jeff was speaking to Catherine.

"I'm glad to see you again, actually," he was saying. "I felt so badly about what happened when we met the other day. Dogs usually love me. Anyway, I'm really sorry if I did something to upset Charlie. Maybe I made a sudden move or maybe it was the tone of my voice . . . "

Catherine smiled. "I wondered if it was your cologne or aftershave that set her off."

Jeff looked stunned. "Wow," he said. "I never thought about that possibility! Animals are super-sensitive to odors, way more than we are. Again, I apologize."

"No harm done. And thank God for that!"

Jeff laughed. "Yeah. Charlie's teeth looked in very sharp shape." Jeff checked his watch. Louise noted that it was a Rolex. "Well," he said, "I've got to run."

"Busy at work?" Louise asked.

"Always. My dad is a tough taskmaster. But that's one of the reasons he's so successful. And speaking of Dad, I'd better hurry—he's expecting me."

With a final wave Jeff scooted out of the room.

"Thanks again for the flowers," Louise called after him. "Sheesh," she said, turning to her friend. "It's been like Grand Central Station in here today. Not that I'm complaining. It's nice to feel like you're really part of the community."

Catherine was frowning a bit.

"What?" Louise asked.

"Nothing. It's just that he's actually pretty okay, isn't he, the junior Mr. Otten."

"I told you. Maybe Charlie was having an off day when she tried to attack him. She's entitled. The best of us get the grumpies."

"Yeah. He did seem pretty genuine just now, and sorry, though he had no reason to apologize. Maybe I was too quick to judge. It's been known to happen. And I do feel a bit protective of Isobel. How can I not?"

"And I appreciate that," Louise said. "Believe me."

"Not that she's the daughter I never had but . . . Well, in some way I guess she's the daughter I wish I had had."

"We can share her friendship, to some extent."

Catherine smiled. "Thanks. But I'll let you handle the college tuition."

"Ha! How generous of you! Though actually, I'm hoping Isobel herself will cover a lot of the cost of college with academic scholarships. God knows, she's no athlete."

"On that note, I should get going and leave you to the business of running this inn, just in case all those scholarships don't materialize."

Catherine took her leave.

Louise regarded the bouquet Jeff had brought her and inhaled its heady fragrance. She hadn't seen anything quite so luscious in ages. It could easily be used as a bridal bouquet.

And speaking of which . . . Louise grabbed her phone and placed a call to Flora Michaels, wedding planner to the earthbound stars.

Chapter 28

CITYMOUSE

Greetings, All!

On this lovely July morning I want to pay a long-overdue homage to the women of Se Vende, one of if not the most beautiful and welcoming and interesting stores in Portland.

Sage and Olive are the coolest mother/daughter team next to LouLou and me. They travel around the world choosing stuff for their excellent site on Exchange Street—all sorts of colorful pottery, beautifully crafted hammocks, mirrors in intricately carved frames, and—my favorite!—lots of unique and simply stunning jewelry from Mexico, Israel, Turkey, Vietnam, and other wonderful places I hope to visit someday! (See Gwen's photos below.) And if you're really lucky, Sage's huge gray kitty will be hanging out with her! And maybe you'll also get to meet their friend Cait, who is an artist and a professional belly dancer and a super-nice person, too!

Pop in when you're in Portland and tell them CityMouse (aka, me) sent you!

Now, to mention the outstanding Diana Vreeland yet again . . . She was quoted as having this to say about fashion magazines (way back before blogs and websites, of course):

"What these magazines gave was a point of view. Most people haven't got a point of view; they need to have it given to them."

By the way, it was Ms. Vreeland who, in the opinion of those who know, pretty much invented the role of the powerful, all-knowing fashion editor.

Now, my brief comments on the above: I'm not sure if I wholly agree with the statement I quoted. I like to give people the benefit of the doubt and think that everyone truly does have her own thoughts—not that some direction can't be helpful in shaping a point of view!

I have no desire to be an arbiter of style or fashion for others (hey, I think that's the first time I've used that word—*arbiter!*). People who blog about fashion have become known as "style influencers," and that's a pretty big responsibility to bear.

I'm too humble (yes, really) and too non-ambitious (ditto) to think that I have anything so vitally important to say that it would or should change someone's mind or heart about something as personal and individual (at least, it should be) as style.

Well, CityMouse signing off for now before I talk/write myself into an even deeper mess!

It had taken almost an hour to get to what Jeff had referred to as "the Blackmore estate." When they pulled up into the ridiculously long driveway, it was already crowded with cars—nice ones, at that.

Isobel took a deep breath. She felt nervous and hesitant and she had since Jeff had first told her about the party.

"The Blackmores are important people," he had informed her. "I hope you have something appropriate to wear."

"Oh," she had said. "Well, what sort of . . . I mean, is it fancy dress?"

Jeff had laughed. "Isobel, you're too cute. I told you, it's a lawn party. In the middle of the day."

"Oh. Okay. So, how do you know the Blackmores?"

"They're friends of the family. They're good people."

That made sense. The rich and powerful were friends with the rich and powerful. The rich and powerful didn't hang out at Arby's or Walmart, meeting up with the poor and insignificant. It was the same reason rock stars married models and not the girls who worked at J. C. Penney or the nail salon.

Still, Isobel had not been at all reassured. She had even thought for a brief moment of using her mother as an excuse, before realizing that a lie could get complicated very quickly. Besides, why in the world would her mother refuse to let Isobel attend a daytime party at the home of a respectable family?

But Jeff had taken the decision out of her hands. He had called her mother to assure her that the people hosting the party were decent and that many of the guests were also friends of the Otten family, and that while there would be alcohol he would refrain from drinking, and that they would be home well before dark.

Her mom had seemed pleased that Jeff had come to her with reassurances, and of course she had assumed that Isobel wanted to go to the party. Isobel hadn't had the heart to tell her mother the truth.

Sigh. She had had the worst time choosing an outfit. She had never been told to dress "appropriately" for an event before; it was a lot of pressure! Finally, she had settled on an A-line skirt that came to just below her knee, in a summery plaid of pale blues, greens, and yellows; a pale yellow shirt; and low wedge sandals. Sandals and bag were the color of heavy cream. She kept her jewelry simple—gold-tone hoop earrings; three gold-tone bangle bracelets; and a blue topaz and silver ring that her father had given her for her twelfth birthday. (She might be displeased with her father, but that didn't mean she had to be displeased with a perfectly innocent piece of jewelry!)

When Jeff had come to pick her up, he hadn't commented on her outfit. She took his silence on the subject as approval. Still, when she got into the car he was frowning.

"What's wrong?" she asked, wondering if bare legs were somehow not exactly "the thing" for a party at the Blackmores'.

"That guy." He jerked his head in the direction of the driver's side window. Isobel leaned forward and looked past him.

"Oh, Quentin."

"I know who he is. What's he doing here?"

Isobel had giggled. "Don't the hedge clippers give it away? He works for us! He's sort of a handyman, jack-of-all-trades. It's pretty amazing, all the things he can do."

Jeff had not replied. He drove them swiftly off, with another frowning look in Quentin's direction.

Once parked in the long drive of the Blackmore estate, Jeff

took Isobel by the elbow and they joined the other party-goers on a spacious lawn. Isobel glanced around at the other guests and had trouble discerning a dress code. There were women in shorts and T-shirts, in linen pants and silky blouses; there were women in maxi-dresses and there were women (some of the younger ones) in miniskirts. With few exceptions, the men wore chinos with white or blue oxford shirts, sleeves folded up to mid-forearm, and natty European-style loafers. Jeff was one of the exceptions. His jeans were on trend—dark and slouchy—his shirt was taupe linen (Iso-bel thought he must have an entire closet full of linen shirts), and he wore it buttoned at the collar and sleeves. His low-heeled boots were artfully scraped and bruised. Isobel thought he was easily the best-looking and the best-dressed man at the party.

The house was enormous, one of the largest Isobel had seen, and she had seen a heck of a lot of impressive piles both back in Massachusetts and here in Maine. In spite of its ro-mantic if somewhat grand name—Eagle's Eye Ridge—she found herself forced to describe it (silently, as she didn't want to insult anyone's taste) as a McMansion, more bland bulk than interesting style, more hotel chain than personalized home.

The hosts—and Jeff had not introduced her to them; for a while Isobel wasn't even sure who they were among the crowd—had erected a tent under which had been placed about twenty small round tables with chairs. There was a live band set up at one end, playing a selection of jazz and blues and classic rock, and waiters circulated the lawn with trays of appetizers. A bar served beer, wine, and a limited range of exotic cocktails, none of which were at all familiar to Isobel. There were no dogs and no children. In fact, Isobel thought she was probably the youngest person at the party by several years.

This shindig, Isobel thought, made the Ryan-Roberts party look amateur in comparison—if you cared about comparing such things. Isobel found herself longing for shouting boys with massive water pistols, and pudgy pugs underfoot.

They had been there no more than ten minutes when Jeff turned to her and announced that he had to "do the rounds."

"It's my social duty when I represent my family," he explained.

"Okay," Isobel said. "Do you want me to come with you?"

"No." His reply was emphatic. "Why don't you get something to drink?"

She watched him walk off and join a small group of guys about his age. They all shook hands. Jeff must have said something funny because all three of the guys suddenly laughed. One glanced in her direction, and Isobel immediately felt embarrassed. Of course she hadn't been the object of a joke, especially not one told by Jeff. *Wow, I am being beyond silly today,* she scolded herself.

She turned away and walked to the bar, where she asked for a seltzer with a slice of lime (she usually asked for lemon, but maybe it was time to be wild and crazy!), and while she sipped it, she couldn't help but overhear a conversation between two very well-dressed middle-aged women. They were talking about Jeff's older brother, Michael. The brother Jeff hadn't yet mentioned to her.

Flynn had told her mother that Michael Otten was an impressive person, and had been even as a kid. The women's conversation revealed more of the same. Something about an award he had won for some research . . . Isobel didn't want to linger in the hopes of catching details and risk being caught eavesdropping on a private conversation—especially a private conversation among people who—if their clothes and jewelry were any indication—were very probably "important."

Isobel moved off. She remembered that her mother had mentioned that Michael Otten worked for a big pharmaceutical company and that he was based somewhere in Switzerland. She would like to go to Switzerland someday. In fact—

Her thoughts about travel scattered when she spotted Jeff a few yards off, chatting with another girl. She looked about Jeff's age or maybe, Isobel thought, even a bit older, twenty-one or twenty-two. She was dressed in a skintight short skirt and an equally skintight T-shirt with spaghetti straps, and on her feet were a pair of wedges that had to be at least five inches high. Her hair was sleek and black and very long; her eyes were hidden behind enormous black sunglasses. For the first time in her entire life, Isobel felt a twinge of doubt about her appearance. She felt juvenile and even a bit—dowdy.

Jeff leaned down and whispered something in the girl's ear. Whatever he said made her smile and touch his arm. And then he came strolling toward her, a smile on his face that Isobel could only call secretive.

"Hey, there you are," he said. "I was looking all over for you."

You weren't looking very hard, Isobel answered silently. "Who was that girl?" she asked.

"What? That girl I was just talking to?" He shrugged. "Just some girl."

Isobel struggled to keep her voice even. "Do you know her?" she asked. "I mean, did you know her before today, or did you just meet her?"

Jeff's expression stiffened, and he took a step closer to her. "What's up with the third degree?" he demanded.

"Nothing." Isobel hesitated. She felt a bit intimidated with him looming over her. She took a tiny step backward. "It's just that it looked like you were—like you were flirting with her. It was . . . it was kind of embarrassing for me." *And hurtful,* she added silently. *And humiliating. And utterly shocking.*

Jeff sneered. "You have some nerve yelling at me. I saw you with that guy before, over by the band. You were totally coming on to him."

Isobel felt her stomach lurch with the absurdity of Jeff's proclamation. "I wasn't yelling at you, and I was not coming on to him," she protested. "He said hello to me and I said hello back. That was all. How could you accuse me of . . . of doing something so awful?"

Jeff grunted and shook his head. "You're such a child, Izzy. You have no idea what you're doing, do you? Look, just don't talk to anyone for the rest of the party, okay? These people are my friends. I don't need the embarrassment."

He turned away and then, spun around and pointed a finger at her.

"And by the way," he said, "I saw that photo of you on your blog, the one where you're wearing that skimpy bathing suit. I also don't need people seeing my girlfriend half-naked. I'm an Otten. Remember that. We have a reputation to uphold."

And then he stalked off.

Isobel opened her mouth, as if to respond to Jeff's latest criticism, but even if he had still been there to hear her, she had no idea what she would—or could—say to him.

She closed her mouth. She had never felt so utterly embarrassed. She wondered if anyone had heard their confrontation, but she couldn't bring herself to glance around for witnesses. What would she do if someone caught her eye?

Isobel spent the rest of the party on her own, afraid that another guy would try to talk to her, or that she would catch Jeff with another girl. More than once she found herself fighting back tears. Finally, after what seemed an eternity, Jeff rejoined her and announced that they were leaving. Without another word they walked to his car and got in. Jeff was silent on the ride home. It wasn't usual for him. Or was it? Was what she had witnessed today par for Jeff's course? Was this sort of thing what routinely went on between boyfriend and girlfriend?

Isobel just didn't know. She had been out of her league, spending an afternoon with people who were so much older, people with more experience dating and flirting. People who were drinking. Not that anyone had acted drunk, but even one glass of wine or one bottle of beer could have an effect on someone's behavior . . .

Finally—the ride had seemed interminable to Isobel—they pulled up outside the inn.

"Good-bye, Jeff," Isobel said, her voice soft.

He grunted, and didn't look over at her.

Isobel got her courage in hand. "Thanks for taking me to the party."

This time, he didn't even bother to grunt.

He made no attempt to kiss her. She was very grateful but also very disappointed. Isobel got out of the car and he pulled off immediately.

Isobel felt chastened. Jeff always waited to be sure she got inside safely. But it was still light out and they had had a fight, their first fight . . .

The sound of typing on a keyboard led Isobel back to the kitchen. Her mother was at the table, engaged in Blueberry Bay work, no doubt. She looked up briefly at Isobel, and then looked back to the computer.

"How was the party?" she asked. "Did you have a nice time?"

"Yeah," Isobel said. "But I'm really tired. The sun was super-hot . . . I'm going to go upstairs and read for a while before bed."

"Did you get enough to eat?"

"Yeah, I'm fine."

Without looking up from the computer again, her mother said, "Okay, good night."

Isobel escaped to her room. It had never felt as much like a safe haven until now. Still, she lay awake for hours, her mind racing and turning back on itself. Mostly, she felt guilty about what had happened at the party.

Maybe, she thought, watching the light fade from the sky through the window, she just wasn't ready to date; maybe she should let Jeff go before she did something to really embarrass him. He hadn't even introduced her to the hosts, the Blackmores. He had probably been afraid she would say or do something stupid or immature.

Still, Isobel felt that Jeff shouldn't have been flirting so openly with that girl. But she was a fair-minded person, wasn't she? She and Jeff had never been at a party together before today. Maybe Jeff was just a flirty guy. Some people were and they didn't mean anything serious by it. It was a personality type, really, like the way some people were cutups and others were wallflowers.

Isobel tossed the covers off and minutes later, pulled them back up. She plumped the pillows. She got up and paced. She realized that as bad as the night was, she dreaded the morning more, when she would have to do something, take a step, make a decision . . .

Finally, surprisingly, she slept, and dreamed of nothing she could remember.

Once again, Jeff made the decision for her. He sent her a text at 6 a.m. to ask if he could come by the inn later that morning. Isobel said that he could.

At ten he arrived.

Isobel's mother had gone to Wells to get a haircut. Bella was cleaning up in the kitchen, soon to leave for the day, and the housekeeping staff was busy putting the guest rooms back in order. Isobel met Jeff on the front porch. She realized she had absolutely no idea what to expect from their meeting. She felt more awkward than she had ever felt in her entire life.

"Thanks for letting me come by," Jeff said. His tone was apologetic. At least, Isobel thought it was. At the moment, she didn't feel sure of very much. Her stomach was one big, uncomfortable knot; she hadn't been able to eat a bite of Bella's beautifully prepared breakfast.

Isobel found that the only reply she could give was a nod.

"I guess I had a little too much to drink at the party yesterday," Jeff went on. "I'm so sorry, Isobel. I swear I'll never let anything like that happen again. Please, believe me."

"Okay," she said, though she still wasn't at all sure she believed him. She wondered if it would be fair to take that "okay" back . . .

"You didn't say anything to your mother, did you?" Jeff asked.

Isobel shook her head. "No."

"Good." He put his hand over his heart, as if in relief. "I wouldn't want to worry her over nothing. So, do you forgive me?"

He looked so sad and so serious. The only person Isobel had ever had trouble giving a second chance was her dad—and that was only since he had left them for Vicky.

"Of course I forgive you," she said, and now, she was sure that she meant it.

"Thanks. I mean it." Jeff grinned. "Really, Izzy, the whole thing is kind of your fault. You're so pretty, you make me crazy with jealousy. The only reason I was talking to that other girl was because I had seen you talking to that guy, and, well, I . . . I guess I kind of flipped out. I've never felt about anyone else the way I feel about you."

"Really?" Isobel felt a smile creep to her face.

"Really. And then you were wearing that short skirt, and I swear every guy at the party was giving you the eye."

Short skirt? The skirt she had worn to the party came down to her knees. She remembered Jeff's feelings about that cool orange dress in the resale shop. The dress wasn't at all revealing, but he hadn't liked that, either. And the vintage bathing suit . . . It provided more coverage than most modern one-piece bathing suits did. You could see more skin on Main Street any day in July or August—and you usually did!

Could Jeff really be so conservative in his tastes . . . But if he was, why had he been flirting with a girl in such a tight and revealing outfit? Was his behavior, as he had confessed, all due to alcohol?

Isobel felt a sense of uncertainty taking hold again. Nothing about the whole incident made much sense to her, but . . . Life was uncertain. Everything about it was always up in the air and unresolved. Things changed from moment to moment. Maturity meant learning to accept that.

Jeff reached into the pocket of his jacket and took out a white box tied with a purple ribbon.

"Here," he said, holding the box out to her. "I got this for you the other day. I was going to save it for a while, but I think that now's the right time. You deserve it."

Isobel stared at the box in Jeff's hand.

Jeff laughed. "Go ahead. It won't bite."

With a nervous smile (it had to look nervous because she felt all tingly inside), she took the box from him and untied the ribbon (noting that it was a wonderful shade of purple, like the skin of a plum). Carefully, she opened the box. Inside, resting on a piece of what looked and felt like satin, was a slim bracelet, a bangle scattered with clear, sparkling stones. Isobel was speechless.

"It's white gold," Jeff said.

Jeff didn't say anything about the stones in the piece, and Isobel didn't dare ask. *Probably,* she thought, *they're crystals, maybe Swarovski. Wow.*

"It's beautiful," she said, fighting the urge to cry with happiness. "I—Thank you."

Jeff put the bracelet on her wrist and squeezed her hand gently.

"Better than that ugly brooch you were going on about," he said.

Jeff, of course, meant the Marena piece that woman in town had been wearing. "Well, this is prettier . . . in a more feminine way," Isobel admitted.

"So, are we good?"

Isobel nodded.

Jeff laughed. "I was really worried you were going to dump me. I swear, I didn't sleep at all last night. I couldn't believe I had been such a jerk."

"Me, too," she said. "I mean, eventually I fell asleep but . . ."

Jeff took her hand and pulled her down to sit next to him on the top step.

"Well, everything is back to normal now," he said. "It's all good."

It was all good, Isobel thought. And she didn't want to dwell for one more second on the past.

"I keep meaning to ask you," she said brightly. "Why haven't you told me you have an older brother? I heard someone at the party talking about him."

Jeff frowned. "We're not close. And I wouldn't believe everything you hear about him."

"Why? It wasn't anything bad. In fact—"

"Isobel. Can we not talk about this please?"

"Oh. Sure."

Jeff smiled and squeezed her hand. "Good. Let's just be here together."

But that wasn't meant to be. Just then a car pulled up the drive and came to a smooth stop. A woman slid out of the driver's seat. It was one of the inn's guests. She was tall and thin—she had not-so-casually mentioned to Isobel's mother that she had worked as a model for some years before getting married—and was wearing a wraparound dress in cobalt blue with black platform/stiletto heels. It was an outfit meant to be noticed.

"Who's that?" Jeff asked.

"That's Mrs. White," Isobel said. "Her husband goes off every morning to play golf and she goes off for a bout of retail therapy. I can't say I blame her. Golf seems pretty boring, and shopping is so much fun!"

Today Mrs. White had been to the outlets in Kittery. Isobel

spotted a bag from Banana Republic, one from Coach, and another from a store she didn't recognize. Idly, Isobel wondered what was inside the bags. Mrs. White's style didn't much interest her; Isobel called it "women on parade," a slightly more sophisticated version of "girls on parade," and you saw it all the time.

Jeff let go of Isobel's hand and leaped to his feet. "Let me help you with those packages," he offered.

Mrs. White showed her gleaming, perfectly straight teeth in appreciation. "Why, thank you," she said, holding out her shopping bags for Jeff to take. The diamonds on both hands winked blindingly.

Jeff went ahead of her into the inn. Mrs. White stopped to smile down at Isobel.

"What a nice young man," she said. "Such manners. You don't find that often these days, even in men my husband's age. Somewhere along the line they lost the training they might once have gotten. Either that or they just stopped caring."

"Yes," Isobel said, smiling up at the woman. "Jeff is very polite."

"And so handsome . . ." Mrs. White sighed. "I'd call that one a keeper!"

She followed Jeff inside, leaving Isobel to ponder those final words. Yes, maybe Jeff was a keeper. Maybe what had happened yesterday afternoon at the party was just an anomaly, just one of those things that was the odd result of a series of odd circumstances coming together in a rare and random way . . .

Jeff rejoined her a moment later. He took both of her hands now in his, and looked into her eyes. "Thank you, Izzy," he said. "Maybe I don't deserve to be forgiven, but thank you for doing it."

"You're welcome," she replied. His eyes, she thought, were really so expressive. Eyes as windows to the soul. She wondered who had been the very first person to express that lovely truth.

He leaned down and kissed her gently and lingeringly on the lips. Isobel felt happier, more blissful, than she remembered ever having felt.

"I have to go," he said finally. "I'm needed at Dad's office. But I'll check in with you later, okay?"

Isobel nodded. Happiness, it seemed, had robbed her of the ability to speak.

Jeff then got into his car. Isobel watched him drive off. She felt so, so much better than she had earlier, before his visit. He had been so kind and gentle. And Mrs. White's appreciation of Jeff's gentlemanly behavior had helped her to see and to understand the good things about Jeff that she might have been missing or underestimating.

Isobel sighed in sheer contentment. The bracelet Jeff had given her winked and sparkled in the sun, almost as brightly as Mrs. White's rings! Or maybe not quite, but it was a beautiful piece. If Jeff hadn't given it to her—if she had seen it in a display case in a jewelry store—she might not have considered it as something she would like to wear. But somehow Jeff had known . . . Better than she had known her own taste, Jeff had known that the bracelet would suit her.

She couldn't wait to show the bracelet to her mother. On second thought, Isobel considered, maybe she would keep it to herself for just a little while. She would treasure it like the very special gift that it was—like the flowers Jeff had given her, like the way he held the door for her, like his incredibly exciting kisses.

Isobel looked up at the lovely green leaves of the big oak tree down by the white picket fence and smiled. *I am such a lucky, lucky gal,* she thought.

Chapter 29

"No . . . No! Please!"

Louise's eyes flew open and she gasped, struggling for a normal breath. The sheets were tangled around her ankles. Her nightgown was soaked through. One of the pillows had fallen to the floor.

It hadn't happened for a long, long time.

Louise managed to find the switch on the bedside lamp and struggled free of the sheets to a seating position against the remaining pillow. Her heart was still racing. Her mouth was dry; she reached for the bottle of water on the bedside table and drank deeply, spilling some of the water on her already wet nightgown. It was just about three o'clock in the morning, the dead of night, the time when demons both real and imagined invaded and tormented the soul.

It had been so horribly real—the fear, the dread, and then the panic, the certainty that something very, very bad was about to happen. And then the worst of it all, the absolute inability to move, to run, to escape the dread that was inexorably descending.

It had been so long, almost a year now . . . Still, how could she have forgotten the intensity of the nightmare? She put her hand on her stomach, as if to protect what she had not been able to protect all those years ago, in the cold, hard light of day . . .

This time, caught fast in the bondage of the dream, she had seen Ted's bloody death, had heard the sound of the gunshot that had brutally ended his life. He was only twenty-three when he died. But he had already wasted his life almost beyond salvation. And he had ended the life of his child. The fact that it was an unwitting act didn't matter to Louise. When he had pushed her down that flight of stairs, after beating her and chasing her out of their apartment and through the hallways when she had finally broken away, he had destroyed the life of his own flesh and blood. Not that he had cared. How could he have? Maliciously, he had tampered with her birth control pills. When she found out she was pregnant, he had roared with laughter, and, as quickly as the laughter had erupted, it changed to insults and vile condemnation. "You were stupid enough to make that thing," he had snarled. "Now, get rid of it."

But he had taken care of that . . .

Louise put her hands to her face and pressed her fingers against her eyes. She wished she had some antianxiety pills on hand. Her doctor had prescribed a medication for her after Andrew had moved out, but she hadn't taken it for long. The last thing she had wanted was to risk becoming dependent on prescription drugs. How would having a junkie for a mother have helped Isobel cope with the divorce and its attendant upheaval?

Well, she thought now, getting slowly out of the wreck of her bed, *there's always booze* . . . But the problem with booze was that it made you fat. The inane thought almost made her laugh. To be worried about weight gain . . . Wouldn't life be a joy if your biggest worry were gaining a pound or two?

Louise set to work putting the bed back into some order. While she retrieved and plumped the pillows and shook out the covers, she wondered why the dream, the nightmare, had visited her just now. Stress, of course. Inordinate stress could resurrect the terrors you had tried so hard to face down and put behind you. Flora Michaels was at fault. That was it . . .

When the bed was done, Louise went out into the hall and headed for the bathroom. A few ibuprofen were in order. She glanced toward Isobel's closed door. All was quiet. Ah, the sleep of the young and the innocent and the blameless . . .

When she got back to her room, she changed into a fresh nightgown and collapsed into her bed. Reason was returning. The occurrence of the dream could not be blamed entirely on Flora Michaels, if at all. The real culprit was probably the fact that Isobel was entering the world of dating. That reality must have triggered Louise's deepest fears, the store of bitter memories she thought she had permanently locked away, the nasty old demons she hoped she had exorcised forever.

Louise adjusted the pillows under her head and sighed. Thank God Isobel's first experience with the opposite sex was with such a decent guy. If there was anything bad to know about Jeff Otten, surely she would have heard it by now. Just because a dog didn't like him didn't make him a criminal. And Flynn had vetted him and surely Bella had her ear to the ground, even though she didn't indulge in the worst sort of small-town gossip like so many others. Even the sometimes prickly, suspicious Catherine had come around enough to admit that Jeff did seem to be a genuinely decent person.

And then a thought came to her . . . She felt ashamed it hadn't occurred to her before now. Did Andrew know that his daughter had a boyfriend? She hadn't asked Isobel if she had told her father about Jeff, and she was not in touch with her ex-husband in any regular or consistent way. The child support checks arrived on time each month, as did the check for spousal support. Other than that . . .

And when, Louise asked herself, was the last time she had reproved Andrew for not being in closer or more frequent touch with Isobel? She had been remiss there, probably because Isobel having more contact with her father might mean more contact with Vicky, and that was something Louise wasn't eager to encourage. Of course, as she told herself (and anyone else who would listen) all the time, she would never actively stand in the way of a relationship.

Suddenly, Louise felt she had been neglectful. Maybe her guilty conscience had punished her with the dream, as well it should. She vowed that she would have a talk with her ex-husband. She would urge him to call his daughter more often, especially now that another baby was on the way and his attention would be more and more required at home. That would be understandable, of course, but it would only add to the estrangement that had grown up between Andrew and Isobel.

And that estrangement was troubling enough. Louise had asked to see the birthday card Andrew had sent to Isobel; Isobel had shrugged and said that she had thrown it out.

"But why?" Louise had asked. "I mean, not that you have to keep a card forever, but it's only a day after your birthday. You usually keep—"

"It was nothing special," Isobel had interrupted. "It's not like it was handmade."

"Did he at least write you a nice note?"

"No."

"Did Vicky sign it, too?"

"Yeah. I mean, he signed it for her."

Louise rubbed her eyes now until they hurt. Why hadn't she taken Andrew to task for not even having written a note to his daughter? Sixteen was a special birthday; even someone as unconventional as Isobel admitted that. And she couldn't help but wonder why Vicky, the mother of two girls, hadn't urged Andrew to make the day special.

Then again, she had no idea what part Vicky played in Andrew's current relationship with Isobel. Did Vicky know how he ignored her? Did she demand that he do so? Or did she encourage him to maintain his relationship with his child?

Louise sighed and turned out the light. She doubted sleep would come again. That was all right. She feared that if it did come, the nightmare would come with it. One horrible dream a night was quite enough. Better to lie awake and have your guilty conscience berate you.

Chapter 30

CITYMOUSE

Hey, Everyone!

Today, I'm returning to an oldie but goodie, the Three Corners Flea Market held every Saturday in a big old dusty field in Brunswick. Gwen and I were last there back in April, and for some unaccountable reason I neglected (and just realized this!) to tell you about and to show you some of the fun-eriffic things we discovered!

So scroll down for a look at:

*An awesome brocade jacket that weighs about twenty pounds (no joke!); the vendor told us that it dates from the 1940s. I tried it on (very carefully!) and felt like a screen siren out of some moody old black-and-white film . . . But alas, the price was astronomically out of our range, so the jacket remained.

*A simple and elegant strand of jade beads. Gwen suggested we buy it for Miss

Kit-a-Kat, which we did! The green of the stone goes so well with the green of her eyes.

*A lone teacup hand-painted by the vendor's great-grandmother. (Why she was selling such a treasure she didn't say and I didn't ask.) I hope you can see the delicate brushstrokes. What a lovely and lively depiction of a spray of lilacs!

*And last but not least, take a look at this funky crystal chandelier! Can you imagine what it would take to keep such a sparkly thing sparkly?? CityMouse admits to not having the required patience for such a responsibility.

Well, Dear Readers, that's all for now. I hope everyone has a fantastic day!

Isobel closed her laptop. She would have had something new and interesting to write about if she had gone with Gwen to that antiques mall in South Portland. But Jeff had invited himself along, and Isobel, knowing that she would have spent the entire time worrying that he was bored and dealing with Gwen's being annoyed that Jeff was there, had told Gwen she didn't feel well. So Gwen had gone on alone.

It was not an ideal situation, lying to a friend, and then flaking out on her readers by dredging up stuff she had already discarded as not blog-worthy (not uninteresting, but not super-exciting, either) and making it sound funtastic. (In fact, the brocade jacket had been moth-eaten and the chandelier decidedly dingy.) The whole enterprise felt dishonest. It was the first time Isobel had resorted to that sort of thing, and it didn't sit well with her. But she just hadn't seen any other way.

But it was okay, Isobel told herself resolutely. The important thing was that she would be spending the afternoon with her boyfriend. Her boyfriend who was crazy about her.

Just ahead of Jeff and Isobel on Main Street was a group of older people; there were three women and a man. The man and one of the women were walking with the aid of canes; the other two didn't appear to be that much more mobile than their friends. Each of the four wore those big dark wraparound sunglasses a lot of older people wore. (Personally, though Isobel thought they were kind of awful-looking, she also thought they made a lot of sense. Sometimes when she was in Portland, she had to squint down to slits and put her hand over the top of her sunglasses just to see enough to cross a street without getting run over by a car!) Though the day was very warm, almost ninety degrees, the man wore a Windbreaker and each of the women wore a cotton sweater. That made sense, Isobel thought. Old people were said to feel the cold pretty easily. And all of the local restaurants were seriously air-conditioned.

"If old people can't walk faster than a freakin' crawl, they should stay home," Jeff declared.

Isobel was stunned. "Hey," she said, "come on. Everyone gets old. If they're lucky."

Jeff shook his head. "I know. I was only kidding. Jesus, you're a sensitive girl. Don't you have a sense of humor?"

Isobel felt her cheeks flush. "Oh. Sorry. I mean, yeah, I guess I am pretty sensitive." People had been telling her that since she was little, after all. Still, she didn't see what was funny about people walking with the aid of a cane . . .

"You know," Jeff said, putting his arm through hers, "I didn't tell you before because I didn't want to sound like I was trying to impress you or something, but back in Vermont

I do a lot of volunteer work at a local nursing home. A lot of the residents are in their eighties and nineties, and even more of them can only get around in wheelchairs."

"Oh," Isobel said. She felt chastened. "You do?"

Jeff shrugged. "Yeah. It's no big deal. I do whatever is needed, help people get in and out of bed, read to them, play cards." Jeff laughed. "There's this one old guy, I just know he must have been a professional poker player at one point. He swears it's only luck, but that guy beats the pants off me every time."

Isobel imagined big, handsome Jeff sitting across a table from a little old man in a worn-out cardigan, youth and age personified. The image made her smile. "That's so nice of you," she said.

"I do what I can. Hey, I'm glad you're wearing the bracelet. I hope you never take it off."

Isobel smiled. "Not even when I shower?"

"Not even then. Not ever."

Isobel held out her arm to better see the piece. The stones twinkled in the sun. She wondered again how much he had paid for it. The money didn't matter, of course. It was the thought that counted, the fact that the bracelet had served as an apology for his having gotten mad at her at that party and unjustly accusing her of coming on to another guy.

The memory brought with it a twinge of discomfort, not really anger but something like it. What? Isobel skillfully pushed the feeling away. Everybody made mistakes, and Jeff had apologized in a pretty major way.

Besides, it really was romantic, Jeff wanting her to wear the bracelet always, like you would wear a wedding ring, something you cherished and treasured and didn't take off until the day you died . . .

It was a bit odd, Isobel thought, that she hadn't shown her mother the bracelet. And that she still wasn't entirely sure why she hadn't. It wasn't like she was hiding the bracelet from her; she had worn it every day since Jeff had given it to her. In fact, she was kind of surprised that her mother hadn't already commented on it. Her mother was usually pretty observant. Then again, she had been so busy planning for the wedding; she could be forgiven for not noticing a new bauble.

Suddenly, Jeff put his hand on the back of her neck and gently turned her face up to his. "Those are real diamonds, you know," he said. "Only the best for my girl."

"Oh. Oh, I—" She felt tears come to her eyes. Before she could say more, Jeff released her and pulled his phone from his pocket. He scowled down at the screen.

"I have to get going," he said.

Isobel's spirits sank as quickly as they had risen. "I thought we were going to get lunch."

"Something came up."

"At work?" Isobel asked.

Jeff glanced up and down the block as if looking for someone or something to appear. "Yeah, sure. Can you get home on your own?"

"Oh. You can't take me home first?"

Jeff looked back at her. "This is important, Isobel," he said. His tone was a bit patronizing, a bit stern. Isobel felt as if she were being gently scolded for failing to understand the gravity of whatever it was that was happening. Then again, he was older and he was working for his father, someone everyone knew was a big businessman . . . And he had bought her a gold and diamond bracelet . . . That wasn't something a boy got his girl. That was something a man got his woman.

"Um, sure," she said. "Sorry. I guess I could call someone. It's no problem."

"Thanks, Izzy. You're the best. I'll call you later."

Jeff dashed off in the direction of his car. She had hoped for another kiss, but his business was obviously pressing.

Since she had started dating Jeff, Isobel had done some research about the Ottens and their empire. She hadn't seen anything on the company's website about connections in Dubai—maybe that was top-secret corporate information!—but what she had seen was pretty impressive. In fact, with Jeff working for his father's company she was surprised he had any time at all to spend with her. *Well,* she thought, *he must really like me!*

Isobel didn't need to call someone for a ride. As luck would have it, Flynn Moore was in town and spotted her on the corner before she had a chance to decide whom to call.

"My friend had an emergency at work," she told him, climbing in to his immaculately clean pickup truck. "I told him I'd be fine getting home on my own."

"Then it's a good thing I happened by," Flynn said with a smile.

As they drove, Isobel snuck surreptitious looks at Flynn. His hair was thick and silvery, what you could call a "mane" of hair, swept back off his forehead. His eyes were very bright blue, like the blue of a Paraíba tourmaline. (Isobel had seen pictures of the stone, though none in person. The blue was so intense it was almost disturbing, in the way extreme beauty could be disturbing.) There were deep wrinkles around his eyes when he smiled, which was often. She thought they added to Flynn's physical charm.

Isobel's mother had told her that Flynn was sixty. Though he looked to be in great shape, he walked with a bit of a limp. Its cause was a mystery to Isobel. Maybe he had arthritis. Maybe he needed or had had a hip replacement. Maybe he had been in a skiing accident a long time ago . . .

Isobel wondered if Flynn had children or nieces and nephews or even grandchildren. Gosh, she didn't even know if Flynn had ever been married! It was odd how things worked in a small town. On the one hand, everyone knew everyone else's business, or seemed to know. On the other hand, some lives managed to remain mysteriously private. She suddenly wondered if she would ever possess the key to the mystery of Flynn Moore.

Flynn dropped her off at the inn with greetings to her mother. Once inside, Isobel grabbed something to eat (one of Bella's scones left over from breakfast, and a carton of red raspberry yogurt, did the trick) and then ran up to her room, where she flopped down on the unmade bed. She had a lot to think about.

The knowledge that Jeff worked with the elderly made her appreciate his attentions even more than she already did. Once she got her license she could volunteer somewhere, too, a nursing home or maybe she could work at a shelter for battered women. Her mother would be especially proud of her for choosing that avenue.

Isobel turned onto her side. She wanted to be wise. She knew that wisdom was something, a quality, maybe a gift or even a talent, that was supposed to come only with age. But she hoped she would be wise, at least a little bit, before her hair was gray and her back stooped. What was the point of achieving wisdom if, by the time you achieved it, you were too old to actually put it into practice?

And what was the point of having wisdom if you were too old to command anyone's attention so that you could share it? Because did young people ever listen to old people? Not people her mother's age, but really old people. Young people should, of course, listen to those older, but Isobel was pretty sure, at least from what she had witnessed, that they didn't.

Isobel sighed. She wished she had known her grandparents. She had brought that photo of her grandmother in the wild paisley dress up to her room and put it in a frame on the dresser. Maybe her grandmother had harbored a secret desire to be other than she was, which, according to Louise, was a timid and retiring woman. The dress certainly seemed to be a clue, unless, like Louise guessed, it was a purchase made under pressure from a friend. Hmm. A friend who sensed that Nancy Jones had an inner spirit aching to be set free? It was too bad that Isobel would never know.

Suddenly, Isobel knew what she would buy with the gift certificate Catherine had given her for her birthday—a copy of Ari Seth Cohen's book, *Advanced Style*. It was chock-full of photographs of stylish women in their sixties, seventies, eighties, and for all Isobel knew, even their nineties. That was one of the good things about being interested in style. It was a passion that could last throughout a lifetime.

Isobel glanced at the old-fashioned windup alarm clock on her desk. It was already three thirty. She hoped that everything was okay with Jeff. He had looked pretty concerned or distracted when that call had come in and he'd had to hurry off. She guessed he must feel an awful lot of pressure working for a father who was so high-powered and influential. She had never felt pressure from either of her parents to succeed in any particular way. But maybe that had more to do with her than with her parents' being cool. Isobel liked to think of herself as someone who didn't easily succumb to the standards of other people, even people she loved or admired. She liked to think of herself as someone who consciously chose to march to the beat of her own drum.

An unexpected ray of sunshine penetrated the room, illuminating Isobel's bracelet. She held out her arm and admired it once again. She felt warm and happy and drowsy. Before long, she had drifted off to sleep.

Chapter 31

Mother and daughter were in the kitchen the following morning. The breakfast room had been cleared and the tables reset for the next day. Bella had gone home, and the house-keeping staff was hard at work in the guest rooms, hallways, parlor, and library.

Louise was ironing napkins; it was one of those domestic chores she had always found unaccountably soothing. Isobel sat at the table flipping through a fashion magazine, her empty cereal bowl still beside her. Louise could see a few splashes of pink-tinted milk and grimaced. She wished she could get Isobel, usually pretty health-conscious, to give up eating Franken Berry cereal, but the girl refused. Honestly, it didn't seem to be doing her any harm, though what havoc they would find at her next dentist appointment was any-one's guess.

Sunlight streamed through the windows. It was going to be a scorcher, Louise noted. If she was lucky, she might be able to snatch some time that afternoon to escape to the beach and cool her feet in the Atlantic.

Suddenly, she noticed a sparkle flashing from Isobel's left wrist as she turned a page of the magazine.

"Where did you get that bracelet?" she asked, carefully placing the iron in its stand.

Isobel looked up from her magazine and laughed. "Oh, I

wondered when you'd notice! I've been wearing it for days. Jeff gave it to me."

"Jeez, this wedding has me totally distracted. What was the occasion?"

"No occasion. He just gave it to me."

Louise felt a twinge of discomfort. "It looks pretty expensive, especially for a no-occasion gift," she said.

Isobel shrugged. "His family has a lot of money. And Jeff works for his dad so he probably has cash of his own. Anyway, you know I don't care about how much things cost."

No, Louise thought, *but he might.* Maybe that was an unfair leap to make, assuming Jeff would want payment of some sort for the gift . . . She had no reason to think ill of Jeff Otten and every reason to think well of the family in which he had been raised. And there was no way the bracelet was anything but silver and crystals. It couldn't have cost so terribly much, even with the price of silver still being pretty high and crystals enjoying another moment of popularity. Still . . .

"Still," she said, "it seems a bit odd that he would give you such a big gift so soon after you two started dating." Andrew, she thought, hadn't given her an important (his term for expensive) gift until they had been dating a year.

Isobel grinned. "Are you saying I'm not worth it?"

"Of course that's not what I'm saying. You're worth the heavens and all beneath them."

"Ha!"

"Just promise me you'll let me know if he gives you another extravagant gift, okay?"

Isobel shrugged again. "Sure, whatever."

Louise was not thrilled about that answer—it sounded vaguely insincere—but she had no choice but to believe in and trust her daughter's words. Right?

Isobel left the kitchen soon, after being reminded to put her bowl in the dishwasher. Louise went back to her ironing.

*   *   *

Later in the day, Louise sat at the kitchen table with a cup of iced coffee. It had been a busy day of troubleshooting at the inn (Mr. and Mrs. Daley reported a clogged toilet and later, a clogged sink) and putting out fires relating to the wedding from hell (the bride, Morocco or Jamaica, had blown up at her fiancé and called off the wedding; an hour later, everything was back on, leaving both Flora Michaels and Louise recovering from minor heart attacks). She never did have the time to escape to the beach.

Now that she had a spare moment to think about something other than the problems of strangers, Louise's mind turned again to the bracelet Jeff had given Isobel. Really, it was odd that Isobel hadn't shown her the bracelet right away. Isobel was usually so impatient, exuberant, and open.

Louise wondered. Maybe Isobel was indeed uncomfortable about Jeff's gift, but reluctant to admit it. Odd. She remembered now how Isobel hadn't told her about the first time she had met Jeff . . . Was this new pattern of behavior something about which she should be concerned? Well, Louise thought, probably not. It was a good thing that Isobel was embracing independence. And the easiest way to alienate a young person was to breathe down her neck with questions. So be it.

Louise's phone announced the virtual presence of Flora Michaels. She sighed. It was the fourteenth text of the day, and it wasn't any friendlier than the first thirteen. The two women had been working together for weeks now and they were no more friendly than they had been during that first fateful phone conversation. With any other person Louise would have tried for some personal connection, but Flora Michaels, by every word and every gesture, discouraged— no, forbid!—friendship or, at the very least, amiable relations. So be it.

Still, Louise had a sudden desire to force-feed Flora Michaels a box of Franken Berry. It was probably the only thing sugary enough to sweeten her up.

Chapter 32

CITYMOUSE

Bonjour, My Friends!

I'm so excited to share with you all this outstanding hat Gwen and I found at a tiny little antique shop we'd never even noticed before. Just look!

It's like a puffball made of white feathers—isn't it hilarious?

But it's also kind of fabulous and intensely glamorous. When LouLou saw it, she remembered seeing photographs of Princess Grace of Monaco wearing a hat just like it. We went online and found the occasion—Princess Grace and Prince Rainier were visiting President Kennedy, and oh boy, the look Grace was giving Jack in one of the pictures . . . All I can say is that if I had been Jackie (and LouLou agrees!), I would not have been pleased!!!! And I guess if I had been the prince I would not have been pleased, either. Well, people felt that JFK was a really good-looking guy, so I guess that sort of thing happened all the time. Even now you hear stories about his affairs and whatnot. Personally, he doesn't do it for me and affairs are wrong, but . . .

Anyway, here's another picture of the hat, this time on top of Gwen's head! By the way, when we found the hat it was resting in its original cardboard box; if you look closely, you can see the box off to Gwen's right, that black and white round thing.

I can't imagine where one would have worn this hat—other than to meet the president! (And frankly, it seems an odd choice for meeting a head of state, but hey, what do I know about protocol among the rich and famous?) Maybe to a posh luncheon with one's friends, at a high-end, very proper restaurant on New York's Upper East Side, where everyone is dressed *"à la mode"* and *"mauvais gout"* is unheard of?

Sigh. How social and sartorial conventions have changed!

Now, let me end with some food for thought. I came across the following quote (online, of course) from Helen Gurley Brown (yes, another quote), and it got me thinking—as, I'm guessing, it was meant to do!

"Beauty can't amuse you, but brain work—reading, writing, thinking—can."

As I can't really know what exactly Ms. Gurley Brown meant by this statement—and since I have no idea of the context in which she uttered it—it's difficult to comment with any intelligence . . . But I'll give it a try!!!

For me, thinking, reading, and writing ABOUT beauty is one of, if not the most, amusing things there is! Contemplating the very idea of aesthetics can occupy me happily for hours . . .

I love the poem by John Keats entitled "Ode on a Grecian Urn," with those famous final lines that read:

Beauty is truth, truth beauty,—that is all
Ye know on earth, and all ye need to know.

Now I know there's debate about what, exactly, Keats meant by that (everything in the world of art is debatable, I guess) and about how those lines are really meant to be read, but if I think that if you take the lines at face value, the message—that Beauty and Truth are one—is of the greatest importance for our souls.

Well, I hope that amateurish foray into art or literary "criticism" (ha!) makes some sense to you, my Dear Readers. If it doesn't—don't tell me!

Au revoir, my fellow Style Seekers!

Later that day, Isobel and Jeff were sitting in the gazebo behind the inn. Isobel loved sitting there on almost any day of the year, even in winter; it was such a romantic setting, calling to mind long, flowing dresses, picture hats, and men in high white collars. Jeff, however, didn't seem thrilled. His expression was flat; he sat stiffly, his hands on his knees.

"Oh wow, look at that huge dragonfly!" Isobel exclaimed. The insect was darting crazily just out of reach. "Isn't it gorgeous?"

Jeff shrugged.

"You're not a nature lover?"

"No."

"You don't have a favorite flower? Like, a petunia?" she teased. "Or maybe something more bold and masculine, like a sunflower?"

Jeff didn't respond to her teasing questions. "I've been reading your blog," he said.

"You have?" Isobel smiled. "You might be the only guy who does."

"Why don't you ever mention me on the blog?"

Isobel was caught short not only by his question but also by his tone, which was decidedly that of someone who felt very, very hurt. "I—"

He cut her off. "You mention every other person you know around here. I thought I was important to you."

"Oh wow," she said, reaching for his hand. He let her take it, but he didn't squeeze back. "You are important to me. I just . . . I didn't think you were all that interested in style and fashion. I mean, in women's style and fashion, which is mostly what I write about."

"Isobel, I'm interested in everything that interests you."

"But you don't have to be."

"Yes," he said. "I do."

Isobel laughed. "But I'm not interested in everything you are."

"You should be. That's what it means to be a couple." Jeff pulled his hand away from hers and stood up. He ran a hand through his hair in a gesture of great frustration. "That's what drove me crazy about my last two girlfriends," he said.

"They just didn't understand. They were so wrapped up in their own lives they didn't have any time for me. For us. I thought you and I were different."

Isobel felt very confused. She was not so sure one person in a couple should be genuinely interested in every single thing that interested the other person in the couple. It sounded kind of stifling, not to mention improbable. Still, she didn't want to be an ex-girlfriend anytime soon. And what did she really know about the whole relationship thing, after all? She had never even been in one before now!

She considered for a moment. What were Jeff's interests, anyway? As far as she knew, he had none. Or for some reason he wasn't sharing with her what he enjoyed doing in his spare time. Come to think of it, he had never even told her his major at school! She must have asked him—it was such a basic, common question—in fact, she knew that she had, so what had he answered? For the life of her, she couldn't remember. She felt bad about that.

"Well, okay," she said then. "So, tell me about something you like to do. Tell me about your hobbies. Tell me about your passions."

Jeff made a rude, dismissive sound. "Why should I bother? You already said you don't care about the stuff I care about."

Isobel felt her stomach sink. "That's not at all what I said! Come on, Jeff. Tell me. Maybe I could be interested in your hobbies. It's always good to learn about new things."

"Forget it. I'm only the one who gave you a diamond bracelet. Why should I matter?"

"Jeff, no . . ."

"If you'd rather write about some dead guy than your boyfriend, I'm outta here."

He turned and stalked off, leaving Isobel stunned and even more confused than she had been at the start of the disastrous conversation.

"Jeff, wait!" she called, but he didn't turn back. A moment or two later she heard his car roaring off.

The day suddenly seemed less bright, the dragonflies less interesting, the flowers less colorful. Isobel wondered if maybe Jeff was right; maybe she wasn't paying enough attention to him. Well, there was a way to show Jeff that she cared. She would add him to her next blog post!

But what to say? Maybe she could mention his earrings, but in and of themselves they were ordinary. Maybe she could write a brief history of men's jewelry and the famous guys throughout history (maybe just the western world, to keep things in check) who wore jewelry. Shakespeare wore earrings, didn't he? Lots of Elizabethan guys did.

No. No history lesson on CityMouse.

And the fact was that she would be embarrassed to tell her readers about the bracelet. She was afraid that to describe it precisely—and honestly—would sound like bragging and she was not a braggart.

Maybe if she let her mind wander a bit, inspiration would come. In the meantime, Isobel thought about those other girl-friends Jeff had mentioned. She didn't want to think about them, but she couldn't seem to help it. Had Jeff given those other girls expensive presents, too? Had he had sex with all of them?

Sex. Isobel wondered now if Jeff's hurt feelings could be frustration in disguise. So far they had done no more than make out. But Jeff was definitely not a virgin. He had to want a lot more from her, though he hadn't been pressuring her, not really.

The weird thing was that even though she was seriously at-tracted to him—the very thought of him brought tingles to her stomach—Isobel just didn't feel willing to take the next steps. It wasn't that she was afraid of sex. It was just—well, she wasn't quite sure what was holding her back from mov-ing their relationship forward. But something was, some in-stinct maybe, and that was good enough reason for her. For now.

Isobel left the gazebo and went inside.

*   *   *

Isobel spent a good deal of the night pondering the notion of soul mates; of twinned and twined hearts; of infatuation and intense devotion and undying love. These were not topics meant to lull you into dreamland.

Did everyone who was truly in love lose him- or herself in the other person, or maybe in the third entity, the relationship? Was it necessary to "lose yourself"? Traditional notions of romance would seem to say so. The woman, especially, was to become a part of the man, a piece of something larger, no longer "only" herself. Really, it was a bit offensive and seriously old-fashioned—and experience had pretty much shown that nine out of ten times it ended in disaster for the woman—but it also did sound kind of heroic in a weird way, sacrificing yourself for the greater good, which was *LOVE* in capital letters. Lovers were two halves of a whole . . .

In the middle of the night, she had gotten out of bed to sit at her desk with her laptop. She thought it might be wise to see what great poets and novelists had to say about the matter. You could always rely on great poets or novelists to tell a truth in a way you would remember.

Isobel chose a "famous quotes" site at random and selected "quotes about love." There was something from Emily Brontë; Isobel thought it was probably taken from *Wuthering Heights*. It sounded like something Cathy would say about Heathcliff. But she hadn't read the book in a while so she wasn't really sure.

"Whatever our souls are made of, his and mine are the same."

There was also a line from a work by Leo Tolstoy. She didn't know what novel this might be from, or even if it was from one of his novels. She had yet to venture into the works of the famous Russian writers.

"He felt now that he was not simply close to her, but that he did not know where he ended and she began."

And then, from *Romeo and Juliet,* there was a line the teenaged Juliet speaks to her teenaged lover:

"The more I give to thee, the more I have, for both are infinite."

Her head spinning, Isobel had shut down the computer and crawled back into bed. Maybe love took more than she had in her to give. And maybe . . . Well, was she actually in love with Jeff? She thought that maybe she was. She got all tingly when he was next to her. Wasn't that a sign of love? Or was that merely a sign of sexual attraction? She thought about him when he wasn't with her. Then again, she thought about Gwen when Gwen wasn't with her.

Isobel shifted under the covers. She felt so awfully young and naïve. She so hoped she hadn't permanently alienated Jeff with her immaturity. She had learned as a firsthand witness how delicate relationships could be, even those that were supposed to be—or that, at least, looked to be—strong, like her parents' marriage. If that had failed after twentysome odd years and an official and public vow of foreverness, how much more likely was it that her own fledgling relationship with Jeff would fail because of her inability to understand a simple need and request?

Very early in the morning, Isobel fell into a deep sleep. But after only three hours, she was out of bed and back at work on the blog post. Finally, inspiration struck. At least, she was able to craft a few sentences she felt pretty sure Jeff would like.

Jeff had said he would come by the inn at twelve o'clock. Isobel took her laptop down to the kitchen to wait for him. He was as good as his word, walking through the kitchen door at precisely noon. He didn't apologize for having stormed off the day before, but Isobel didn't expect him to. He had been upset, yes, but justifiably. She knew that now.

"I have to show you something," she said immediately.

Jeff looked wary. But maybe that was her imagination.

He sat at the table, Isobel standing at his side, and she showed him the new post. Isobel read the important part over his shoulder.

> "And here now is something I want very much to share with my Dear Readers—this lovely photograph of my lovely boyfriend, Jeff Otten. He's a member of one of the very important and philanthropic local families and in my opinion (and in the opinion of everyone else here in Ogunquit!) a super nice and kind and smart person!"

He finished reading in a few quick seconds. And then he frowned up at her.

"You should have asked me if I was okay with this."

Isobel's stomach dropped. She shook her head. "But you told me you wanted me to mention you . . ."

"Did I give you permission to say anything you wanted about me?" Jeff snapped.

The word *permission* struck Isobel like a slap. Were adults allowed to give each other or to withhold from each other permission? Other than bosses and army officers and priests and rabbis and other authority figures like that?

"But it's nothing bad . . ." she protested feebly.

"And this picture. When did you take this picture of me?"

"Well, actually, Gwen took it. It's from when we were hanging around the other day."

Jeff jabbed the screen with his finger. "She had no right to take my picture. Who does she think she is? She invaded my privacy. I should—"

"Wait, Jeff, I asked her to take it! It's not her fault, really."

Jeff was silent for a moment. And then he said, "Can you take it down? The entire post?"

"The whole thing? But I only mention you in a few lines."

"Isobel, I want you to take it down."

Isobel felt the tiniest thread of fear but brushed it aside. "Well, all right," she said.

"Now. Before I leave."

"I'm sorry, Jeff," she said, hurrying to take a seat at the table. "I didn't mean to—Did I offend you somehow? I don't understand."

"You don't need to understand. You just need to accept that I don't want that post out there."

Without further protest, Isobel took down the post, Jeff now standing over her as if, she thought, to be sure she did what he had asked.

"Now was that hard? Thank you." Jeff bent and kissed her forehead. "I've got to go."

Isobel tried to smile. "Okay. Does your dad need you at the office?"

"Yeah. I've been working on some important reports he wants right away."

"Okay. Oh, before I forget. Gwen's parents got us free tickets to see *The Pirates of Penzance* at the Playhouse this Saturday night. They're supposedly really good seats, too. And Gwen said they could probably get another two if you think your parents would want to come."

"This Saturday? No," Jeff said, "we can't go. I'm taking you to hear a band at the Dolphin Striker in Portsmouth. Besides, I'm not into musical theater."

Isobel hesitated. It was the first she had heard of plans to go to Portsmouth, and Gwen's dads had gone to the trouble of getting tickets, but the last thing she wanted to do was upset Jeff again with another silly blunder. "Oh," she said finally. "Okay. What about your parents, then?"

Jeff laughed. "Izzy, really? My parents don't bother with local theater. If they want to see a professional show, they go to Boston or New York."

"But the Ogunquit Playhouse gets some really big names, like—"

"Izzy. I said no. Look, I really have to run. I'll check in later."

He left through the kitchen door. Isobel still sat at the table, laptop closed in front of her. She looked down at the sparkly bracelet on her wrist and frowned. Were all men so— so fickle and sensitive?

Isobel rubbed her eyes. They felt tired. She felt tired.

She wished she could talk to someone about what had just happened with Jeff. Her mom was beyond busy, and she had told Isobel that she hadn't been sleeping well lately. She would try her best to concentrate on what Isobel was saying, she was always good that way, but to go to her mother about something so minor—and it was minor, after all, Jeff's being sensitive (that was a more accurate word than *fickle*)—would be unfair.

And she could forget about talking to Gwen. Gwen didn't like Jeff, and Isobel was sure that Gwen wouldn't give Jeff's side of the misunderstanding—it hadn't been a fight, really, not even an argument—proper consideration. "It's all his fault," she would say immediately. "He was being unreasonable. You did nothing wrong." It was great to have someone unconditionally on your side, except when it wasn't.

Catherine, however, might be a good person to ask for advice. She was smart and sensible and in her own admission had "been around the block," an old-fashioned expression Isobel found hilarious. But Catherine might feel weird about keeping their conversation from Louise, even though Isobel would assure her that she wasn't trying to hide anything from her mother.

No. She foresaw potential messiness if she involved Catherine.

As for her friends back in Massachusetts . . . Though some of them kept in touch through CityMouse, the nature of her relationship with them had changed. What intimacy there

had been was pretty much gone. That had probably been inevitable. Sometimes when you didn't see a person on a daily
basis, so much of what made the friendship real was lost. It
wasn't always that way; lots of people maintained long-
distance friendships over a long period of time. But maybe
the friendships she had made with those girls back in Massachusetts hadn't been as strong as she thought they had been.
Well, she had been a child then, really. And things always
changed. The only thing in life you could count on was not
being able to count on something or someone forever . . .

Isobel got up from the table and took her laptop up to her
bedroom. Once there, she locked the door behind her and lay
down on the bed.

She was determined to figure this out for herself. Adults
didn't go running to someone else for advice about every single little glitch in their daily lives. Adults looked their problems square in the eye and wrestled them to the ground. Like
what her mother had done when her father had left them.
She hadn't sat around whining. She got on with her life. Like
Isobel would get on with hers.

Chapter 33

"You might be interested in this."

"What?"

Louise and Isobel were in the kitchen the following day. While her daughter grazed through a bag of SunChips (*ah, youth,* Louise thought enviously), Louise sorted through her collection of plastic food storage containers and lids. She didn't know how it happened but at least once a week a lid went missing. It was very frustrating.

"I bumped into the owner of that cute little boutique on Beach Street this morning."

"The woman with that adorable little white dog I want to eat with a spoon?" Isobel asked.

"Yeah. Anyway, she told me she'd been chatting with Sally Otten at their church after services last Sunday and Mrs. Otten told her that Michael, her older son, the one who lives in Basel—"

"Yeah, yeah, what about him?" Isobel demanded.

"Patience. Well, word is that he was promoted to president of something or other at his company—sorry, Paula Murphy isn't the most coherent of storytellers—and that he won an award from some prestigious council on ethics in the pharmaceutical industry. Again, the details were a bit fuzzy."

"Still," Isobel said. "Wow."

"That's what I said. I'm surprised Jeff didn't mention Michael's latest triumphs to you."

"I'm not. Jeff told me that he and his brother aren't close."

Louise nodded. "I guess I can see that. They are seven years apart. That difference doesn't matter much between adults, but growing up they must have lived in virtually different families."

"Yeah."

"And it can be more difficult to bridge that gap when both siblings are the same sex. There's competition and all . . . Maybe Jeff and his brother will grow closer later on in life. Maybe once they get married and have kids."

"Yeah, who knows? Guys are hard to figure out sometimes."

Louise raised her eyebrows. "Tell me about it. Hey, is anything troubling you? Is everything okay with Jeff?"

"Oh yeah, everything's fine. It's just—"

"Where's the manager!" It was a bellowing demand, not a question, and it had come from the front hall.

Louise put her hand to her forehead and rubbed. "Oh crap, it's Mr. MacCready again. Really, that man can't go five minutes without a complaint. If it's not the butter being too hard to spread without shredding his fresh-baked muffin, it's the toilet paper being too harsh for his precious you-know-what."

"The toilet paper, huh?"

Louise shrugged. "Slight exaggeration. Wait, you were about to say something. 'It's just' what? Godzilla can wait for five minutes."

Isobel laughed. "If I was going to say something I totally forgot what! You'd better go tend to Godzilla, Mom. Creatures like that tend to make a big mess when they're upset."

"You're right. Once more into the breach . . ." She hurried off to deal with Mr. MacCready and his latest unreasonable demand.

Later that day, after The MacCready had been pacified (the sprig of fresh lavender on his bed had irritated his sinuses and he wanted new sheets immediately) and the latest wedding crisis had been temporarily wrestled into order (no, it was unlikely that the inn would be able to hire a local lobsterman to display his boat in the backyard for the amusement of the guests), Louise found herself lounging on the front porch, enjoying a precious few moments of leisure. There was a slight breeze in the air, and Louise thought she could smell the salt of the ocean in it.

She thought back to her interrupted conversation with Isobel earlier. She felt sure Isobel would talk to her if anything really important was troubling her. Since Isobel was old enough to understand, Louise had stressed the importance of communication without reservation or shame or the fear of punishment. Certainly, choosing not to tell a few relatively minor incidents to her mother (was the gift of an expensive bracelet an "incident"?) didn't mean that Isobel would choose not to tell a big worry or a serious fear.

Suddenly, Louise remembered being in the car that day with Isobel and pointing out Jeff at the garage. Isobel had responded as if she had never seen Jeff before, but she had, she had met him in town days before . . .

Wait a minute, Louise thought. *What had happened when?* She had had so much on her mind in recent weeks, days tended to run into one another; just last Wednesday she had thought it was Thursday and had taken the garbage to the curb in anticipation of a pickup. She wasn't at all sure she could she rely on her memory of the sequence of events involving Isobel and Jeff. She certainly hoped she was confusing the time line, because if she wasn't, then she had caught Isobel (albeit after the fact) in an outright lie.

Louise was distracted from this unpleasant thought by a guest pulling up to the inn and climbing out of her car. Ms. Jackson was a large woman in every sense—tall and broad and solidly built. Her smile and her good nature were as big as her physical self.

Louise got up and opened the door of the inn for her. "Hello, Ms. Jackson," she said. "How was your afternoon?"

The woman beamed. "Wonderful. And there's nothing like spending the day in the sun to whet one's appetite. I'm absolutely famished!"

Louise smiled and followed her inside. "Well, there are some cookies in the parlor . . ."

"Excellent!" Ms. Jackson exclaimed, making a beeline for that room. "They should hold me over until dinner!"

And a cookie wouldn't kill me, either, Louise thought, her worries about Isobel flown.

Chapter 34

CITYMOUSE

Hello, Everyone!

Recently, I ran across a quote from Anjelica Huston (online, of course, where so many of us tend to live too much of our lives) about the inimitable Diana Vreeland. She said that Ms. Vreeland "... made it okay for women to be outlandish and extraordinary."

I don't know enough about the social history of the last century to say if Diana Vreeland was the most important influence in encouraging women to be outlandish and extraordinary, but even if she was only one of many strong women who helped less-strong women be proud individuals, well, that's a big feather in her cap!

Again, I am reminded of the term *jolie laide*, used in reference to both Anjelica Huston and Diana Vreeland. How much better to be *jolie laide* in mind and spirit, too, than to have a cookie-cutter personality and character and mind-set!

Now, here's a photo Gwen took about a week back of a woman we spotted the last time we were down in Portsmouth. The woman—who was visiting the East Coast from southern California—was very amenable to our taking her picture. Her name was (is) Roberta Worthington and she told us that the lime-green-with-splashes-of-black-all-over-them skinny jeans she was wearing were actually a pair she had bought way back in the eighties (!) and pulled out once a summer every single year since. Fun tidbit: The first time she wore the jeans was to a Duran Duran concert!!! Can you imagine?? Her slouchy black blazer was a purchase from the early nineties and her bag—*fantastique!*—was "just a little Louis Vuitton thingie" she had picked up at a vintage shop about ten years ago. In short, nothing but her T-shirt and underwear (she told us this; we are not impolite enough to ask about someone's undergarments!) were new! Even her slim-line loafers (no socks necessary) dated from 2005. Clearly, this woman takes very, very good care of her clothes and never gains or loses more than a pound or two.

Well, I must run. Until next time!

Isobel posted, closed the laptop, and sighed. She didn't feel outlandish or extraordinary at all. She felt dumb. And sad. And she had been feeling dumb and sad since the post incident with Jeff. She felt sure he was still disappointed in her for ignoring him on her blog, and then for saying the wrong things about him.

The situation with her father and Vicky wasn't helping her mood, either. The last bit of correspondence she had received from the new Bessire family had been a brief and perfunctorily pleasant e-mail from her father and later that same day, a joke forwarded by Vicky, something about a husband and a wife and a homeless woman. Isobel hadn't found it in the least bit funny.

Victoria Bessire. It was odd to be sharing a name with a stranger. Bessire was her name, her mom's name, her dad's name, and now, it was Vicky's name, too. And it would be the name of the baby who was due to make his or her appearance in October.

Hmm. Isobel thought that old argument about patriarchal dominance might be worth revisiting when she was eventually out on her own. She wondered if Diana Vreeland had been born with that last name or if it was her husband's. Had she even been married? She would have to look that up. Someday. She guessed it really didn't matter.

Isobel got up from the chair and began to pace through the stuff accumulated on the floor of her room. If only things could go back to the way they used to be, when she and her mom spent all of their time together and were a real family, because yeah, even when it was just the two of them they were a real family. A family wasn't about the number of people in it or about whether the parents were both male or both female or one of each sex. A family was about the connection. That was everything.

Still, life had been so much less complicated before the divorce. And before—she had to admit it—before Jeff. But if Isobel was having a hard time adjusting to this new life, her mother seemed to be thriving and happy, in spite of the challenges she faced with the inn. And Isobel was glad for her mother, really. And at some point her mother would probably want to date. She was young and attractive and smart and good. She deserved someone just as wonderful.

But what if her mother got married and took the guy's name? Isobel would be the only Bessire in the new family . . .

Isobel sighed. Growing up had never seemed particularly difficult until now. But maybe that was because, until her relationship with Jeff, she had never really been challenged, like an adult is challenged. With an adult relationship came responsibility, everybody knew that. It wasn't all gifts and candlelight. Some of it, maybe a lot of it, was the difficult work of getting along on a daily basis, dealing with moods and crises and the flu and bills that couldn't always be paid on time.

Adult relationships were about love; love was the only thing that made all the difficult parts of a relationship worthwhile. And Jeff hadn't yet told her that he loved her . . . Well, Isobel thought, guys could be notoriously bad at expressing their real emotions. Everyone knew that.

Desultorily, Isobel got dressed. She and Jeff and Gwen were going to the movies. Isobel did not expect to have fun. It was difficult work, juggling the needs of two people who despised each other.

It was not a movie Jeff should have wanted to see, a story about a middle-aged woman finding true love after the sudden death of her longtime husband. Isobel had planned to see it with Gwen, but when she had mentioned her plans to Jeff, he had invited himself along. Gwen had not been thrilled, especially when she learned that he insisted on driving, but she hadn't cancelled, either.

Once in the mall theater, Isobel had made to sit between her best friend and her boyfriend, but with a quick maneuver, Jeff took that place instead. He had whispered to Isobel almost the entire time, which had at first seemed fun and then, pretty quickly, had seemed rude and embarrassing. Besides, how could she concentrate on the movie with someone talking in her ear?

But Isobel hadn't known how to stop it. She didn't know whether it had bothered Gwen, who said nothing about Jeff's whispering once the movie was over and they were strolling aimlessly through the mall, Jeff, once again, between them.

"Did Izzy show you the bracelet I gave her?" Jeff said suddenly.

"Which bracelet?" Gwen asked, turning to see Isobel beyond her boyfriend.

"The one she's wearing," Jeff answered.

Isobel felt oddly embarrassed. "I'm sure you've seen it," she said lightly. "I've been wearing it every day."

"No," Gwen said. "I haven't." Isobel thought she said it sharply. "Let me see."

Isobel held out her arm.

Gwen was silent for a long moment. Her expression was bland. "It's very pretty," she said finally.

"White gold and diamonds," Jeff said.

"Very nice."

Jeff's phone indicated that he was wanted. "Sorry," he said, already walking off a bit. "Gotta take this."

"Of course I'd seen the bracelet," Gwen said the moment Jeff was out of earshot. "I just assumed it was something your parents had given you ages ago. Why didn't you tell me Jeff gave it to you? It's kind of a big deal. Too big," she added.

Isobel had no idea how to answer Gwen's question. Not really. Maybe she had said nothing to Gwen for the same reason she hadn't mentioned the bracelet to her mother until she had noticed it on her own. Still, what was that reason?

Lamely, she said, "It's not too big a deal."

Jeff returned before Gwen could argue her point.

"Everything okay?" Isobel asked.

"Yeah. Why shouldn't it be?"

Isobel shrugged. They continued to walk on through the mall, past shops crammed with cheap plastic accessories for girls and cheap plastic sports paraphernalia for boys.

"Hey, Izzy," Jeff said suddenly. "You should get a tattoo."

Isobel looked at the window display of the store outside of which Jeff had come to a halt. There was an assortment of human skulls. Some were carved of stone; others looked very much like plaster casts of the real thing. There were framed photos of customers' tattoos. One guy's back was entirely covered by an elaborate image of a gorilla standing on his legs and beating his chest with his fists. Someone's forearm was simply black, as if it had been dunked into a vat of permanent ink. Isobel looked to the person at the counter inside. She couldn't tell if it was a man or a woman, not that it mattered. The person was wearing a black, short-sleeved T-shirt and dark, baggy jeans; on his or her head was a bandanna and in his or her ears were massive plugs instead of regular earrings. What was visible of skin was entirely covered in ink, some of it red and yellow.

"Tattoos aren't really my thing," she said, turning away. "I mean, I've got nothing against anyone who has a tattoo, and a lot of tattoos are really awesome, but . . ."

"Then, come on, but what?" Jeff prodded. "What do you mean, not your thing? Are you afraid of needles? Is that it, Izzy, afraid of a little pain?"

Gwen's lips tightened. "Pain is not pretty," she said. "And infection is no joke."

"Do you have a tattoo?" Isobel asked Jeff, dodging the needle issue (of course she was afraid of pain, any normal person was!), and hoping to erase Gwen's last provocative comments from the record.

Jeff grinned. "You'll see it soon enough."

His response made her blush. (Gwen, behind Jeff's back, rolled her eyes.) Jeff had been getting more insistent, like what had happened in the movie theater, not the whispering but the . . . She wouldn't think about it now.

"Come on," Jeff went on. "Something small and meaningful. Something personal."

"Like what?" Isobel didn't know why she was allowing this conversation to go on. But she didn't know how to stop it, either. *You could just say, "I don't want to talk about this anymore,"* she told herself. But maybe that would be rude or unnecessarily dramatic.

"Like your favorite flower," Jeff answered. "Or," he added with another grin, "the name of your favorite guy."

"But they're so—permanent." Isobel laughed nervously. "I'm always changing my mind. One day Oreos are my favorite cookie, the next day it's Chips Ahoy!"

Jeff sighed in that way Isobel had come to recognize as his I'm-trying-to-be-patient-with-you way. "Look, Izzy, the point is to make a commitment. The point is to take the plunge, know who you are, go for it, and not look back."

"She knows who she is," Gwen snapped. "She's a person who changes her mind a lot."

Jeff's face flushed, and Isobel thought she saw his mouth tighten and twitch in a way she did not like at all.

Oh, she thought, *please don't let them fight!* "I'll tell you what," she said quickly. "I'll think about it, okay? Besides, I have to check with my mother before getting a tattoo. I promised her a long time ago that I would." She had promised no such thing. She had always been against getting a tattoo. But neither Jeff nor Gwen said another word. The lie had worked, at least for the moment.

"Let's go home," she said now. "Okay?"

Neither of them objected. Neither of them spoke again, either. Half an hour later, Jeff pulled up outside the Blueberry Bay Inn.

"I'll take Gwen home, then I'll come back," he said.

"No thanks," Gwen said quickly, getting out of the backseat. "I'm going to stick around for a while. Maybe stay for dinner."

Jeff gave Isobel a look she couldn't quite interpret, except to know that he wanted her to get rid of Gwen. But Isobel could say nothing. She suddenly felt utterly exhausted. Finally, she opened her mouth, to say what she had no idea, but Jeff cut her off.

"Then I'm out of here. I'll check in with you later, Izzy."

"Okay," Isobel said, climbing out of the car.

Jeff took off, perhaps a bit too quickly, Isobel thought. How could she find out if Jeff had ever gotten a speeding ticket? Was that sort of thing public knowledge?

Gwen went up onto the porch while Isobel greeted a guest returning from a day at the beach. "There should be tea and cookies in the parlor now, Mr. Browning," she said.

Mr. Browning smiled. "That sounds lovely," he said. He clumped up the porch stairs, loaded down with the accoutrements of serious relaxing—a folding lounge, a cooler, and a duffel large enough to carry towels, a change of clothes, and several hardcover novels.

"No one goes to the beach anymore without lugging half of their possessions with them," Isobel said, attempting a smile. She sat in the rocker next to the one in which Gwen had sunk. She felt a bit awkward. She just knew Gwen was going to quiz her about Jeff.

"Mmm," Gwen said. "Look, why does Jeff always want you to be someone you're not?"

And there it was. "What are you talking about?" she said, more to postpone having to give a real answer than because she was genuinely puzzled by Gwen's question.

"I don't know, like that whole thing with the tattoo. He kept pushing you even though you told him you don't like tattoos and don't want to get one."

"Oh, come on," Isobel said, wearily. "He was just kidding around."

"I don't think he was. I think he was dead serious. I think he very much wanted you to get his name inked on your arm. Or someplace less—obvious."

Isobel didn't reply.

"And then that time when you told me you really didn't want to go to that party and he pretty much dragged you along and . . ."

Isobel forced a laugh. "He did not 'drag' me along. I changed my mind." *And he spoke to my mother beforehand,* Isobel added silently. *I had no choice but to go. At least, it felt like I had no choice.* "And I had a pretty good time after all," she added. That was a lie.

"I thought you said that most of the people there were pretentious."

"Did I? Well, maybe a few were." Isobel had told absolutely no one about Jeff's behavior at the party and had created a bit of a tall tale about the event in general. What else could she have done? No one would have understood the truth. "I think I was just nervous. I didn't know anybody there but Jeff."

"Since when does that bother you?" Gwen demanded. "You're the friendliest person I know."

"That doesn't mean I'm not uncomfortable in certain situations."

"And what about his calling you Izzy? I thought you hated that nickname! I thought you hated all nicknames."

"I do, usually," Isobel admitted. "But it's okay when Jeff says it. It's affectionate."

"It sounds ridiculous."

"That's just your opinion," Isobel snapped. "What's up with you, anyway? Are you jealous that I have a boyfriend and you don't?"

Gwen looked stricken, as if she had been slapped with a palm and not just words. Isobel felt awful.

"I'm sorry," she said. "That was a stupid thing to say.

Really. It's just . . . "At that moment the frustration Isobel had been laboring under threatened to crush her. She hated being stuck in the middle, defending one to the other. She hated it. "It's just that you never have anything nice to say about Jeff. It makes things very difficult for me. It's very un-fair of you."

And Jeff never had anything nice to say about Gwen, ei-ther. He thought she was fat. He thought her family situation was abnormal. He thought Gwen had too big an influence on her, whatever that meant.

But Isobel wouldn't let Gwen know how Jeff felt. She wasn't mad at Jeff. She was mad at Gwen. Let Gwen fix things. Gwen was the one who had complained about having to see the movie with Jeff "tagging along."

Yeah, so she was favoring Jeff over her friend. So what? Jeff was her boyfriend. That was special.

It was some time, during which neither girl looked at the other, before Gwen spoke.

"I'm sorry, too," she said, standing. "I didn't mean to be unfair. Look, I'm going to grab a ride home with Quentin."

Isobel felt a little sick to her stomach. She and Gwen had never fought before. Ever. She had never fought with any-one—except for her father.

She wanted Gwen to stay. She wanted Gwen to go.

"I thought you were going to stick around for dinner," she said, still not meeting her friend's eye.

"Nah, I should get home. I just remembered my parents want us to go out to dinner with some friends of theirs visit-ing from New York. Tell your mom I said hi."

Gwen strode down the porch steps and over to where Quentin was tossing some lumber into the bed of his old but well-cared-for pickup truck. Gwen spoke to him and Isobel saw him nod. A moment later, they climbed into the truck and drove off.

Isobel watched them go. She had a queer feeling as they

disappeared around the curve in the road. She felt abandoned. She felt left behind. She felt—ridiculous.

And then her phone alerted her to a text. It was Jeff.

G STILL THERE? it read.

NO, she replied.

B THERE SOON, was his answer. **LUV U.**

Isobel smiled. Good. She loved him, too.

Chapter 35

Louise sighed and picked up the crumpled, dirty napkin from the floor of the porch. People were slobs, she thought irritably. Even her clientele, who, generally speaking, were well-off and well-educated, thought nothing of leaving crumpled, dirty napkins on the porch or of placing wineglasses directly on a wooden side table when a stack of coasters sat nearby. Maybe they all had housekeepers at home following them around with a sponge. Still, there was such a thing as common courtesy and respect for other people's property. Or didn't parents and schools teach those things anymore?

Her interior rant was brought to a halt by the unexpected arrival of Isobel's gentleman caller. *I wonder*, Louise thought, watching Jeff emerge from his car, *if I'll ever have a gentleman caller again. If I do, he had better be neat and clean around the house.*

"Hey, Mrs. Bessire," Jeff said when he had reached the top step.

"Hey, Jeff," Louise replied. She noted that he was impeccably put together, as always. She wondered if that was due to his mother's training, or if he was one of those men who was born with a good style gene. "Here to see Isobel? I'm afraid you missed her. She went down to the beach with a book."

"No, actually," he said, "I'm here to see you, Mrs. Bessire.

I know you're crazy busy with this big wedding coming up, and I thought you could use a little treat."

Jeff held out a large brown box tied with a ribbon. Louise had seen it in his hand but had assumed it was for her daughter. She accepted it gratefully. Chocolate from Harbor Candy Shop was a big deal. Nobody in her right mind would dispute that.

"Wow, thank you, Jeff," she said. "That was really was nice of you."

Jeff shrugged. "My mother taught me the importance of chocolate on an everyday basis, not only in a crisis."

"Smart woman. Chocolate was just what I needed. Thanks again. And, please call me Louise."

Jeff smiled and bowed his head ever so slightly.

"Thank you, Louise. Well, I'd better get going."

"How is working for your father going?" Louise asked politely. She assumed, of course, that he was heading back to the office, wherever that was. No doubt Jack Otten maintained a home office, as well as one in Portland or Boston or New York.

Jeff gave her a brilliant smile. "Just fantastic," he said. "Thanks for asking."

"Where did this come from?" Isobel was holding up the box from Harbor Candy Shop.

"Your paramour came by with them," Louise said airily, turning from the kitchen sink with a little smirk. "A little present for me."

Isobel beamed. "He did? Wow. That was really nice of him." She opened the box and selected a candy. "Oh. My. God," she said, mouth full of chocolate and caramel and nut. "These Turtles are amazing."

"Tell me something I don't know. Try a dark chocolate nonpareil. To. Die. For."

Isobel did, and immediately sank into a chair at the table.

When she emerged from her stupor, she said, "So, you like Jeff, right, Mom?"

"Yeah," Louise said, drying her hands on a towel. "I do. Why? Are you having doubts about your feelings for him? Because if you are, you shouldn't be afraid to talk about it. To me or to Gwen and then, if it's necessary, to Jeff."

"No, not at all," Isobel said hurriedly. "Everything's fine with Jeff, really. It's just that, well, I get the feeling Gwen doesn't really like him. I think she's jealous he wants to spend so much time with me. Frankly, I'm kind of upset with her about it. I mean, we swore we would never let a guy come between us."

Louise glanced at the bracelet on Isobel's left wrist. To Gwen, it might be a symbol of a friend's moving on . . . She tossed the towel onto the plastic drain board and joined her daughter at the table.

"Maybe it's not jealousy Gwen is feeling," she said. "Maybe it's really that she's sad things are changing between you girls, and maybe it's just a little hard for her to accept. After all, you two have been inseparable for a long time."

"Yeah, maybe," Isobel admitted. "It makes sense, I guess. But it's still frustrating. Sometimes I feel like I'm being torn apart."

"Does Jeff like Gwen?" Louise asked.

Isobel nodded vigorously. "Oh yeah. He thinks she's great."

Louise took that statement with a grain of salt. Best friends and boyfriends were often a volatile mix. As long as Gwen and Jeff each made an attempt to get along for Isobel's sake, things would be well enough, if not perfect.

"Give Gwen time and try to be understanding. Be sure you spend time alone with her as well as with Jeff, okay? If the situation were reversed and Gwen suddenly had a boyfriend, you might feel the same way as she does now."

"Okay. You're right."

Louise reached for the box of candy that sat between them. "Okay, just one more piece. Damn, this stuff is good."

"Mom!" Isobel cried. "Save some for me!"

"It's my gift."

"Given to you by my boyfriend!"

"So? It's every woman for herself when it comes to chocolate."

Isobel faked a frown and grabbed the last Turtle before scurrying out of the kitchen.

Louise smiled after her daughter. She really hoped that Isobel's friendship with Gwen would survive this transition. Gwen was a truly special person. And she had faith in her daughter's ability to adapt to new situations. Hadn't she always done so easily?

Chapter 36

CITYMOUSE

Good day!

I hope everyone is happy and healthy and enjoying the dog days of summer—though I must admit I don't know what "dog days" means—I must look it up! The English language has so many interesting expressions and "turns of speech" with such bizarre origins . . . Someday I'd love to own a real copy of the *Oxford English Dictionary,* all however many volumes. The books themselves, I mean, not access to an online source. There's something special about turning pages . . .

And for some visual entertainment—Gwen took these shots back in late May when the azaleas were first in bloom. I like to imagine a dress made of a material as papery and lovely as these white blossoms. The dress would be a diaphanous creation, something to be worn on a very special occasion, like to an early morning wedding on the beach or to an evening concert in a beautiful green field or—

Well, duty calls and I must scurry off, like the CityMouse that I am . . . Until next time!

Isobel groaned. She simply had not been able to find anything really interesting to say on the blog today. She knew she was reaching with this post—in fact, the post was awfully lame; she suspected that most of her readers had never even heard of the *OED*—but part of her just didn't care. Her brain was just empty. And as for her energy, it was at low ebb.

For example, two weeks before, she had seen an ad in one of the local papers about a new resale shop opening on Route 1 and instead of calling Gwen immediately and making a plan to get to the store as soon as possible, she had thought, *Well, someday I'll get there.*

Well, maybe her general lack of enthusiasm for all the things that she usually enjoyed was because of the heat and humidity, both of which Isobel hated. They could make you sick and listless. That was a scientific fact. So were hormones, and for all Isobel knew her body was still going through some adolescent changes. Hey, her mother was always saying how she was still suffering through PMS, and you didn't want to get Catherine started on the subject.

Isobel sighed. This sense of existential boredom was boring. When was her life going to kick back in again? She had always bounced back from sadness or adversity with what even she recognized was astonishing speed. So what was wrong now? Maybe, she thought, with a twinge of guilt, she just missed Gwen.

Gwen really was smart, maybe because of how she had spent the first years of her life. She had had to learn to read situations clearly and on her own. She had had to learn how to form independent opinions based on the evidence presented to her, however scant or dubious. Maybe being annoyed with Gwen for having her own opinions about Jeff was stupid. Maybe Gwen really did see something about the relationship that Isobel was missing . . .

It was disturbing, but she forced herself to think about what had happened at the movies the other day—besides Jeff's whispering. He had held her hand in his lap and a few times she had had to push his hand (and hers in it) away because it had seemed to her that he was getting a little too close to . . .

At the time she had thought that the movement of his hand was unconscious—maybe he was restless, sitting still for almost two hours—but it had made her uncomfortable nonetheless.

She had refused to think about it after the movie, but the more time that passed the more the memory kept intruding. What if Gwen had seen? What if a stranger had seen and reported them to the management and they had been thrown out? What if the police had been called, or even mall security? It was too dreadful to think about. Her life would be over. How could she ever recover from something so base and humiliating?

But Isobel was not at all sure she wasn't making a mountain out of a molehill (another tired, old cliché she probably overused). Her overreaction was probably another example of her relative immaturity. One thing she was very sure of, and that was Jeff's feelings about her reluctance to have sex. He was getting impatient with her. The other day he had snapped at her when she had pushed him away. They had been kissing and Jeff's hand had wandered down from her waist . . . After that, he had immediately driven her home, ignoring her half-articulate apologies.

But he had said in that text that he loved her . . . Maybe it wasn't as romantic as saying the words to someone's face, but these days it was just as valid. Right? And love meant being patient with a person . . .

Isobel twitched. There he was, on her phone, texting that he was on his way to see her.

Isobel met him on the porch. Her mother was out grocery shopping. As far as Isobel knew, all of the guests were out, too. James and Jim never wasted a sunny day hanging around the inn when they could be working on their tans.

Jeff looked distracted again, or distant, or disturbed. Isobel couldn't trust herself to properly identify his expression.

"I read that post you wrote about Portland," he said without a greeting.

"Which one?" Isobel asked. "I've posted a lot about Portland."

"The one where you go on about that foreign-sounding store."

"Oh right. I got a lot of nice responses to that post."

"Well, I don't want you to go to the city without me. It's dangerous. Besides, the place is a toilet."

"It is not!" Isobel cried, half-laughing at the absurdity of what Jeff was saying.

"It's crawling with homeless people and drug addicts and booze fiends. Those people are the scum of the earth. I don't want you having anything to do with people like that."

"What?" Isobel blurted.

"You heard what I said."

"But when I go to Portland I'm going into shops and the museums and restaurants," she argued. A tiny, tiny part of her wondered why she was even bothering to argue against such a—such a ridiculous demand. "Besides, homeless people aren't dangerous. They're mostly just—sad."

"Isobel," Jeff said, his voice louder now and his tone emphatic, "I know what I'm talking about. I'm just thinking of you and your safety. I don't want anything bad to happen to you. You should be grateful for my concern and not fight me on this. Remember, Isobel. I love you. And you love me, too, right?"

There were the words, live and in person. "Of course I love you," she said. "And of course I'm grateful. Really."

The sound of high heels alerted Isobel to Mrs. White, who was coming out of the inn just then. Her hair had obviously been newly colored. It was almost white-blond and looked as smooth as silk.

"Why, hello," she said brightly. Isobel had the distinct feeling that her greeting was meant for Jeff alone.

Jeff smiled. He got to his feet and walked down the porch steps with Mrs. White. When they reached her car, he opened the door for her. He must have said something funny because Mrs. White laughed and put one manicured hand briefly on his arm before sliding behind the wheel.

Isobel felt a teeny bit weird about what she had just witnessed. She wouldn't dream of touching Mr. White's arm, even if he was young and good-looking. Especially if he was young and good-looking. He didn't belong to her. He belonged to his wife. Well, as much as a human being could "belong" to another human being.

But—as Jeff had reminded her—she was young and relatively inexperienced in the ways of the world . . . At least, in the ways of romance. She really couldn't argue that.

Jeff bounded back up the steps of the porch. "I've got to get going," he said. "I'm meeting my father and one of our lawyers at the York Harbor Inn."

He leaned down and kissed her forehead. When he stood up, he looked at her sharply.

"What's wrong?" she asked.

"You should think about dyeing your hair platinum."

Isobel laughed a bit too loudly. Jeff went down to his car and drove off in the same direction Mrs. White had taken. Which, Isobel told herself, meant absolutely nothing.

She sat there on the porch steps for a while, thinking. Jeff's comment about platinum hair was a bit weird (maybe he was color-blind; anyone with a decent sense of color could see that she would look completely washed out as a platinum blonde!), but what really bothered her was that his concern for her safety seemed so out of proportion. Even her own father—back when they had lived together—hadn't been as overprotective, and she had been so much younger then, so much more vulnerable. At least, her father had never said or done things to make her feel like he was—not protecting, but—well, guarding her. Not keeping bad things out but keeping her in.

A loud hiss from the rhododendron bushes, followed by a shriek and a beating of wings, alerted Isobel to the presence of Ivan the Terrible. Talk about creatures needing protection! No local bird or small four-legged creature was safe from Ivan's harassment.

Isobel wondered. Maybe Jeff's father was overly protective of his mother. Maybe that was where he had learned his tendency toward, well, smothering. Or, his tendency to be too much of a gentleman? Could someone be too much of a good thing? He had held the car door for Mrs. White, and earlier, he had carried her packages up the steps and inside. He had brought Isobel flowers and had given candy to her mother. Surely those little courtesies couldn't be signs of something wrong?

Still, Isobel absolutely would not—could not—tell her mother or Gwen or Catherine or James or Jim or anyone else she knew about Jeff's—what? His warning? They would say that he was overprotective and old-fashioned.

And, of course, she could never share what he had said about the populace of Portland. Without hesitation every single one of them would condemn Jeff for his narrow-minded attitude. And honestly, could she blame them? Sure, there were a lot of unfortunate people in Portland, but that was because the city was so good at providing the help those people needed like shelters, food pantries, SROs, and probably lots of other services Isobel didn't even know about.

Maybe Jeff had led a seriously sheltered life; maybe all he needed was to learn more about urban culture. After all, he had grown up in cozy little Ogunquit and was going to school in rural Vermont. He had probably never had any lengthy experience with city life. She supposed it could be scary for the uninitiated.

Isobel sighed. She wanted Jeff to be patient with her, so she would need to be patient with him. Patience should be a two-way street, right?

Oh, life was suddenly all so complicated!

She absolutely did not want to break up with Jeff (he was so good-looking and could be so charming and nice and generous and he loved her—that counted for a lot!), but she was feeling a bit exhausted by their relationship, like she was always making a mistake with him, like she was walking through a minefield (it was as good a cliché as any), afraid that the next step would bring an explosion.

And she had just told him that she loved him . . . Had she lied? No. She did love him. And yet, he was still so unknown, so foreign to her. He still hadn't told her what he liked to do in his spare time. She had no idea if he followed a sports team, what he read, if he liked to go sailing or build things or play chess or whether he played a musical instrument. He was like a closed book. But books were easy to open and to browse. Not so much people.

And the way she and Jeff looked at the world was so different too. For some reason Jeff wouldn't (or couldn't) explain, he was prejudiced against gay people; Isobel was absolutely not prejudiced against anyone and staunchly pro-marriage for everyone. Maybe it was wrong to be with a person who didn't share your core values and beliefs. And if it wasn't exactly wrong, it was fatiguing. And sometimes, though it was hard to admit, it was embarrassing.

But then, just when Isobel thought that maybe, possibly, she should walk away from the relationship, Jeff would do or say something so nice that all thoughts of ending the relationship just flew away. Yes, she thought, more sure now, maybe all Jeff needed was an education, and if so, who better to give it to him than his girlfriend?

And maybe—Isobel thought this seemed very plausible—maybe Jeff's parents had been so focused on Michael, the perfect son, they had neglected their younger child. Without meaning to, of course. That would explain why Jeff never liked it when Michael's name was mentioned. And it also might explain why he was working for his father this summer. Finally, with Michael away, Jeff could spend some quality time with his father, could prove to him that he was as valuable as his older brother.

This was a new perspective. Jeff as fundamentally powerless in his position as the younger son of a powerful man . . .

Unbidden, memories of what she had learned over the years about how to spot an abusive person came back to her. Abuse didn't have to be about punching and hitting, though it often manifested itself that way. It was really about a misuse of power, and that could take a lot of different shapes, including neglect. And a girl could abuse a boy or a woman could abuse a man as easily as the other way around. It was human nature to be tempted by power. Unfortunately, some people, usually the ones who secretly felt powerless or victimized, justly or unjustly, were overwhelmed by the need to wield it.

Isobel felt a chill in spite of the warm July sun. Whoa. Wait. Did that make Jeff, a neglected child, a potential bully? The thought shocked and appalled her.

No, it did not. Absolutely, no way, it did not. Because if Jeff was a bully, that meant that she was a victim and that just wasn't possible. Isobel Amelia Bessire, an abused girlfriend, a bullied girlfriend? No. Way. Not with her strong personality. Not with the training she had gotten from her mother and from her father. Not with her adamantine insistence on independence and individuality.

Her relationship with Jeff was exactly like all romantic relationships, Isobel decided firmly. Periods of constant negotiation and turmoil were followed by periods of peace and equality, and then by periods of more wrangling and argument until the next plateau was reached. For a while. That was the nature of a plateau. It didn't go on forever. Eventually, it came to an end and you fell off.

And if that was true—if that was how long-term relationships worked—then she had better get used to things being complicated. It was time to put aside childish ways. So she didn't like everything about Jeff. There were things about her that Jeff didn't like, either. Her clothes, for one. Her hair color, for another. Her best friend, for yet another.

Isobel jumped to her feet. It was a waste of time to sit around babbling to oneself. Better to be productive. And she had promised her mom she would inventory the supply of guest towels . . .

Just as she reached the front door, Ivan the Terrible, somewhere on the prowl, let out a viciously loud scream. Isobel flinched and hurried inside.

Chapter 37

Louise and Isobel were sitting at the kitchen table that evening, watching television. There would be no hanging out in the parlor until after the fall season had come and gone and Louise and Isobel could expand into the otherwise public spaces of the inn.

Louise dragged her eyes back to the screen; they had wandered to the far more interesting microwave. She hadn't been able to focus on what was happening; it seemed to be a show about a couple. The couple had some friends. They all lived in a city she didn't recognize. And for some reason she couldn't fathom, one of the characters was a cross-dressing minister, which was supposed to be funny.

"But, darling," the lead female character (played by their bride) was saying now, "you know I always eat spaghetti with my hands."

There followed a bit of canned laughter. And then the lead male character (played by their groom), delivered the next line in what was obviously his trademark manner—hands on hips, head to one side, his voice a broad parody of exasperation.

"Tell me you didn't just say that!"

There followed more of the canned laughter, and Louise reached for the remote to mute the sound for the duration of the commercials.

"This is," she said, "quite possibly, the worst television

show I have ever seen. Ever. This show has jumped the shark at its conception. How many seasons has this garbage been on? What is the world coming to? And more in that vein."

"If I had seen this before Flora Michaels first contacted us," Isobel said in reply, "I would have told you to say 'no' very loudly and very emphatically."

"Wasn't this Gwen's idea, that we watch this?"

"Yeah."

"She should be watching it, too, as punishment. Did you catch how Dax—"

"Who?" Isobel asked.

"The star. The groom. Dax. Or is it Jax?"

"I think it's Mack. Whatever his name is, he couldn't act his way out of a paper bag."

"Kylie isn't much better," Louise noted. "She brings a whole new meaning to the term *wooden*."

"I think you mean Kyra."

"No, I know it's not Kyra. Mackenzie?"

"I don't think I can stand to watch the final scene, can you?"

Louise hit the POWER button on the remote. "Absolutely not. Want anything to drink? How about some popcorn?"

"Mom, you can't drink popcorn."

"Ha-ha. Well?"

Isobel shrugged. "Sure. Do we have any garlic salt for it?"

Louise set about putting a bag of popcorn in the microwave and locating the plastic container of garlic salt (she kept it in the house for Isobel; personally, she hated it). Then, she poured herself a glass of wine, a delicious sauvignon blanc from the Loire Valley Catherine had introduced her to, and took a pitcher of Bella's lemonade out of the fridge for Isobel.

They were settled together again at the table when Isobel said, "Tell me about how you and Dad met?"

"Haven't I told you that story a million times?"

"A million and one. But I want to hear it again."

Louise shrugged. "All right, here goes. But I'm giving you the condensed version. I was out of college about a year. I had a job at one of the big bookstore chains; I'd just made manager. One day, this handsome guy who looked a few years older than me came in. Even so, I only noticed him because I thought it odd the way he was wandering up and down the aisles as if he had no idea what sort of book he wanted to buy."

"And he didn't," Isobel asked, "did he?"

"Nope. I was beginning to wonder if he was a very inexpert thief when he suddenly started striding with great purpose toward the information desk where I was checking some files online. When he was close enough to hear me, I asked, 'May I help you?' "

"And he . . ."

"His face turned the color of a plum and he said, 'Yes, please. Will you go out with me?' "

"And you said . . ."

"And I said, 'How will that help you?' I wasn't trying to be mean. I guess I was just surprised."

"And he said . . ."

Louise laughed. "He said, 'I have no idea. But I think you're very pretty and I would like to get to know you. Please.' It was the final 'please' that did it."

"So, you took pity on him and said yes."

"I guess so. And the rest, as they say, is history."

Isobel looked thoughtful. "Did you guys fight a lot in the early days?" she asked.

"I don't know about a lot," Louise said. "The early days are usually the blissful ones for a new couple. But arguing is an integral part of a marriage. You can't live with a person day after day after day and share meals and a bed and a bathroom and not get on each other's nerves now and then. And then there are the outside challenges that can cause fights, like a job loss or a troublesome family member or even needing a new car."

"Is that why you and Dad always had such wildly different cars?"

Louise smiled. "He wanted form, I wanted function."

"Sometimes Jeff and I disagree," Isobel said.

"Well, that's normal. As long as when you do argue, each of you listens to what the other has to say. So, what sort of things do you disagree about?"

Isobel shrugged. "I don't know. Just things. Nothing important."

"Misunderstandings?"

"Yeah. Mostly."

"You should be careful of too many misunderstandings. That points to bad communication. But who am I to talk? My marriage failed."

Isobel reached for her mother's hand. "The divorce wasn't your fault, Mom. You know that."

"Do I? Well, okay, it wasn't entirely my fault, but it takes two to tango—yeah, a cliché—and maybe there was something I was doing or not doing that contributed to your father's looking elsewhere for a companion."

"I guess," Isobel said, though she sounded doubtful. "Though I hate to think of you staying up nights blaming yourself. After all, you weren't the one who cheated and lied."

"Don't worry," Louise assured her. "I don't waste any time blaming myself. I just recognize that maybe I was a part of the dynamic of failure. Probably."

"Sometimes I feel so mature," Isobel said suddenly. "And other times, I feel like a babe in the woods. I feel like I know absolutely nothing about stuff I should know all about."

"That's pretty common at your age, you know. Being a teenager is uncomfortable and from what I remember, supremely frustrating."

Isobel smiled a bit. "Well, misery loves company, I guess."

"Are you really miserable?" Louise asked, concern furrowing her brow.

"No, no, I didn't mean it like that. I just meant to say that I'm glad I'm not a freak for feeling like two different people smushed into one head."

"You, my dear, are not a freak. Anything but!"

Isobel smiled. "Even after what happened with you and Dad, are you happy now when you remember those old days?"

Louise nodded. This was something she had thought about often. "It's funny," she said, "but yes. Well, maybe *happy* isn't the word; I don't feel happy now about stuff that happened so many years ago. But I can remember feeling genuinely happy back then and that's valid. Meaning, even though things didn't last happily ever after with me and your father, the good times were real and I believe them."

"I'm glad. I mean, it would be horrible if all those good times turned out to mean nothing in the end just because they didn't last forever."

"Yes, it would be horrible," Louise agreed. "And while we're on the subject of relationships, have you and Jeff had sex yet?"

Isobel blushed. "No," she said. "Not yet. I'm taking my time. Jeff's cool about it."

"Good. But you have the birth control pills your doctor prescribed, right? And a condom with you at all times. And—"

"Mom, really, I'm all set. Honestly. I'm not about to do something stupid, trust me."

"I do trust you. It's just that when it comes to sex—"

"Mom!"

"Let me say it. When it comes to sex, even the smartest person can become an idiot in the blink of an eye."

Louise reached across the table and took her daughter's hand. In response, Isobel scooted her chair closer to her mother and gave her a long, big hug.

Louise was deeply pleased; it had been some time since Isobel had hugged her so fiercely. Isobel was indeed in some ways still a babe in the woods, naïve and almost dangerously enthusiastic at times. Louise was flooded by memories, both emotional and physical, both joyful and sad, of the days when Isobel was a baby. How precious those days were, never to return . . .

Isobel released her mother. "Thanks," she said. "You're a good mom."

"You know, we could probably watch another episode of the show online if you want."

Isobel shrieked. "Mom! Are you trying to punish me?"

"No, no, sorry. Bad joke. Why don't we see if we can find a good PBS mystery?"

"Oh, I'd love to see an episode of Hercule Poirot! The clothes! The interior design!"

Louise laughed and picked up the remote. "Don't get your hopes up." She turned on the set and rapidly pressed the button for their local PBS station. "Oh. My. God," she said, staring over at her daughter. "Did you look at the listings earlier? There's an episode of Poirot just about to begin."

Isobel grinned. "Of course not," she said. "All I did was get my hopes up."

Chapter 38

CITYMOUSE

Greetings, Everyone!

Today I want to share news of a cool new (well, new to me) kind of jewelry metal called Alchemia, or "zero karat gold." (Get it? From the word *alchemy,* which was an ancient attempt to transform base metals into gold. Well, thanks to the History Channel, I happen to know that since 1924 scientists have been doing just that, but in brightly lit labs, not in dark and secret lairs.)

Gwen and her family were up in Portland yesterday, and they stopped in one of their all-time favorite stores called Motifs. (It's on Commercial Street, if you're interested. Paula, the owner, has the most excellent taste ever.) There Gwen found a super-attractive ring with a blue topaz and a kyanite (it's a blue stone, too) in a band and setting that looked like gold . . . But the ring was so affordable the Gwentastic Gwen knew it couldn't be real gold. And that's when the super-nice woman helping her, Kirsten, explained that the designer, Charles Albert, uses a nickel- and lead-free alloy that looks like 18K gold!

Needless to say, Gwen snatched up the prize and her father Curtis took these lovely pictures of her wearing the ring. I love how the bright/light blue of the stones plays off the gunmetal color of her nail polish, don't you?

You can check out the jewelry of Charles Albert online—of course, I already have; his skull rings are gorgeous—and plan your next stunning and stunningly affordable purchase!

'Til next time, CityMouse is signing off.

Isobel posted, closed down her laptop, and sighed deeply. It was another anemic entry. Not that the topic was boring— the ring was really beautiful and the store was fantastic—but her writing had amounted to a sort of lame advertisement and nothing more.

Life just seemed a little dull lately, like the edges had been blunted or the center of things blurred. Her interest in the things she loved continued to flag, and her focus was bad and getting worse. New York Fashion Week was coming up in early September and usually, by now she was in a frenzy of anticipation, as eager to see what was being worn by the people in the audience as what the designers had come up with. But this year, she found that she didn't really care about getting a glimpse of that faraway street style and the fantastical runways.

She didn't think she was actually, really, clinically depressed (she had been able to laugh at that ridiculous TV show), and she certainly didn't have anything remotely resembling suicidal thoughts and thank God or whoever for that!

And she had enjoyed the talk with her mom; her mom had confirmed that yeah, relationships were difficult. Still, Isobel hadn't been able to bring herself to tell her mother all of the things that had been bothering her about Jeff . . . Rather, about her inability to understand him properly. It was no good to blame other people for what amounted to your own failure.

Isobel glanced critically around her room. Jeff would be there soon and she still couldn't find her phone. She knew she had had it the day before. She was sure of it. She had rummaged through her room at least three times, and turned out every bag she had carried in the past two days, and even those she hadn't worn in weeks. But the phone had not emerged. She made one more visual sweep of the room. Nothing.

"I'm getting absentminded in my old age," she muttered to herself. "That, or I'd better learn how to get organized."

Isobel heard a car crunching on the gravel of the driveway and hurried downstairs. Jeff was always on time and he didn't like to be kept waiting. Lots of people were like that. She ran down the porch steps and slid into the passenger seat of his car.

And there was her phone, on the floor.

"What's my phone doing here?" she asked, reaching down for it. "I've been looking all over for it."

Jeff pulled out of the driveway. "You must have dropped it the last time you were in the car."

Isobel shook her head. "No. I distinctly remember having it in the kitchen yesterday . . ."

Jeff laughed. "Then what's it doing here? Izzy, you know how absentminded you are. Anyway, what's the big deal? You found it, right?"

"I guess," Isobel agreed. But inside, she wasn't so sure. Could Jeff have taken her phone to check up on who was calling her, or on whom she was calling? No. That was absurd.

"What's the deal with that Raisa chick?" he asked as they drove along.

Isobel startled. "How do you know about Raisa? I never mentioned her to you."

"Yeah, you did. Remember?"

She did not remember. What she did remember was that she had missed a call from Raisa Morris, an old friend from Massachusetts, and had planned on getting back to her but for some reason she had not.

Well, maybe she had mentioned Raisa to Jeff once. It wasn't impossible. Still . . . Isobel was loath to believe that Jeff could have taken her phone to check up on her correspondence. Wouldn't that be stealing? Didn't he trust her? And why hadn't he noticed the phone on the floor of his car, and called her mother about it so that Isobel wouldn't be worried she had lost it for good? And he was always sending her text messages and expecting immediate answers. If he had been trying to reach her last night and getting no response, wouldn't he have come by the inn to see if she was okay? Or, again, called her mother?

Something wasn't right, or maybe it was that she couldn't quite grasp what was going on. It was probably another symptom of the sort-of depression she was experiencing; everything appeared all blurry and confused. Jeff wasn't the responsible one here. She was. She was the guilty party.

"So, what's up with her?"

"Who?" Isobel asked.

"Duh. Raisa?"

"Oh. Nothing. She called me the other day and I meant to get back to her but I forgot."

"Maybe you should wear a string around your finger so

you won't forget to do the stuff you mean to do." Jeff laughed. "But knowing you, you'd forget why the string was there in the first place."

Isobel attempted a smile. There wasn't much point in arguing with him. He always seemed to have the final word. "Where are we going?" she asked.

"For a drive."

"I know, but where?"

"You'll see."

A half second of annoyance was replaced by dull acceptance. Jeff could be as stubbornly silent as he could be loud and verbal. It was just the way he was.

"You know, Izzy," Jeff said suddenly. "I was thinking about what happened to your family. I mean, I know the man is your father and everything, and it's in the Bible that everyone should respect his parents, but that's only if the parents deserve respect. How can you respect a guy who cheats on his wife—and with his buddy's wife? That's a double betrayal. He screwed his wife and his friend."

Isobel felt a bit sick. "I never told you that part," she said. "About Vicky being the wife of my father's colleague."

"Sure you did. How else would I know?"

"But I'm sure I didn't—"

"Izzy, please. Are you calling me a liar?"

"No, of course not."

"Anyway, I have a zero-tolerance policy on cheating. There's no legitimate excuse, ever."

It frightened Isobel a bit, Jeff's knowing about Vicky, and the vehemence with which he had condemned her father. But at the same time, he had tapped in to the very real anger she felt toward Andrew Bessire.

The fact was that she hadn't seen him in months, and that had been for only an afternoon. She had taken the bus down to Boston one cold March day to meet him for lunch at Union Oyster House (her father's nod to old times?). The meeting had not been a success. They were awkward with

each other, and there was none of the old feeling of Daddy
and Daughter against the world. After lunch he had asked
her if she wanted to go shopping. But he had looked at his
watch before asking and it was clear to Isobel that he hoped
her answer would be no. She hadn't disappointed him. He
walked with her to South Station but hadn't waited to see her
off. She had cried a bit on the bus ride home, but by the time
the bus reached the station she had managed to put the disastrous day behind her. She had greeted her mother with a
smile and a hug and had reported that the time she had spent
with her father was "nice." After a few gently probing questions that had resulted in pleasant though uninformative answers, her mother had said no more.

"Why are you so quiet?" Jeff was asking.

"No reason," Isobel said automatically. And then, she re-
vised her response. "Well, actually, I was thinking about the
last time I saw my father. It wasn't a success."

Jeff reached over and squeezed her hand.

"I swear I will never cheat on you, Izzy. You're safe with
me. Forever."

Safe. Forever. It didn't sound so bad . . . Though what it
had to do with the failing relationship between her and her
father wasn't clear. "I'll never cheat on you, either," she said,
again, automatically. Well, she wouldn't. She would never
cheat on anybody.

"Swear it."

"Okay," she said. Why not? "I swear I will never cheat on
you."

Jeff nodded. "That's good. I'm glad we got that settled."

Isobel managed a smile and wondered. Was Jeff implying
that he wanted to marry her someday? It was almost always
this way. She was almost never sure of the meaning behind
his words.

Isobel was hardly aware of the passing scenery, lovely
though it was. She thought she should probably feel good
and comforted by Jeff's pledge—and by the vehemence with

which he had made it, but she didn't quite. Nice girlfriend she was. Her boyfriend vows eternal loyalty and all she could feel was—what? Trapped? Annoyed? Resigned?

"Dickhead."

Jeff uttered the word beneath his breath. A sports car had pulled up alongside them at the light. Isobel knew what was coming. Jeff revved the engine. When the light turned green the car raced ahead.

She clutched the armrest. She wished he wouldn't speed. But she was afraid of asking him to slow down. She had a feeling his response would be perverse, that he would speed up even faster. Jeff was willful. That wasn't necessarily a bad trait—his father was probably willful, too; how else would he have become such a success?

"Loser," Jeff crowed, as they left the other car far behind. "Right?"

Isobel nodded. "Right."

Chapter 39

Louise brought two cups of fresh coffee to the kitchen table and put one down in front of Catherine.

"Want to know the latest from wedding central?" she asked, pulling out a chair.

"Naturally."

"Flora Michaels said the bride thinks it would be 'cute' if the staff dresses in period garb for the wedding."

"What period?" Catherine asked. "Mmm. Good coffee."

"Well, that wasn't quite specified. The bride, as you might have surmised from her choice of career, isn't exactly academically inclined."

"I see. Well, what did you tell Ms. Michaels?"

"I told her that under no circumstances would the staff—by whom she meant me and Isobel only, by the way, not those 'scruffy males'—dress in anything other than their own contemporary attire. Appropriate for a special occasion, of course."

"And how did Flora Michaels—and the bride—take that bit of news?"

Louise sighed. "We're still in negotiation."

"By 'scruffy males' I'm guessing they mean Flynn and Quentin."

"And neither one is the least bit scruffy!"

Catherine seemed to be musing. Then she said, "Though I

can see Flynn looking rather smart dressed in, say, one of those tight waistcoats, circa 1776."

"And Quentin in a stovepipe hat?"

"Yeah, that's not going to happen, is it? Although he does have a Johnny Depp thing going on with that lovely face . . . Maybe a pirate costume? Were there American pirates? And maybe we could get Jeff to dress up. Wasn't Thomas Jefferson blond under that powdered wig?"

"I have no idea. I'm pretty sure he was tall, though. But speaking of Jeff . . ." Louise told Catherine about the bracelet he had given Isobel.

Catherine frowned. "He gave her an expensive piece of jewelry after only a few dates? I have to say, that's a bit worrisome. What's his rush?"

Louise shrugged. "I don't know. At least it wasn't a ring."

"Huh. Thank God for small favors."

"Well, I'm not entirely sure the bracelet really is expensive," Louise amended. "It looks it, but these days you can get good knockoffs for not much money at all."

"The illustrious Otten family doesn't need to resort to knockoffs."

"Well, that might be the point. Jeff is probably used to a different level of lifestyle than we are. What seems expensive to us might seem like the deal of the century to him. In his mind, he could have given her a mere trinket, a token of his affection."

"Are you trying to convince yourself or me?"

Louise smiled a bit. "Maybe both."

"Mmm. Well, how does Isobel feel about the gift? That's what's important."

"As far as I know, she hasn't taken it off since he gave it to her. But . . ."

"But what?"

"Nothing. It's just that she didn't tell me about it until I noticed it one day. I thought that was kind of odd. Restraint isn't one of her strong points."

"No, it certainly isn't," Catherine agreed. "Hmm. I wonder . . ."

"Me, too. I've been 'round and 'round in my head trying to puzzle out her motives."

"Have you thought of asking her?"

"Of course. And she said she didn't say anything to me because she didn't think it was a big deal."

"Well, maybe that's all there is to it. Isobel is an—how to put this? She's an individualist. Her reasons and motives for doing or not doing something are often not the norm."

Louise smiled ruefully. "You mean that my daughter is a character."

"Yes, I do, and you should be glad of that. You've raised a child who is not afraid to be who she is. That's huge."

"Thanks. Though I'm inclined to give most of the credit to Isobel herself."

Catherine shrugged. "Well, maybe it doesn't matter who's responsible. All I know is that it will be a pleasure to witness Isobel growing into the full person she's going to be."

Louise felt tears forming. "I don't think you could have said a nicer thing to me."

"Don't start to cry," Catherine warned, blinking quickly. "I'm just about to get my period, and if you cry I will most certainly start to bawl."

Chapter 40

CITYMOUSE

Hi, Everyone:

As any reader of this blog—or any other style and fashion blog knows—crystals are enjoying a moment and have been for a few years now. Personally, I can't see them ever being considered passé—they are bright and shiny and so much more afford-able than diamonds, precious, and even many semiprecious stones. And really, the sparkle of a good crystal can rival the sparkle of a CZ. (At least, in my opinion.)

In our Maine Mall in South Portland there's a Swarovski store, and I know they can be found in malls all over the country—or, at least, I hope they can! If you can't get to an actual store, you could check out their online store. And so many designers are using crystals (lots of them Swarovski crys-tals) in their jewelry that no one who wants to wear some sparkle should have an ex-cuse for not wearing some sparkle!

Signing off for now, with love, CityMouse.

"Um, is this it?" Gwen asked.

The girls were hanging in Isobel's room. Gwen, sitting at the desk, had turned to face Isobel, who was sitting cross-legged on the bed.

"What do you mean?"

Gwen shrugged. "Well, it's just that your posts are usually, you know . . ."

"What?"

"Longer," Gwen said carefully. "For one thing."

"Yeah, well, brevity is the soul of wit. Shakespeare said that and if—"

"My dads are in theater," Gwen interrupted. "You don't have to tell me what Shakespeare said and what he didn't."

"Okay. So, what's the big deal?"

"Nothing. It's your blog. You can do what you want with it. But—don't you think we should add a photo to the post? We always have at least two or three photos . . ."

"I don't think it matters much."

"I could easily shoot a piece of jewelry. Your mom has that cool ring, the one with the five clear crystals. I could style a—"

"Don't worry about it." Isobel snapped.

"I'm not worrying about it. I'm just—"

"Gwen. Really. We don't need to bother with a photo!"

Gwen turned back to the laptop and closed it. The room fell silent.

Isobel remembered. A few weeks ago, Gwen had suggested Isobel expand the blog by getting advertisers and teaming up with a brand for promotion. Isobel had been excited about the idea. She had talked to Jeff about it, of course. But he hadn't shared her enthusiasm at all.

"Come on, Isobel," he'd said. "You're not exactly a business-person type. This blog habit, it's harmless and keeps you out of trouble. But it's only a pastime. It's kid stuff. Don't be stupid and try to make it into something it's not. Besides, it already takes up too much of your time. The Facebook page, the Twitter account, all that time wasted hanging out with

Gwen in those musty places selling crap to people stupid enough to think it's rusty gold."

When she had tried to answer, to protest, he cut her off.

"What about me?" he had asked, and not for the first time. "Aren't I worth all of your attention?"

When they had first started to date, questions like those had amused Isobel. She had taken them as largely rhetorical. And she had thought that Jeff was cute when he was needy.

But she was beginning to understand the intensity—the utter seriousness—underlying his words. It worried her a bit. Just a bit.

But maybe he was right—again. Maybe she wasn't spending enough time focusing on him.

"Earth to Isobel?"

Isobel startled. "Oh," she said. "Sorry. What were you saying?"

"I was asking if you're excited about our trip to Longfellow Books Tuesday night."

Right. She had planned to drive up to Portland with Gwen and Will (Curtis was taking Ricky to a Red Sox game at Fenway Park) for a reading by one of their favorite Maine-based authors. Joan Nicholson wrote wonderful stories about life alone in her camp (no running water; a wood-fired stove; no cell phone reception or Internet) almost three miles from the nearest road.

But Jeff didn't want her to go. He told her he hated Joan Nicholson's work. And he told her he had made plans for them to do something Tuesday night. He hadn't told her what those plans involved, but he had seemed really disappointed and really annoyed that she was even considering leaving him on his own.

"I forgot to tell you," Isobel said now, feigning nonchalance. "I can't go."

"What do you mean, you can't go?" Gwen demanded.

"Just that I can't go."

"But you were so psyched about the reading. And we were

planning to get gelato at that place on Fore Street. And you've got that gift certificate from Catherine."

Isobel looked down at the bracelet Jeff had given her. "I changed my mind, okay?" she said. "I'm allowed to change my mind."

"You changed your mind? If that were true, then you would have said you don't want to go. Why can't you go? Jeez, Isobel, does this have anything to do with Jeff?"

"Of course not," Isobel lied. She felt a bit angry—no, a lot angry—that Gwen was challenging her. "And by the way," she blurted, "I decided I don't want to do CityMouse anymore."

The moment the words were out of her mouth, Isobel wished she could cram them back in. But shock and pride, a strangely powerful combination, made her feel committed to the decision she had announced aloud.

Gwen's eyes widened and then narrowed. "What? I can't believe I'm hearing this. Why?"

"You always wanted it for yourself, anyway," Isobel said with a snort. It was a ridiculous accusation, ridiculous and mean and untrue.

"I think you're losing your mind," Gwen snapped. "City-Mouse is your baby, your special project, and it's always been that way. I've never wanted it to be otherwise. I've always been perfectly content being the sidekick. You know that!"

Isobel could find nothing to say. She shrugged.

Gwen got up from Isobel's desk chair. "Look, I don't know what's going on with you," she said, "although I have a pretty good idea. I do know we're not getting anywhere in this conversation. I'm going home."

Gwen stalked to the door and slammed it behind her.

Isobel flinched.

Chapter 41

"It's me, Louise."

"I know," Andrew said. "My assistant doesn't put through anonymous calls."

"Oh," she said. "Of course."

"So, how's business?" he asked. Not how are you. Not how is my daughter.

"Great," Louise replied brightly. "Business is great."

"Good."

Andrew didn't have to know the whole truth. So far she had managed to keep the celebrity wedding a secret from him. She most definitely did not want his advice, well meaning though it might be. She most definitely did not want to feel what she had felt so often during their marriage, that she was ill-equipped to handle a task at hand. She didn't really think that Andrew intended to make her (and others) feel bad about their abilities; he just couldn't seem to help being officious. It served him well in business, if not always in his personal relationships.

And she most definitely did not want Andrew to tell Vicky the business genius about her project.

"How is Vicky feeling?" Louise asked, priding herself on being woman enough to ask.

"Pretty good. She's past the morning sickness. And she's convinced the baby is a boy. She says she's carrying differently this time."

"So, you're not going to know the sex for sure until the baby is born?"

"That's how Vicky wants it. This is her show, after all."

Louise rolled her eyes. "Well, I'd say you had something to do with the show's production."

Andrew laughed. "So, to what do I owe the pleasure of this call? The checks should have gone out already. Is there a problem with them?"

"No, no. I got the checks yesterday and they're safely deposited."

"Then, what's up?"

"Andrew, when did you last speak with Isobel?"

There was a bit of silence, into which Andrew cleared his throat. "Well," he said, "I guess it's been some time now, maybe a couple of weeks."

"More like over a month, at least. And texts and e-mails don't count. Really, Andrew, what's wrong with you?"

"Nothing's wrong with me, Louise," Andrew protested. "Frankly, I get the feeling Isobel doesn't have a whole hell of a lot to say to me."

"Maybe she'd have more to say to you if you showed some interest in her life. Fake it if you have to."

"I don't have to fake an interest in my daughter's life! For Christ's sake, Louise, I'm not an unfeeling monster."

Louise bit her tongue. She really didn't want a fight; at best it would be unproductive and at worst, it would leave her with a bad headache.

"Look," she said wearily, "just make more of an effort, okay?"

"Is there some particular reason why you're pushing this? Is Isobel in trouble?"

The patience it required to deal with this man . . . Louise sighed.

"She's fine. At least, she says she's fine but I think she's under some strain. Maybe it's because of what's going on here with—" Louise caught herself just in time. "With it being our busy season. Anyway, it certainly wouldn't hurt for you to call her if you don't have time to Skype. Please, Andrew."

"All right, of course. When is she usually home?"

"She's a teenager, Andrew. She has her own schedule. Just call her on her cell."

"Fine. Look, Louise, I have a meeting in ten minutes. I've got to go."

"Fine," Louise repeated.

She ended the call with a mixture of relief and frustration. No sooner had she left the kitchen than she was greeted by a familiar querulous cry.

"Mrs. Bessire? Mrs. Bessire?" It was Mr. Starck, a guest in one of the rooms on the third floor. He was a google-eyed little man, tubby and tiny with a penchant for whining. At the moment he was coming at her with his arms held straight out in front of him, two large white bath towels draped across them. An offering of sorts, Louise thought idly. As if I'm a goddess and he's a supplicant . . .

"My bath towels aren't dry," he announced.

Not an offering. A complaint. "When did you last use them?" Louise asked pleasantly.

"About two hours ago. I always shower first thing in the morning."

"Well, it is a humid day," Louise said, mustering all the patience she possessed. And after that phone call with Andrew, it wasn't a lot. "They'll need a little longer to dry completely."

"But I'm just back from the beach and I want to shower again now." His whiny tone was also partially puzzled. Why, he was really asking, wasn't the world exactly how he wanted it to be? Why?

Louise faked a smile. She was getting very good at faking smiles. "Then let me get you some fresh towels, all right?"

She put out her arms for the towels. They felt perfectly dry.

"I'll be right up," she said to Mr. Starck. He pouted and scurried off to the stairs.

Louise headed down to the basement. She would toss the towels into the dryer for a few minutes. If that didn't satisfy him, he could go—

Louise sighed. Her guests were her responsibility. They paid the mortgage and a host of other expenses. Besides, she had chosen this business. She had gone into it with eyes wide open if partially blinkered. And a whole succession of Mr. Starcks would still be a hell of a lot easier to handle than one Flora Michaels.

With a loud and satisfyingly dramatic sigh, Louise threw the towels into the laundry bin and selected two fresh towels from the linen shelves. If Mr. Starck wanted dry towels, he would have them.

Chapter 42

Isobel was pretty sure of what she would find, but she went online anyway.

Gwen had not posted. For the first time in almost two years, CityMouse was silent.

She knew Gwen hadn't believed her about why she wanted to give up the blog. Gwen was not dumb.

There was a new question and comment from one of her most devoted readers; the girl was from a small town in Illinois. Isobel felt a responsibility to her, but she just couldn't work up the energy to respond. Not now, anyway. Soon.

She closed the computer and sat there at her desk, hands in her lap. She felt listless. She thought she might never have felt listless before in her entire life. It was a very unpleasant way to feel.

Isobel sighed. The relative radio silence from her father continued. She had sent him an e-mail the week before. (She still hadn't mentioned Jeff—why should she?) He had gotten back with a hurried greeting and a promise of "more later." Two days later she had gotten a hefty check from him with the instructions to spend it on "something fun." She had yet to cash it or to tell her mother about it.

Isobel opened the laptop again and checked Vicky's Facebook page; she checked it regularly now, even though it was like poking an open wound. It was studded with pictures of her father with Vicky and the girls in a variety of locations—

at the beach, on someone's huge boat, at a lake. Some pictures looked suspiciously like they had been taken in Newport. (For all Isobel knew, her father had told Vicky that she was the one who had cancelled out on the visit to Newport.) In the most recent photos you could see that Vicky was pregnant.

Isobel closed the laptop again. It was ridiculous, this situation with her dad. Like, the fact that they hadn't Skyped since just before that disappointing afternoon they had spent together in Boston back in March. Sure, she could suggest a video chat but she didn't feel up to being rejected. And even if her father did agree to a video chat there was no guarantee he would pay attention to their conversation. The last time he had been totally distracted. The girls kept interrupting (he hadn't asked them to stop), his cell phone kept ringing (he hadn't turned off the ringer), and when she had asked him if he had read her blog recently he had said, "What blog?" and then, "Oh, oh right, jeez, sorry, honey. No, I haven't been keeping up with it."

She had felt annoyed and humiliated.

Suddenly, sitting there at her desk, Isobel felt an intense surge of anger. Her cheeks, she realized, were ablaze. Why had it never occurred to her to wonder what her mother thought of her father's neglect? Had her mother even noticed that her father had gone missing? Had she tried to persuade or force him to be a better correspondent? What kind of mother was she if she didn't even . . .

Isobel put her hands to her face. Her cheeks were still hot. No. It was wrong to be upset with her mother. Of course her mother loved and supported her. If her mother wasn't on her side, then who was on her side? Nobody, that's who.

Not even Jeff?

Her phone alerted her to a text. It was from him.

WE R TAKING DRIVE, it said.

She forced herself to stand, to go into the bathroom and wash her face, to put on a clean T-shirt. Maybe a change of scenery and some fresh air were what she needed. Her life at the inn had become claustrophobic and unhappy. Just that morning she had come close to snapping at a very nice woman who was staying with them for a week. All the woman had done was say hello and ask if Isobel liked living in Ogunquit year-round. Harmless.

And how long had it been since she had eaten anything? Isobel wondered as she closed her bedroom door behind her. Maybe she would ask Jeff if they could stop and get something to eat . . .

She did ask but they didn't stop for lunch until they were in a tiny little town somewhere in New Hampshire. They sat at a booth in the town's only restaurant, a diner half the size of Bessie's in Ogunquit. It was close to two o'clock and they were the only customers.

They had been seated for less than two minutes when a skinny, acne-ridden boy who looked no older than Isobel came to take their order.

"It's about time," Jeff snapped. "You blind or something? We've been sitting here for almost fifteen minutes."

The boy's face turned scarlet, emphasizing his terrible acne. Isobel's heart bled but she said nothing in protest of Jeff's rude behavior.

"Sorry," the boy mumbled.

Jeff sniggered. "You should be. I could get you fired for letting customers sit here waiting around while you, what, played with yourself in the bathroom?"

Isobel flinched. Still, she said nothing. Neither did the boy.

"Get me a burger, medium, and a tuna salad sandwich for her," Jeff ordered, tossing the menus up at the boy. He caught one. The other fell to the floor.

"Moron," Jeff said.

Isobel realized that her hands were trembling. She put them in her lap. Jeff busied himself with his iPhone. When her sandwich came she just looked at it.

"Why aren't you eating?" Jeff demanded. "Is there something wrong with the sandwich? That idiot waiter probably—"

"No, no, please, Jeff," she begged, finally finding her voice, "there's nothing wrong with the sandwich. Please." She forced herself to take a bite and swallow, and then another, before she put the sandwich down on the plate.

Jeff devoured his hamburger and fries. When he had finished, he said, "I see you haven't posted anything new on the blog in the last few days."

So, he had been checking. Well, he had the right to read the blog. Anyone could read it. Or look to see if it was still there.

"Yeah," Isobel said, attempting a light, nonchalant tone. "I was getting kind of tired of it after all . . ."

Jeff nodded. "Good. Really, Izzy, I felt like I was losing you to a computer. You were getting pretty obsessed with it all. Frankly, I was worried about you."

"Worried?"

"Yeah. I was afraid you were losing touch with reality. You creative types are notorious for going a bit cuckoo." Jeff grinned. "It's part of your charm but only in small doses."

Isobel said nothing. She glanced to her right, out onto the main street of the tiny town. She wondered if there was any way she could get home on her own from here . . .

"I like what you're wearing," Jeff said. "Not one of your goofier outfits. Seriously, I don't know where you come up with some of your ideas about how to dress."

Isobel turned back. It was true. She had automatically put on what was probably the most ordinary pair of pants and the most conservative shirt she owned. Other than Jeff's bracelet, she wore no jewelry. She just hadn't had the energy or the interest to be creative. Did she really look goofy when she thought she was being innovative? Maybe Jeff wasn't the only one who laughed at her. Could she have been an object of fun or ridicule all this time and not even known it?

The waiter appeared again (he was brave, Isobel thought, but of course it was also his job; he had no choice but to be attentive) and asked if Isobel wanted to take what was left of her sandwich with her.

"No," Jeff said shortly. "She doesn't." When he had gone off, Jeff looked at her with a squint. "It's probably better you didn't finish," he said. "You don't want to get fat. Do you know my mother wears the same size she wore back in high school? That's discipline. I respect that in a woman."

Isobel said, "Mmm."

Jeff took out his wallet and threw just enough cash on the table to cover their meal. He left nothing for the waiter.

"But we can't just leave—" Isobel began. The look on Jeff's face stopped her.

"He's not getting what he doesn't deserve. Come on."

Jeff grabbed her hand and half-hauled her out of the diner. Isobel, mortified, prayed the waiter or the manager wouldn't come running after them. She didn't know what Jeff would do to them . . .

Once they were back on the road, a horrible thought came to Isobel. Could Jeff have taken her so far away for lunch because no one knew him at that little hole-in-the-wall diner? It was a safe place to humiliate a stranger without witnesses . . .

Isobel glanced over at Jeff, at his straight profile, his perfectly groomed hair, his manicured hands on the steering wheel. It was a disloyal thought, despicable really, but she couldn't come up with any other reason for their being so far from home, and that was a failure not only of her imagination but also of her usually kind and generous spirit.

Isobel looked back to the road ahead of them. Sometimes she wondered what Jeff saw in her, a ditzy, naïve, and possibly undisciplined girl.

Jeff leaned on the horn and shouted, "Stupid motherfucker!"

Isobel flinched. She knew the words weren't meant for her, but words hurt, even those overheard, even those shouted at a stranger, a middle-aged woman behind the wheel of a Jeep. As far as Isobel could tell, the woman had done nothing wrong.

"She could have killed us!" Jeff ranted, slapping the steering wheel with his palm. "People are idiots. The road is a dangerous place, Izzy, especially for someone like you."

"Like me?" she asked, her voice small. "What do you mean?"

"Scattered. You know, like I said before, you're one of those creative types. It's better for you to be in the passenger seat than behind the wheel, trust me. If you had been driving a moment ago instead of me, we'd both be roadkill."

One of those creative types. Maybe she was, though she hadn't been feeling very creative lately. But she was competent, wasn't she? You could be a creative type and still be fully functional. She did well in school and she—"But I—" she began, not sure of what she would say.

"Now, don't argue, Izzy. You can't even keep track of your phone. Not that I don't find it all pretty cute, the absent-mindedness, the forgetfulness. And come on—your jewelry talks to you, tells you it wants to come out of its box for the night? Sheesh, Isobel. If I didn't know you so well, I'd think you were certifiable."

She tried to laugh but what came out was a bit of a cough. "But what if I need to get somewhere?" she said. "I mean, it's not like there's any public transportation available where we live, unless you count the summer trolleys."

"I'll drive you anywhere you need to go," he told her.

"But what about when you go back to school in September?"

Jeff glanced at her. "Why would you want to be going anywhere if I'm not with you?" His tone made the question rhetorical.

They continued the drive in silence. Isobel stared blindly out the passenger's window. She told herself that Jeff's offer to drive her wherever she needed to go was a gesture of love and service. And then she remembered how he had abandoned her in town that time he got a text that demanded his attention. And then she remembered that he didn't want her to go to Portland without him . . .

My God, if Jeff had his way she would wind up becoming a recluse! *Stop it, Isobel*, she scolded silently. *Stop being so dramatic. Stop being so much of a creative type.*

And then Jeff was pulling the car to a stop in front of Blueberry Bay Inn.

"I wish I could stay around," he said, "but I promised my dad I'd go with him to a business dinner at Arrow's. You're staying in tonight, right?"

"Of course." *Where could I go?* Isobel thought. *I don't have a license and my best friend is mad at me . . .*

"Good. I'll check in as often as I can. These guys we're meeting can be pretty intense, but don't worry—I won't forget about you."

Isobel smiled but it felt forced. "Okay," she said.

She found both her mother and Catherine in the kitchen, drinking coffee.

"There you are," her mother said. "I was wondering where you'd gone off to."

Isobel shrugged. "Well, here I am."

"Do you want something to eat?"

"No, that's okay. I had a big lunch," she lied.

"So, where were you? Were you out with Jeff?"

"Yeah."

"How is he doing?" Catherine asked.

"Fine."

Isobel wished she hadn't come into the kitchen She felt trapped, like a prisoner being questioned by her captors.

"Oh, by the way," she blurted, completely without intention, "I've decided I'm not going to take my driver's permit test next week."

"But why?" her mother asked. "Haven't you been studying?"

Isobel shrugged. "Oh, I memorized the entire book. It's not that. I just don't feel the need to drive yet, that's all."

Her mother looked seriously puzzled. "But Isobel, it's impossible to get around without a car. How many times have you reminded me of that? And you've asked me, about a bazillion times I might add, if you could get a car of your own for your next birthday."

Isobel didn't reply. Sometimes, she thought, silence is really the best policy. Especially when you were lying.

Catherine cleared her throat. "Forgive me if I'm overstepping my bounds, Isobel, but are you scared of driving? It can seem pretty daunting when you're starting out."

"Oh no," she said quickly. "That's not it."

"Well," her mother said, with a shrug, "I can't force you. But I also can't be your chauffeur forever."

"I know," Isobel said. "It's no big deal."

Isobel hurriedly left the kitchen before she could dig herself any deeper into a pile of lies and stupidity. She was at the foot of the stairs when the doorbell rang. "I'll get it," she called back to the kitchen. The front door was always unlocked during the day. The guests should know that, but maybe it was someone inquiring about the inn's rates . . .

Isobel pulled open the door to find Gwen standing there. It was the first time since they had become friends that she hadn't just walked in.

"Oh," Isobel said. "Hi."

"I can't stay," Gwen said, remaining where she was, on the threshold. "I just thought you should know that someone has been sending me threatening texts."

Isobel felt her shoulders twitch. "Since . . . Since when?" she asked.

"Two days ago."

Isobel saw now that her friend's eyes looked haunted, wary. "That's awful, Gwen," she said, her voice catching. "I'm so sorry."

"Yeah."

"But I don't understand. Why did you think I should I know?"

"Because we're friends."

Isobel flushed. "Well, that, of course, but—"

"You don't get it, Isobel." Gwen's voice had risen sharply. "The texts could be from someone who knows the both of us."

"Oh." The implication being that Isobel, too, might be his (or her) next victim. Was that what Gwen was saying? "What do the texts say?" she asked, though she really didn't want to know.

"I don't want to repeat them. They're—ugly."

"Who do you think they're from?" Isobel asked. Her heart had started to beat furiously.

"I don't know for sure."

"Can you guess?"

Gwen looked away.

"Did you tell your parents?" Isobel asked, afraid to know the answer to this question, too.

"No," Gwen said. "Not yet."

Not so very long ago Isobel would have urged Gwen to go to her parents. But things were different now. She herself was keeping so much from her mother . . .

"Just ignore the texts," she said, with a lot more conviction than she felt. "It's probably just a stupid joke, anyway."

"Yeah. Maybe. Still . . ."

"Yeah."

"I gotta go." Gwen turned and walked rapidly back out to her car.

"Be careful," Isobel called as she drove off, but Gwen's windows were up and she doubted Gwen heard her.

Isobel closed the door. She wanted to lock it, bar it, but it was still early and guests expected to find an open door and a welcome.

"Please," she whispered to no one. "Please don't let it be him, please."

She thought of the waiter Jeff had tortured earlier, of the horrible name he had called that woman driver, of how he had accused her of flirting with someone at that awful party they had gone to, of the critical things he had said about Gwen and her family. There was violence in him, something more than just impatience or high spirits.

Isobel took a few deep breaths and willed herself back to reason. Her suspicions were out of proportion; the scant evidence she had was faulty; the suspicions were totally groundless.

They had to be.

She heard Catherine taking her leave. She didn't want to face anyone right now. She couldn't. Catherine usually came and went through the back door but just in case . . . Isobel ran up the stairs and locked her bedroom door behind her.

Chapter 43

Louise was passing by the breakfast room when the sound of a familiar male voice stopped her. She knew that Isobel was in there, setting the tables for the next morning. She hadn't known that Jeff had come by.

No matter. She began to walk on when something Jeff was saying made her freeze. No, she thought, it couldn't be. "Your mother's friend, Catherine..." and then, "everyone in town knows she's a whore..." finally, "I can prove it if I have to."

Isobel was speaking now. Louise listened hard but couldn't make out her daughter's murmured response.

Shaken, she hurried on toward the library where she sank into a chair. Jeff was a nice guy. He had apologized to Catherine for the incident with Charlie. He had brought Louise flowers and candy. There was no way he could have spoken the words she thought she had heard. She had misheard, and badly. Louise felt ashamed of herself, not only for accusing Jeff without real proof but also because if indeed he hadn't said those awful things she had heard—or thought she had heard—then the words had actually been a product of her own overworked mind.

Still, she would have to confront Isobel. She had to know for sure if what she had thought she had heard was what had really been said. If it was, Isobel was sure to be horrified and angry. But would Isobel tell her the truth? She had lied about other things this summer . . .

Louise waited in an agony of impatience for Jeff to leave, and as soon as he did, she went in search of her daughter. Isobel was in the kitchen. Louise noted that she was again wearing something ordinary, which was extraordinary for Isobel—a navy T-shirt and a pair of chinos Louise hadn't even known Isobel owned. Still, it didn't unduly concern her. Young people, especially creative, passionate people like Isobel, tended to adopt habits and trends and then drop them just as easily as they had acquired them.

"Isobel," she said, "I have to ask you a question."

Isobel shrugged. "Okay."

"When Jeff was here just now, did he say anything about Catherine? Anything—unpleasant?"

There was a clatter as the spoon that Isobel had been holding dropped to the floor. "What?" she said.

Louise bent down, picked up the spoon, and put it in the sink. "Well," she went on, carefully, "I was in the hall just outside the breakfast room and I couldn't help but overhear—"

Isobel cut her off; her voice was raised to an unnatural pitch. "He absolutely did not say anything bad about Catherine! How could you think that he would? How could you think that I would let him?"

"I didn't think that he would," Louise protested. "Frankly, I was shocked. I figured I must have misheard. It's just that—"

"And how could you eavesdrop on us?"

"I'm sorry, Isobel," Louise said, and she meant it. "I didn't set out to listen to a private conversation, really. But when I caught—"

"When *you thought* you caught—"

"Okay, when I thought I caught Jeff saying something hateful about my friend . . ."

"You felt you had to question me about it."

"Well, yes," Louise admitted. "You would do the same, I'm sure, if you thought you heard someone speaking badly about Gwen."

"Thanks a lot, Mom. Really. Your trust is greatly appreciated."

Louise had never seen Isobel so angry; her face was aflame with color. She supposed her anger was justified. Still, it was distressing to witness—and even more distressing to know she had been the cause of the anger.

"I'm sorry," she said again. "Please, let's try to forget this ever happened."

Isobel shook her head as if in disgust and stalked toward the kitchen door. At the last moment she turned.

"By the way," she announced, "I'm thinking about getting a tattoo."

"A tattoo?" Louise repeated stupidly. "I thought you hated the whole idea."

Isobel shrugged. "That was then. This is now."

Isobel had never spoken so disrespectfully. *God*, Louise thought, *my innocent snooping really hurt her, and badly.*

"Well, I'm not sure how I feel about—" she began, but she was interrupted by a call from Flora Michaels. The woman's timing, like everything else about her, was uncannily bad.

Louise sighed. "I'm sorry, Isobel. I have to take this. We'll talk later."

Without a reply, Isobel left the kitchen.

Louise dealt with the wedding planner with as much grace as she could muster, which was not a lot, particularly considering she seemed to have called simply to shout out a bad mood. Finally, Flora Michaels's spleen was entirely vented and she ended the call, leaving Louise free to worry about something much closer to home. Her daughter.

Well, she thought, there were a hell of a lot of worse things Isobel could do than get a tattoo. As long as the image was nothing violent or grotesque or vulgar. Tattoos were no big deal these days. Practically everyone had one, from bikers to stay-at-home mommies.

Still, the tattoo issue wasn't the most worrisome thing, not compared to Isobel's decision to postpone her driver's test. In spite of what Isobel had told Catherine, maybe she was afraid to get behind the wheel . . . But why not just admit that she was afraid?

Louise sighed. So much seemed uncertain these days. What she had overheard that morning . . . If she had been right, it was an awful, disgusting thing to say about Catherine and patently untrue. But if her own mind had come up with those revolting accusations, well, that was even more disturbing. Stress could do terrible things to a person; look at the resurgence of the nightmare. It could make a person paranoid and suspicious of good people; it could cause her to form ugly thoughts about a loved one.

Louise rubbed her temples. She wondered if she should see a therapist once this awful wedding was history. She decided it might not be a bad idea.

Chapter 44

Isobel sat slumped in the chair at her desk, laptop closed in front of her. She rubbed her temples, but the pain in her head didn't budge. The questions and comments from her readers were piling up, but she just couldn't muster the energy to answer, not even the energy to thank a reader for taking the time to reach out.

She was glad that Jeff was coming to pick her up; she needed a change of scenery. Her bedroom, the entire inn, felt tainted somehow, like a prison, someplace alien and unsafe. Only weeks before it had felt like a refuge . . .

Not that being with Jeff was that much better. Lately, his behavior had been increasingly erratic. But in a weird way she almost didn't care. She felt so enervated she almost didn't care what he did or whom he insulted or what he said to her about her general incompetence.

She heard Jeff's car pull into the drive and went down to meet him. This afternoon, he seemed to be in a good mood. At least, he wasn't speeding (yet) and he hadn't spoken ill about anyone she loved (yet). They drove in silence for a bit. Isobel wondered where they were going but didn't ask.

"I want you to see my home," Jeff announced suddenly.

"Really?" Isobel said. "Wow." The news pleased her, though not as much as it once might have. "Thanks."

Jeff looked over at her and grinned. "For what?"

Isobel didn't answer. Before long they had turned on to a

long private road, perfectly paved, at the end of which stood the Ottens' house. Isobel's breath was taken away. It was truly beautiful, a rambling yet majestic old stone building with an enormous porch wrapped around three sides and two turrets soaring into the sky from the third story. The Atlantic shimmered and undulated in the background. The sheer drama of the scene—the azure of the sky, the sparkling navy of the sea, the deep green of the lawn—had a strong effect on Isobel. She felt more alive than she had in weeks.

"You grew up here?" she asked when they had gotten out of the car. "With this magnificent view of the ocean?"

"Yeah."

"Wow. It's like something out of a fairy tale, but better."

Jeff laughed. "You're too easily impressed, Izzy. This is nothing compared to what I'm going to have in ten years' time."

He led her around the back of the house first. There was a tennis court and an in-ground pool overlooked by a deck with an entire kitchen (not just a grill) and bar, and cushioned lounge chairs and small tables and standing heaters and a big fire pit.

"You didn't tell me you had a pool!" Isobel exclaimed. "Do you use it much?"

Jeff shrugged. "Not anymore. When I'm not working, I'm with you. We could go for a dip later if you want," he said.

"Oh, but I didn't bring my bathing suit."

Jeff grinned. "So what?"

"That's okay," Isobel said quickly. "I'm not really in the mood to go swimming. By the way, where's your mom?" If Mrs. Otten was around, there was no way he could force her to go skinny-dipping. Not that she would allow herself to be forced to do anything she didn't want to do but . . . Jeff could be persuasive.

"In Boston," Jeff said. "She goes down about twice a month to see some old friends."

"Oh. That's nice. I'd like to meet her someday."

Jeff gave Isobel a look she couldn't interpret.

"What's wrong?" she asked timidly.

"Nothing," he replied. "Except that I don't plan on introducing anyone to my parents other than my fiancée. Frankly, they don't even know you exist."

Isobel felt stung. And stupid.

Jeff suddenly laughed. "Don't worry. You stand a very good chance of being a member of the Otten family someday."

"Oh."

"You don't believe me?"

"Of course I believe you," Isobel said. What else was there to say?

"Good. Just go on being my good little Izzy."

They went inside then, and Jeff told her that the staff had the afternoon off. He led her through room after room on the first floor—a beautifully appointed morning room (his mother's domain), formal dining room, enormous kitchen, a living room with three couches, and finally into what Jeff called the study (his father's domain). One wall contained floor-to-ceiling bookshelves. Another wall was almost entirely covered with awards, official photographs, and framed diplomas. Isobel quickly scanned them and saw only the names and images of Jack Otten and his elder son. Both, she noted, were very good-looking men. Before she could ask where Jeff's awards were, he took her arm and led her out of the room. They were now in a hall, the walls of which were hung with paintings and prints. Just in front of her was a gorgeous framed print in brilliant, jewel-like colors. It looked Arabic but Isobel didn't know enough about art of the eastern world to place it in time or style with any accuracy at all.

"Do you ever travel on business to Dubai with your dad?" she asked.

"Where?"

"Dubai. You said your father travels to Dubai on business."

"Oh yeah," Jeff said. "No. I don't like traveling outside the United States."

"Really?" Isobel said. "I want to travel everywhere. Europe, Asia, the Middle East. I'd love to go to Israel someday. Of course, there's a whole lot of the U.S. I'd like to visit, too. The Grand Canyon, San Francisco, New Orleans."

Jeff didn't respond.

"My mom heard that your brother lives in Switzerland," Isobel went on. "Did you ever visit him?"

Now Jeff did respond, and his expression darkened into a scowl.

"I told you never to mention him."

"Oh. But I thought—"

"You're not supposed to think!" Jeff shouted. He took a step closer to Isobel, his face now red with fury. "You're supposed to do what I say."

"I want to go home now," Isobel said. She was surprised she had the nerve to speak; she hated that her voice was trembling.

Jeff took another step closer. "We all want things we can't have," he said harshly.

"My mother is expecting me."

Jeff laughed. "Your mother abandoned you for that stupid wedding. She wouldn't notice if you were missing for days."

Isobel gasped; she felt as if she had been punched in the stomach. "How dare you say that about my—"

"Shut up!"

His fist slammed into the wall just to the left of her head, hard enough to cause the gorgeous Arabic print to tilt wildly. And then he stormed off down the hallway.

She didn't know why—she was in shock, she was afraid, she felt sick—but Isobel followed him closely enough to see him bolt out the front door and slam it behind him.

She watched through the window in the door as he drove off, abandoning her.

She heard a whimper and realized that it came from her own throat. "Don't cry, don't cry, don't cry." She chanted the words dumbly, and after a moment or two she felt some bit of sense return to her.

She had no idea when Jeff would return, or even if he would return. The staff was out, as were Jeff's parents. It was too far for her to walk home and too dangerous with summer highway traffic.

She was trapped. She felt another whimper rising in her throat.

No, Isobel told herself, summoning every bit of courage she had left. She could not succumb to panic. She would not. She was not trapped; she was not Jeff's prisoner. She had a brain. She would use it.

She could call her mother or Catherine or James or Jim or even Flynn to come and get her. Sure.

And then she would have to explain why she was alone at Jeff's house. She would have to tell them what had happened, the whole story, right from the start—or she would have to lie. Again.

It did not occur to her to call the police.

Isobel stood in the massive front hall of the Otten house as if bolted to the floor. The nasty things Jeff had said about Catherine at the inn came roaring back to her. Her mother had overheard correctly. But Isobel had lied to protect Jeff. Or had she lied to protect herself? What, she wondered now, would he have done to her if she had told her mother the truth? What would he do to her now if she told anyone the truth? Because Jeff would find out that she had betrayed him. She was sure of that.

She could not call anyone for help. That was just the way it was. Isobel felt a deadly inertia overcome her as she waited, miserably, for Jeff to return.

When he did return, almost two hours later, Isobel was sitting on the front steps of the house. Her heart began to race, painfully, when she saw his car approach up the drive.

She wondered if a sixteen-year-old could have a heart attack. She stood abruptly when he got out of the car, the better to run if she had to run. Though why she hadn't run away earlier she just didn't know.

Yes, she did know. She was Jeff's prisoner whether he was there with her or not.

Jeff walked slowly toward her. His expression was unreadable; that was nothing new.

"Look," he said without preamble, "I'm sorry I stormed off earlier."

Isobel couldn't open her mouth. She thought she smelled alcohol on his breath, but she couldn't be sure what was real with Jeff and what she was imagining.

"I had to blow off steam," he went on. "You wouldn't have wanted me to stay, would you? You made me so mad I thought I was going to punch you. I did you a favor by getting out of here, you know. You should be grateful that I care so much."

"I'm sorry," Isobel said. She wondered why she was apologizing. She dared not admit to him that she was frightened. She suspected it would only make him angry again. But anything might make him angry again . . .

In the space of a few weeks Jeff had become an entirely unknown quantity, unpredictable and threatening. Maybe he had been that way all along and she just hadn't seen the truth. Oh, but why hadn't she seen the truth? How could she have been so mistaken about him?

"I'll take you home now," Jeff announced.

Isobel was afraid to get in the car with him, and afraid not to. She wondered if she would make it back to the inn or if there would be an accident. If he had really been drinking, if he did still want to hurt her, would he instead take her someplace isolated where no one could hear her scream . . . Isobel clicked the seat belt into place and gripped the strap over her shoulder.

Jeff started the car. "We're cool, right?" he said, staring hard at her.

Isobel had to clear her throat before the word would come out. "Yes."

"Good. You know, Isobel, I don't know what I would do if anything happened to you."

"What could happen to me?" she said, with a sick and aborted attempt at a laugh.

"Anything. Anything can happen to anyone. Life's a crap-shoot, Izzy. Don't ever forget that."

Neither one spoke on the drive home. When they pulled up outside the inn, Jeff leaned over to kiss her. Isobel's deepest instinct was to pull away but she fought it. As long as she was in the car she was still under his control. She kissed him back, feeling repulsed and dirty.

When he had roared off, Isobel ran upstairs to the bathroom she shared with her mother and locked the door behind her. Her hands were trembling. She caught a glimpse of her face in the mirror above the sink. She didn't recognize herself.

Izzy.

She was violently sick to her stomach.

Chapter 45

Louise was in the library, reorganizing the tourist pamphlets and tidying the bookshelves. A familiar footfall in the hall made her look up.

"Isobel?"

Her daughter came into the room.

"You look tired," Louise said. "Do you feel okay?"

Isobel shrugged. "I'm fine. I just didn't sleep well."

"Oh. Sorry about that. I hope you didn't inherit that habit from me."

Isobel half-smiled.

"Are you still thinking of getting a tattoo?"

Isobel shrugged again. "No. Maybe. I don't know."

"Because I won't forbid you. I just want to be involved with finding a reputable place."

"Don't worry about it. It was just something I said."

"Okay. But if you decide to go through with it, you'll let me know?"

"Yeah. I'm going to go get something to eat," Isobel said, turning to leave the library.

Louise watched her go. Her daughter looked as if she had lost some weight—and Isobel didn't really have any extra weight to lose. Maybe one of Bella's muffins, left over from breakfast, would tempt Isobel.

Sheesh, Louise thought. This impending wedding was

really having a negative trickle-down effect on everyone at the inn. Even unflappable Quentin seemed a bit tense lately, almost wary, as if he were watching and waiting for something to happen.

Either that or her own stress was making her imagine it all.

Louise finished in the library and went back to the kitchen. If Isobel had been there, getting something to eat, she had left no trace. That was odd. She wasn't known for her neatness.

A knock at the door preceded Catherine's arrival. "You busy?" she asked.

"No, come in."

Catherine did. "I'm here for no purpose at all," she said, "except maybe for a cup of your infamous coffee."

Louise got them both a cup and they sat at the kitchen table.

"Here's something interesting," Louise said. "Isobel's always sworn she hates tattoos, but the other day she announced she was thinking about getting one."

"Well, there's nothing so odd about that, is there? People do change their minds."

"Sure," Louise admitted. "But I don't know. Lately, so much of her behavior has been—unlike her. Erratic. I mean, since when has she taken to shrugging? Shrugging is for people without the energy to come up with a real, solid something to say."

"Do you think it's something hormonal?" Catherine asked. "You know, mood swings?"

"She's never experienced mood swings before, but I guess it's possible. Lord knows I've still got them."

"Maybe something's bothering her. Have you asked? Okay, I'm sure you have."

"And she says that everything is fine. I can't force the truth from her—assuming she isn't already telling me the truth, that everything is fine, just changing."

"Change is never easy. And keep in mind even the smallest bump in the road seems monumental to a teenager."

Louise nodded. "You know, I did something the other day I know I shouldn't have done. But honestly, it was unintentional." She told Catherine about the eavesdropping; she didn't tell her the nature of what she had heard.

"No one likes her privacy violated. Especially not teenaged girls."

"I know. But still, she was so angry . . ."

"Do you think Jeff could be pushing her to get a tattoo?" Catherine asked suddenly.

"Jeff? I don't know. He doesn't strike me as the tattoo sort. Then again, everyone's the tattoo sort these days. They've become so mainstream."

"I have one," Catherine said. "Don't look so shocked. Even corporate types let loose sometimes. At least, that's what I told myself when I made the decision to get inked."

"Just tell me it's not a skull and crossbones."

"Nope. I have nothing against contemplating a skull as a *memento mori*. But I draw the line at using them for decoration. Same thing with crosses."

"Mmm. Have you noticed how Isobel's been dressing in the past few weeks?" Louise asked.

"Yeah. How could I not? But maybe she just got tired of being flamboyant and innovative. It's a lot easier to dress like everybody else is dressing. Being yourself takes a lot of work. Unless, of course, yourself is like everybody else's self . . ."

"But Isobel, tired of quirky style? It seems so unlikely."

"Jeff again?" Catherine suggested.

Louise shook her head. "I don't know. I hope not . . ."

"I think we might be looking for trouble where none exists. I'm not saying we shouldn't keep our ears and eyes open, but . . ."

"You're right." Louise sighed. "I've been letting this wedding make mush out of what I have in place of a brain."

Catherine, usually not the most demonstrative of women, leaned over and put her arm around her friend and squeezed. "You're doing a great job all around, Louise," she said. "Stop beating yourself up or you'll be no good to anyone. I mean it."

"Yeah," Louise said. "You're right. You always are."

Chapter 46

Isobel sat slumped on the edge of her bed. She felt like a failure. She felt as if she had an illness, something shameful, something she had to hide from sight or be punished for it, something for which she should be ostracized from the community of normal girls who didn't let boys treat them like dirt.

There was simply no more denying the truth. She was dating an abuser. She was dating a bully.

And the fact that her mother had always been so open about her own past with an abusive man, the fact that her mother had always taught her to tell someone about abuse immediately, made the situation that much more awful. How could she disappoint her mother? How could she tell her that the education she had given her daughter had somehow failed, that her child had become a victim?

She had defended Jeff so fiercely against her mother's accusation that he had spoken cruelly about Catherine. What she should have done—if she could have done it—was cry out to her mother for help. Instead, because she had never known what to do with her anger, she had turned it against her mother, the one person who might have saved her . . .

Isobel looked at the bracelet Jeff had given her and shuddered. She saw it now as a shackle, not as a symbol of love or affection. She saw physical evidence of a purchase—her trust, bought with money—not evidence of an act of generosity.

The bracelet and all it represented repulsed her. But she was afraid to take it off, to throw it away. If Jeff saw her without the bracelet, what might he do to her?

She saw clearly now all the disturbing incidents she had excused or rationalized. Jeff had probably even lied about volunteering at the retirement home. Could he have lied about working for his father?

Gwen had been right when she had accused Jeff of wanting her to be someone else—his toy or his puppet. His possession. His emotional prisoner.

As if in a trance, without conscious will, Isobel left her room. She walked back to the kitchen though she wasn't hungry and she didn't want to see her mother, who so often could be found there. But she did want to see her mother. To be sure she was safe.

Her mother was unloading the dishwasher. "Hey," she said.

Isobel managed a smile. "Hi."

Louise closed the door of the dishwasher with a sigh. "Why is it that I hate this stupid chore so much?" she said. "It's not disgusting, like cleaning toilets. It's not even difficult, like vacuuming corners."

Isobel shrugged.

"Well, whatever. Hey, I haven't seen Gwen around much lately," her mother said, as she reached for a cup from the dish drainer. "Is she okay?"

"Yeah," Isobel said, as casually as she could manage. "She's fine. She's just busy."

Busy avoiding me, Isobel thought. Because now she was certain that those threatening texts Gwen had received had come from Jeff. She wished she knew the nature of the harm they had threatened. *Stay away from Isobel or I'll—what? Hurt you? Hurt your family?* And for all she knew Jeff might still be cyber-harassing Gwen . . . or worse.

Her mother poured coffee into her cup. "You two haven't been updating the blog as regularly."

"Yeah, we got a bit . . . It was a lot of work . . ."

"Oh." Her mother frowned. "That's too bad. I mean, it's too bad that the work wasn't enjoyable anymore. That's what you meant, right?"

"Yeah. Well, maybe someday I'll get back into it . . ."

"Oh. Well, I'm glad Gwen is okay. I miss hearing the laughter between you two."

"I didn't think you noticed me anymore," Isobel said with a shaky laugh, hating herself for sounding so pathetic. *Don't let anything show,* she demanded of herself. *Keep it hidden! Keep this madness far away. What she doesn't know can't hurt her.*

"What?" Her mother frowned. "Now, that's unfair. I know I've been crazy busy with this awful wedding, but that doesn't mean I don't pay attention to your life."

"I know. I was only kidding."

"And I'm sorry. I really will try to be more attentive. You're what's most important to me after all, not the business."

"Thanks, Mom." Isobel willed the incipient tears to go away.

Louise finished her coffee and took a set of keys from a hook on the wall by the back door. "I've got to run to the hardware store. Want to come with me?"

"No, that's okay."

Her mother left the kitchen, and a few moments later Isobel heard her drive away.

Lies upon lies upon lies, she thought. *Who knew I'd become such a consummate liar?* She hated herself for it.

Isobel listened closely for any sounds of life. There was nothing. She was alone in the inn. It wasn't unusual for the guests to be out in the daytime, enjoying the beach or shopping or having drinks and a meal at a café on the water's edge. But for the first time since she had lived at Blueberry Bay Inn, Isobel felt scared. Not so much of the emptiness but of the fact that she lived in what was essentially a public space. Just the other day she had come across a guest examining a cut-glass vase that stood on the mantel over the fireplace in the parlor. It was a vase her father had bought for her mother years earlier. Her mother loved that vase, and here was a total stranger handling it as if it were his own. She had to exert every ounce of self-control she could muster not to rush at the man and snatch the vase from his hands.

Her life was on exhibit.

She was entirely exposed. How could she ever successfully hide from Jeff? Guests—virtual strangers—were in and out all day. Any one of them could be a spy sent by Jeff Otten. Maybe that sort of thinking was paranoid, but maybe it wasn't.

She just knew he had taken her phone the other day . . .

Isobel slowly climbed the stairs to the second floor. Only weeks ago she routinely raced up and down these very same stairs. Now, she couldn't imagine ever having the energy for such exertion.

Slowly, carefully, she opened the door to her room. She stood at the threshold, hesitant to enter. The room was its characteristic mess, but she knew her room, her sanctuary. And she was sure—almost sure—that someone had been in it. There was something out of place, there was something missing. If she looked hard enough she would find the disturbance, she would find the absence . . .

Slowly, carefully, she stepped inside. Yes, something was—wrong. She wondered if her mind was now playing tricks on her. But how would she know?

How could she ever be sure?

Chapter 47

The nightmare had come again, this time more awfully than ever before.

Louise sat on her bed, her knees drawn to her chest, her arms wrapped around them. Sweat trickled down her face. She felt sick to her stomach. Because this time, before she could struggle to wake, both she and her baby had died.

She had heard once that if you died in a dream, you had really died in waking life. How ridiculous. How could such a thing be proven? Anyway, here she was, very much alive in her bed at the Blueberry Bay Inn, while in that other, brutally vivid dream world she lay dead at the foot of a flight of stairs, arms and legs sprawled awkwardly, neck turned at an impossible angle, blood seeping from her mouth.

But there she had also stood, a terrorized figure, staring down at her own unmoving, bleeding self, until that figure had screamed Louise awake.

Louise listened for movement in the hall, but there was only silence and the loud beating of her heart. Hopefully Isobel hadn't heard her scream. And James or Jim. The men had become friends, but they were also paying guests, and as such they didn't need to be exposed to the landlady's nightmares.

Thank God, she thought, stretching out her legs, which were beginning to cramp, for old, solidly built houses.

The two of them, mother and daughter, dead. Could the latest manifestation of the dream mean something new? Was her subconscious trying to tell her that there was something threatening the daughter who had survived to be born—and thereby threatening Louise?

No. She didn't believe in dreams as premonitions or psychic messengers. Her therapist, the one she had seen after the fall and miscarriage, hadn't believed that, either. He had emphasized that dreams were merely a rehashing of unresolved emotional issues. It was easier to believe that than to credit dreams with supernatural powers of a sort. But still . . .

Louise shuddered. The images had been so vivid this time, colors loud and vibrant, sounds—like her own scream—ear shattering.

She made a decision. In the late fall, after the inn had closed for the season, she would take Isobel away for a few days. Maybe they would go north to Montreal or south to New York. Any change of scenery would do them both good, and Isobel was such a good student she could afford to miss a day or two of school.

And who knew, but maybe a change of scenery would also reignite Isobel's passion for CityMouse. New shops, new sights and sounds, new stimuli might be just what Isobel needed. It did seem odd—and very disappointing—that she had so thoroughly abandoned the blog after putting so much time and effort into it for two years . . .

The headache that inevitably followed the nightmare was making itself known. Quietly, Louise went out to the bathroom for a cool cloth. There was still no sound from either room. Good. Back in her bedroom she changed into a fresh, dry nightgown and sat back against the pillows, the cool cloth on her forehead.

Yes, she and Isobel needed to get far, far away. That much, Louise knew for certain.

Chapter 48

Everyone thinks my life is so perfect. I live in a pretty little town in a charming old house with a big shady porch and a gazebo out back and a white picket fence out front. I have a big allowance. I don't have to work after school, and my grades are good enough so that I should get into any college I want. But what people see on the surface is almost never the true story. If people only knew that my life is really a hell. I don't know how I got into this hell and I have no idea how to get out of it. I—

She deleted the words immediately. No one would read them. She would go to her grave with this secret.

A surge of anger rose in Isobel's breast. This was her mother's fault. It was her mother's fault that she was trapped in this tiny town. If she still lived in Massachusetts, she could—what? Escape? Hide?

The anger died quickly, as it always did, to be replaced by a feeling of intense resignation.

With willpower she didn't know she had, Isobel left her room and carefully, cautiously, left the inn. She was as sure as she could be that no one had seen her leave. At the road she turned toward town and the public library. Cars and pickup trucks and men and women on bikes passed her, but Isobel barely noticed the traffic.

The day before Jeff had accused her of flirting with Quentin. He had backed her against a wall, loomed over her in a sick reversal of protective intimacy.

She had denied the charge vehemently. "Besides," she had added, "Quentin likes Gwen. He has no interest in me."

"No guy could possibly like Gwen," he had replied with an expression of revulsion. "Not even that loser Quentin. She's fat and weird."

Now Isobel was scared for Quentin, too. Quentin was strong but Jeff was big, and where Quentin would fight fair if forced to fight at all, Jeff would fight dirty. About that, she had no doubt at all.

Since the day he had left her prisoner in his home, Jeff's bad behavior had escalated. Now there was no softening of the blows, no reversal of a harsh verdict like there had been earlier in the relationship. He spoke unapologetically now, and Isobel had come to realize that all those reversals and explanations he had offered had been sops, meant to fool her into believing that he was someone he was not. A normal person.

Twenty minutes after leaving the inn, Isobel turned onto the path before the charming stone building that now held no charm for her. She was pretty sure that Jeff never used the library. In the weeks she had known him, she had never seen him with a book or heard him mention one he was reading. Still, she glanced over her shoulder before entering the library, afraid that she had been followed, if not by Jeff himself then by one of the friends she had never met or heard of.

"Isobel, hello," the librarian, Nancy, said, with a welcoming smile.

Isobel forced a smile to her own face. "Hi."

"How's your mother holding up with this big wedding looming? The whole town is talking about it."

"Just fine, thank you."

"That's good news. Can I help you find a book?"

"No, thanks. I just need . . . I mean, I want to use a computer, if that's okay."

Nancy directed Isobel to a computer and went back to her desk. Isobel wondered if the librarian would trace her online history once she had gone. Maybe she was required to; Isobel just didn't know. But the possibility frightened her. She debated abandoning her search for information that might help her out of the horrible situation in which she found herself. But somehow, she screwed up her courage and stayed. If someone confronted her about being where she was and doing what she was doing, she could always lie. She could say that she was researching information for a friend back in Massachusetts.

It took about thirty seconds for Isobel to realize that there were hundreds of websites devoted to domestic abuse in all of its forms. Where to begin? "At the beginning," Isobel murmured, choosing the first site on the list.

Twenty minutes later, Isobel felt hot and dizzy. There was so much information. Some of it could be helpful, depending. Some of it was not helpful at all. Several of the websites she had already glanced at advised a victim—or a person who thought she might be a victim—to use her intuition. Isobel almost laughed out loud at that. She had ignored her intuition for so long that it had finally fled, abandoning her to a constant state of doubt and confusion.

Other websites advised a victim to tell a friend about the abuse. But that well-meaning bit of advice was also useless to Isobel. If she told a friend about Jeff's behavior, then that friend—Gwen or Catherine, even Flynn or The Jimmies—might also become one of Jeff's victims. He was a vindictive person, she knew that now, and emotionally unstable.

Yet another website demanded in no uncertain terms that the victim "get out of the abusive relationship!" This time, a chuckle did escape Isobel. Well, that was easier said than done! Who had written that spectacularly unhelpful and insulting bit of "advice"? If she knew how to get out of the abusive relationship, she wouldn't be crouched over the public library's computer, looking for answers to that desperate question!

Isobel shut her eyes and tried to steady her breathing. There was no point in getting angry now . . . After a moment she opened her eyes and clicked on yet another website.

"A large portion of men and women who experience rape or physical violence first do so when they are between the ages of eleven and seventeen."

Isobel read this statistic and felt the panic rise in her chest. Oh God, she thought. Was there a way for people like her to avoid the fate of being abused as an adult? There had to be. Her mother seemed to have avoided it but maybe her mother was hiding things from her, like she had been hiding things from her mother . . . Could her father have abused her mother, too, not just that long-ago boyfriend? No. Isobel couldn't bear to think about it. If that were the truth, it would surely kill her.

With every ounce of will she possessed, she forced herself to read on.

The bad stuff, she discovered, was even closer than far-off adulthood. Victims of teen dating violence were more likely to do poorly in school; to binge drink; to attempt suicide. And—this was appalling—many of the victims grew up to act violently as adults.

Isobel felt sweat prickle under her arms. So, chances were good she might become a victim once again or, a fate even more awful to contemplate, become an abuser herself. Was her future preordained, all because she had accidentally bumped into this charming, deceptively powerful person . . .

Or had something in her past already sealed her fate, some fatal flaw of character with which she had come into this world? Did the fact that her mother had been abused by a boyfriend condemn Isobel to the same future?

It was all so horribly confusing and so very, very depressing. And yet, Isobel pressed on. Knowledge was power; she believed that. Or she once had believed that . . .

Abuse, she read, could be a learned behavior. Often, the abuser was simply following in a parent's footsteps. Did Jeff's father, Jack Otten, abuse his wife? Was that where Jeff had learned how to bully someone he supposedly cared for? If that were the case, it would take some of the blame away from Jeff. It wouldn't exonerate him, but it might help explain why he had been treating Isobel so badly.

But what if there was no abuse at home for Jeff to mimic? What if Mr. Otten treated his wife beautifully? What if some people were simply born bad? What if Jeff had no real reason for behaving the way he did; what if he just believed that he had a right to do whatever he wanted to do? Was there any hope for such a person? Was such a person suffering from a certifiable ego disorder? Was it evidence of psychosis or of something much worse—evidence of evil?

Before that moment Isobel had never, ever given serious thought to the notion of evil. Before now she had associated the word with superstition and a Dark Ages sort of ignorance and gory, exploitive horror films. In short, she had dismissed the notion of evil as an unpleasant, destructive fiction.

Now, she wasn't so sure.

There was one more bit of research she wanted to accomplish. With another look over her shoulder to be sure that no one was watching her, she typed in the words *restraining order*. She had heard her mother telling anyone who would listen that a restraining order wasn't a magic bullet. Still, it might be better than no protection at all, so she learned where and how to get one. She learned what security it could and could not provide.

And then she thought: When Jeff learned that she had taken out a restraining order against him, wouldn't it make him even more furious and more likely to hurt her? Hadn't she just learned from her reading that any resistance, any show of independence, was likely to drive an abuser to more violence?

Isobel rubbed her forehead. If only there was someone she could turn to who could fix this awful situation, someone who could pluck her safely and forever out of harm's way, someone beyond the range of Jeff's frightening influence.

Someone like her father? Would he come to her rescue? No. He would not. Because, Isobel reminded herself ruthlessly, he had two other little girls to love, and a new baby on the way. He had effectively abandoned Isobel, after duping her for almost an entire year, so why would she even imagine turning to him in a crisis, like she had when she was a child? She was angry with herself for this weakness. Her father was a coward. A person didn't become a hero unless he wanted to become a hero.

Isobel shut down the computer. She felt more frightened and less hopeful than she had before she had done the research.

She thought that the librarian looked at her keenly as she passed the front desk with a quick wave of farewell. Did she know? Could she tell? She felt a crazy urge to stop and blurt the truth to Nancy but knew that it would only draw another innocent person into the web of danger. Isobel had become toxic.

Once out on the sidewalk, she peered warily up and down the street for any sign of Jeff. She would get home the way she had come, though the journey along the long stretches of narrow, winding road was dangerous. She simply couldn't risk Jeff seeing her in a car with anyone and taking out his anger on him—or on her.

The sidewalk was teeming with happy tourist families, wearing brightly colored T-shirts, eating ice-cream cones, and carrying Boogieboards. The contrast between the care-free vacationers and herself, caught in a hellish trap, felt too enormous to bear.

She stumbled; she wasn't even aware that she had taken a step. A hand reached out and grabbed her arm. With a cry, she jerked her arm away.

"Sorry," the old man said, his face flushed with sunburn or embarrassment. "I thought you were going to fall."

Isobel mumbled words resembling "thank you" and turned toward home.

Chapter 49

Her eyes were rimmed in red. The skin around them looked bruised. The rest of her face was pale.

It had been a bad night, worse than ever. The dream had come in another new and ghastly form. This time, Louise had seen Isobel's teenaged face on the dead baby. It was by far the most appalling version of the nightmare yet. Louise honestly didn't know how she could survive anything worse.

She had stumbled down to the kitchen that morning, earlier than usual, in desperate need of coffee. Three cups and several hours later, she felt no better.

Catherine, who had just come by, confirmed that Louise looked as bad as she felt.

"You look awful. Sorry, but you do. Are you sick?"

"No," Louise said, too tired to take offense at her friend's honest though blunt comment. After all, Bella had said much the same thing. "I just didn't sleep well. Again. It's the stress of this wedding."

"Speaking of which . . ."

"Did you talk to Calvin Streep?" Louise asked. She hadn't had the nerve or the energy to fight Flora Michaels's assistant the day before when he had issued a particularly outrageous demand. She had complained about his behavior to Catherine; Catherine had asked for his contact information and promised to "set things straight." Louise had not protested her assistance.

Catherine laughed. "Oh, I talked to him."

"And?"

"And he's a pompous little ass. But don't worry. Everything is settled. In your favor, of course."

Louise put her hand to her heart. "Oh Catherine, what a relief! I don't know how to thank you."

"You should have asked me for help with this sort of thing before now. Those two have been completely out of control with their crazy demands."

"I wanted to do it all on my own," Louise admitted.

"That's usually not a good way to do business."

"Now I know."

"Yes. Now you do. Well, I can't stay. My car is out front, with Charlie in it. I'm taking her to the vet. I get so disgustingly nervous, even when it's just a routine checkup. Charlie is calm as a cucumber while Mommy sweats and shakes."

Louise smiled. "The parenting instinct is strong. The thought of our child in pain is almost unbearable."

"Maybe it's a good thing I never had a baby. I'd be dead of a heart attack before her third birthday and she'd spend most of her life in therapy as a consequence."

With that final lugubrious comment Catherine left. Louise didn't realize how Catherine's presence had helped calm her until she was gone. The memory of the nightmare wasn't the only thing bothering her. Andrew had sent her an e-mail the afternoon before with an excuse (work was crazy; he had had a bad cold) for not having been in more touch with Isobel. She had lost her temper and shot back an angry and unconsidered reply, to which there had been no response. Well, Andrew was a smart man; self-preservation was high on his list of priorities.

It should be high on her list of priorities, as well. But how to banish the macabre image of Isobel's current face where the baby's should have been? She knew it would haunt her forever; eventually it might destroy her.

Louise gasped. She thought she had seen movement just

outside the kitchen door. Cautiously, she peered through the window, but there was no one and nothing there.

She knew beyond a doubt that something in her life was very wrong. But exactly what was very wrong was maddeningly beyond her grasp.

Chapter 50

Isobel lay in her bed, curled up in a fetal position. She would have to join her mother and Jeff in the kitchen soon. (He had dropped by unannounced, and her mother had invited him to stay.) Already, her mother had knocked on her door, urging her to come down for dinner.

Slowly, she sat up. This was no way to live a life, that much she knew. She had been living in a state of constant fear since the day Jeff had abandoned her at his house. Since then, she had learned very quickly to read his smallest gesture, like a dog with a cruel and inconsistent master, always looking for a clue that would tell him whether to flinch, cringe, roll over, or run away.

Because what did you do when you were afraid of something and you wanted desperately to survive it—and you knew that you couldn't or wouldn't simply run away from it? You watched it. You studied it. You hoped to eventually know enough to outsmart it.

Since that day Jeff had been hinting that he had been watching her more closely. "Paying more attention to her" was what he said, but Isobel knew what that meant. Jeff was spying on her. At least, he wanted her to think that he was. She didn't know for sure if he had found out about her library search. She didn't think he would believe her if she told him she had been trying to help a friend in need. Not with his suspicious mind . . .

But the spying wasn't the worst thing. Earlier that day, at his house, Jeff had forced her to perform oral sex on him. She had been afraid to say no. He was rough during the act; her neck and shoulders ached from his grip. When it was done, he told her how good she had been and had held her close.

She had been rigid with fear in his arms.

"You know I love you, Izzy, right?" he had whispered in her ear.

"Mmm."

Jeff's grip had tightened. "I said, right?"

"Right," she had managed to whisper.

"And you love me, right?"

"Right."

But this wasn't love at all.

With her will in tatters, Isobel went down to the kitchen.

"Finally," Jeff said.

Isobel took her seat between them.

"Did Isobel tell you she's no longer writing her blog?" Jeff asked as he helped himself to a second serving of green beans.

"Yes," Louise replied. "She said it was becoming too much. Right?"

Isobel nodded.

Jeff turned to her. His expression was a mix of bemusement and concern. "I have to say, I was totally surprised when you told me," he said. "I never thought you'd give up the blog. It meant so much to you and we had talked about your plans for expansion."

Isobel was almost impressed. Jeff was brilliant in the role of innocent boyfriend, expressing concern for his girlfriend, being nice to the mother he had accused of abandoning her daughter. Who was she to equal his skill?

Jeff was saying something. Her mother was laughing.

Isobel poked at her food. Everything felt surreal. She wanted to leap from the table and shout, "Stop! It's all a lie!"

She wanted to curl up and die. It would be so much simpler than fighting on . . .

Quentin came through the kitchen door just then, carrying a tool case. His right eye was almost swollen shut; the bruise was angry, black, purple, and red, and covered almost all of his cheek.

Isobel gasped. She knew absolutely that Jeff was responsible for Quentin's injury.

"Oh my God," her mother cried. "What happened?"

Quentin turned partly away. "It's nothing. Got careless."

"You should be more careful," Jeff said, jocularly. "You don't strike me as the clumsy sort, but appearances can be deceiving, right?"

Quentin's lips thinned into what could be interpreted as a smile or a frown or a grimace.

"Do you want an ice pack?" Louise asked. "I can—"

"No." Quentin's answer was abrupt. "Thanks. I'm going to fix that drain upstairs now." He left the kitchen as quickly as he had entered.

"You know," Jeff said, leaning confidentially toward Isobel's mother, "if that Quentin fellow isn't working out, I know a few guys you might hire."

Isobel literally leapt from the table. "I need to use the bathroom," she said. She ran to the powder room and locked the door behind her. Her heart was racing. She leaned against the wall for support; her entire body was trembling.

Gwen. Catherine. Quentin. Jeff hated them all. Only Isobel stood between her friends and more violence against them, verbal or physical. How had she become the protector of everyone she loved? In only weeks she had become an adult before her time and in a way she had never thought possible. It wasn't right. It wasn't supposed to be this way.

When she went back to the kitchen, her mother was still sitting at the table with Jeff. They were eating ice cream.

"I don't feel very well," Isobel said from the doorway. She

couldn't look either her mother or Jeff in the eye. "I'm going up to bed."

"What you need is a good night's rest," Jeff said solicitously. "I'll check in with you later."

That night Isobel had lain awake trying to imagine a way to break away from Jeff. She couldn't. Every scenario she constructed ended in his successful pursuit. Even if she waited until she turned eighteen and could legally disappear into a big city, change her name if necessary . . . Jeff would still find her. He had the power.

And all night long he had sent her e-mails and text messages in which he made it clear he didn't believe she was sick. He warned her not to betray him. He reminded her of what they had done at his house the day before. He told her of what other things they were going to do, soon.

Morning finally dawned. Isobel was both grateful (she could stop pretending to herself that she was capable of sleep) and fearful (it was another day in which she would have to see and deal with Jeff).

She went down to the kitchen though she wasn't in the least bit hungry. If her mother was around she would try to eat something for the sake of appearance.

Her mother was there.

"Are you feeling better this morning, Isobel?" she asked, a frown of concern on her face.

"Fine," Isobel said. "Must have been a twelve-hour virus or something."

"Can I make you some eggs?"

"No, thanks. I'll . . . I'll just have some toast or something."

She took two slices of bread from the bread box and stuck them in the toaster.

"I've been thinking about going out west for college," she said, her back to her mother. "Maybe California or Seattle."

"What? First of all," her mother said, "you're only going

to be a junior this fall. It's a bit early to be making decisions about college, isn't it? And second, I thought you wanted to stay on the East Coast, near me. And your father."

"It's never too early to think about college," Isobel countered, turning now to face her mother. "And besides, I've been thinking. I want a big change in my life. Change is good, right? Look how we left our life in Massachusetts and moved to Maine because you wanted a fresh start."

"Well, that wasn't quite the same . . ."

"Why wasn't it the same?" she challenged.

But her mother's phone announced that someone else demanded her attention.

"It's Flora Michaels," Louise said with a sigh of annoyance. "We'll talk about college plans some other time. I've got to deal with this."

Her mother left the kitchen, phone to her ear.

The toast popped. Isobel put the pieces of bread on a plate and left the kitchen. She heard her mother's voice from the library. For the first time she realized that the only person in her life Jeff had never vilified—except for that once, the first time at his house—was her mother. In fact, she had asked him the other day why he never called her Izzy when they were with her mother. He had said that using her full name was a sign of respect.

Isobel had wondered what exactly he had meant by that but hadn't bothered to ask.

Jeff texted her.

She responded immediately. She had to.

Chapter 51

Louise was exhausted. She had been afraid to sleep the night before, afraid to be swept into the nightmare that grew increasingly dark and dangerous with each manifestation.

She had sat vigil over her sanity until against her most strenuous will she fell into a light sleep around 5 a.m. Her alarm clock woke her at six thirty, rousing her from a vague waking dream involving a bride in a tattered dress and, for some reason she couldn't understand, Andrew in a chef's coat, fixing the bride dinner.

She was in the kitchen, watching a news show, when Isobel came in.

"Bella made scones this morning," she said to her daughter. "Cinnamon and raspberry."

"That's okay. I'm not really hungry."

"Just letting you know that I've got my eye on the last cinnamon one, so if you're going to change your mind you'd better change it fast."

Isobel smiled a bit and took a seat at the table. "That's okay. You can have it."

"Oh, I want to hear this." Louise raised the volume on the TV. Kathleen Shannon of Channel 6 in Portland was doing a story about domestic violence; the story highlighted the city's social services for abused women and advised women in trouble on how to get a restraining order and otherwise seek help.

At the commercial break, Louise lowered the volume again. "It's just so sad," she said. "But I guess there will always be abusers out there. I'm not naïve enough to think otherwise."

Isobel didn't respond.

"Are you okay?" Louise asked, finding Isobel's silence unnerving. Usually, she was such a chatterbox.

"Fine," Isobel said.

"I know it's hard to listen to these stories. It's hard not to feel some of the pain and shame those women feel. And the anger and the fear."

Isobel nodded.

Louise looked back to the television and raised the volume. The weatherman was predicting rain. "I feel bad that I haven't had time to volunteer since we moved to Maine," she said. "I should be out there helping other women."

Isobel suddenly stood, bumping against the table and rattling the spoon in her mother's empty cereal bowl. "I forgot I left my laptop open," she said, and dashed out of the kitchen.

Louise's phone chirped. There was a text from Flora Michaels. Could there be little marzipan pigs the flower girl could scatter like petals as she walked the aisle, she wanted to know. Louise supposed it was possible and texted back that she would speak to the owner of Harbor Candy Shop about the special request.

Another text a moment later specified that the little marzipan pigs should be black. Was black the cool color for brides this season? Louise wondered. Either way, it was a harmless enough, if bizarre, desire.

The universal appeal of weddings . . . Even if you weren't personally acquainted with the bride and groom, you couldn't help but marvel at how a couple entered marriage with such enthusiasm. It was human nature to seek the positive. And it was also human nature, Louise thought now, to display a sort of arrogance about the future. I'll be smarter, I'll have more patience; he'll never hit me, she'll never leave me.

Louise cleared away her breakfast things. Had Isobel eaten anything at all that morning?

Someday Isobel might marry, Louise mused; it seemed likely, given her romantic nature. And she would display the same giddy certainty that all would be well in her married life.

Louise turned on the dishwasher and went to the broom closet for the broom and dustpan. Jeff Otten, she thought, as she began to sweep under the table, was certainly a nice young man, but he did seem a bit paternal in his treatment of Isobel. True, he was a few years older but that shouldn't make much of a difference. The real issue might be that with his family money he might be used to getting his own way, to making decisions on his own and to issuing orders that were followed without question.

She wanted Isobel to find her own way in life and to make her own decisions, and that could be very hard to do when someone was—or expected to be treated as—the leader in a relationship. A partner was what Isobel needed. It was what everyone needed in a romantic, committed relationship. Not a father or a mother but a sidekick, a friend, someone who would appreciate you for the individual you were.

Louise dumped the contents of the dustpan into the garbage and returned the broom to the closet. All she wanted to do next was to sleep, but sleep, too, would come when celebrity couple Kick and Monty had finally tied the knot at Blueberry Bay Inn.

Chapter 52

CITYMOUSE

Hello, Readers:

This is Gwen, Isobel's sidekick and co-adventurer in style seeking and style making.

I wanted to let you know that Isobel is taking a sabbatical of undetermined duration to pursue another special project and in the meantime, I will try my best to fill Isobel's unique and therefore unfillable shoes by posting once a week.

I promise that Isobel will see any and all messages of good cheer and good luck any of you readers might want to send her.

So, for today, here's a photo of a vintage purse I found among my fathers' horde of theater props and costumes. It was used in a production of *The Importance of Being Earnest,* staged in New York (off-Broadway) way back in the early 1980s. The beadwork is exquisite—I hope you can see it clearly—and the lining (sorry, no photo of that) is

raw silk. As Isobel is fond of saying, "They
don't make them like they used to!" And by
"them" she means any object of beauty
and quality.

Well, thanks for bearing with my feeble attempt at interesting writing. Until next
week, Gwen.

Isobel closed her laptop and let the tears flow unchecked. She
deeply appreciated Gwen's kind gesture; Gwen knew that
Jeff was behind all of her odd and hurtful behavior. God, she
wanted so badly to see her friend, but it was better for them
to stay away from each other until—until what? Until Isobel
could find a safe way out of this mess . . .

The day before Jeff had—mercifully, for Isobel—been unable to see her. He said he was going to Boston with his father. Isobel had wondered if he was lying but didn't care. His
absence was a brief respite in the madness that was her life.
Still, Jeff had harassed her from afar, calling and e-mailing
and sending her texts every half hour or so. She wondered
what his father thought about it all, or if he had even noticed,
and decided she didn't care about that, either.

Now, oddly, he hadn't been in touch with her yet that day.
His silence scared her. And it gave her the tiniest glimmer of
hope. What if Jeff had gone back to Vermont, tired of her,
tired of working for his father? What if he had been in an accident and had died . . .

She couldn't even feel guilty for thinking this.

But her luck would never be that good. Once, only weeks
before, she had thought she was "one lucky gal." How miserably naïve she had been. She would never be so naïve
again, or so innocent.

Isobel left her room and wandered aimlessly downstairs.

She heard a sound from the parlor and peered cautiously inside.

Quentin was there, bent over an overturned chair, screwdriver in hand.

"Hi," Isobel said. Her voice sounded weak to her ears.

He looked over his shoulder, and the expression in his large brown eyes seemed more solemn than usual.

"Hey," he said. He turned back to work.

"Your eye looks a little better," Isobel said. She felt ashamed and responsible. She wondered if Quentin had had to go to a doctor about the eye. She wondered if his mother had health insurance.

"Yeah," he said.

"Have you seen Gwen?"

"Yeah." He kept his back to her during this exchange.

"How is she? I mean, I haven't seen her in a while."

"She's okay."

There was another ponderous moment of tension, and then Quentin turned around.

"Is your mom around?" he asked. "I haven't seen her today."

"No. She went into town."

"My cousin Lara used to date Jeff Otten a few years back," he said without preamble.

Isobel wanted to run away but she felt rooted to the spot. "Oh."

"He used to hit her. One time, the last time, he broke her nose."

Isobel reached out for the back of the chair closest to her. She felt light-headed.

"Mr. and Mrs. Otten bought off my aunt and uncle to keep them from going to the police," Quentin went on, his tone almost matter-of-fact. "Paid them enough to cover Lara's medical expenses. And a bit more."

Isobel heard this with a heavy heart. She knew that Quentin was telling the truth. Still, even after all she had been through, she didn't want to believe it. It was too, too awful. "Oh," she said feebly.

"My aunt and uncle are farmers. It was a bad year following a bad year. They didn't have the money for a doctor to fix Lara's nose. Besides, Lara was too embarrassed to go public. You can't blame them for keeping their mouths shut. Though sometimes I find myself thinking they're just as guilty as Jeff. And maybe I am, too. Maybe I should have told you this sooner. But I have a tendency to believe that people can change for the better. Maybe, I thought, Jeff Otten's grown up some. But I don't know."

A conspiracy of silence, Isobel thought. And all to protect—what? A family's good name? A social façade? The privacy of a violent young man?

Isobel felt as if she had been hit in the face with a brick. She didn't know what she could possibly say to Quentin. "I'm so sorry about your cousin," she managed finally.

"Yeah. Me, too."

"Why did you tell me this?" she asked then. Though of course she knew very well why Quentin had told her. He knew or at least suspected that Jeff was abusing her. And he might not be the only one who knew. Was she really fooling anyone by keeping quiet? Yes. She was fooling her mother. And Catherine. And Flynn. And herself.

Quentin smiled a bit. It was a kind smile. "I thought you should know what you're involved with," he said.

She knew she should thank Quentin. He deserved her thanks. But she couldn't give it.

"I just hope I didn't speak up too late," he added.

But the look in his serious brown eyes before he turned back to work told Isobel that he knew he had, indeed, spoken too late.

Chapter 53

It was well after midnight. Louise was sitting at the kitchen table with a mug of warm milk. It was an old sleep aid her mother had sworn by. She frowned down at the mug. It was probably more effective when you used whole milk rather than the watery one-percent version she had in the house. She pushed the mug aside.

Isobel was upstairs, hopefully asleep. She looked almost haggard lately. She had admitted to not sleeping well. And God damn it, Andrew hadn't come through for Isobel like he had promised to, no big surprise there.

Louise sighed. Then again, had she been there for her daughter this summer? Not much. What had Isobel said to her just the other day? "I didn't think you noticed me any-more." Well, the wedding was in ten days, and once that was done with . . .

A sudden pounding on the kitchen door made Louise jump and yelp all at once. She looked around, and through the glass in the door she could see a familiar face leaning close. The face was familiar, but the expression was one she had never seen on it before. What was it? Panic? Fear? Anger?

Louise leapt to her feet and threw open the door. Jeff, she thought, must be in trouble. Maybe there had been a car accident, maybe he was hurt . . .

But face-to-face with her daughter's boyfriend, she could clearly see that he was drunk. His eyes were bloodshot and unfocused. His hair was on end. There was a dark stain, still damp, on his fine linen shirt. He swayed and grabbed the door frame with his left hand.

Louise's gut recognized this for what it was. She had seen it before, a long, long time ago. This was trouble. She spoke, trying to keep her voice calm and soothing.

"Hello, Jeff," she said. "What are you doing here? It's after midnight."

"I know what freakin' time it is," he spit. "I want to see Izzy."

Chapter 54

Though she had been in bed for hours, she was still not asleep.

The words of Jeff's last e-mail kept running through her mind.

"You're a lying whore. I know you're having sex with someone else. I'm going to hurt you if you don't give it up to me. I'm going to hurt you anyway."

It was a dirty and menacing message from a person who claimed to love her, but not a particularly surprising one. But he hadn't shown up at the inn all day. Now, the silence felt more dangerous than any active harassment. At any moment he could appear, crash through her bedroom door, jump out at her from around a corner, and she would be helpless to resist. He was so big . . .

Finally, her body and spirit simply worn out enough to quiet her brain, she dozed off. But it wasn't for long. Isobel shot up in the bed and sent the covers flying. She didn't know exactly what had woken her so abruptly. But she did know that her mother was in danger. She knew that as absolutely as she knew that her name was Isobel.

She grabbed her bathrobe from the foot of the bed, a tattered old terry-cloth garment, and belted it quickly around her. Her feet still bare, she tiptoed out of her room to find the hall dark. There was no light from under James's and Jim's door. There was no light from under her mother's door, either, but Isobel gently knocked and pushed it open.

The bed was empty; it had not been slept in.

Isobel went back into the hall and listened in the dark.

After a moment, she thought she heard a low voice from far off . . .

As quietly as she knew how, she snuck down the stairs. When she reached the front hall she heard it more clearly now. Jeff's voice. He was in the kitchen.

Some instinct directed her to slide out the front door and dash around back rather than barge into the kitchen from the hall. The kitchen door was open, as were the windows. Keeping to the edge of the frame, she peered through one of the windows and gasped.

Jeff was drunk. That much was obvious; he was swaying and slovenly. And he was alone with her mother.

Isobel was sure her mother couldn't see her from where she stood by the table. Jeff had his back to the window. Good. She didn't want to alert either of them to her presence. She needed the element of surprise if she was to do anything . . .

"Isobel isn't here, Jeff," her mother said, calmly, and clearly. "Why don't you go on home—"

Jeff laughed, though it sounded more like a bark. "I'll do what I want to do, and what I want to do is to see Izzy. Now."

"I told you," her mother said, her tone still even, "Isobel is not here."

Jeff took another step forward, weaving slightly but still on his feet. Isobel thought he had never looked so huge, so dangerous.

"Liar!" he shouted. "I know that bitch is here and you're hiding her from me!"

Isobel's teeth clenched so hard she thought they might shatter. She grabbed at the pocket of her bathrobe and realized that she had snuck downstairs without her cell phone—

stupid! She was afraid to leave her mother alone with Jeff while she ran back upstairs to call the police. She was afraid—

"I'm not lying," her mother was saying. Isobel thought that her voice betrayed some tension and fear now. "And I'm not hiding her, Jeff. Look, it's late. I really think you should go now."

And then Jeff slammed his palm against the fridge, knocking several of the magnets to the floor. "Tell me where that whoring bitch is or I'll mess you up!"

Isobel's hands flew to her face in horror. Her mother reached into the pocket of her robe and pulled out her phone. "I'm calling the police—"

"Thank God," Isobel murmured.

But before her mother could press those three numbers, Jeff lunged at her, grabbing her arm and shaking her roughly enough to cause her head to snap back. The cell phone went flying and landed behind the trash bin.

The terror Isobel had felt was gone in an instant. The decision to act was made by her limbs. Isobel ran into the kitchen, screaming for help.

Jeff turned, startled by her sudden and loud entrance, and snarled. Roughly he pushed Louise from him. She stumbled backward, hit her head on the table, and fell heavily to the floor.

"Mom!" Isobel dashed toward her mother, but within a step, Jeff had grabbed her by her arm. "Let go of me!" she cried.

But Jeff was strong. And he was angry, out of control now.

Isobel struggled wildly for a moment until, through the clamoring of her panic (her mother might have a concussion, she might be dying!), she heard the unmistakable sound of an engine screeching to a halt and then, Charlie's frantic barking.

"I'll kill that stupid dog right after I kill you!" Jeff spat between clenched teeth. His breath was foul with alcohol. Isobel felt her stomach heave.

He released Isobel's arm and clamped both hands around her neck and squeezed. Isobel choked and felt her eyes pop. She grabbed at his forearms and fought vainly to dislodge his hands from her throat. And then she began to black out. She had never blacked out before ... Her vision grew fuzzy and then dim and her knees sagged and ...

And then she was vaguely aware of a light that hadn't been there a moment before, and voices ...

Jeff suddenly released her, and Isobel felt herself being carried to a chair at the table. And then her mother, conscious, was being lifted into the chair next to hers ...

It was Jim, dear, brave Jim ... He was now on his cell phone ... And there was James. He was holding Jeff's arms behind him ... She turned away.

And over by the door stood a disheveled Catherine with Charlie straining her leash, barking to raise the dead ...

"Oh my God!" Catherine cried. "Louise! Isobel! Are they all right?"

James frowned. "They will be," he said.

Isobel saw Catherine put a hand to her heart. "Charlie woke me up. She was whining something awful, and suddenly I got a feeling ..."

Charlie had ceased her barking but she continued to growl menacingly at James's prisoner. Isobel saw Catherine tighten her grip on the leash.

"I have half a mind to let Charlie have her way with this piece of crap," James muttered. "But I don't want to deprive the justice system of its fun, either."

"Get your hands off me!" Jeff yelled, trying in vain to free himself from James's iron grip. "I'll have my father's lawyers fucking destroy you all!"

"Save it," James said in a voice that carried a big enough authority to make Jeff go silent, at least for the moment.

"It's over," Isobel muttered. She was breathing heavily. Gently, she touched her throat. "It's finally over."

"Izzy!" Jeff's voice was harsh and loud.

She squeezed her eyes shut. She couldn't look at him. The very sight of him repulsed her.

"Izzy! Listen to me!" he demanded.

Isobel put her hands over her ears but was still able to hear the sound of sirens approaching. She kept her eyes closed and her hands where they were until the police had hauled Jeff away.

Chapter 55

Catherine came over to the inn mid-morning the next day. The two women were sitting at the kitchen table drinking what was a fourth cup of coffee for each of them. Neither had gotten more than an hour or two of sleep.

Princess Charlene lay on the floor, her head on Louise's feet. Isobel was finally, mercifully, asleep in her room.

Catherine had insisted on going with Louise and Isobel to the hospital the night before, while James and Jim stayed awake with Charlie until the women's return.

The bruises on Isobel's neck, though nasty to look at and painful, weren't serious. Louise was more banged up—there was an ugly cut on her forehead and a series of bruises along her right side—but miraculously she had avoided getting a concussion when her head had hit the table.

"Thanks to my thick skull," she had declared to the attending doctor, just before breaking down in a torrent of tears.

There was a knock at the kitchen door. Louise startled; she thought it would take some time before a knock at that door didn't frighten her. Catherine got up to open it. It was Flynn. The look on his face was one of shame and embarrassment, but he met Louise's eye squarely when he spoke.

"I can't tell you how sorry I am, Louise. I should have known. I just should have."

"So the word is out," Catherine said, closing the door and pouring a cup of coffee for Flynn.

"Small town."

Louise managed a smile. "You can't blame yourself, Flynn. If you had known anything bad about Jeff, you would have told me. I'm the one who should feel sorry, and guilty, and I do, I feel both."

"Now, enough with the guilt," Catherine said gently. Charlie thumped her tail in agreement.

Flynn joined the women at the table. "I thought you should know I paid a visit to Jack Otten this morning."

"Oh?" Louise thought that had been pretty brave of Flynn. And if Jeff was anything like his father, maybe a bit foolhardy, too. "Did he . . . I mean, what did he say?"

Flynn sipped his coffee before answering. "In short," he said, "the man told all. Seems Jeff's past includes more than a few cases of robbery, as well as bullying. The kid's been in and out of counseling programs for years, but nothing seems to stick. In my day we called a boy like Jeff Otten a bad seed. Nothing to be done about him but let him find his way to jail. Apparently, Jack and Sally have been fighting that inevitability in whatever ways they know how."

Catherine whistled. "The stuff of a soap opera."

"So I'm guessing that Jeff wasn't actually working for his father," Louise said. "He gave me a business card, you know. It looked official enough, but . . ."

Flynn grimaced. "Jack Otten wouldn't let his younger son near the business with the proverbial ten-foot pole. No, that card must have been a fake, just like every other thing about the kid."

Something occurred to Louise. "Was there any mention of a recent robbery?" she asked Flynn. "A bracelet of white gold and diamonds?"

"Oh my God, the bracelet he gave Isobel," Catherine said.

"Don't tell me he gave her stolen property. Man, I'd like to kill that son of a bitch."

Flynn nodded. "Stolen but subsequently paid for. The shop owner knew who had taken it. He had the theft on surveillance tape. Jack Otten paid up. It wasn't the first time."

"Why did people continue to cover for him?" Catherine demanded. "The bad behavior must have been going on for years."

"I can't say for sure," Flynn admitted, shaking his head. "I'm guessing the Ottens paid well for silence. And a lot of people like Jack and Sally. They've been good to the community. And then there's Michael. Everyone likes Michael. Guess people didn't want one bad apple to spoil the reputation of the entire family."

"Allowing a violent young man to prey on vulnerable girls and steal from his neighbors is hardly being good to the community," Louise retorted.

"No," Flynn admitted. "It isn't. But don't assume everyone was in on this conspiracy of silence. Jack told me plenty of folks let it be known they wouldn't cover for Jeff if he came near their family or their business."

"It's nice to know there are still some people with moral fiber," Catherine said huffily.

"Did he ask for my silence?" Louise asked. "In other words, did he name a price?"

Flynn frowned. "Not in as many words. He wanted to know what you had decided to do. I told him I didn't know."

Louise remembered how hard it had been to tell the truth when she was the one who had been abused. But she had done it, and Isobel could, too. One thing was for certain. The Bessire women could not be bought.

"It's up to Isobel," she said. "I'll back her whatever she decides to do."

Flynn finished off his coffee and rose. "I'm sorry again about all this," he said. "Whatever I can do to help now, you promise to let me know."

Louise held out her hand and Flynn took it solemnly. Then he left, after scratching the Princess behind her ears.

"Will you tell Isobel the bracelet was stolen?" Catherine asked when Flynn had gone.

"I think I have to, don't you?"

"Yeah. Frankly, it doesn't suit her anyway. She should sell it and buy herself something she really likes. Something that says—*I am Isobel.*"

Louise managed a bit of a smile. "Did you know that Jeff called her Izzy?"

Catherine shuddered, and it was for real. "I think," she said, "that I might have to let Charlie have her way with him after all."

Chapter 56

CITYMOUSE

Welcome once again, Dear Readers!

CityMouse is back after her hiatus, and very happy to be here!

So many thanks to Gwen for so many reasons. Every girl should have a friend and partner in adventure as good and kind and as smart and brave!

There's much to catch up on, and I hope you'll be patient with me as I do that catching up.

For now, let me leave you with a quote from the late, great Coco Chanel:

"The most courageous act is still to think for yourself. Aloud."

Hugs and kisses, Isobel, aka CityMouse

It had been a week since that fateful night, the night when everything had changed again, but this time for the better.

Isobel and Gwen were hunkered down in Isobel's room, on her bed, survivors of a crisis that had almost torn apart their friendship for good.

"I've never cried as continuously as I've cried since the night Jeff stormed into our house," Isobel admitted. "I feel like I'm crying for every sad thing that ever happened in my life, from losing my favorite toy when I was two to—well, to losing my perfect family a few years back."

Gwen reached out and squeezed Isobel's hand. "I'm so sorry," she said. "I wish I could turn back time . . . Remember how I told you I'd heard that Jeff was a troublemaker?"

"Yeah. The day Jeff came by with the daylilies. The stolen daylilies."

"Pilfered from Mrs. Baker, right. I still can't believe she went to the police about a few stolen flowers! But I'm glad she did."

Isobel laughed. "Gardeners are a special lot. Passionate doesn't even begin to describe them."

"Anyway," Gwen went on, "a few weeks after that I asked my parents if they had ever heard anything more specific about Jeff. They had, but couldn't be sure any of it was true or just malicious gossip, considering their source."

"Who was . . . ?"

"A woman who manages one of the laundry places for tourists in Wells. Seems she dated Jack Otten briefly way back when, before he married his wife. I guess she's still angry with him for breaking up with her. My dads say she's always ready with a bad word about everyone in that family."

"Oh. Nothing like a woman scorned . . ."

"Right. Only her tales about Jeff turned out not to be tall, after all. Anyway, at the time I was afraid I was being unfairly prejudiced so I decided not to say anything more to you. Clearly, I made the wrong choice. I'm so sorry, Isobel. I can't say that often enough."

Isobel smiled. "That's okay. I wouldn't have believed you if you had shown me written proof and photographic evidence of Jeff's being a jerk. Do you know what I found out? The day before he attacked my mom and me, I didn't hear from him at all. Turns out he was with one of his criminal buddies in New Hampshire, robbing local stores and generally being a public nuisance. They even got pulled over for speeding, but somehow, probably because of Jeff's so-called charm, they didn't get a ticket."

"How do you know all this?"

Isobel smiled. "Flynn, of course. Hey, will you tell me what those threatening texts actually said?"

Gwen grimaced. "Trust me, you don't need to know the details. But they were definitely from Jeff, and that's when I knew that whatever rumors had been going around about him were true. I'm ashamed, Isobel. I know I should have told my parents but I was so afraid. See, Jeff had threatened to hurt you if I continued to see you."

Isobel leaped off the bed. "What! But I thought Jeff had threatened to hurt you if we spent time together. I think he felt threatened by you, and by our relationship. What an idiot I was!"

"Me, too! Here we were, both trying to protect each other . . . It's a sick, dark comedy. And I had no idea of how to get you away from Jeff, or of how you could get yourself away, or even if you wanted to get away!"

"I didn't want to get away," Isobel admitted, sinking down again on the bed. "Not for a while. And then . . . I did. Desperately."

Gwen sighed. "How could this have happened to us, of all people? We're smart and savvy and yet . . . we allowed some jerk to control our lives."

"Like my mom says, people like Jeff, liars and abusers, are very, very skilled at manipulating people. Even super-smart people get fooled by them."

"Yeah. It's frightening. Well, one good thing came out of all this."

"What?" Isobel asked. "Aside from the fact that we both learned some valuable lessons."

"Yeah, but more importantly, no more 'Izzy'!"

"I shudder to think that I allowed him to call me that! And get this. Flynn told my mom that Jeff wasn't working for his father at all. And he isn't going back to college, either. He got kicked out for cheating. Seems it wasn't his first offense. Big surprise."

"I wonder what he would have told you in September when he failed to drive off into the sunset?"

"Some lie, I'm sure," Isobel said. "But I was beyond believing anything he said. All I wanted was to get away from him without putting anyone in harm's way. Myself included. Do you know I actually believed him when he told me he volunteered at a retirement home!"

"Doing what, poking the residents with a pointy stick? What a piece of crap."

Isobel laughed. "How eloquent!"

"Don't hate me for asking this. But aren't you still afraid of Jeff, even a little?"

"No." Isobel's reply was emphatic. "Now, I'm furious. Finally. And I don't feel one little bit bad about being angry."

"Good. I'm really glad to hear that. Though I have to admit, I'm still a wee bit afraid of him. Crazy, isn't it?"

Now, Isobel squeezed Gwen's hand. "You know," she said, "Quentin spoke to me. It was right before Jeff's midnight performance in our kitchen."

"What do you mean, he spoke to you?"

"I can't break a confidence, but I can say he told me he knows someone who was hurt by Jeff. A girl. He said he hadn't spoken to me before because he was hoping Jeff had changed. But I guess some people just don't. Or can't. Or won't. Anyway, Quentin apologized for not warning me sooner. I guess he was just trying to be fair."

Gwen sighed. "Good people trying to do the kind thing—

to give a guy the benefit of the doubt—and what was the result? Disaster. It really sucks."

"Quentin is a good person. No lying, no pretense. You
have good taste, Gwen. Have you noticed his face is kind of
delicate in that Johnny Depp kind of way?"

"Have I noticed? Am I blind? And that smile! I think I'm
going to squeal! And I am so not the squealing type! People
who dress like I do generally don't go around squealing."

Isobel laughed. "So, are you two formally a couple?"

"No, but I'm hoping. Do you know, he thinks it's cool that
I have the guts to dye my hair weird colors?"

"Really?" Isobel sighed. "Boy, are you lucky. Not that you
don't deserve it. Quentin likes you just the way you are. Jeff
liked his own image of me, an Isobel that didn't actually
exist."

"I wonder if that's common with abusers. I mean, I wonder if they tend to see people how they want to see them. Or,
if they're incapable of accepting that another person is an entirely separate being and that she has the right to be that entirely separate being."

"Abusers as egoists?" Isobel said. "It's an interesting notion."

Gwen clapped her hands together; because she was wearing ten rings, one on each finger, it made quite a noise. "I
think we need to have some fun. Now."

"Fun is a Gwentastic idea!"

"Then it's settled." Gwen held out her hand for her friend
to take. "Ice cream from Goldenrod Kisses. Let's go."

Chapter 57

Catherine and Charlie came by the inn one morning a little over a week after Jeff's performance in the Bessire kitchen.

"Here," she said, handing Louise, who was sitting at the table, a travel magazine. "There's an article in there about some of the most awful inns in the country. I laughed out loud."

Louise smiled. "Thanks. I'm in the mood for something amusing right about now . . ."

"Look, Louise." Catherine took a seat next to her friend. "I have to apologize to you again. I feel like I really let you and Isobel down."

"Don't blame yourself—" Louise began but Catherine cut her off.

"No, hear me out. I'm furious with myself for not knowing something was wrong with Jeff. I should have known. I was too complacent. And I should have listened to Princess Charlene. She knew the truth, and she wasn't afraid to make a ruckus about it."

Louise sighed. "And all I did was make excuses for Jeff . . . I'll never ignore Charlie's warnings again."

As if in approval of that vow, Charlie put her front paws up on Louise's knees and smiled.

Catherine and her companion left soon after for their second morning constitutional. Louise remained where she was; she had felt beyond tired since the night of Jeff's intrusion.

Jeff Otten. Her instincts had been dulled by his charm and his good looks. It hurt her to admit it now, but she had felt relieved that Isobel had a boyfriend to occupy her time. Even when Isobel's behavior had begun to change, Louise had convinced herself that Isobel was just experiencing episodes of the usual adolescent angst—and she had turned her attention to the business of the inn.

Now she knew that the return of the nightmares (there had been none since Jeff's attack) had indeed been warnings from her subconscious. On the surface Ted Dunbar and Jeff Otten were so very different. But some deep instinct had tried to warn her that handsome, polite Jeff was at bottom the same person as Ted. A coward and a bully.

There had been moments since Jeff's attack on her family when Louise felt she would never break free of the guilt and shame that gripped her for not having seen what was happening to her daughter. Her worst sin was that she had succumbed to her own largely unconscious prejudices. In her volunteer work she had counseled the message that "it could happen to anyone," and yet, deep down, she just hadn't been able or willing to believe that it could happen to her own flesh and blood. She had been unforgivably blind and unconsciously arrogant, quick to assume the worst about that couple down in Kittery earlier in the summer yet failing to identify her own child as a victim.

How could she ever make it up to Isobel? She felt it would take a lifetime to atone for her neglect. As a small start, she had rescheduled their special day in Portland, with a visit to the spa, lunch, and shopping. Catherine and Flynn had agreed to play innkeepers for the day . . .

"Hi, Mom."

Isobel came loping into the kitchen and sat in the chair Catherine had vacated.

"How are you?" Louise asked. "And don't say fine. Give me something real."

Isobel smiled. "Okay. Are you ready for a revelation?"

"I have to be."

"Toward the end I started to get really angry with you for having brought us here to Maine, even though I know that an abusive relationship can happen anywhere. But I felt so trapped and so isolated . . . I just didn't know who to blame . . . other than Jeff, of course, but for some reason I couldn't blame him, not for a long time."

Louise swallowed her tears. "That was hard to hear, but I'm glad you told me. No more withholding the important stuff."

"Right. It's time to be brave."

"I'm just sorry you had to learn bravery through fear. I had hoped to teach you another way . . ."

Isobel smiled. "You did, Mom. You do all the time. It wasn't fear that made me run into the kitchen when I saw Jeff grab you. It was love. Okay, and it was also anger. I mean, all I could think of in that split second was, how dare he touch my mother!"

Louise took her daughter's hand. "And all I could think in that moment was, *Is she crazy? Run away!*"

"There's something I just don't understand, Mom. How could Jeff's mother keep her mouth shut knowing her son had a history of hitting girls? I mean, I know she's his mother and mothers don't like to think badly of their children, but . . . It just doesn't make sense to me."

"You were expecting a show of female solidarity?"

"I guess I was," Isobel admitted.

"Well, the maternal bond is strong enough to cause a fair amount of poor judgment at times. I'm not sure how much we can blame Sally Otten. Though she and her husband certainly weren't doing Jeff any favors by bailing him out of trouble over and over again. All they were doing was making it easier for his behavior to deteriorate. And on some level, I'm sure they knew that."

"How do you stand being a parent? It must be brutal!"

Louise laughed. "At times it is brutal, even with a wonderful child like you. But it's worth the trouble, trust me."

"I wonder if Mrs. Otten would have acted differently if she had a daughter. I mean, then she would have had to do something to stop Jeff, right?"

Louise shrugged. "Hard to say. Remember, we know almost nothing about her. Maybe Jeff was the apple of her eye when he was little and she can't let go of that image. I suspect we'll never know what really goes on in that house."

A *thump* from the hall announced the arrival of the mail being dropped through the slot in the front door. "I'll get it," Louise said. When she returned to the kitchen, she was already sorting through the stack of envelopes. "There had better be a check in here from . . . Well, speak of the devil. Or rather, his mother."

"What is it?" Isobel asked.

"A letter from Mrs. Otten. It's addressed to you."

"Oh." Isobel's expression was hard to read.

"Do you want me to read it first?"

"No, it's okay." Isobel took the letter from her mother, opened the envelope, and read the contents of the single sheet of heavy, old-fashioned writing paper. The note left her unmoved. "Here," she said, handing it to her mother.

Louise scanned the page. "It's carefully worded, all right," she said after a moment. "She admits no personal responsibility or guilt, but at least she doesn't ask you to go easy on her precious little boy. 'I'm sorry you had to endure such a trial.' Well, I guess she knows the game is up."

"I actually feel a little bit sorry for her," Isobel said, taking back the letter and folding it into the envelope. "It can't be pleasant to know your child is a criminal. Maybe she even blames herself for the way he is."

"You know, there is another possibility we didn't consider. Well, that I didn't consider before now. It might explain Sally Otten's letting Jeff run wild."

"What do you mean?"

Louise grimaced. "Maybe she was—is—afraid of Jeff. Maybe he was abusing her, too."

Isobel clapped a hand to her mouth. "Oh no, that's too awful! But it would explain her keeping quiet, especially if Jeff had threatened her."

"It would be a dreadful way to live, a prisoner to your own child, in your own home. And who knows what part Jack Otten played in the whole scheme. Besides enabler."

"Do you think someone like Jeff will ever change?" Isobel asked after a moment. "I mean, really change?"

"I have no way of knowing that. I suppose only a psychiatrist could determine what someone like Jeff Otten is capable of becoming, good or bad."

"You know," Isobel said, "near the end I was thinking of him as evil, like he was possessed by a demon spirit. And I'd never even believed in evil or demons before that."

Louise put out her arms and Isobel went into her embrace. "Oh Isobel, I'm so sorry. I so wish I could magically erase the past months!"

"Me, too. But maybe not. Maybe I learned some valuable lessons thanks to creepy Jeff Otten. Like, how to stand up for myself. And how to say no, even if it makes another person angry." Isobel laughed, but it was a shaky laugh. "Well, I'm not so sure I'm okay with anger yet . . . It really frightens me . . ."

"We'll get past this," Louise said. "I promise. Do you believe me?"

Isobel nodded. "I do."

Chapter 58

Isobel was writing the final lines of the latest CityMouse post.

> Let me end with yet another fabulous *bon mot* from the mouth of Diana Vreeland:
>
> "Blue jeans are the most beautiful thing since the gondola."
>
> Well, I don't know how the good people of Venice feel about that (!) but I do know that it's high time I gave jeans (blue, white, or any other color) a shot, as to date I've mostly ignored them. I think a shopping trip is in order!
>
> Good-bye for now from CityMouse.

Isobel posted the blog, complete with photos of Gwen in a variety of fantastic jeans they had found while rummaging Goodwill. (There was a pair of super high–waist jeans that made them both hysterical.) And then she yawned so widely it became a laugh. Maybe a nap was in order; so much had been happening she felt exhausted even thinking about it all!

Like the fact that Jeff had been arrested, charged, and then released into his parents' custody. Rumor had it they had sent him to stay with an aunt and uncle in Colorado. Once again, they had salvaged the wreck that was their younger son. But if Jeff did ever show his face again in Ogunquit, he would be remembered as the guy who had attacked the Bessire women in their own home. Local papers had run the story, and Channel 6 had, too. The truth was known.

More importantly, at least as far as Isobel was concerned, her father had opened the door to better communication between them. Her mother had called him with the news about what Isobel had suffered at Jeff's hands. The conversation had been volatile; her mother had admitted to Isobel that they had blamed each other pretty harshly before calming down enough to begin the grieving process together.

Two days later Isobel had received a long, handwritten letter from her father. (Boy, was his handwriting bad!) She looked again at that letter now. His tone was one of abject apology. Isobel believed he was truly sorry for not having paid enough, or the right sort of, attention to her since the divorce.

"I put too much on you," he had written at the end, "assuming you were too smart and tough to ever be really vulnerable. But that was self-serving, a convenient excuse to let me off the hook of guilt. I disrupted your life, your mother's, our family's life. I need to take emotional responsibility for that. I'm just sorry I had to learn that lesson as a result of your being hurt. Please forgive me, Isobel."

Well, it would take time and effort to bring their relationship back to a solid state; Isobel accepted that. And she knew she would have to get past the desire to blame her father for the vulnerable state in which Jeff had found her; that it had made her more susceptible to his emotional machinations was beyond a doubt. But that was not to say that she might not have become Jeff's prey even if her father had still been around. She had been so attracted to Jeff, so willing to be with him no matter what sacrifice that required—including some of her most cherished passions and beliefs.

Ugh. It was all so—weird. But she was really beginning to feel that she was moving beyond relying solely on her father's (or any man's??) attentions to give her a good sense of self-esteem. She absolutely could not allow herself to be treated badly ever again, or to rely so utterly on one person's good opinion.

Ding! Someone had sent her an e-mail. Isobel smiled. It was her dad.

Chapter 59

The big day had finally arrived. Mother Nature (probably afraid to piss off Flora Michaels) had cooperated by providing plenty of sun, a cooling breeze, and low humidity.

Louise had splurged on a new dress, a simple silk sheath in a peachy tone that worked perfectly with her classic patent-leather nude pumps. Isobel was wearing her grandmother's paisley dress for the occasion (Louise had taken up the hem). So far, Isobel told her mother, she hadn't gotten any psychic transmissions or felt any residue of hidden personality from the dress, but she was hopeful.

"Did we ever get their names straight?" Isobel asked her mother, as they stood on the porch, watching guests take seats on the front lawn. Louise had pointed out that it would be more practical and private to have the ceremony on the back lawn, but practical and private were not big considerations for Hollywood types. The more cars that slowed to watch and take pictures—and create a traffic jam that would annoy the neighbors—the better.

"No," Louise said. "The other day I called the groom Hake."

Isobel frowned. "I think that's a type of fish."

"It is. Often used for fish and chips. But get this. Each one uses a stage name. Know what their real names are? Mary Smith and Robert Brown."

"Ha!"

Louise regarded the wedding party gathered before them. The bride's dress resembled a confection made of spun sugar and marshmallow. It was easily four feet wide across the hips and the train went on for a good seven or eight yards. The headpiece was a crown about a foot high and encrusted so heavily with crystals Louise was momentarily—and painfully—blinded when the blushing bride had made her appearance. Her bouquet—a densely packed mass of red and pink roses—was heavy enough to cause severe damage to anyone stupid enough to get hit by it (Louise thought: *Take note, bridesmaids!*). Her shoes were an entirely impractical choice for a wedding taking place on a summer lawn—five-inch stilettos. With each step the bride took toward the minister she sank a wee bit and then was forced to yank the foot free. It made for a rocky and not very attractive gait.

The groom wore a standard-issue black tuxedo with a spray of red berries on his lapel. "I think those berries are poisonous," Isobel had remarked to her mother. "Should we say something?" Louise didn't see the point. "He's not dumb enough to eat them. I think . . ."

The maids of honor—there were nine of them, each one blonder than the next—wore nine different shades of pink, from the most anemic blush to the most shocking of shocking pink. The effect was slightly nauseating. "From calamine lotion to Pepto-Bismol," Isobel pronounced. "From chicken pox to an upset stomach. Why didn't she stick to one shade?" Each woman carried a single red rose. "I bet the thorns are still on those stems," Isobel said darkly.

The groomsmen—nine, each one with very dark, carefully coiffed hair—wore black tuxedos similar to the groom's, but with a cummerbund to match the dress of his partner. Ditto the nausea.

The flower girl, who could have been no more than two years old, was grotesquely made up like a toddler beauty pageant contestant. The skirt of the dress she had been stuffed into—pink, of course—stood out stiffly, like a balle-rina's tutu, and was as scratchy as a Brillo Pad. Louise knew this, much to her dismay, because at one point that morning the bride, in a fit of annoyance, had thrust the squirming child, already decked out in her finery, at Louise, who had no choice but to accept her. "Keep it away from me," the bride had ordered. "I think she needs her diaper changed."

Poor little thing, Louise thought now. She was far too young for the responsibility of being a flower girl, all alone, pacing slowly toward the precariously erected bridal canopy under which the minister awaited. She had thrown a fit after one step and had to be removed from the scene by her supremely annoyed parents, who no doubt had been hoping for some free publicity for their little darling.

But all was not amiss. The miniature carousel had been nixed (thanks to Flynn), as had the flock of pink doves (ditto; he had had a friend on the town council write a letter claim-ing that such things were unlawful in the town of Ogun-quit)—in favor of the black marzipan pigs (Isobel, thank God, was over her strange detestation of black, and had managed to snag a few pigs for herself) and a relatively real-istic ice sculpture of a swan. (That it was already melting was the bride's headache, not Louise's.)

Isobel went off to find Gwen. A moment later, James and Jim, on their way to a friend's house, stopped on the porch to greet Louise.

"Congratulations, Louise," James said. "You pulled this off magnificently."

"Well, I don't know about that," she demurred. "But at least that ridiculous bridal canopy hasn't fallen on anyone and nobody's thrown a punch. Yet."

Jim laughed. "We wish we could stay to gape, but we have a previous engagement. See you when all is said and done."

The men went off and Catherine joined her now. There was no way in hell, Catherine had informed Louise, that she would miss this event. If Flora Michaels dared to point out that she hadn't been invited, she would simply ignore her.

"They deserve each other," Louise said, watching the bride and groom as they stood facing each other in front of the minister. "I don't know who is more self-absorbed, Tack or Manila. Watching them these past two days has been quite the edifying experience."

"How long do you give the marriage?" Catherine asked.

"A few months, a year maybe?"

"Sounds about right. What a waste of time, effort, and money. And emotion, assuming the bride and groom actually have any feelings for each other, besides disdain."

"Each is just a vehicle for the other's ride to ephemeral fame," Louise said philosophically. "You know, in the end I might be the only one really profiting from this event."

It was possible. Her name and the name of the inn would be printed in all of the magazines and tabloids that would carry the story of Crack and Burgundy's wedding, and business might very well boom because of it. Already a journalist from a slick home design magazine had come to interview Louise and photograph the inn in all of its late summer glory. Another publication had booked a visit for mid-October, in order to catch the Blueberry Bay Inn at the height of Southern Maine's leaf-peeping season. And yet another periodical was due to take photographs around the Christmas holidays, in spite of the fact that the inn wasn't open for business after November first. "You might want to rethink that," the editor had advised Louise. "People enjoy sneaking away for a cozy winter weekend. You know, roaring fires, sparkling snow on branches, all that crap."

Catherine nudged Louise with her elbow. "Flora Michaels looks pretty bad."

Flora Michaels, who was standing by a stand of black-eyed Susans at the foot of the porch, was wearing a caftan-like garment that engulfed her skeletal body in a disturbing mélange of orange polka dots, yellow stripes, and gold squiggly lines. The Incubus was also present. Louise thought Flora Michaels admirably subdued once the actual event had gotten under way. Maybe deep, deep down beneath those prominent bones a heart beat after all . . .

"What's new about that?" Louise asked. "She can hardly support that . . . that thing she's wearing."

"No, I mean, she looks sick. The makeup is pouring off her face in tan streams. Fascinating but—Oh crap, she's on the ground."

Louise and Catherine scurried down to where the wedding planner lay in a heap of garish fabric. Flynn appeared from nowhere and scooped her up (muttering that she weighed no more than a medium-sized Maine coon cat). He then carried her inside to the parlor, where he unceremoniously dumped her on the couch and left to scout out a cold beer.

When Flora Michaels revived after a few minutes of Catherine's fanning her face with a magazine, Louise helped her to a sitting position. Catherine then poured water down her throat and gave her a lecture on proper hydration and nutrition. Neither Louise nor Catherine assumed the lecture would do any good, but it was out there.

"I'd like to use the business end of a hose on her face," Catherine mused quietly as Flora Michaels lay back again to continue her recovery. "See what's under all that goop."

Calvin Streep, his own plump face shining with sweat above his impeccable seersucker suit and white shirt, chose that moment to peek into the room. His face contorted in disdain when he observed his employer stretched out on the couch.

"She'll be fine," Catherine said with an insincere smile. "In case you were worried."

"She's not my concern anymore," Calvin Street replied, with something approaching glee. "I've quit. I've taken a position as executive personal assistant to the head of Olympian Studios. No more pathetic weddings for two-bit actors in poky little towns."

"How nice for you!" Catherine crowed.

"Break a leg," Louise added. When Calvin Streep had slithered off, she added, "No, really. I mean, fall down and break a leg."

Isobel and Gwen appeared in the parlor then.

"Is she okay?" Isobel asked, peering down into Flora Michaels's makeup-streaked face.

Catherine shrugged. "She'll live. And we'll never have to see her again after today."

Louise nodded vigorously. "I'm never saying yes to this dragon lady ever again."

"This is the big, bad wedding planner?" Gwen sighed. "Wow. That's a lot of trouble in a pretty small package."

A burst of applause, some obnoxious whistling, and a few catcalls from outside reminded the women of the sacred ceremony being performed on the front lawn.

"I guess it's a done deal," Isobel commented.

Catherine turned to Louise. "You'll consider my business proposition, I hope."

"What proposition?" Isobel and Gwen asked at the same time.

"Catherine has suggested she become a partner in the Blueberry Bay Inn."

"It will take some of the pressure off your mother," Catherine explained. "Let her concentrate on the people part of the business. And frankly, I'm getting bored with spending my days painting. Monet, I'll never be."

Louise laughed. "So, I guess we're in the hospitality business to stay. You okay with that?" she asked Isobel.

"Sure. I think we all make quite a team."

"Hey," Gwen said, "how can I get in on this enterprise?"

"You can take pictures of the inn for the website," Louise said. "The ones there now aren't as good as they could be. I didn't know any really good photographers when we first moved here. I'll pay you, of course."

Gwen beamed. "My first professional gig! Thanks, Mrs. Bessire."

"I think this calls for champagne," Isobel proclaimed.

Louise smiled. "A glass for each of us. Team Blueberry Bay deserves it."

Epilogue

The weak mid-November light forced its way through the windows of Isobel's room. The famous New England fall foliage was long gone; the air was crisp when it wasn't damp; the earth was gray and brown; the first snowfall was said to be not far off.

Isobel was looking forward to spending the weekend after Thanksgiving with her father, Vicky, the girls, and little Andrew Jr. How typical, Isobel thought, not entirely without fondness. Vicky, her father had told her, had wanted to name the boy Jared but he had stood firm. Well, her father's quirks didn't bother Isobel so much any longer. She had more important things to focus on.

Like rebuilding—and enjoying!—her life.

An interesting thing had happened. Quentin's cousin Lara had come by the inn one afternoon to apologize for not having told the truth about Jeff when he had broken her nose. She was a pretty girl, a few years older than Isobel. She and her cousin shared the same gorgeously wild brown curls and soulful brown eyes. She was nervous throughout their meeting, literally wringing her hands. (Isobel had never actually seen anyone do that, though she had read about it in novels.) Lara admitted that she still wasn't ready to go public, and might never be. Isobel understood why.

The bracelet had been dealt with. The local jeweler—the one from whom Jeff had stolen the piece—confirmed that the diamonds were indeed diamonds, and the gold was indeed gold, maybe the only two things Jeff hadn't lied about. Of course, there was no way Isobel could keep it; it was tainted beyond rehabilitation. Her mom sold it for her on eBay, and with the money it fetched, Isobel invested in better software for the blog. With another portion of the money Isobel bought a Marena pin she found at her first live auction in Vermont. (Gwen had driven, though Isobel had just gotten her permit.)

Gwen and Quentin were together as a couple now, and Gwen was as attentive to her friendship with Isobel as ever. Isobel knew all too well how hard it must be on her at times, juggling two important emotional priorities—but at least in this case, Isobel and Quentin actually liked and respected each other!

Flynn and Catherine were spending much of their time together, too, though Catherine had declined to say if he was "the one." "It doesn't seem to matter so much anymore," she had told Louise and Isobel. "Flynn is a great guy, and we enjoy each other's company. That's fine for now. Maybe it will be fine for always."

James and Jim, Isobel's Knights in Shining Armor, had gone home to their castle (that's how Isobel liked to imagine it) in the Hudson Valley, with reassurances that they would return the following summer. A sizable deposit had sealed that promise. They kept in touch via e-mail and had invited Louise and Isobel to pay them a visit at Christmastime.

And Jeff Otten? He was still in Colorado, causing who knew what sort of trouble. But even if he came back to town, he could never hurt Isobel again because she had changed— she had!—and she would no longer let anyone treat her with such disrespect. Sometimes, alone in her bed in the middle of the night, it still surprised her that a person—only a person, not a demon—had been able to achieve so much power over her, and in such a short period of time.

A person who had been born of a mere woman. Isobel

often thought of the time in early October when she and her mother had seen Mrs. Otten in the produce section in Hannaford. Isobel didn't recognize her, never having met her, but Louise had met her, once, and her face had taken on a strange look.

"Jeez, Mom," Isobel had asked. "What's wrong?"

"Nothing. Except that's Mrs. Otten, over by the oranges."

She was a pretty, slightly plump woman somewhere around Catherine's age, Isobel guessed, dressed expensively and conservatively in a tweed skirt suit. She didn't look like a victim, but what did that mean? She also didn't look like a conspirator, and yet, that's what she was, aiding and abetting her son in his crimes.

Part of Isobel had wanted to walk right up to Mrs. Otten. "Hi," she would say. "I'm Isobel Bessire, your son's latest victim." But she didn't have the nerve or the level of hate it would take to confront Jeff's mother in that way. Isobel had just watched Mrs. Otten choose some fruit and walk away.

Isobel, as a survivor, was learning how to be aware of toxic people, but at the same time to retain a healthy degree of trust in humanity's innate goodness. It wasn't always easy, but if her mom had learned to do it, so could she. If bazillions of people through history had learned, then so could Isobel Amelia Bessire! And she was learning to accept that even a smart and savvy person could make a mistake in judgment, and that it shouldn't be a cause for self-loathing. Next time she had the slightest doubt about someone's behavior toward her, she would tell, because talking was good . . . almost as good as writing!

Isobel sat at her desk and opened her laptop.

Greetings, Fellow Style Seekers!

Today I want to talk about scarves . . .

CityMouse was back with a vengeance!

Please turn the page
for a very special Q&A with
Holly Chamberlin!

Q. *The Summer Everything Changed* is very much a story about a mother and daughter, a topic you have visited in several other novels, for example, *Last Summer* and *Tuscan Holiday*. Is this a subject you intend to return to in the future?

A. Oh yes. The mother-daughter dynamic is a rich and varied one; I could write a story a month for the rest of my life and never repeat a detail. Fortunately, I have a good relationship with my mother so I have no personal ax to grind or demons to put to rest—we've battled it all out long before now! The novels allow me to explore—at a safe distance—a relationship that is classically fraught, complicated, and sometimes painfully intimate.

Q. Was it difficult to write about the topic of teenage domestic violence?

A. Yes, it was an emotional drain; there were times I wanted to snatch Isobel from her abuser's grip and had to keep reminding myself that it was all a fiction and that I was, in fact, in charge. Talk about characters taking over an author! And writing this novel was a challenge in another way. I had to figure out how to tell a story that would engage the reader and keep her engaged—and not unduly depressed—while it was becoming increasingly dark and dangerous. Hopefully, I met this challenge successfully.

Q. Isobel, your teenaged heroine, is an interesting combination of sassy and secretively fearful, of spirited and secretly hesitant. Do you think she is unusual, or do you find that many teenaged girls are not as confident and as self-assured as they seem?

A. I believe that all too many adolescent girls and young women are a painfully mixed-up bundle of contradictory beliefs and behaviors. In portraying Isobel as intellectually independent at the same time she is emotionally dependent and even naïve, I think I portrayed quite a common—and unfortunate—type. Frankly, I drew on my own experience to create her. As a teen, I could ace a test and write a great paper, but at the same time I was intimidated by intimacy, full of self-doubt, and fearful of identifying and speaking my needs lest I be rejected or considered somehow bad or wrong or troublesome. Women have come a long way—but not far enough.

Q. Did you relate at all to Louise, Isobel's mother, or to Catherine, Louise's friend?

A. To some extent a writer "relates to" or has a relationship with every single character, if only to say, "God, what an awful person she is; I'm not at all like that!" In this case, feeling some sympathy toward two adult women wasn't so difficult. For example, like Louise, who among us hasn't ignored a crisis in our own home because of laziness or stress or some deep-seated psychological reason we'd rather not acknowledge? And, like Catherine, I am middle-aged and don't have children, so there is some of my own angst in her story. That said, every character in the book is just that—a character, not me, not my mother, not my friend, not anyone else who lives and breathes.

Q. Can you tell us what's next for Holly?

A. Well, I'm currently writing a novella that will be published as part of a collection along with a few other writers. And

I'm working on another novel. Like *The Family Beach House*, *Summer Friends*, *Last Summer*, and *The Summer Everything Changed*, the story is set in Maine—but that's all I'm telling you! Okay, and it involves mothers and daughters—that's no surprise.

THE SUMMER EVERYTHING CHANGED

Holly Chamberlin

ABOUT THIS GUIDE

The suggested questions are intended to enhance
your group's reading of Holly Chamberlin's

The Summer Everything Changed.

DISCUSSION QUESTIONS

1. When we meet Isobel we learn that she is a notoriously open and honest person. Not long after, we see her begin to keep secrets from her mother, a new habit that takes even Isobel by surprise. Louise decides that this is merely a sign of her daughter's increasing independence. Does this view have some merit? Or do you think Isobel's keeping secrets from and then lying to her mother is an unconscious indication of anger or frustration? Is it perhaps an unconscious indication of a need for some control over her life after the divorce and move to Maine?

2. Isobel's dear friend, Gwen, comes from a stable home environment, albeit after years in the foster care system. Isobel attributes Gwen's good sense and judgment to her early childhood experiences; Gwen might argue that being the daughter of two loving and committed parents has helped make her strong. Talk about how the girls are different and yet alike, and about how nature and nurture have each played a part in forming their characters.

3. Catherine mourns the fact that she never had a child. She also feels angry about the insensitive and judgmental remarks various people have made regarding her personal choices. Talk about how having a child or not can, and often does, deeply determine a woman's sense of purpose or fulfillment. Do you sympathize with Catherine's decision (in some ways very practical) not to have a child without also having a loving husband?

4. Louise deliberately puts off facing her sense of something being "wrong" in her world until after the celebrity wedding, an all too common and understandable—if unfortunate—way of coping with undue stress. Later, Louise harshly criticizes herself for being blind to the truth about her own daughter while being acutely wrapped up in the troubles of others. Discuss Louise's culpability—and/or her innocence—in her daughter's distress.

5. Consider Isobel's natural exuberance; her native trust in people's goodness; her habit of avoiding and minimizing her pain; her fear of risking someone's displeasure by displaying anger, even when she feels she has a legitimate complaint. How much of her complex personality might be attributed to her family's changing dynamics? When are parents not to blame or to be held responsible for a child's mental and emotional habits and character? In other words, when does a child become responsible for her own responses to the world?

6. Talk about the role of a father in a daughter's life, especially during the confusing years of adolescence. In what ways can a father help or hurt his daughter's burgeoning sense of self and independence? In particular, talk about how Andrew's relationship with Isobel might have contributed to her falling victim to Jeff's attentions and eventually, to his bullying. Should Louise have taken a more active role in compelling her ex-husband to be a more attentive parent? Or was this not her responsibility? What about Vicky's responsibility—if any—to her stepdaughter?

7. It is said that a sense of self-esteem comes from what we achieve, not from the compliments we receive. By

belittling Isobel's efforts with CityMouse, a project that has great meaning for her, Jeff attacks Isobel in a very vulnerable place. It could be argued that the most violent damage Jeff inflicts on Isobel is psychological. Referring to your own experiences or those of friends and family members, talk about the various forms of abusive or bullying behavior to be found in a domestic relationship.

8. Isobel's blog entries often speak to her strong belief in the importance of individualism, yet under pressure from Jeff, Isobel is led to betray herself and her own uniqueness. To this day, many otherwise strong and intelligent women fail to be true to themselves and their own beliefs when confronted with bullying tactics both at home and in the workplace. Considering your own experiences, what one piece of advice would you give to girls on the cusp of becoming young women?

9. The shame of being identified as a victim prevents many people, both men and women, from speaking out about an abusive situation. Can you understand Quentin's cousin Lara's reluctance to reveal Jeff as her abuser? Can you understand why her parents accepted money in return for keeping quiet? Can you understand Isobel's fear that exposing Jeff as a bully might put those she loves in danger? Bullying is the abuse of power. What other reasons (real or imagined; practical or fantastic) might an abused person claim for keeping silent?

10. After Jeff has been arrested and the truth about his treatment of Isobel has come out, Louise and Isobel speculate about Jeff's mother and the role she played in his career as a bully and an abuser. Talk about the part Sally Owen might have played in forming her

son's character. Is she perhaps partly to blame? Is she possibly blameless? What do you think she hoped to accomplish by sending Isobel the note, in which she acknowledges but fails to apologize for her son's behavior?